"Something bad is going to happen. I feel it."

Sam knew without even looking that Emerald's pearly teeth would be worrying her lush bottom lip. It was something she always did when she was agitated and therefore something she always did when they were together. He had a knack for keeping her riled. Even from across the room, her hot-blooded temper and wild sensuality dragged at him like a riptide, pulling him so far under her spell he could barely breathe.

"Hello? Sam? Are you hearing me?" she demanded, waving her delicate hands at him as she spoke. The effect was akin to a matador waving a red cape at a bull. He wanted those hands and that mouth doing things to him. Surely steam had to be rising off him.

He heard her all right. He just didn't know what in the hell he was going to do with her.

The Lure of the Wolf
"Raw emotions give way to desperate choices, which adds up to breathless reading pleasure!"

—*Romantic Times*

"Wonderful. . . . A unique world . . . that is both intriguing and sensual."

—Paranormal Romance Writers

Touch a Dark Wolf
"A unique take on the werewolf world, and a thrilling ride."
—Lora Leigh, bestselling author of *Harmony's Way*

JENNIFER ST. GILES

Kiss of Darkness

POCKET BOOKS
New York London Toronto Sydney

Pocket Books
A Division of Simon & Schuster, Inc.
1230 Avenue of the Americas
New York, NY 10020

This book is a work of fiction. Names, characters, places, and incidents either are products of the author's imagination or are used fictitiously. Any resemblance to actual events or locales or persons, living or dead, is entirely coincidental.

First Pocket Books paperback edition April 2009

POCKET and colophon are registered trademarks of Simon & Schuster, Inc.

For information about special discounts for bulk purchases, please contact Simon & Schuster Special Sales at 1-800-456-6798 or business@simonandschuster.com.

The Simon & Schuster Speakers Bureau can bring authors to your live event. For more information or to book an event, contact the Simon & Schuster Speakers Bureau at 866-248-3049 or visit our website at www.simonspeakers.com.

Cover illustration by Franco Accornero

Manufactured in the United States of America

10 9 8 7 6 5 4 3 2 1

ISBN-13: 978-1-4165-6339-6
ISBN-10:   1-4165-6339-3

To the heroes and heroines around the world
who fight for freedom and for good, bringing light into
the darkness and love to the lost.

Acknowledgments

My thanks to my editor, Abby Zidle, for making this book the best it could be. To Deidre Knight for keeping me sane in the insanity. To Jacquie D. for keeping me going every day until I found the light at the end of the tunnnel. To Wendy, Rita, and Stephanie for always being there. To my sister Tracy who gives with her whole heart and never stops doing everything possible to make my writing career a successs. To Annette, who selflessly gives of her heart, love, and amazing photography talent to bring my stories to life. To Dayna for believing in me and for inspiring Emerald and Sam. To my parents for giving so much of their life to make my life possible. To my husband for making it possible for me to write. And finally to my children for filling my heart and for understanding and putting up with a mom who always seems to be under deadline.

Prologue

"MEGGIE, WAKE UP, poppet. We have to be goin' to a safe place, now," Emerald whispered to her daughter as she brushed back the soft curls from her face. All snuggled into her Magical Realms comforter she looked like a sleeping sprite surrounded by unicorns and fairies dancing on rainbows. Megan's room was a treasure land of everything "magical" she could find, as if she already knew she was part angel.

Blinking several times, Megan opened her eyes. They were more solemn than any five-year-old girl's should ever have to be. She pulled her Booboo Bunny close and rubbed her cheek against the pink fur. "Da comin', too?"

She'd heard the argument tonight. Emerald sighed and bit her lip, fighting the burning sting in her eyes. She thought she'd cried all the tears she possibly could. "No. Da canna. Da's not well, poppet," she said, shaking her head.

Tears filled Megan's eyes, making them bright green pools of pain that tore Emerald's heart. "For-eber?" Megan asked, her breath catching on the word.

"Forever is a very long time," Emerald said softly. There'd been so many things that she thought would be forever. Eric's love for her. Hers for him. She didn't believe in forever anymore.

Megan said nothing as Emerald helped her dress in warm clothes, but as they left her room, she trembled. The big teardrops sliding silently down her daughter's cheeks sent another surge of anger through Emerald. Damn Eric. Damn herself and the bloody evil that was stealing everything away from them.

She hadn't forced Eric to accept her help, and now it was too late. Her terrifying vision along with tonight's argument had solidified her fear. She might not have been able to read Eric's thoughts, but the twisted hunger for blood—her blood—was boiling inside him.

Her husband was no longer human, and she had no more illusions.

She and Megan were no longer safe.

Eric's soul now belonged to Michael Wellbourne. He'd left several hours ago and wouldn't be back until dawn, until the last moments of Samhain and the wicked celebration at the Devil's Mound had come to an end. Since then, Emerald had packed the car with everything she and Megan needed to go into hiding, and now it was time to leave. Yet there was so much of her in their little cottage—a photo here, a labored embroidery there, a gift rich in memories on the shelf that she didn't dust often enough. She felt as if she were ripping herself apart as she walked out the front door.

She tightened her hold on Megan's hand and pulled the "magic" comforter closer. As long as miracles and magic existed in the world, there was hope. This wasn't the end. Somehow, some way, she'd find a way to save Eric yet. She had to. For her sake as well as for Megan's.

Her daughter walked bravely, clutching her bunny and her favorite bedtime book, *Precious Princesses*. Eric had bought it for Megan's fourth birthday. Emerald swallowed the lump of emotion clogging her throat. Eric had called Megan Precious Princess from the moment she was born. So much so that when Megan was little and Emerald had told her daughter she was being a naughty girl because she kept standing on the seat of the shopping cart, Megan wrapped her arms around Emerald's neck, gave her a huge smile, and said adamantly, "I not naughty. I precious princess."

So many memories. So many lost dreams. Her house stood on a hill overlooking the fog-ridden Salisbury Plain, Stonehenge, and highway A303, the fastest route to London. From that city she could disappear to anywhere in the world.

Sucking in deep breaths of the chill air, she opened the car door and helped Megan in, but her hands shook so badly that her daughter ended up buckling herself into her car seat.

Doona think about it now. You canna, Emerald told herself as she got into the driver's seat and backed way from everything she believed her life to be. Her vision blurred as she pulled out onto the road.

"Wait," Megan cried, and Emerald hit the brakes, blinking away her tears before she turned to look at her daughter. Megan held out her pink bunny. "Da might need Booboo Bunny." Her tiny mouth quivered, but she held her shoulders stiff and kept her eyes fierce.

Dear God. Emerald fisted her hand around the steering wheel and prayed for strength. Megan didn't know Eric wasn't human anymore. Even Eric himself didn't know. But Emerald knew, had known even before her horrifying vision. She'd sensed the final shreds of the man she loved being torn away this past week and she'd been unable to save him.

According to Angel Lore it might have been possible to stop it all a month ago, at the very beginning when Eric had first been bitten by Michael Wellbourne, a Vladarian Vampire. But Eric wouldn't listen, even before the poison in his blood took hold of his soul. Wouldn't let her try and help him fight the evil with her powers. He'd been too proud to begin with. Then he'd claimed the power burning inside him made him stronger, better equipped to fight the monsters of the damned. To his credit, he'd eliminated a record number of vampires in a short time, but last week that had suddenly changed. And all of his insistences that he could handle the situation, all of his denials over how strong the evil had become inside him, were lies. Eric the

Vengeful, the world's foremost Vampire Slayer, was now what he'd once hated and killed. Was now reveling with the enemy and embracing the damned.

But he was still Megan's father.

Looking heavenward, Emerald thought about backing up to the house so Megan could leave her bunny for Eric. But when she saw a black wedge-shaped shadow cross in front of the blood orange moon, she froze, terror gripping her. It was exactly what she'd seen in her vision, an army of huge batlike creatures silhouetted in the sky before they attacked her and Megan. She shuddered hard, trying to force from her mind the images of torture and murder.

It wasn't real, she thought, shaking her head. It wasn't about to happen now, was it? In her vision she and Megan had been attacked while sleeping in their beds. Yet as she blinked and looked again, there was no mistaking the army of the damned. The foul creatures were heading in their direction fast.

She shoved the gas pedal to the floor, racing down the winding road toward the highway and London. Once the creatures discovered their prey had left, they'd come looking. She had no doubt. Their evil hunger in her vision had been unmatched by anything she'd ever known: Not even the demons from hell that she used to regularly fight had been as bad.

"Wait!" Megan cried out. "Go back."

"We canna, Meggie. We'll have to send Da the bunny later."

"A present? We can send Booboo Bunny to Da as a present?" Megan asked, sounding completely taken with the idea.

"Yes, poppet. Yes, we will."

"But why not now?

"There are bad creatures coming."

"Are they very bad creatures?"

"Yes."

Emerald hurtled into the darkness, heart pounding and stomach wrenching. She wasn't going to make it to London where she could hide in the mass of humanity. And she couldn't fight an entire army alone, not without drawing power from another source. Her powers were rusty. She'd barely used them since becoming pregnant with Megan. Motherhood had taken precedence. No demon fighting. No power tapping. Nothing more than an occasional misty vision, until last night. The thought that their lives would now rest on her powers made her ill.

Sanctuary. She'd have to find sanctuary instead. A place sanctified and blessed where the damned wouldn't be able to reach her. The church in Amesbury? Could she make it? It was two miles away and she'd need time to break into the church too. Turning onto the highway, she glanced back toward home.

The top of the hill had become a huge bonfire. Flames were devouring her home, shooting high into the night as they consumed everything.

"Dear God!" she cried, running off the road in her shock. She pulled right, barely avoiding a crash as horror and panic gripped her. How had the creatures moved so fast? How had they caused such a devastating fire so quickly? It was as if they'd opened the earth and unleashed an inferno from hell.

Where were the creatures? She looked about, frantic.

Sensing the grave danger, Megan cried for her and unbuckled herself. She came over the seat and grabbed Emerald's arm.

"Meggie. Oh, God, Meggie. Get buckled now!" Emerald drove with one hand and buckled Megan in the middle seat next to her with the other. She was petrified for her daughter.

"Mommy! Hold me."

"I am in my heart, poppet. Can you feel my angel wings?" she asked, projecting magical comfort and protection over her daughter.

"Yes. And Nana's from heaven too."

Emerald prayed that was true. She kept searching behind her, couldn't see the creatures, yet she could feel their evil press-

ing in on her. The night suddenly turned darker. Dear God . . .
that black cloud rolling her way . . . moving faster than the
wind . . . it couldn't be. As she watched, two creatures, larger
than the rest, rushed ahead of the pack, moving at hyper-speed
toward her.

She pumped the gas pedal, trying to go faster, but it was all
the way to the floor. It wasn't going to be enough.

The Stones, Em.

She hadn't heard the angelic sound in so long that she almost missed the soft tinkling. Her mother's voice. What stones?
Did she mean Stonehenge? The Druids' Stones were just ahead,
little more than a hundred meters off the roadway. But that
would be suicide. She and Megan would be alone . . . expected
to the creatures with no help.

Go, Em. Go to the Stones.

But—

Suddenly a bone-chilling screech tore through the night.
Two thumps sounded on the roof of her car. The roof began to
cave inward, buckling until a black claw punched through. It
sliced into Megan's car seat.

Deafening screams filled the car. Hers. Megan's. The creatures'. Everything ran together in a blur. She and Megan were
going to die. Horribly.

The heavy creatures shifted on the roof. Then a black face
appeared in the windshield. Looking down into the car from
above, he smiled, fangs dripping with blood. She knew its eyes.
Eric. Another face appeared. Wellbourne.

Oh God!

THE STONES! GO NOW!

Emerald wrenched the wheel and careened off the road toward the ancient stones. The car bounced hard, jostling Megan
forward toward the dash. Megan's scream was suddenly cut off.

Crying, Emerald grabbed for her daughter, caught her shirt
and pulled her back.

"Meggie! Meggie! Talk to Mommy, Meggie."

Megan didn't answer, but fell slack into the seat. What happened? She hadn't hit anything.

"Meggie! Oh, God, please." Emerald didn't stop the car but plowed forward across the rutted field and through the ghostly fog toward Stonehenge's monoliths.

The creatures moved to the hood. Facing her, one clung to the windshield, blocking out everything. Huge and black with wings, it stared at her with Eric's eyes. No. Not Eric's anymore. Eric's gaze had never held the vitriolic malice glowing from this creature.

Everything went cold. Her heart, her soul, her skin. Even her breath frosted in the air. She became so cold that she couldn't move, couldn't steer or brake or look away from death. Grinning, the creature smashed in the windshield. Tiny pieces of cutting glass blasted everywhere, stinging her face and arms, welling up blood. The creature's icy, evil hunger pierced her soul, wanting to master her, rule her, and devour her.

It reached for her throat, fangs ready.

Chapter One

Trapped between *the spirit realm and the mortal world the black wolf cried out, howling into the twilight. His haunting plea for help, for freedom, echoed throughout the misty barrier that separated mortal from immortal, but he could not be heard. Not among his brethren. Not among the humans he could see so clearly. Only the lost souls on Spirit Wind Mountain heard him, spirits as imprisoned as he. He was a warrior bound by invisible chains, unable to answer the sworn call of his Blood Hunter's soul to protect Logos's Elan and the struggling mortals, unable to fight the great darkness unleashing itself upon the mortal ground.*

Present Day
Twilight, Tennessee

"I have to go to town, Em. I'm sheriff. Twilight's my responsibility." Sam Sheridan clenched his teeth, fists, stomach, and anything else he could clamp down on, wondering just how sharp an edge a man could walk before he split apart. It was worse than ironic that after everything he'd been through—the military, imprisonment, torture, and years of personal hell—that a pint-size bit of mystical fluff was going to do him in. Make that a nicely figured bit of mystical fluff with wet-dream jeans and a soft green shirt that hugged every curve he wanted to touch.

"You canna go. Not now," Emerald Linton said as she planted herself in the middle of the doorway to the one-room cabin he'd made into his office. "Leaving here would be a mistake. You'd be opening yourself up for an attack from Cinatas. And once you're away from the protective shield, the growing darkness I feel from the gathering Vladarians *will* feed the vampire infection inside you."

"It's been four days, Em." Closing his eyes, he fought for patience. She was determined to keep him at the old ranger camp they were holed up in, and he was fast approaching the point of no return—the point where he'd start kissing her and never stop. A vampire's lust for blood couldn't be any stronger than his lust for her. He'd been trying to avoid her since he'd returned from Belize bitten and supposedly damned for eternity. So far nothing had happened in the ninety-six hours, forty-two minutes, and—he glanced at his watch—ten seconds since Luis Vasquez had sunk his teeth into Sam's neck. No fangs had developed. No bloodlust had overtaken him. He'd like to think it was because he'd killed the Vladarian Vampire seconds into the bite and not because Emerald's protective shield was holding any changes at bay.

Even if he wasn't infected, it wouldn't change his hands-off policy where she was concerned. They had no future together, never had a chance at one from the moment they'd met nine months ago. She was a woman with a child in tow and he'd been damaged goods from the start, never knowing when and where he'd have a PTSD flashback from the past. Or if he'd hurt someone in the dark hours of the night.

He did know without a doubt that the vampire bite had nothing to do with his visceral desire for Emerald. He'd been itching for her since he'd first seen her. His gaze raked up Emerald's body, managing to avoid her imploring, misty green eyes. Every time he looked into her eyes, he went a little crazy inside. Itching didn't come close to describing his need for her. Ravenous did.

More than once he'd considered giving in to his need, just having an all-night sex fest and getting her out of his system. But he didn't think he'd have the resolve to walk away the morning after, and she'd feel even more of a need, maybe even then would have the right, to "fix" him. And he was unfixable.

Drawing a deep breath, he tried to refocus on the reason she was in his face at the moment. "Have you had a vision about me, Em? About today? Is that what this is all about now?"

She didn't immediately answer and her hesitation jerked him to attention. He brought his narrowed gaze to hers, searching the liquid green depths that always left him drowning in her allure. He'd never known her not to be pigheadedly sure about her magic mumbo jumbo. After a long moment she shook her head then focused on his desk, fear and an odd vulnerability clouding her eyes. "No, no vision this time. I just feel something bad is going to happen. You canna go."

He had to go, for both their sakes. She'd be angry, but then that was a good thing. If she was ticked at him then the odds they'd end up in the bed behind him went way down, right? He'd been operating on that philosophy since he met her, but it was failing to do the trick these past few days.

He could feel her from all the way across the room. Her hot-blooded temper and wild sensuality dragged at him like a riptide, pulling him so far under her spell, he could barely breathe.

Sucking in another deep breath, he caught a whiff of her scent and cursed. The pure essence of Irish lavender mixed with a mysterious but irresistibly alluring aroma hit him hard. It was a heady aphrodisiac potent enough to wake the dead.

"Hello? Sam? Are you hearing me?" Emerald demanded, waving her delicate hands at him as she spoke. Even though her bracelets tinkled like heavenly bells, the effect of her siren-red nails was like a matador waving a red cape at a bull. Surely steam had to be rising off him.

"Yeah, Em, I'm feeling you," he said, his voice cutting through his throat like shards of glass. He heard her all right. He just didn't know what in the hell to do with her.

He knew backward and forward what he *wanted* to do with her.

He shot up from his seat. He had to get out of there fast and he had to put her out of his mind, even if it was just for a little while, or he was going to do something they'd both regret—like make use of the bed shoved against the wall.

"I don't think you are, Sam," she said, her lilting voice imploring him. "Dark, powerful forces are gathering all around us."

Shamefully, the forces bearing down on him had nothing to do with evil and everything to do with sex. Yep, they were in a battle for their lives and for the lives of thousands if not millions of others. Yep, they barely had any privacy holed up in a small ranger camp with her daughter and seven others, including two elite warriors from the spirit realm called Blood Hunters. Yep, he should be thinking about a million other things besides her and him being hot and heavy, but he wasn't. And that was exactly why he had to leave. He had to do something to put his focus back on their situation. Making an appearance at the station house in Twilight and doing a little recon on the Falls Resort, Dr. Cinatas's stronghold on Hades Mountain, fit the bill.

Squeezing his eyes shut and searching for strength, he counted to five, then tried to reason with her one last time. "Em, feeling something bad might happen isn't good enough for me. There's something bad happening just about every split second all over the world. I can't toss aside my responsibilities just because you've got a 'feeling.'"

"This isn't a joke, Sam," she said. "You know it's more than just a feeling with me. You know that sometimes I just *know* things. The evil surrounding us is stronger than ever before. I sense it out there beyond the shield."

"None of that changes the fact that I'm the sheriff. I *have* to check on the town. The station has been getting dozens of calls from old man Hatterfield about the 'black cloud' over Hades Mountain, and 'goings-on' at the Falls Resort there. We both know it isn't his moonshine talking. Cinatas is up to something and I have to go. The citizens of Twilight pay me to keep them safe."

"You canna do anything for anybody if you're dead," she cried. "You're officially on vacation until next week, remember? We all agreed that until we had some idea of how Cinatas and the Vladarians would react to our attack in Belize it would be best to stay under the protective shield. They'll be wanting revenge." She held a finger up for each point. "You destroyed the Vladarians' blood supply and killed Luis Vasquez, one of their own. You, Jared, and Aragon wiped out their Belize stronghold. Because of Aragon, Pathos, their leader for hundreds of years, is gone forever. And none of that is counting what we did to Cinatas's Sno-Med operations here and in Manhattan. What part about *they want us dead* doona you understand?"

He had to bite back a grin at that question, realizing he'd probably said something similar to her during one of their many disagreements. She was right. Dr. Anthony Cinatas and his Vladarian bloodsuckers would come after everyone with both barrels blasting. But Sam just couldn't sit here any longer waiting for "it" to happen—not if he could get a handle on what that "it" might be.

"Em, the protective shield is great—a real miracle. But we can't cower here with our heads stuck in the sand. If we don't try and find out what they're up to, I can guarantee they're going to come up behind us and bite us in the ass." He gathered his keys, hoping the jangle would bring an end to the argument. "Jared, Aragon, and Nick agree."

She didn't say anything, but turned to look into the outer room, giving him the freedom to study her profile. Bad move. Sunlight spilling over her cast her into shades of gold, making him greedier than King Midas.

"When did you men have this conversation and why dinna you tell the rest of us?"

"Late last night, so there hasn't been time to talk yet," Sam explained. Though battle ready, the Blood Hunters—Jared and Aragon—hadn't been as antsy to act as Sam and his deputy, Nick. Four days to men who'd been alive for millennia amounted to less than an eye blink, but the former spirit warriors did agree that more information was needed. "With no vision, how do you know that what you're feeling is even connected to me or not?" he asked.

"Instincts? Intuition?" She threw her slender hands up into the air, clearly frustrated. "Whatever you call it doesn't matter. I just know something bad will happen."

Sam had figured out a long time ago that all women spoke two languages simultaneously. The words that they said were one language and what they meant was another story. Like when they said "nothing" was bothering them, it always meant that "something" big was up.

At least it was that way until Emerald zoomed into town in a red Mini Cooper that screamed "squash me" to every semi and logging truck barreling down Twilight's Appalachian two lanes. He saw red every time he thought of her and her daughter tangling up with another car, and he saw red every time he went toe to toe with her mystical speak. It was a whole different language, and it left his head spinning. Give him a "nothing" that meant "something" and he was all right, but give him a "something" that meant "everything in and out of this world" and he was at his wits' end.

" 'Something's' not good enough. I've gotta go."

"Sam, please." She turned and their gazes met again. Hell, he was in big trouble; tears filled her eyes. The emotion in her plea twisted him inside out.

You're drowning, man. You're a total goner with the will of a marshmallow. Just lock the door and go for it. Forget the town, forget the threat. Forget the fact that you're twisted up inside and just take her. Get your fill. It doesn't matter that you can't offer her anything more than sex.

A cold sweat broke out all over his body. He had more honor than that. A man didn't take a woman unless he could give back full measure of what she's willing to offer and Em wasn't a one night stand. "Hell, Em, look at it my way for once. I can't live my whole life according to your mumbo jumbo."

She recoiled as if he'd hit her. "My . . . mumbo . . . jum—oh! How can you still say that after all that's happened? After so many things have been proven true? After all you've seen—the Red Demons, the shield . . . How can you not have any more belief in me than that?"

Damn! How did he always end up hurting her feelings? "Em. I didn't mean it that way. I just can't live by your 'feelings.' Not when—"

Her BlackBerry chimed and she dug it out of her pocket. "Hold on," she said, glancing at the screen.

Sam thought he would blow a gasket. They were in the middle of an argument and she was going to give advice? If Emerald had one fault it was that she tried to take care of everyone all of the time. And that damn BlackBerry she answered twenty-four/seven for her sex counseling clinic in Ireland was part of it. He didn't care if somebody over there had a kink in their dick at the moment. "Looks as if we both have more important things to do today. You're in my way, Em."

She gasped. "Fine, Samuel T. Sheridan. You can do whatever you want. I doona care." Whipping around on her heel, she marched out of the building. The tears streaming down her cheeks told him that she did care—a lot. But he bit back the urge to call out to her, not trusting himself to even exhale until the door slammed.

He was safe. For now. Checking his 9 mm Glock, he slid on his holster, gave his desk a quick once-over to make sure he wasn't forgetting anything. Then he escaped from his office before Emerald changed her mind about leaving him to his own devices. Burying the niggling voice urging him to go after her, he went in search of his deputy, ace helicopter pilot Nick Sinclair. Nick needed to be on extra alert while Sam went to town.

He found Nick in the dining hall, cleaning their stockpile of weapons. The cache wasn't nearly enough to fight the battle they'd be facing. Sam already had sent out a red alert to all his military connections that he was looking for hardware. He hoped they'd have a load soon.

"Aragon and Jared should be helping you break down and clean the guns," Sam said. The spirit warriors were sharp and battle savvy but could use a little more experience with modern weapons. Considering how fast they'd assimilated to life on earth, it wouldn't take them long to become experts.

"Jared and Erin are on the Net, trying to track down all of Pathos's real estate holdings. So far they've found a humungo estate outside of Vienna. If we can figure out where besides the Falls the bloodsuckers congregate, we can deal a mortal blow to them and their operation. Erin wants to pinpoint all the Sno-Med clinics and research centers worldwide as quickly as we can, too. With the vampires' supply of Elan blood destroyed, they'll be looking to replenish it by offering free medical screening to the masses again. If we know when and where they plan to hold their health expos then we have a better chance of stopping them. Aragon and Annette are with Stef. She had a bad night." Nick looked back at his gun. "Annette thinks I should keep out of Stef's sight."

Nick said the last with a sense of angry despair, and Sam clasped the young man's shoulder in a reassuring squeeze. Sam wasn't exactly sure what he should say about Annette's sister. In his opinion everyone was expecting too damn much from the girl too soon. She did have to realize that starving herself to escape the pain of existing after being in Vasquez's clutches wasn't hurting the bad guys. Sam knew how she felt, but he'd fed on revenge and the need to fill in as a father for Nick. Reed Sinclair had died getting Sam out of that hellhole in Belize, and it was the least Sam could do. "Believe me. It's not you, man."

Nick shrugged, clearly disbelieving, and Sam released him, sighing.

Nick continued to oil the gun a moment more then said, "The thing is, I feel partially responsible for what happened to her."

Sam glanced at his watch then straddled the bench opposite Nick. The town could wait a minute or two. "Yeah, right. Annette's investigation is going to show you were on Sno-Med's staff and killing women with experimental blood treatments. That you were in cahoots with Stef's boss, Rankin, to off his wife with the deadly treatments. Then you kidnapped Stef and Abe Bennett and sent them to Vasquez to cover your ass."

Nick rolled his eyes. "You know what I mean. I knew five seconds into my blind date with Stef that she wasn't a player, but that didn't stop me from maneuvering her into my bed. I was horny and there was just something about her, a goodness that I . . . hell, wanted to touch. I can't explain it. If I'd left her alone like I should have then she wouldn't have been so upset about sleeping with a guy she hardly knew and she might not have been out searching for peace at the Sacred Stones so early in the morning and vulnerable for Rankin's attack."

That was a mouthful from Nick, which only attested to how torn up he was over Stef. Sam sure as hell knew what it was like to want what you shouldn't have, and unfortunately Nick was learning a hard lesson. "Rankin would have gotten Stef and Abe no matter what. So you can't put that onus on yourself. As for your guilt over Stef, you're right in some ways. A real man doesn't take a woman unless he can give her what she is looking to give him. But Stef is an adult. She could have said no."

"With me pushing all of the right buttons?" Nick replied. Apparently a woman didn't have a chance to resist when Nick turned on the charm.

Sam shook his head. Some things never changed. He narrowed his gaze at Nick. "Seems to me everyone wants something out of Stef—wants her to talk, to eat, to heal. Maybe what you need to do is decide how you feel about her and your one night together. Are you her lover, her friend, or a stranger? Then act on that basis to give her what she needs rather than wanting *her* to forgive *you*. She might not have any forgiveness in her."

Nick looked stunned and sat staring blankly at the pieces of his M-16. "You're right. This isn't about me, but about her. I care about her, but . . . hell, I don't know if there is anything else."

"Don't let guilt lead you into promising what you don't have to give, but at least be someone who cares," Sam advised.

Nick snapped the rifle barrel into place. "Have you talked to her about Vasquez? About what the bastard might have done to her and Abe?"

Sam shook his head. "She knows I was Vasquez's prisoner for two years, but she won't talk to anyone about her captivity. Vasquez had Stef for six months. I can guarantee she's been through some heavy shit. It isn't going to be all better anytime soon. Maybe never. What little we've learned has come from Marissa, but Vasquez kept his niece locked up with her grandmother most of the time in a nunnery on the compound. Other than the screams of those being tortured and what Marissa imagined caused them, she didn't see what went on in the camp. She just knew her uncle was evil and she and her grandmother would be the ones screaming if they didn't do what he said."

Reluctantly, Sam's mind went back to Belize and what he'd lived through at Vasquez's hands. Though Stefanie didn't bear the physical scars that Sam did, he knew the scars on the inside were the worst. Shuddering hard, he clenched his fists. "You want a snapshot of what it was like? Vasquez enjoyed physical torture, but he excelled in destroying the spirit and soul, mainly by making you watch someone else pay the price for your actions. Once a woman at the compound brought me food and treated my lacerations from Vasquez's whip. He caught her helping me. The punishment was forcing me watch him . . ." Sam shuddered again then swallowed the choking lump in his throat. "Let's just say she died hard after a long time. My guess would be Stef's friend Abe died hard, too. And she had to watch."

"Jesus. How can bastards like that be allowed to exist?"

Sam didn't answer. There wasn't any answer.

Sam's cell phone vibrated. It was the station. "What is up with Myra?" he muttered. "She's called no less that a dozen times since yesterday about old man Hatterfield's complaints. Usually she lets me know once and then fields the rest until I come into the station."

Sam flipped open his phone. "My ETA is twenty," he told her as he connected the line. "What's up now?"

"You were supposed to be here by now," her voice was deliberately sultry. "The coffee is . . . ah, very hot . . . and ready, but now you've got company." Sam frowned at his phone. What the hell was that?

Nick obviously heard. He rolled his eyes.

"What kind of company?"

"Oh, just the FBI."

"Did they say what about?"

"No. Maybe we can have coffee after," she said suggestively.

"I'll be there shortly." Sam gritted his teeth, dismissing Myra's lunacy to focus on why the FBI was here.

"Want me to come along?" Nick asked.

Sam shook his head. "I can handle the suits. They're probably here to finish clearing Erin's arrest warrants."

"I'm not talking about the FBI, I'm referring to Myra. Sounds as if your absence has revved her libido and sent her off the man-hunting deep end."

Sam snorted. "She's harmless."

"Harmless as a barracuda," Nick muttered. "Here, take this for backup." He dug out his wallet and tossed a foil packet. "She's probably waiting naked in your office and the FBI thing is a ruse."

Sam caught the condom, shaking his head in exasperation. It wasn't the first time Nick had tossed one at him. He'd been doing so with increasing frequency since learning Sam had been without any sort of relationship after being a prisoner in Belize. In Sam's mind his flashbacks put him out of the dating game. It wasn't until Emerald showed up that he'd had any sort of desire for things to be different. "No need to worry. Myra's not my type."

"Man does not live by bread alone and you've been starving yourself for over eight years. I know a powder keg ready to blow when I see it and you're it. Find your type and do something. Maybe then you'll stop taking everybody's head off just because they were unwise enough to speak to you."

He left the dining hall and headed for his patrol car in a bear of a mood. He was getting it from all sides this morning. The FBI had better be camping out on the doorstep for Myra's sake or he'd fire her. Not that Sam *wanted* any government suits sticking their noses into Twilight. Until definitive proof of Cinatas and Sno-Med's illegal and murdering activities was found, the unconventional war he and the others waged against the bloodsuckers wouldn't sit well with the law.

Over the past few weeks Sam had dealt directly with the FBI twice. Once to prove Erin Morgan hadn't been responsible for the murder of four patients and the burning of Sno-Med's Manhattan clinic. The second time was over a freshly electrocuted corpse found on the side of the road in Twilight. The dead man had been a serial killer who'd been executed in the electric chair two years ago in South Carolina, then buried there by the state. The Feds were still scrambling around, trying to figure out how the corpse ended up in Tennessee, looking as if he'd been executed an hour ago. Sam knew, but telling the Feds would get him a one-way ticket to a padded cell. Who would believe anything that had been happening? Warriors, werewolves, undead vampires in influential positions around the world, assassins, and a petite woman with enough magic to make a shield worthy of *Star Wars*.

"The gack-headed idiot!" Emerald muttered as she rushed from Sam's office for the privacy of the nearby woods and rested her back against the rough bark of a pine tree. She needed a minute to pull herself together. She shivered, despite the warmth of the bright morning sun filtering through the leaves.

Why today of all days had Sam decided to leave the camp? Why today of all days had she awakened with an overwhelming sense of imminent doom? The two had to be connected, but all she had to go on was her intuition. No matter how hard she tried, she'd been unable to conjure even a tiny glimpse into the future.

She'd felt this deep sense of dread only twice before. Once had been six years ago when her husband had tried to kill her and give their daughter to Michael Wellbourne. The second time had been last year when Michael's brother, William Wellbourne, discovered where she and Megan had been hiding and came after them. Both times Emerald's visions had alerted her to the danger and they'd escaped to safety, but this time, all was darkness.

The energy needed to draw power from the nearby Sacred Stones to form the protective shield over the camp had drained her resources and was likely why she'd been unable to tap into her precognitive abilities. She'd experienced a similar problem after fighting Eric and Michael Wellbourne at Stonehenge. It had taken her six months to recover her ability to scry into the future. She had to find another source of power. This floundering in the dark was driving her crazy. She hadn't realized how much of her confidence was dependent on her visions.

All she had right now were her nightmares of Eric's vampire infection and her intuition. Both of them screamed that Sam was headed for trouble. Suddenly Emerald's mind shifted into gear. If she couldn't beat him, why not join him? At the very least she'd be around to help protect him. Stowing away would be her best option. He wouldn't ditch her on the side of the road, so he'd have to come back to the camp or keep her with him. Halfway to his car, she heard his cabin door open.

Heart racing, she dove behind a pine tree and cursed herself for waiting too late to act. But instead of coming her way toward his car, Sam went in the direction of the dining hall, and she took that as a divine sign to go with her wild plan. The second he disappeared from sight, Emerald ran for his squad car.

It was stupid of her to expect he'd hold back from something he thought he had to do. He wouldn't be Sam if he did. Nine months ago, she'd driven into Twilight and he'd pulled her over for a traffic warning. She'd never forget it. He'd stepped from his flashing squad car and sauntered her way, oozing power and sex appeal as his honed muscles stretched the seams of his uniform. Her breath had come to a screeching halt and her pulse went from sixty to two hundred in one point five seconds. He reached the side of her car, all tall, dark, and foreboding, looking like a god next to her little Mini. He'd tipped his hat in a show of respect that zinged her insides, but it was his deep rumbling voice saying "Ma'am" that surged a sensual heat through her erogenous zones. He'd swept her away right then and there. She could still feel the tingle to this day.

It had been quite a shock to be so turned on by a total stranger, especially with her daughter sitting in the seat next to her. But that hadn't been as nearly as shocking as seeing his eyes. He'd lowered his mirrored Ray-Bans to pin her with blue eyes so remote and cold that she'd literally shivered from the frost. In that split second, she'd had a vision of him that grabbed her heart and wouldn't let go. A vision of a lone warrior, covered in wounds, who stood alone on a glacier facing a malignant army of thousands. The warrior died a horrible death and had been dragged into the pits of hell.

Since their first meeting, they'd gone toe to toe on everything under the sun. He was determined to be the Lone Ranger and she was bent on saving him from that fate. She believed she could, but then he'd returned vampire bitten just like Eric had been and her faith had taken a nose dive. Nightmares of Sam becoming as damned and evil as Eric filled her dreams.

For once, Emerald thanked the heavens for her short little frame as she climbed into the back of Sam's squad car. The Red Demons had done a number on it last week, beating up the body of the car and shattering the back passenger window. She'd thrown an old blanket over the backseat to shield anyone from missed slivers of glass until the window could be repaired and the car thoroughly cleaned. Hopefully it would keep her hidden from Sam for now.

Crouching in the floorboard and pulling the edges of the blanket over her, she dialed Annette up on her BlackBerry. Annette answered on the first ring. "Listen, luv. Don't ask questions, but run outside and distract Sam with conversation while he's getting into his car. He's insisting on going to town and I'm stowing away to join him."

"Are you crazy?" Annette asked.

"Just bloody do it. I don't have time."

"I'm hunting him down now," Annette said, lowering her voice to a whisper. "Are you sure about this?"

"No, but I'm too worried to let him go alone. This feeling of doom I have is connected to him."

"So you're going to march into the jaws of the shark as well? What kind of sense does that make?"

"I know what he's up against when it comes to the paranormal and his vampire bite. He doesn't. Will you and Marissa keep Meggie with you today? She can read to Stef again. I'll call her as soon as we get to town, okay?"

"All right, but I don't like it. I see Sam. Bye."

Emerald turned off her BlackBerry and waited for Sam, feeling ridiculous about hiding in his car, but she couldn't see any other way. She pressed the back of her hand to her damp brow, and her angel bracelets tinkled. She hadn't taken off the protection her mother had given in years, but she couldn't afford for Sam to hear them now. Slipping them from her wrist, she stuffed them into her pocket.

Thankfully, she didn't have long to wait. Within minutes, she heard Sam's and Annette's muffled voices. Sam opened the car door.

Annette was in midsentence. ". . . as you're getting that stuff you might as well bring the sterilizer for the surgical instruments. And the rest of the bandage supplies would be good, too. They're in the cabinet against the back wall of the supply room—gauze, tape, sterile pads, elastic wraps, and the nonstick Teflon pads I use on burns, and—"

"Hold it," Sam interjected. "What about the kitchen sink? Or better yet, why not have the whole clinic trucked up here?"

Emerald could clearly imagine Sam' scowl. Annette had probably asked him to bring everything in her clinic.

"That would be perfect," Annette replied.

"That was a joke," Sam said. "You know as in ha, ha."

"Yeah, mine, too," Annette said. "My bad mood is because I haven't had my coffee yet. What's yours?"

"Wrong side of the bed," Sam said. "You lost me after about item number fifteen. Can you call Myra with that list? I'll send a deputy over to get them and I'll bring them back with me this afternoon. Will that work? I'm in a hurry right now."

"Yeah. Um, will you do me another favor?"

"More?" Sam asked.

"Be careful, all right?"

"Sounds like Emerald got to you, too."

"She's worried about you and with good reason. Besides, she hasn't been wrong yet."

"I know. That's what bothers me the most," Sam said. "Not that she's right, but that she's as worried about me as she is. She has enough to deal with already. I'm not letting her add me to her responsibility list."

"Too late. You're already there, whether you like it or not."

Emerald heard Sam climb into the driver's seat and the space she hid in suddenly seemed to shrink. Bloody hell. This was stupid. She braced herself, ready to lever up from her cramped position, but paused to hear Sam's response.

"I'm not going to let her mess herself up trying to help me. I'm staying as far away from her as I can. Don't get me wrong, I'm taking her warning seriously—but it doesn't change the fact that I'm the sheriff of Twilight. These are my people and I have a job to do. If an epidemic hit the town, you'd be out there treating the sick no matter what the danger, right?"

Annette sighed. "Dead on. Just be careful, okay?"

"Count on it," Sam said.

Emerald heard Sam shut the car door and crank the engine. He moved about four feet then rolled down his window. "Nette," he called out. "Tell Em . . . hell. Tell her I'll check in every couple of hours."

"She'll appreciate that," Annette replied.

Then Sam pushed on the gas and the car began a bumpy journey over the dirt road leading from the camp and the Sacred Stones at the top of Spirit Wind Mountain.

Emerald stayed tucked into her little space, sure she'd made the right decision. She understood Sam all too well. He was the sheriff, so he'd sheriff. What he didn't understand was that she was an angel, well, part angel, and as such she too had a responsibility. To save her friends. Unless the evil became too great. Then she would have to kill.

Chapter Two

SAM ROLLED to a stop about fifty yards away from camp, stuck his head out the window, and sucked in a deep breath of pine-scented morning air. Emerald's lavender fragrance was so engraved in his brain that he could still smell her. He'd like to think it was just her blanket covering the backseat that he smelled, but it was more than that. He could still almost feel her. Maybe once he left the protective shield he'd be free of her.

The line marking where Emerald's protective shield ended and the "real world" began was just ahead of him. The boundary had become clear within hours of her whirling the shield into place last week. Something about the shield slightly altered the color of the foliage, turning the forest's greens and browns to deeper, richer colors, creating what Sam called the "Disney Effect." According to Jared, the change in colors was because the goodness from the Sacred Stones saturated everything under the shield, which included Sam. But it was time for him to face the real world. Grasping the steering wheel tightly, he eased off the brake and rolled forward.

The second he passed through the shield he could feel the difference. A faint sense of malice hit him and steadily grew the farther he went down Spirit Wind Mountain, as if he was getting closer and closer to a dead skunk—faint on the edges but mushrooming into a nuclear stink bomb the closer he got. Only what assaulted Sam wasn't an odor, but a throbbing sensation of evil more potent than any he'd sensed before.

His pulse raced as the memory of hanging upside down and being whipped unconscious flashed through his mind. Vasquez had been sadistic. Vasquez had been evil. But the malevolence bombarding him now was worse because the attack hit directly inside him, leaving him mentally grasping for a way to defend himself. A cold sweat broke over Sam's body and he shivered all the way to his soul. The urge to turn back to the camp overwhelmed him and he slowed the car, fighting for control.

This was insane. He had to be imagining it. It had to be another psychosomatic manifestation trying to control him. Right? Instead of paralyzing pain down his spine he was now feeling darts of evil piercing his soul.

He was such a pansy-assed loser.

Rather than pulling a one-eighty and running back to camp, he braced his hands on the steering wheel and hit the gas. Come hell or high water, he wasn't going to chicken out. He couldn't give in to this new symptom of his psychological weaknesses.

The commitment to proceed eventually relieved some of the oppressive waves of ill will hitting him, which proved to him it was all in his mind after all. If the evil had been real, it would have gotten worse. One thing bothered him though. Everything around him seemed different somehow. Either that or he was more aware of his surroundings on a level he'd never been on before, and he prided himself on being pretty damn alert.

He could hear everything, even over the hum of the car's engine: the rush of a roadside creek, the chatter of a squirrel scurrying along a fence top, the wind of his wake fluttering the leaves of white oaks and poplars. He could smell everything, too. The car. The gas. The oil. The asphalt. The trees. The grass. The sunshine. Everything had a discernable scent to it. And he could damn well still smell Emerald as if she was right there . . .

"Son of a bitch." Another deep breath confirmed his suspicion and he hit the brakes. The back end of the squad car fishtailed before he ground to a halt right in front of the town line marker: WELCOME TO TWILIGHT, TENNESSEE. WHERE EVERYTHING IS POSSIBLE.

The sign should be amended to read WHERE EVERYTHING IN

HEAVEN AND HELL IS POSSIBLE. And it should be flashing a red danger signal, too.

Maybe not everything was possible. He couldn't seem to escape a pint-size blonde.

Emerald's entire being was focused on breathing and not writhing from the power of the darkness freezing her soul. The closer Sam drove to town, the worse the pain had become. She knew what it was. She'd felt the gathering forces of darkness outside the protective shield growing stronger and stronger over the past week. But she hadn't realized their full potency until leaving the shield. Or was it because she wasn't wearing her angel bracelets?

She'd lived in Twilight for almost a year now and had been aware of its special qualities. The scrambling of the magnetic and electric fields surrounding the area created an atmospheric fog that made it easier for supernatural beings to pass through the spirit barrier into the physical realm. There were other mystical places on earth, places where the spirits for good prevailed, like Stonehenge, and places the evil forces controlled, where bad things happened. Twilight, with its Sacred Stones on Spirit Wind Mountain, had been predominantly a place of good. Now she didn't know. The darkness seemed to have taken over, with forces more potent than she'd ever faced before.

Icy pain clawed at her in overwhelming waves of malice, and she fought for balance. She *had* to block out the darkness and get a grip before they reached town or she'd be worthless in helping Sam. If it was this bad for her and she knew what was going on, how much worse was it for Sam? Rising above her own discomfort, she sent her senses in search of his spirit and felt he'd already made the jump from fighting the sensations attacking him to nearly accepting them. The blood drained from her already dizzy brain.

Sam! Fight it, she silently urged his spirit.

Suddenly he cursed and hit the brake hard.

Emerald's face plowed into the back of the car seat and her breath whooshed from her lungs. Then her stomach gave a sickening lurch, not only worried that he'd hit an animal but that he had heard her as well. The jig was up.

Sam snatched the blanket away and glared at her over the back of the seat.

She blinked up at him. He looked even more unhappy to see her than she'd expected.

When in doubt, come out slugging.

"What in the bleedin' hell happened?" she asked as she popped up from the floorboard. She glanced about, looking for why he'd stopped on a dime as she pressed her fingers gingerly to her left cheek. At least she still had a cheekbone, but it was sure to be black and blue.

"You. That's what happened. I . . . felt you. I can . . . smell you," Sam said softly, more softly than she'd ever heard him speak. His arctic blue gaze nailed her and she immediately knew what the dead eye of a killer storm had to be like—that moment when everything was unnaturally still, and all she could do was watch the destruction about to hit.

"Oh." Emerald bit her bottom lip.

" 'Oh'? Is that all you can say? I'm trying very hard at the moment to remember that I am the good guy here. What the hell kind of stupid fool stunt is this, Em?"

She rolled her shoulders, feeling an ache in her neck. "Talk about fool stunts. You could have just calmly pulled to the side of the road to out me instead of nearly breaking my bleedin' neck."

Sam's exhale carried the force of a steam engine about to explode. "That may happen yet. Last chance to explain and it had better be good."

Emerald shrugged. "Mohammed wouldn't stay on the mountain, so I came along to protect him."

"The only thing I need protection from is you," Sam muttered. He shut his eyes and looked as if he was searching for patience, but then popped them open and glared at her again. "You know, I don't even think I can count high enough to keep myself from throttling you. What right do you have to put yourself in danger for me? You've got a child to look after."

Emerald flinched; his strike hit deep. She constantly struggled to balance her responsibility to fight the dark forces growing in the world with keeping her daughter removed from that fight. It hadn't been easy, especially when both she and Megan were on William Wellbourne's hit list. One of her first visions about the Blood Hunters coming to earth was of them defeating the powerful Vladarian Vampires. When William Wellbourne discovered their hiding place last year, she'd had no choice but to act on that vision and come to Twilight. Her daughter shouldn't have to spend her whole life hiding in fear. "I am looking after Meggie. She's safe under the shield with a doctor, two warriors, and a sheriff's deputy at her fingertips should she need any help. Which is exactly where we would both be if you'd stop being such a stubborn gack."

Sam tipped his head back against the car seat and pinched the bridge of his nose, as if to cut off a sharp pain. "We've argued this until it's a dead horse. If you can't get it then there's nothing else I can say. I can look after myself and I can do it better when I don't have to worry about someone else getting hurt. As soon as we get to the station, you're going back."

Sighing, Emerald climbed into the front and settled in the passenger's seat. "I get it. And were we talking about physical threats only, you'd be right. But you canna tell me you can handle that." She pointed out the windshield of the car, swallowing hard as a knot of cold fear grabbed her by the throat.

In the distance over the top of a partially obscuring ridge top Emerald saw the source of the cold evil scraping her half-angel soul raw. She'd known the dark forces had been gathering. She'd felt it, but she'd assumed it was Cinatas and the Vladarians at the Falls Resort. This was more than just them there. More than she imagined possible. Over the nearest ridge, the roiling, black cloud dominated the sky, radiating waves of malevolence like an erupting volcano. Putrid malice straight from the bowels of hell spewed toward heaven.

"What the hell?" Sam said, cranking the car engine, and hitting the gas. "That can't be that black magic crap over Hades Mountain we're seeing already."

"I'm afraid it is," Emerald whispered. Two weeks ago a blackish mist had formed an obscuring barrier over the Falls Resort, a spell spawned from hell that enabled all manner of demonic creatures who ordinarily couldn't exist in the physical realm to roam in its shadow.

Sam steered the car ahead and tried to watch the black cloud at the same time. "If that's the Hades Mountain cloud, then other folks besides Hatterfield would be complaining about it. And Myra at the station damn well would have told me. She doesn't miss an opportunity to inform me of anything 'important' day or night."

Emerald didn't reply but kept her gaze centered on the black cloud as Sam rounded the sharp curve in the road. The town of Twilight came into full view, a tiny place with one stop light at the intersection of State Route 44 and the rural road leading to the city of Arcadia. Hades Mountain sat opposite them, across the wide valley. The mountain had two peaks, a high one where the Falls Resort was located and a much lower one off to the right. Reaching upward as if the demonic forces were building a malignant Tower of Babel toward heaven, the black cloud completely enveloped the top peak and most of the left side of Hades Mountain. The right side was clear. Separated from the black monster and scattered in patches throughout the valley lay misty patches of dark clouds.

This was more than a gathering of Vladarians.

"Sam," Emerald said softly. "I think it's a good thing you decided to come to town."

"You want to tell me what's going on up there?" he asked as he coasted down the steep incline into the valley.

Emerald shivered. "To fuel that much concentration of evil on earth, either the Devil has come to Twilight or half of hell is up there on that mountain." She shifted her gaze to Sam. "I'm afraid the clouds hovering over Twilight mean Cinatas and his vampires are after more than just us at the ranger camp. They want the town."

"What do you mean they want the town?"

"There have been times and places where demonic forces have taken over whole groups of people."

"And you know all that just from Druid visions and feeling things?" Sam asked harshly.

She looked away. She'd been hiding too much too long behind her guise of Druid magic. Ever since she put up the protective shield, she'd been on borrowed time in keeping her angel power secret. Jared and Aragon already suspected the source of her magic wasn't earthly. Druid priestesses, Wicca and such were merely conduits of magic and power either from the energy of the physical world or from other paranormal beings. Though she could draw on power from those sources to help her, her angel nature enabled her to create power and goodness to fight against evil.

Thankfully, Sam didn't press for an answer. He hit the gas pedal and hurried toward the station, oozing almost as much explosive tension as the dark cloud over Hades Mountain.

Reaching the edges of town, he cut his speed. There were more people milling about than usual—something she would expect during a special celebration, but not for a Saturday morning. Parking lots of the restaurants and the local bar, the Wet Whistle, were full. Groups of teenagers as well as other folks were gathered about, not appearing to be doing anything in particular but just oddly *there,* with discontent written all over their faces. As she and Sam passed, folks stopped to stare but didn't smile or wave. It was eerie. "Is it Founder's Day or something?"

"No. Just a regular Saturday as far as I know, which makes two things Myra has neglected to mention to me. It's not like Myra at all." Sam pulled into the sheriff's station and backed into a slot, leaving his front toward the street and a quick getaway. The he nailed her with another piercing glare. "As soon as I find out what's up here, you and I are going to talk about that black cloud and how you know what you know. Then you're going back to the camp, pronto."

Emerald didn't answer as she exited the squad car because the sensations of evil suddenly rose to a level of terror. This new assault came from the direction they'd just traveled, opposite Hades Mountain. She tried to chant in her mind the ancient words from Angel Lore that would keep the deep chill of darkness from paralyzing her with fear, but couldn't. It had hit her too strong and fast. She managed only to turn and face what she knew to be coming.

She could hear Sam calling her name, but she couldn't answer, couldn't run to him. She tried to warn him, but only a muffled cry came from her throat. Barreling into town at high speed was a white limousine.

She felt Sam at her side. He'd grabbed her arm to get her attention, but she couldn't take her eyes off of the limo racing their way.

"What the hell is it?" Sam demanded, then turned to look at the roaring limo. "That son of a bitch must be doing eighty. He's going to kill somebody." Releasing her arm, he ran toward the street, stepping out and waving his arms to get the driver's attention.

Sam was in danger. She was in danger. Not from being hit by the limo, but from whoever or whatever was inside it.

The limo driver hit his brakes. Smoke rose from the tires as they squealed on the asphalt. The limo stopped not more than five feet from where Sam stood.

Help, Emerald's soul shouted, her body seemingly frozen by the killing cold assaulting her.

She remembered the bracelets in her pocket. Fingers trembling, she dug them out and slid them on. As the clasps magically melded together, a faint sense of warmth and power surged through her, freeing her. She moved toward Sam, her body shivering badly.

Ignorant of the danger he was in, Sam marched toward the limo with his hand resting on the grip of his holstered Glock. He clearly intended to drag the driver from the car and likely take him by gunpoint to the jailhouse behind them.

Heart pumping wildly, she sent out a heated, mental attack against the darkness radiating her way. She forced herself forward and grabbed Sam's arm, pulling at him with all of her might as she thrust herself between him and the limo. He was in midstep, and her sudden jerk set him off balance. He stumbled hard to the left, giving her a murderous look as he went down on one knee.

There would be hell to pay for this stunt, but Sam had no idea what he was up against. Focusing hard, she sent wave after wave of angelic heat at the limo. When she added the ring of her bracelets, she heard the demons in the front of the limo cry out in pain. Then one of the tinted back windows rolled down, bringing her face-to-face with the hate-filled red gaze of William Wellbourne.

Burgenland, Austria

Life had been a bitch. He'd died. Then the fun began. For Dr. Anthony Cinatas, being undead and inheriting his father's legacy had made him a sort of Unholy Roman Emperor. The adoration of thousands on their knees was within reach. Everything was perfectly mapped out. Pathos had left nothing to chance.

Being of were blood, Elan blood, and now of vampire blood—thanks begrudgingly to Ashoden bin Shashur, who'd bitten him as he lay burned and broken in Sno-Med's ashes—Cinatas had become a superior immortal. The Vladarian Vampire had thought to make Cinatas his blood slave, but Pathos, like an avenging demon, had put a quick end to that. He'd shown up inside the Black Demons' stronghold in hell, claimed Cinatas as his son, and had Shashur executed—tortured into nonexistence by the Red Demons.

Cinatas now owned everything, since Pathos had been condemned to spend eternity lost in space, so to speak. Once Cinatas exchanged the cursed rubber mask he wore over his burn scars for a face transplant, life would be really good. Glancing through several more pages of cover models, he found another one that came close enough to what he used to look like, so there wouldn't be too many questions asked. Four men for him to interview. One would take the bait and die. Eeny meeny miney mo, he settled on Conrad Pitt as his first choice. Picking up the phone, he notified the surgeon's office and set the wheels in motion. Shortly, he'd be a new man. Getting one of the models' faces wouldn't be a problem. Offer the man the job of his dreams and he'd come running. Too bad life was full of accidents, and sometimes people just disappeared.

He'd have the transplant on the surgeon's private island near Dubai in the Persian Gulf and then recover here at Zion, the estate that now belonged to Cinatas. Stronghold, heaven, utopia, there weren't words enough to describe the place, other than to say God or Satan couldn't possibly have any better. Make that Logos and Heldon, Cinatas amended. He was now operating in a realm other than the mortal.

Located a short helicopter ride from Vienna, Zion's size and opulence was in keeping with the castle Hofburg, the former residence of the imperial Hapsburgs. But its pièce de résistance was the war room. Every superpower in the world would be envious of the state-of-the-art equipment that allowed a man to rule heaven, earth, and hell.

A newsbreak flashed on the computer screen, catching Cinatas's attention. It was puzzling that out of all the data fed to the war room from around the world, only information about the pope went to Pathos's personal computer. All other data, worldwide, was fed minute by minute onto a gigantic global map in the war room and denoted by coded icons. With the wireless mouse next to him, Cinatas could click on a black star in Baghdad and read about a suicide bombing of a market, or a skirmish between pirates and a UK cargo ship off the Somali Coast. Blue dots gave political information. Green squares were for environmental news, gold stars reported on Hollywood gossip. Red triangles denoted Pathos's offspring—who had yet to be activated—or his personal hired agents, all of whom were well placed in key political/ruling positions—a worldwide army of red just waiting to be used.

Why did Pathos have so much interest in what the pope did? Clicking onto the newscast, Cinatas read some stupid sentiment about directly blessing all of his devoted subjects. Through specially made golden urns blessed by the pope, the sacraments of the Eucharist were going to be transported to all dioceses around the world. This article gave mention that a special sacrament would be delivered to a cathedral in Cincinnati, Ohio, in two days, the first of many as the consecrated host would then travel throughout North America. Millions would flock to elaborate ceremonies, begging to be blessed. Cinatas imagined followers clamoring for him, kissing the hem of his garments, and looking to him for damnation rather than salvation.

A knock at the door interrupted his euphoric moment and a

wave of anger washed over him. Nyros. Pathos's personal assistant was fast becoming a thorn in Cinatas's side. The door opened to admit the Red Demon on whisper-soft, shoeless steps—only Cinatas was clean enough to wear shoes upon the carpets, especially once he had the décor changed to pure white. He kept his eyes shut, refusing to acknowledge Nyros until he was sure the demon had subjugated himself properly to Cinatas's presence. Day in and day out, Nyros had to be repeatedly reminded not to speak until spoken to.

Ten minutes later, Cinatas opened his eyes. The demon stood patiently waiting with his gaze cast properly downward. Things were looking up. "Nyros, you have good news for me, of course? Everything I've commanded is done?"

The demon hesitated and Cinatas clenched his fangs. Days ago he'd given Nyros several important tasks and the demon had yet to complete them to satisfaction.

"Your flight to Tennessee awaits your convenience. Wellbourne has arrived in Twilight along with Vladarians from the European faction, the Royals, and the Eastern Bloc. They are on their way to the Falls now."

"Good."

"But there are problems, Master. Several demons report an impenetrable shield protects the camp where Erin Morgan hides."

"They better not have tipped her off. The attack must be perfect," Cinatas warned. He'd deliberately delayed arriving at the Falls until the last minute to keep Morgan in the dark, just in case she had spies watching out for him. "I'm sure the Vladarians can handle the shield problem." The limp dick demons probably didn't know *how* to penetrate.

"Samir and Herrera will be late, or we'll have to delay until they arrive."

Cinatas narrowed his eyes and stared hard. Surely he'd heard wrong. Was he completely surrounded by incompetents? "There cannot be a delay. I wait for no one."

"The trouble is that Vasquez's demise has ignited a war among the oil rich vampires as to who will claim Vasquez's SINCO holdings. His shares in the oil company are worth billions and he left it all to his niece, Marissa Vasquez. She has been missing since the fall of Corazón de Rojo. The Vladarians are searching for her throughout the Belize jungle. Samir claims Marissa was affianced to him, thus Vasquez's share should be under his control until he can marry her. Vasquez's second in command, Herrera, is making the same claim."

Cinatas pinched the bridge of his nose, leaving an unnatural crease in the mask he wore. He tried to remind himself that great evil came from cold, calculated control as he bit back the vitriolic rage coursing through him. Did he have to do everything? "Tell them they are to arrive or they'll be denied their next transfusion of Elan blood and *I* will claim both this Marissa Vasquez and her SINCO inheritance. It is essential for all to witness my victory over Erin Morgan and her friends. Have I not explained this to you?"

"Yes, master, you have but—"

"There are no buts!" Cinatas yelled, working himself into a tirade. Nobody could hear anything unless it was shoved down their throat. "In less than three weeks that bitch of a nurse Erin and her group of friends have compromised my authority. They forced me to burn down Sno-Med's Manhattan clinic. They escaped imprisonment and were responsible for burning down the research center in Arcadia, obliterating years of my data on blood proteins. And I shouldn't have to remind you of the humiliation we all suffered in Belize. Pathos captured and exiled from the universe. Vasquez killed. The entire supply of Elan blood for the Vladarians destroyed. They've humiliated me and the Vladarians before the world of the damned. They have to pay or we will be lost. It is essential for everyone to be there. How many times do I have to tell you that if *a man cannot control those who serve him, then he de-*

serves to die?" Damned blood boiling, fangs throbbing, Cinatas glared at Nyros.

The adage was one any great conqueror would live by. Image was everything when it came to ruling, and he had to restore his reputation or he'd end up fighting every faction in hell for power. Already many Valdarians were starting to rebel despite the fact that Cinatas had a choke hold over the vampires' supply of Elan blood. Since Logos had sentenced Pathos to an eternity of nothingness, there had been far too many gatherings of different Vladarian factions. They had to be plotting to take over. The coronation Cinatas had planned would help, but he needed to make it something the undead and the damned would never forget.

"Yes, master. Pathos would agree," Nyros finally replied. "I am as eager as you are to restore our honor and avenge his death. A very special torture awaits Annette Batista and the Blood Hunter Aragon. Last night Pathos told me in detail what he wanted done to both of them."

Cinatas started to reply, but then Nyros's exact words registered.

"Last night? Don't you mean last week?"

"No, master. Lord Pathos reached me in a dream. He walks in the shadows between all realms, subsisting in nothingness. But I will find a way to save him. I've taken the liberty of petitioning Heldon to meet with you. You must beseech him to help save Pathos from the fate of a faded warrior. Having once been Logos's right hand, Heldon is sure to know how."

Cinatas blinked, surprised he didn't immediately go up in flames from the explosive rise of his rage. Beg Heldon to save Pathos? Give up all of the riches and power he'd just fell so gloriously into? *No way in hell.*

How dare Nyros!

And why had Pathos contacted Nyros instead of his own son? Was it possible Pathos was party to Cinatas's thoughts? *No.*

If that were true, then Nyros wouldn't be standing so calmly before him. He'd have tried to kill Cinatas.

Cinatas stood, smiling at the demon. Nyros's presumption was intolerable. As soon as Cinatas gleaned all that he needed from Nyros about Pathos's holdings, the Red Demon would be disposed of. "Your loyalty and efficiency have been noted, Nyros. Have all the Red Demons arrived at the Falls?"

"Yes, as well as factions of Blue, Green, and Yellow Demons, as you requested. They await your victory and coronation."

"Good." That was at least one thing done right. To have so many demons supporting his coronation as "emperor" of the Vladarians would make all of them think twice about trying to take over. Vladarians were such impure and disloyal creatures. One day Cinatas would follow through with Pathos's plan to eliminate them. Until then, he'd make good use of their egos to further his plans to defeat Heldon, which meant everything he had in mind for Erin Morgan had to happen. "And the staging for the blood sacrifice? All is as I detailed? I want things perfect for Erin."

"It will be ready, master. I have the demons working around the clock to create the perfect temple," Nyros assured.

Pathos had been a diabolical bastard without compare. In supplying sperm banks worldwide over the years, he'd given birth to an entire army of offspring. They were all listed in Pathos's Book of Life at Zion. The tome held facts and details about the lives of his offspring and how to best activate them for duty in his "plan" for a new world order on earth and in hell. He'd also learned why Erin Morgan had been under the protection of the Vladarian Order. She was a sperm bank bastard of Pathos's, which made her Cinatas's half-sister. Before Erin had connected herself to a Blood Hunter and taken up Logos's side in the universal battle for preeminence, Pathos had planned for her to be his queen. Now she had to die. Even if Cinatas wasn't in a rage for revenge, Erin had both *were* blood and Elan blood in her. All she would need was a vampire bite to match his superior state of being, and he could not allow that to happen. Nor could he allow her to produce offspring. It was going to be Cinatas's distinct pleasure to inform Erin of her illustrious damned ancestry before he sacrificed her.

"Erin will be the first of many blood sacrifices at the Falls. All of Twilight will run red with the blood spilled for my power," Cinatas said softly. There were a number of obstacles in his path to rule over hell and earth, some Pathos had known about, and others he couldn't have foreseen. But Cinatas was smarter. It was a good thing his father put everything into his competent hands.

"Everyone will soon cry hail to the power and glory of me," Cinatas said, then laughed heartily. "That calls for a glass of merlot before I leave, Nyros. I can't wait for Chateau Petrus to be mine." Hundreds of years of expertise had gone into making Petrus and its merlot grape one of the most coveted vineyards in Bordeaux. Now that he had the power and the money, the exquisite red wine produced at Chateau Petrus should be his for his exclusive consumption. "When will the attorneys have the papers ready?"

"Master, Moueix and Lacoste have refused to sell at any price. They are proving more difficult than we originally thought."

Cinatas clenched his jaw, speaking stiffly. "Is there not one thing you can do without having to have every detail spelled out to you? Their objections must come to an immediate end by any means necessary. I want that vineyard. Send demons to coerce them, kill them, whatever. Just do it."

"Master, we cannot risk losing our anonymity in the mortal sphere. Pathos strived for centuries to bring the damned secretly into world prominence and all his efforts will be—"

Cinatas grabbed the demon by the throat. "Pathos is no longer here, is he? He left everything to me, correct?" The demon reluctantly nodded, and Cinatas released him. "Then I don't want to hear another Pathos anything. We do things my way now. Do you understand? I'll be landing in Nashville in twelve hours. Meet me there with the helicopter. The Petrus matter will be resolved by then."

"Yes . . . master. I will see to it immediately." Nyros disappeared with a sucking pop, transporting himself through the spirit barrier somewhere. Hopefully to Petrus.

Cinatas sat back down at his desk with his fist clenched tight. He hated the damned's mode of travel to familiar places. The feeling of nothingness and insignificance within the universe when he crossed the spirit barrier was overwhelming. He wouldn't lower himself to it just for the sake of speed and convenience. And as screwed up as things were in the spirit realm of the damned, who was to say his particles wouldn't get scrambled in the shift? Then there was Pathos's warning that too many crossings too close together could cause spontaneous combustion. He hated the disadvantage though. And hated that Nyros popped in and out and didn't wait for Cinatas's dismissal as ordered. Cinatas never got his glass of merlot, either.

If a man cannot control those who serve him, then he deserves to die.

These imbeciles would not defeat him.

William Wellbourne blinked twice at the petite woman standing on the sidewalk, at first thinking that his longtime hunt for the bitch who'd killed his brother had him seeing things. But the sudden onslaught of spiritual heat to his icy soul and the piercing sound of angel bells told him he was seeing right. The wind blew his way and he caught scent of her angel blood. He bared his fangs at her, his groin swelling as the imagined taste of her filled his senses. Bloodlust and revenge made for a heady elixir. It was all he could do to stop himself from lunging at her.

The Elan blood that vampires preferred to feed on was sweet sustenance, with enough power to rejuvenate a vampire for months, as opposed to having to hunt and feed several times a day on ordinary mortals. But angel blood was pure ambrosia, and more importantly, by making an angel a blood slave he'd gain control of her powers.

Two demons in the front of the limo cried out in pain from the scorching blast of goodness Emerald hit them with. The other Vladarians in the car jerked to attention as if they'd been slapped, then covered their ears. They turned warily toward the powerful source of heat and sound.

Wellbourne hated angel bells. Their effect on vampires was not unlike those of a malignant dog whistle. Everyone could hear the bells, but only the damned were driven insane by the heavenly frequency.

"Drive," Wellbourne shouted at the chauffeur as he began to roll up the heavily tinted window. He didn't want the other vampires getting a clear look at Emerald, but he didn't have to worry about that now. The lawman with Emerald whipped her behind him and aimed his useless gun. Wellbourne met the man's gaze, felt a familiar vampiric chill emanating from the bloke, then jolted with shock. The lawman was a vampire. Rage coursed through him. Was the bitch already a blood slave to the bastard? Was she his?

The driver hit the gas.

"*Chto za huy!*" Rasputin, the head Vladarian from the Russian faction, cursed in shock.

"A taste of the forces we're up against, perhaps?" Wellbourne said, looking to put the other vampires off the sound and scent of an angel. "Didn't everyone feel the power of a vampire slayer?" Vampire slayers caused a similar heat discomfort to a vampire's system, just nowhere near as potent as an angel's. Nor did they have maddening bells.

The suggestion that the vampires might have to face slayers

as opposed to mere mortals in Cinatas's war set the Vladarians into a snit. Everyone hated Pathos's son and the bastard's determination to lord over them. Forcing them all to come to Twilight was a mistake.

None of them wanted to be here—except, of course, Wellbourne, now that he'd seen Emerald.

Surely he had imagined the lawman's vampirism. Emerald had been protecting the man, and she'd never do that to a vampire. She'd killed her own husband when he'd turned. He'd have to get rid of the lawman though, after torturing him until Emerald was putty in his hands, of course. The angel bitch and her whelp were his to enslave, and nobody was going to interfere with that.

He thought he'd succeeded in distracting the others from Emerald's impact until he caught Valois's glare. The blue-blooded Royal's lineage went directly back to the Bastard of Normandy. Of all the others, Valois was most likely to have crossed paths with an angel in the mortal realm. Some said he'd had a hand in burning Joan of Arc at the stake.

"Za trap, I tell you. All of us coming here together. Itza trap to kill us all," said Yaroslav, Rasputin's comrade.

"Bladdered on vodka, mate?" Wellbourne asked, latching onto the distraction. "We're safer with Cinatas than with Pathos," he said. "Pathos only tolerated us because we were useful. Cinatas is different. He's a narcissistic megalomaniac, which means he *needs* us to feed his ego. He won't be offing us until he has thousands of others at his feet. Wouldn't you agree, Valois? Cuthbert?"

Wellbourne directed his gaze at the blue-blooded Royals. They weren't much different from Cinatas in needing an entourage of brownnosing subjects to keep their egos pumped.

"I'd say," Cuthbert agreed. "The only problem is the bastard is as unstable as a nuclear reactor in meltdown."

Valois's fixed his gaze on Wellbourne, his smile deadly. "I'm more interested in what spirit beings are in Twilight to battle us than in Pathos's pathetic spawn. I've fought vampire slayers before, but have yet to encounter one so strong as that. Any ideas as to what she was, Wellbourne? I thought I heard bells, too."

Valois had locked in on the presence of an angel in Twilight and wasn't going to let it go.

"No. I don't. I did hear squealing, but sounded like someone hitting the brakes too hard," Wellbourne replied, then flashed his fangs at Valois to warn him off. Emerald was *his* angel bitch.

Valois flashed his fangs as well.

Wellbourne apparently didn't have the luxury of waiting for nightfall. He pulled out his BlackBerry and sent a discreet text. The damned were never to be trusted.

Sam saw Emerald thrust herself in front of him as she pulled him off balance and tripped him. He saw red even before his knee slammed into the concrete. He couldn't believe she put herself between him and the white limo that radiated bad news like a subwoofer on steroids. Rage unlike anything he'd ever known erupted inside him and flooded his body with adrenaline. Not even Vasquez's torture had hit him on so visceral a level. The top of his head felt as if it would explode from the blood and power pounding through him. His every muscle bunched with murderous tension as he grabbed the street sign next to him, pushing hard against it to gain his feet.

The sign bent. What the hell?

He didn't have time to think about it now. He gained his footing, shoved Emerald back, and drew a bead on the limo with his Glock—but he was too late. The limo's window was on the way up and he caught only a glimpse of the man in the back before it charged forward. It was enough for him to see fangs and a she's-all-mine murderous glare directed at Emerald. Finger on the trigger, Sam's need to kill consumed him.

He was a gnat's ass away from shooting when Emerald touched his arm. "Sam, don't. Doona give into the darkness," he heard her say over and over. Slowly, a cool green haze washed away the red, leaving him standing on the street, shaking.

He hadn't fired his gun but he'd come close. Insanely close. Criminally close. The anger surging in him hadn't let him go until Emerald stepped in. He still didn't trust himself to speak. Didn't trust himself to move.

Dear God. The core of his being shook with fear. What had happened to him? What was happening to him?

He'd known something more than the black cloud over Hades was wrong the moment he'd stepped from the squad car and looked at Emerald. All the color had drained from her face and raw fear had appeared in her eyes. But it was more than seeing Emerald frightened that had the hair standing up on the back of his neck. It was the icy cold that struck him full in the gut.

Then he'd seen the limo racing like a bullet, ready to nail one of his townspeople, and anger had sent him rushing into the street to stop the son of a bitch. It wasn't until the limo screeched to a standstill that he realized the creepy cold radiated from it.

Breathe. Breathe. Breathe. A quick look around left him astounded. People were about, across the highway in a parking lot, down the street at the coin laundry, but nobody seemed to have noticed what happened. Usually everybody in the small town made everyone else's business their own.

Something was wrong in Twilight.

He had the limo's license plate imprinted in his brain, which meant he could track down the bastards without having to chase them. Good thing. He'd probably be lethal behind the wheel at the moment.

Dozens of questions about what Emerald had just done

screamed through his mind, but he didn't trust himself to speak to her, yet. Not until he had a firm handle on his temper, which meant the FBI—or Myra, if she was lying—would get the brunt of his rage. Nice.

"Sam," Emerald said. "I'm sorry. I didna mean to—"

"Later, Em. I can't think yet," he told her, still gulping in deep breaths of air.

"Come on," she said softly, taking his hand. She led him up the steps of the station and into the shadowed recesses of the entrance. For once she kept quiet, as if she really understood how tenuous his hold was. Even the tinkling of her bracelets grated on him.

What had happened to him?

He tugged her back before she could open the door, intending to take a moment more to gather his cool. But when he looked at her, she had that lip thing going again and all thought and reason abandoned him. Seeing her teeth sunk into her lush bottom lip snapped something inside him. All the desire he'd kept a tight lid on for months meshed with all of the emotion roiling in him and he lost it.

Taking hold of her shoulders, he leaned down and kissed her, sliding his tongue swiftly over her plump lip, then sucking the sweetness of it into his mouth. Her heady lavender and spice scent, mingled with womanly arousal, filled his lungs and set his senses on fire.

Blood roared in his ears, rushing south to his swelling erection. He could smell, taste, and feel her on a level he'd never experienced before in his life. It was all-consuming. Wrapping his arm around her, he pulled her hard against his burning need. She gasped in response and his tongue invaded deep, sweeping the softness of her mouth.

She moaned, angling her neck back to take more of him, and he stepped between her legs, pressing his thigh to the V of her hot sex. Her breasts brushed his chest and he had to touch her, had to feel their ripe fullness. Taste her. Suck her. Thrust into her until nothing but mindless pleasure ruled them both.

"Sam, please," she said, splaying her hand against his chest, breathing as heavily as he was.

That was all he needed to hear. She wanted him as desperately as he wanted her. He'd known it forever. So why in the hell hadn't they gone at it? He couldn't seem to remember why and wasn't the least bit interested in thinking right now. He backed her to the wall and shoved his hand up her soft shirt to even softer skin. Her nipple hardened as he cupped her breast and he groaned deep, shoving his arousal hard against her.

Emerald suddenly smacked her fist into his chest.

He blinked at her, trying to see through his desire-hazed vision. "Em?"

"I meant please *stop*, you gack. Not please more." She pushed at him again and he loosened his hold, surprised to find his hand palming her breast. Reluctantly, he slid his hand from her shirt and eased back, finally seeing clearly enough to realize they weren't even in private. Anybody looking in from the street or the parking lot would have at least seen them kissing, if not the full details. And anyone exiting the sheriff's station would have gotten an eyeful. Damn, where in the hell was his mind?

"I canna believe you kissed me like that. After all this fooking time you up and kiss me now?" She glared at him, chest heaving with ire.

"I'm sorry," he said. "I don't know what happened. I shouldn't have—"

"Yes, you bloody well should have. But you should have kissed me months ago when it would have been *you* kissing me."

"What?" She wasn't upset that he'd mauled her in public? He shook his head, sure she'd lost her mind. Last time he took a head count of two, he was himself both upstairs and below the belt. "What do you mean I'm not me?" When she didn't immediately answer, he exhaled in exasperation. "Never mind, we don't have time right now anyway. Tell me later."

However crazy it sounded, kissing Emerald had restored some of his equilibrium, as if it was the first right thing to happen in a long while. This time he took her hand and led her into the station house.

The minute he stepped inside, he did a double take, wondering if he had the wrong place. The scent of pine cleaner was familiar, but that was all. It was like he'd stepped into an episode of the *Twilight Zone*. Cups and plates littered the desks, junk lay everywhere. Deputy Sandy, upstanding married father of two and deacon in the Baptist church down the road, lounged against Myra's desk. He had his uniform shirt untucked and unbuttoned and was licking white powder off a doughnut dangling like bunch of grapes from Myra's hand.

Myra jumped up the minute she saw Sam, leaving the doughnut stuck in Deputy Sandy's mouth. Sandy stood and with a nonchalant nod sauntered from the room, eating the doughnut as if he hadn't been doing anything wrong. Myra was more tarted up than Sam ever remembered seeing before. She'd always skirted the edge of scandalous dress for a backwoods town, but today's display of cleavage and leg was over the top, even for her.

Sam had been gone for just a few days, not decades. What the hell was up?

"Where have you been? Myra asked him. "I was about to call you again——" Myra caught sight of Emerald and her eyes hardened with a *you've-been-with-her* look. "Fishing vacation, huh? I wouldn't have made you late."

Emerald tried to pull away, but Sam held tight and stared hard at Myra. She'd never been this blatantly rude before.

It was true that Emerald had that well-kissed look about her, but still. "Excuse me," Sam said. "I think you owe us both an apol—"

"Your loss. The coffee would have been really . . . hot," Myra said, interrupting him. Then she shrugged a shoulder, turned on a ridiculous four-inch heel, and cat-walked to her desk. "The FBI was antsy so I put them in your office," she said breezily.

House rule was nobody waited in his office. He should fire her on the spot, but first he needed to find out what in the hell was going on. Gritting his teeth, Sam headed down the hallway with Emerald in tow. He tried to remember what files were on his desk but was distracted by the sight of Deputy John Michaels playing basketball with the water cooler cups in the break room. Who was out on patrol? Today was Bud Carlton's day off.

"The FBI?" Emerald asked, her voice scratchy, as if she had trouble getting the words out. "What do they want?"

"I don't know. They showed up about twenty minutes ago. It could be anything from clearing up the murder warrant against Erin to more questions about the Tsara's corpse to— Hell, who knows anymore. Got any skeletons in the closet, Em?"

He expected her to roll her eyes in disgust. Instead, the fear in her expression hit him right between the eyes. Exactly what was she hiding?

A quick glance through his office door showed a suited man and woman sitting in the chairs before his desk. They weren't FBI. Military was written all over them. They were after him for doing in Vasquez in Belize. Shit. Sam had known it was coming. He'd just hoped he would have had more time. Nobody backed out of a deal with Commander Kingston.

"Sam." Emerald set her hand on his arm just as he opened the door. He turned back to face her and she leaned toward him, bringing her mouth close to his ear. Her deep green eyes were so full of concern that he had to fight the urge to pull her into his arms and kiss her all over again. Desire and something more pulsed through him at her touch, warming him when he hadn't even realized he needed it. "Doona smile," she whispered. "Your fangs are growing."

He pulled back. Shocked. The man and the woman in his office stood up expectantly, but he just stared at them, frozen in place.

Emerald slid past him and introduced herself, filling the gaffe.

Fangs? She might as well have dropped a nuclear bomb in his lap. He ran his tongue over his teeth, and sure enough they felt different. His incisors were sharper and seemed slightly longer. For a moment the world narrowed to a thin tunnel surrounded by black fear as he saw himself turning into the same kind of monster Vasquez had been.

It just wasn't possible. He could never be what Vasquez was. He clung to that thought as he entered the room, walking on shaky legs to his desk. After easing himself into his chair, he propped his boots up on the corner of his desk before speaking to his unwanted guests. It was rude, but it was all he was capable of at the moment. Besides, they'd already lied about who they were. He didn't owe them any hospitality.

"You two get lost on the way to Fort Bragg?" Sam asked, cutting right to the chase. The North Carolina military base was the home of Special Forces Command known as US-ASOC. Sam had spent a lot of time there. He knew the people and the drill.

The man and woman raised their brows, then shrugged.

"We apologize for the deception," the man said. "Your file pretty much indicated you wouldn't have consented to see us otherwise."

"That's right," Sam replied. "So now would be a good time to leave." The sooner he got them out of there the sooner he could get to the issue of how Emerald knew what she did, what was wrong with his employees and . . . his fangs.

"I'm Sergeant First Class Grayson, and this is Staff Sergeant Bond," the man said persistently, nodding at the woman. "Commander Kingston sent us. He would like to see you."

"He knows where to find me," Sam said.

"I think you misunderstand the purpose of our visit, Sheridan," Grayson said. "We've got transpo waiting. You can have a chat with the commander and be back in time for dinner."

"No, you don't understand," Sam countered. "If Commander Kingston wants to see me then he can fly his ass here. I'm no longer his puppet to jerk around. Now unless you all have anything else you want to talk to me about, I have work to do."

"Thought you were on vacation this week," replied Grayson. "Fishing, your dispatcher said."

Did the man have a death wish? Sam wondered. "Yep, I was fishing," he said, hardening his gaze at Grayson. "But I ran out of worms big enough and came to town for more bait. You volunteering?"

Grayson stiffened like a dry corncob. Surprisingly, Staff Sergeant Bond grinned.

"Master Sergeant Sheridan," Bond said, speaking for the first time, and pulling out his old rank. If she thought it would strum any strings of loyalty, she thought wrong. "I'm sure you know how busy Commander Kingston is, especially in comparison to the low demands of small town law enforcement. Surely taking a short ride with us won't inconvenience you too much and it would save us a tremendous amount of time."

Yep, not much going on around here. Just vampires and demons and werewolves and corrupt corporations with murderous doctors.

Sam gritted his teeth, and his incisors pressed uncomfortably against his bottom teeth. The image of fangs sinking into soft skin flashing through his mind and the sudden urge to feed on warm blood from hot flesh grabbed him by the gut, shocking him so deeply that he shot to his feet, startling everyone. Grayson and Bond stood, too, their stance wide, as if braced for an attack.

Sam figured he looked as volatile as he felt. "Small towns and their demands can really surprise you," Sam said tightly. "There's nothing you can do or say to change my mind, so let's not waste each other's time."

Grayson edged his way toward the open door as if he didn't quite trust what Sam would do. Smart man.

"We'll give Commander Kingston your response and be in touch," Grayson said. "Where can we find you?"

"Still fishing," Sam replied. "Myra can reach me."

"I wouldn't fish too far from home," Grayson said. "You won't like it if Commander Kingston has to go hunting for you."

Not so smart a man. Sam nearly snarled at the man. "I'm not liking it now. So that's not going to be any more skin off my back."

Staff Sergeant Bond moved in front of him. Eyes narrowed, she searched his face, as if she sensed something unusual about him. Little did she know what lurked beneath the surface of his skin. He thought about flashing his fangs at her.

"You've got quite a reputation, Master Sergeant Sheridan," she said.

Sam met her gaze dead-on. "It's just Sheridan now. And I wouldn't believe everything you hear."

"Seems they nailed the death wish right," she said. After snapping a salute at him, she turned toward Grayson and they both left his office.

Emerald quickly got up and shut the door. "You want to tell me what all that was about?" she asked advancing on him.

"Long story and nothing compared to this shit," Sam said, feeling his incisors with the pads of his fingers. "I want to take pliers and yank my teeth out. God. You won't believe what I just felt like doing."

Emerald closed her eyes and visibly drew a deep breath. When she opened her eyes again, they were swimming with fear and sadness. "Yeah, I would, Sam. I canna know exactly, but I have a good idea. You're feeling, smelling, and hearing things you never have before. You've got strength you didn't know you had. And your emotions are out of control. Passion, rage, hate, hunger, anything you feel will overpower everything else. You canna control it." She set her hand on his arm. "You might already be thinking about blood. Tasting it. I told you what might happen once you left the shield. The vampire infection is growing. Probably even faster than it normally would because of the evil radiating from the Falls Resort. It's affecting everyone in town. They're doing things, choosing things that'll lead to the destruction of good. Eventually, everything and everyone in Twilight will spiral into self-destruction unless the darkness is stopped. You will, too, even faster because the infection in your soul is working from the inside out. You canna stop it."

Looking into her eyes, he could see that she wasn't just spouting off textbook information. She intimately knew what she was telling him and all of it was dead-on. It scared the hell out of him.

His set his hand over hers. The contention that had been sparking between them forever seemed absent at the moment. Whether their kiss had eased it or the dire reality they were facing had defused it, he didn't know. All he knew was he needed a connection to her. "How, Em? How do you know all of this?"

Her eyes went dark, shadowed with secrets. "It's complicated," she said, turning away from him.

He caught her shoulder and turned her back. He could see

the fear in her eyes mingled with the secrets and gentled his touch. Every time he made contact with her a sense of warmth washed over him, one similar to finding a comforting hearth fire on a cold winter's day.

"What the hell in our lives isn't complicated right now?" he demanded softly, the corners of his mouth tugging up. "Tell me, Em."

Emerald stared at Sam a moment, studying the strained lines of tension in his face, the confusion in his eyes, the brave half smile in the face of it all. He was lost and grappling for answers and still trying to comfort her. Some of them she could answer and others she didn't want to answer. Why Sam? Her heart cried out. Why had he been bitten? Was it some cruel twist of fate that had her repeating what happened with Eric all over again? Would she and Sam be doomed to the same fate? And what about Wellbourne? He'd come after her just as soon as the sun went down tonight, she knew that. Vladarian Vampires were the most corrupt, the most depraved of vampires.

But thinking about Wellbourne right now made her think about Eric and what she'd had to do to him, what she might have to do to Sam. And that was just wrong with her body still throbbing from Sam's desire and her lips still burning from his kiss.

Sam was the first man to awaken her heart, her passion after being alone for six years. She'd like to think he'd just been too prickly for her to ignore. That their heated encounters stemmed from his orneriness and not from suppressed and frustrated desire. But thinking it didn't make it true.

She was furious that he'd finally kissed her too late for her to know anything for sure. Sam hadn't been driven beyond his iron control to kiss her until the vampire infection fueled by that bloody black cloud had pushed him into it. She had no idea whether it was Sam or the vampire wanting her.

Unfortunately, her wayward heart didn't care. Like it had the first time she'd seen him—and envisioned him a lone warrior in pain against a great, unholy army—her heart flipped and cried out for him. She wanted to comfort him, save him. She wanted to touch him everywhere, kiss him forever, and feel him deep inside her driving their pleasure all the way to heaven.

It saddened her that she'd never know his touch without the shadow of the cold infecting his soul. She didn't know if she could save him, and that scared the hell out of her. There were things she had to tell him and then some things she just couldn't. She couldn't take the chance that he'd turn from her.

But he needed her.

"You first, Sam. Who's Commander Kingston and what does he want?" she asked, stalling.

Sam sighed, clearly exasperated, but gave in. "Commander Kinston is the puppet for corrupt, high-ranking officials who knew Vasquez was a monster and that my men and I were among his many tortured prisoners. But they chose to ignore it because Vasquez was head of the SINCO oil cartel, which gives OPEC its only competition and keeps the cost of crude oil from skyrocketing. Nick's father, Reed Sinclair, went against orders and with a handful of mercenaries got me out of Vasquez's hellhole. Reed died during the escape and my welcome home party was Kingston. He gave me the choice between military prison for life or swearing to keep my hands off Vasquez. What he most likely wants, since I've taken Vasquez out, is my head on a block."

"You knew that and yet you still went to Belize and took Vasquez on? Why did you do such a fool thing when you knew what the cost would be?" She wanted to grab him and shake him but brushed her knuckles along the shadowed edge of his chiseled jaw instead. From what she'd seen of Sam's relationship with Nick, it was clear Sam had taken over as a father for Nick.

"Because Vasquez was my monster to kill," he said. "Knowing what he was, knowing that he remained free, kept me as much a prisoner as he had. Learning that he was a vampire and had Annette's sister captive voided my word to Kingston in my mind. Killing Vasquez freed me from the past. I haven't had a flashback since. I'd do it again though, so don't ask me to be sorry. I only wish I'd done it sooner. Maybe then you and I—"

He turned toward her touch and his lips met her fingers. There was a load of emotion tinged with regret in his gaze and an electric dart went right to her center. But he opened his mouth and guided her finger over the sharp edge of his growing incisors. "The military is the least of my worries at the moment. It's your turn, Em. Start talking. How do you know so much about all of this?"

"I doona even know where to start." She pulled from his touch and turned away, fighting off a shiver as the image of Eric and his fangs flashed through her mind.

"The beginning might help," Sam said. She could feel his gaze tracking her as she paced across the room. "You said a vision of Jared arriving at the Sacred Stones is what brought you to Twilight, but I've always felt there was more to it than that. You uprooted your child and moved to a different country, then waited almost a year for the Blood Hunter to arrive."

Emerald drew a deep breath and jumped headlong into the truth. Well, as much of it as she dared tell Sam now. "You're right. There is more. A lot more. I not only had a vision of Jared arriving, but I also had a vision of him with faceless others at his side defeating the Order of the Vladarian Vampires. That is very important to my future and doubly important to Meggie's. But that's not the beginning, Sam. That starts with my parents." She turned to face him and moved back closer, wanting to see his reaction. "The shield. My visions. My magic. It doesn't come from anything Druid, or any other known power here on earth. It comes from the spirit world. I'm part angel, Sam. My mother was like Jared and Aragon, not a warrior but a spirit being from the heavens. She is an angel."

A half laugh escaped from him before he stopped himself and shook his head to clear it.

"You're serious," he said softly. His eyes at first were narrowed with disbelief then widened. "You and Meggie are angels? As in fly in the sky, heavenly trumpet blowing hosts of God?"

Emerald winced. "You canna believe everything you hear about spirit beings. Angels doona have real wings, but they figuratively spread a wing of protection over others. No trumpets, but . . ." She shook her wrist. "Bells, heavenly silver bells. And Meggie and I are only part angel."

Sam's frown deepened as she watched him take it all in and then searched her expression for more. "So all that Druid stuff was—"

"A lie. I'm sorry, but you have to understand that I had to lie. Part of the reason why Meggie and I came to Twilight was that we were being hunted and the vampire after us had discovered where we were hiding. This particular Vladarian is out for revenge against me and my daughter. He's very powerful. We've been hiding from him for six years."

"Damn it." He raked his fingers through his short hair, his gaze back to a familiar glare. "You've been in danger all of this time and didn't say anything to me about it? I could have done something to help. Tracked the guy down, hired people to change his plans, something. At the very least I could have been on the lookout for trouble."

"First off, you wouldn't have believed me," Emerald said. Sam shook his head, and she couldn't help but roll her eyes at him. "Doona look back with rose-colored glasses, Sam. Before Jared came and Cinatas kidnapped us, you didn't believe a word I said. Even then it wasn't until the Red Demons attacked us and I put up the protective shield up that you really put any stock in my abilities. Even today you didn't listen to me. You still came to town."

"You're right about the angel stuff," he conceded. "But the danger angle, I would have bought into. And a FYI for you, I did believe you earlier. But I had to leave. Though from the looks of things I've failed the citizens of Twilight. As their sheriff I'm responsible for their safety . . . and"—his gaze connected with hers—"another five minutes stuck at the camp, I would have been all over you inside and out."

He moved toward her now. There was no mistaking the intent in his blue gaze. He wanted to take up where their kiss had left off. "Who is after you, Em, and why?"

She bit her lip and backed up a step or two, unsure if she was ready to take on a vampire-infected Sam with his passions unleashed.

"The Vladarian vampire who is after Meggie and me is William Wellbourne. He wants revenge because I killed his brother Michael. And you just had the pleasure of meeting him face-to-face. He was in the back of the limo."

Chapter Three

INSTEAD OF *A Nightmare on Elm Street*, it was A Nightmare in Twilight. Nothing that had happened today was real, let alone Emerald announcing in such a matter-of-fact way that she not only had killed a man, but also that the vampire out to kill *her* in revenge had just been on their doorstep not more than twenty minutes ago.

Sam bit the inside of his lip, just to send a jolt of pain through his body and wake him up. But his damn incisor cut the inside of his mouth sharply, and the taste of blood sent a jolt of pleasure through him. He swallowed hard. It was real. All of it. He fought to keep his voice down, fought the urge to shake some sense into her beautiful head. "Did it not occur to you that this guy could very well be on his way to get you right now?"

Emerald shook her head. "Wellbourne would never attack from a position of weakness. Vampires who reach the Vladarian status are pure evil, nothing in them left to be redeemed. This also makes them creatures whose greatest period of weakness is during the day. The heat drains their power, and exposure to the sun for more than just short periods will burn their skin. By the same token, their time of greatest strength is at night. He'll come after me then, but we'll be back to the camp and beneath the shield."

She was serious. He couldn't believe it. He grasped her shoulders, needing her to realize creatures weren't that predictable, but found himself wanting to pull her into his arms and put his own damn protective shield around her. The thought of some vampire tearing into her, touching her, damning her to the same fate as him, wrung him inside out. Anything to do with her inflamed him almost past the point of control. Passion. Jealousy. Protectiveness. Anger. She was right. Everything he felt was so much stronger than before.

"Damn it, Em. It is a wonder you've survived this long without being caught. If I'd been after someone for six years and saw them on the street and they saw me, I wouldn't give a shit what I had to do to get to them. I'd find a way. Don't you think he'll move hell itself to get you? He'll hire someone if he can't do it himself?"

Emerald looked as if he'd struck her in the gut. "I . . . I . . . fook. I've always had my visions before and knew when he was coming, but now . . ."

"Come on." He grabbed her arm, and after checking the hallway, he pulled her from his office. "We'll talk after we get out of here."

Moving across the corridor with Emerald tucked to his side, he drew out his keys and unlocked the steel door to the station's gun room. He snatched two duffel bags off the shelf and started piling in the hardware and ammo, taking a second to make sure the rifles were ready to go.

Maybe it was an obsessive need that stemmed from his military training or his captivity, but when it came to weapons and protective gear, his small town outfit rivaled any big city SWAT team. Even the squad cars they drove were outfitted with all the bells and whistles he could buy.

Some would argue he didn't need all of the equipment he'd collected, but he'd prepared for any scenario and he didn't waste taxpayer money on substandard crap. He'd never given himself a raise either, choosing to put that portion of the budget into the guns, ammo, and protective gear for the county. Maybe it would pay off now.

He shoved a vest into Emerald's hands. "Put that on." He put on one himself then stuffed as many of the vests as he could into the bags. They were top-of-the-line, threat level III-A-worthy body armor.

Within minutes, he'd loaded all he could carry, swung two M-16s over his shoulder, and strapped an array of riot control grenades to his waist. His silver-enhanced, double-action switchblade was already clipped to his belt. It was the best he could do for now.

He drew his Glock and eased out of the room; Emerald at his side. "Stay glued to me. We'll go out the back and take a different squad car in case anyone is watching the front."

"Okay, but Sam, doona make the mistake of believing all that stuff in the duffel bags will wipe out the damned. At best it'll only deter them for a short time."

"Deterrents are good, but it's close to high noon out there. Wellbourne just might send human trash in his place."

Sam saw that Deputy Michaels was still busy playing with the paper cups in the break room, as if he were in some sort of trance. Only now he'd pulled out a pocketknife and was using them as target practice.

"Sam didn't have to worry about locating keys to another car. His force was small enough that he kept a key to all of the squad cars on his key ring. He'd call Myra later and tell her he'd left the station. Because everyone was acting so strangely, Sam planned to keep his whereabouts secret.

"The only way to stop what is happening to the citizens is to destroy the damned feeding the cloud at the Falls Resort," Emerald whispered as he guided her down the hallway.

"You've seen this shit before?" he asked, keeping a sharp eye out for anything as they approached the back door.

"No. My mother told me stories of bad things that happened in the past so I'd know what I might come up against. There are whispers in angel lore of evil consuming places. Whole civilizations just disappearing into chaos. Even to this day I can visit one of those places and feel the dark spirits still permeating the area."

Reaching the back door, Sam cracked it open and checked

every visible angle. He even sniffed the air and analyzed the different scents as nonthreatening before he realized what he was doing.

Emerald gave him a knowing look. He shrugged and pushed the door open.

Moments later, ensconced in Deputy Michaels's squad car with Emerald riding shotgun, he backed out of the rear parking lot. It looked like a clean getaway, yet things felt off to him. His gut said this was too damn easy. He couldn't see it, but he sure as hell felt an ax coming straight for his head.

The hairs on the back of his neck stood on end and he hit the gas, giving everything they flew past a once-over.

Dumpster, check.

Adjoining parking lot, check.

Intersection and cross street, check.

Corner house, check.

Empty field, check.

Barn across the creek, check.

Decked-out Harley chopper roaring past them . . . ALERT. He'd never seen that bike before in Twilight, and the road they were on was too far off the beaten path for a casual outsider.

Watching in his review mirror, Sam saw the driver pull a gravel-spitting one-eighty, smoking rubber off his tires as he gunned it toward them. The SOB was covered from head to toe in black leathers and a black helmet.

"We've got trouble."

"This fast? You're sure?" Emerald whipped her head around.

"Dead sure." On a straight road the bike would have the advantage, but on a mountain road that Sam knew like the back of his hand, he would. Trouble was he needed to have made a right on the street they'd just passed. "Hold on tight," he yelled.

Slamming on the brake, he sent the car into a spin that brought the rear around then hit the gas to pull the car straight, going in the opposite direction, heading right at the chopper.

He centered the car in the middle of the road, ready to play chicken with the biker. The man slowed his speed some, probably shocked that he was now under attack, but he didn't stop. Neither did Sam.

Seconds before impact, Sam positioned the car on the road so the driver had no choice but to hit Sam head on or to swerve to Sam's left. The biker suddenly shifted his right arm, releasing his grip on the handle bar.

"Get down!" Sam yelled, reaching over and jerking Emerald toward him.

The biker popped three bullets into the windshield as he approached, swerving to Sam's side of the car at the last second. Rage exploded inside Sam, coating everything he saw in red. He shoved open his car door and jerked to his left at just the right moment, hitting and knocking the biker down. The man and the chopper went scraping down the asphalt, sparks flying.

Sam wanted to stop the car and go after the SOB. He wanted to tear the bastard apart . . . with his teeth. He'd like to think it was years of training and discipline that kept him from going berserk, but in truth it was only Emerald. He'd be putting her in more danger by going after the biker.

Red still coated his vision and he fought for control. The bullets had pierced and fractured the outer glass of the windshield, but the bullet-resistant polycarbonate layer had stopped them cold. The biker was no amateur. He'd had damn good aim. One bullet would have nailed Emerald at about her right shoulder, winging but not killing. The two meant for him had been head shots. Looks like his obsession with top-of-the-line safety armor had just paid off.

He took the street he needed on two wheels and left a trail of dust behind him. Unfortunately, they had another problem. The left front tire felt low, but he didn't dare stop and change it until he'd put a healthy distance between him and his would be assassin. Though Sam hoped he'd taken the bastard out, he'd seen men get up and ride after worse spills than that.

Emerald sat up, eyes wide with shock. "The bastard shot at us," she whispered. "I'm so sorry," she said. "It canna be more than twenty minutes since Wellbourne saw me. How is it possible that he already has someone after me?" She placed her hand on his arm only to quickly pull it off but then set it back again. Odd. But odder yet, the red haze dissipated, as if the heat of her touch had blown it away. "Could it be someone else? Commander Kingston?" she asked.

"The biker's not Kingston's style," he said. "He'll want to look me in the eye as he turns the legal thumbscrews to put me behind bars at Leavenworth." The road steadily climbed up from the valley floor and he gave her a quick glance before he maneuvered through a sharp turn. "Wellbourne is likely behind the attack, which tells me he is fast, powerful, and deadly. How and why did you kill his brother, Em?"

She was so quiet for a moment he thought she wasn't going to answer. "It was self-defense. Meggie and I were living in England at the time. From our hilltop cottage, I could see the monoliths of Stonehenge on a clear day. It was Halloween and . . . I had a vision of vampires coming to murder Meggie and me. The Wellbournes have an estate not far from there, and an angel blood sacrifice for their satanic cult would have made them more powerful than ever. My only saving grace in being able to defeat Michael Wellbourne was the fact that hundreds of Druid priestesses had gathered at Stonehenge. They'd conjured a powerful force of white magic to ward off the dark spirits of Halloween night. Meggie and I had fled our home but hadn't made it to shelter when Wellbourne and his pack of rabid Underlings attacked us in the car. I left the highway and drove right into the powerful wall of white magic surrounding Stonehenge. Using it as well as some help from my mother, I killed them all."

Sam kept glancing at Emerald, and though the tale was frightening enough as it was, he got the feeling that she wasn't telling him the half of it. But her eyes were so damn expressive, they reflected much more than what she said. Right now they were dark with painful secrets. She wasn't telling him everything, but for the moment it was enough.

"I gotcha. The whole Mafia mentality. He's my brother so even if he deserved what he got, I'm going to make you pay for it," he said, letting her off the interrogational hook. Though there were a lot more questions he wanted answers to, the low tire was worse, and he needed to take care of it before it blew.

Still the questions rattled around in his head. Had Michael Wellbourne just picked Emerald out of the blue to attack or did he already know her before he came after her? And what about Megan? Who was her father? More importantly, *where* was her father? Why wasn't he sharing the burden of protecting his daughter from danger? Not that Sam wanted any man in Emerald's life. Not having the right to feel or think that way didn't stop Sam from turning green, then red, at the thought of another man kissing Emerald's lush lips.

And just like that, hot desire flared in him. He was back at the station with her against the wall, palming her nipple, and priming his erection against her. *Don't go there.* He may have finally kissed her but that didn't change any of the reasons why he shouldn't. It was just the vampire infection sending him over the edge, he told himself, forcing his mind back to locating a good spot to change the tire.

As he drove through the second switchback in their climb up the mountain, he caught a glimpse of four bikers lower down on the first switchback, moving fast. His gut tightened. He wasn't a big enough fool to think the bikers just happened to be sightseers. Ninety-nine percent of him knew they had to be bad news, but he couldn't stomach setting up a rifle and wounding the bikers until they shot at him first. And with

Emerald along, Sam didn't want to get close enough for that to happen again. As armed as he was, he didn't like the odds.

Staying with the car wasn't an option now. They were already on borrowed time with the tire, for one thing. Secondly, with that many after them and his hands tied at picking them off one by one from a distance, he and Emerald needed the cover of the forest rather than the vulnerability of the open road.

"We've got company on the way and a serious tire problem," Sam told Emerald. She turned to look. "They're too far back to see yet." Pulling out his cell, he speed dialed Nick and explained the situation.

"I suppose coming at them with the helo and unloading M-16s at them is out of the picture," Nick said.

"Too noisy," Sam said dryly. More dead bodies around Twilight, and he'd have the FBI after him. "More importantly, there's no time. The bikers will be on us before you could get to us. With Emerald on board, I want to avoid contact at all cost. I have more of a David Copperfield in mind."

"Come again?" Nick asked. "Did you say Emerald is with you? And what about Copperfield?"

Sam gave Emerald a quick glance. "Hope you're up for a hike," he told her. Then spoke back into the phone. "I'm sending the car over a cliff and we're going to disappear in the opposite direction. Give us a helo pickup at Silver Mist Falls in two, no make that two and a half hours. I'll call if we have trouble."

"Roger that," Nick said.

Sam flipped the phone closed and saw just what he needed. The paved turnout on the right would leave zero tire tracks. He pulled off the road and jerked open his car door. "Hurry and get out. I'm leaving you and the duffle bags down in that gully to the right. You stay low and out of sight no matter what. I'm going to crash the car through the left-hand guardrail around the next bend."

"You were serious?"

"Totally. Fifteen minutes tops those four guys will be on us like flies on honey. That last little exchange was entirely too close for my comfort, so losing the car to buy us time and safety is well worth the price. By the time those jokers climb down to the car and find it empty, we'll be long gone."

"Are we sure they're after us?" Emerald asked as she scrambled out of the car.

"We can't afford to assume they're not." Sam grabbed the duffel bags from the backseat and settled Emerald in a well-hidden spot.

Before he could turn to leave, she grabbed him and planted a kiss on his mouth. "Be bloody careful."

"Talk about an oxymoron. I'll call you if I go over the cliff with the car," he said, then ducked from her swat and the "That's not fooking funny" shout that followed him as he ran back to the car, grinning. He didn't know why, but riling her always made his day. Emerald passionate about anything reached down inside him and made him alive in a way he hadn't been in a long time.

He set his mind on sending the squad car over the side of the mountain. The tricky part would be laying rubber on the road to indicate the crash. He barely had the car up to enough speed for the crash as he steered into the next curve. He was about to gun the engine and slam the brakes for skid marks when the tire blew. The car suddenly jerked into a spin.

And skidded right for the cliff.

Chapter Four

EMERALD KNEW that if she wasn't already certifiably insane, she would be before Sam returned. How was she supposed to sit calmly on a duffel bag in the woods while he drove a car over a cliff? She couldn't do it. She had to at least watch. Surely it wouldn't be a problem for her to go peek. As loud as those motorcycle things were, she'd hear them in time to hide again.

She took a step, then stopped, sucking in a deep breath. He'd asked her to stay here. He'd more than proved to her that when it came to any sort of tactical warfare or evasive maneuvers, he knew what he was doing. And there was absolutely zero she could do magically to send the car over the cliff—or stop him from going over either.

If she wanted him to have faith in her abilities then maybe she needed to show some in his when it came to his expertise. Still . . . she swallowed hard, her ears straining to hear something . . . anything.

Then it occurred to her she could call him as soon as she heard the car crash. She dug her BlackBerry from her pocket only to remember she'd turned it off when she'd hid in Sam's car. She hadn't called Megan when she got to town as she'd told Annette she would. Turning on her phone, she saw she'd missed over a dozen calls. Ten were from clients, and the last two were from Annette. Guilt knotted inside her.

Forcing herself to sit back down on the duffel bag, completely out of sight from the road, she called Annette, who answered immediately. "God, Em. Are you and Sam in the car? You have to stop. Get out. Pull over and do something. It's Meggie, she's just had a vision of a crash and she's frantic. I tried to call Sam but it went right to voice mail."

Emerald mentally kicked herself as her whole heart

wrenched for her daughter. She never should have turned her phone off. Her clients had a backup doctor to call, but her daughter didn't have a backup mom, and being where Megan could reach her was really important now that Megan's angel powers were developing, stealing away what little childhood she had left. Emerald hadn't come into her powers until she was seventeen. Megan wasn't even eleven yet.

"I'm fine, Nette," Emerald said. "We're both fine, but Sam is crashing the car on purpose. Ask Nick. He'll explain why. Let me talk to Meggie."

"Here," Annette said.

"Mom? Mom, I saw you in Mr. Sam's car and then I saw the car crashing down the side of the mountain and I couldn't reach you." Megan's voice cracked with emotion and tears. "It was awful."

"I know, Meggie, luv. I'm sorry. But it's okay. I'm fine, so you doona need to worry. Sam is taking good care of me and yes the car is going to crash, but nobody is going to be in it. It is a trick that Sam has to play so we can run the other way and Deputy Nick is going to pick us up in just a little while in the helicopter. I'll be back at the camp by teatime, all right?"

"Yes. Just . . . just don't turn your phone off again, please. I love you," Megan said.

"I won't and I love you more," Emerald countered.

Emerald hung up to the sound of a gunshot echoing in the air. She jumped up, her heart pounding. She took three steps toward the road and then heard the distant roar of the approaching motorcycles, telling her the people chasing them hadn't arrived yet. They were coming sooner than Sam expected, though, which meant they had to be going really fast.

If the goons had yet to arrive then what was the shot? She sent her spirit out, searching for the cold presence of the damned, but detected nothing besides the radiating evil from Hades Mountain. The power in her angel bracelets insulated her enough to make that assault bearable now and her spirit search revealed that Wellbourne had indeed sent mortals after her, a new tactic from him. Without her visions to rely on, she had better start changing how she thought about things.

What if she had waited to tell Sam about Wellbourne? She shuddered. Sam might have been killed and Wellbourne just might have captured her.

The screech of metal and a loud crash sent her heart into a nosedive.

Sam!

She had to look, but the increasing roar of the Harleys had her ducking back behind the brush. A good thing, too, because they came flying by seconds later. Had she gone to the road-side, she would likely have been seen.

Now she didn't even dare call Sam on his phone. The blooming gack. How dare he leave her going nuts over him? What if he didn't have time to make it back to her? What if those goons had caught him on the side of the road?

Whirling around, Emerald located one of the nasty-looking guns Sam had brought. She picked it up, surprised it weighed about the same as a gallon of milk. She put the strap over her shoulder and attempted to aim the gun, yet working with something that was over half as long as she was tall wasn't as simple as she supposed it would be. After several attempts, she managed to hold the gun steady enough to possibly shoot something, if her target stood very, very still. Did she just have to pull the trigger to make it work?

"Em, you're deadly enough without a lethal weapon in your hands," Sam whispered into her left ear from just behind her as he set one finger on her lips to keep her quiet and another hand on the gun, lifting it from her tentative grasp. She shivered as his deep voice stroked her.

"What happened? I heard a gunshot," she whispered back. Though she wanted to smack him for sneaking up on her, she leaned back into him instead, filled with relief that he was un-harmed. She absorbed the feel and scent of him as her knees melted like butter. He stiffened when her body made full con-tact with his, then exhaled roughly, groaned, and thrust his hard, supple frame against her, everywhere. She could feel every contour of his muscled chest, arms, abs, thighs . . . and the bulge between. Then he jerked away, suddenly breathing hard.

"The tire blew. If we'd been in it we would have crashed," he said gruffly. "We'll talk later. Just make sure your BlackBerry is on silent. The bikers are up around the bend, grumbling over who's going to climb down to the car. A call from one of your sexually impaired clients could ruin this whole setup. The bik-ers are armed and they're definitely after us. Heard one of them on the phone demanding to talk to Wellbourne."

Emerald shivered again. This time from fear. She let Sam have the gun, then quickly dug for her BlackBerry, switching it to silent.

"Follow me. Keep as quiet as possible. I stop you stop. I duck you duck. I run you run. Got it?"

She nodded, wondering why she found his macho warrior mode so sexy.

They headed downhill first, which made the walk easy de-spite the underbrush. She was amazed by the way Sam maneu-vered seemingly effortlessly through the foliage, leaving practically no sign of his passing. The mix of pines, poplars, oaks, and maple, thick and full from a bright spring and a lush summer, provided good cover from being seen and from the sun. It wasn't until Sam started an uphill climb that Emerald had trouble keeping up with his longer stride.

"Once we're over this ridge, I'll rest easier," he said, pausing beneath the shade of a large white oak. Sweat beaded his face, and he seemed paler than usual.

"You okay?" she asked.

"What's okay?" he asked, his voice tight. "A week ago I

could do this hike at a dead run carrying twice the weight and not even feel it. Now it's a strain to move at a snail's pace. You mentioned the sun drained a vampire's strength. Is that what's happening now?"

Emerald wanted to wrap her arms around him and pull him close and would have but feared he'd interpret her gesture as pity rather than comfort. The only thing she could say would be to agree. The daytime weakness was only going to get worse. But as strange as it sounded, what he felt now wouldn't be as damaging to him as the power surge he'd experience come nighttime. That was the heady elixir Eric had become addicted to and what eventually led him over the edge. Emerald could only hope the protective shield at the camp would once again slow down the vampire infection claiming Sam's soul.

"On the other hand," Sam continued, "The higher we climb, the more I feel like myself inside, as if some fog in my brain is dissipating."

"That part is the same for me, too," she said.

"What do you mean?"

"All spirit beings and immortals have heightened senses, though some are different from others. You yourself can see, smell, and hear better now than you could before being infected. Angels are extremely sensitive to evil. Feeling its agonizing cold causes severe pain. The farther I am from the cloud over Hades Mountain, the less its malice hurts my spirit, so it makes sense that it would affect you less, too." She deliberately left out that evil in beings hurt her the same way. She didn't want him to have another reason to avoid her touch.

He reached out and brushed her cheek with the back of his hand. "You should have told me. I had no idea it was that way for you. That's what happened to you when you got out of the car at the station. Yet—" He narrowed his gaze at her then cupped her chin, holding her gaze to his. "You knew what it would be like for you even before you left the camp, didn't you?" She had a hard time meeting the accusing intensity of his blue gaze. "You shouldn't have done it, Em. Caused yourself pain for me."

She leaned into his touch, absorbing the cold and sending her warmth to him. "Yeah, I should. You'd do the same for me, probably already have. But I didn't realize it would be as bad as it was. Thank God you decided to go to town, though. We wouldn't have known what was happening in Twilight."

"You may be pint-size but you're no powder puff. Demons . . . vampires . . . is there anything you can't handle?"

"Spiders," she said under her breath, barely able to admit it.

"Spiders? For real?" He laughed, a half chuckling sound of disbelief. "You can face a Red Demon from hell, but are spooked by a tiny spider?"

"Yes. I don't see what's so bleedin' funny about that. They're creepy little buggers that crawl into your shoes or bed. You canna hear them or feel them until they're fooking on you and by then the bastards have already bitten you."

He laughed harder.

Sam rarely laughed, which she supposed was a good thing for her. Not because she was the brunt of his amusement at the moment, but because the way his blue eyes sparkled with warmth and the dimples denting his cheeks made her head spin with stars—an almost orgasmic feeling. Her action drew his attention to her mouth and he stopped laughing to slide his thumb over her bottom lip.

"Careful. You'll hurt that." For a heart-stopping moment she thought he would kiss her again. Instead, he clasped her hand. "Come on. Silver Mist Falls is on the other side of this ridge. It will be cooler there and we can rest until the cavalry arrives. You move at a pretty good clip for a shorty. Nick isn't due for a while yet."

Rest sounded good to Emerald. And so did the time alone with Sam. She searched through her memory, but other than when she'd found him having a horrific flashback in the utility closet at the sheriff's station, she couldn't recall any time they'd really *been* alone together.

He helped her navigate to the ridge top, slowing his pace to her stride and relaxing more than she could ever remember him being. He pointed out different plants and trees, throwing in odd facts about them—edible or not, medicinal usages, poisons. She soon realized Sam knew enough about the forest that he could survive in it without anything from the modern world.

As they reached the top of the ridge, she could hear the rush of water and see a white mist hovering over the valley. The sun sparkled diamonds and tiny rainbows all across the valley. "It's beautiful, Sam."

"Wait until you see the waterfall. It's one of the most unusual falls in the world. There's a hot water spring and a cold water spring that feed the falls, making the steam. In the moonlight, the mist appears silver." He urged her forward. As they descended the air grew warmer. "I think it's safe to take the vests off now," Sam said, pausing to slip his off and to help her with hers. After, she insisted on carrying them.

Soon the steamy mist in the air dampened her face and the sound of the rushing water grew louder until she found herself standing at the edge of a hidden paradise—a deep cool water pool surrounded by smooth stones and verdant forest. She dropped the vests at her feet, totally absorbed by the place. There was a sense of magic to it, earthy magic, not heavenly, but still pure and good.

They stood on a smooth, flat rock that made their own private little shelf between larger boulders, one about knee high, the other about twice that. She could easily imagine herself living in so peaceful and magical a place, stretching out on the rocks on a sunny day and dipping into the warm water for a soothing bath. For a long few moments, she stood there, mesmerized, drinking in the beauty. Then she turned to Sam to share her wonder.

In the shadow of an overhanging tree and mottled with leafy-patterned sunlight, Sam kneeled at the water's edge. He'd taken off his shirt and boots and was cupping handfuls of water over his head. Eyes shut. Water clumped thick lashes. Mouth curved in pleasure and dripping with moisture. Water sluicing over every sculpted muscle of his broad shoulders and rippled chest. A silver cross on a leather cord rested against the dark, silky hair matting his chest that trailed into a sleek line down to the waistband of his now wet pants. Wet pants bulging over the fullness of his sex. Wet pants hugging the power of his thighs. It was all exactly what she wanted, what she'd waited six years to feel, and more than she could take without warning.

She saw stars as the orgasmic dizzy feeling washed over her and she lost her balance. Desperate for a lifeline, she grabbed Sam's shoulder, but her fingers slid right off of him and she felt herself falling and landing in a shockingly pleasant pool of water. Not too cold. Not too hot. But just right. She would have been perfectly fine, except for the fact that she inhaled a second too late.

Timing was everything.

At least Sam had it right. He was in the water and had her head out of the water before she could blink or even come close to drowning as she coughed up the water that had managed to go down the wrong way.

Situated behind her, he had his arm wrapped around her chest and her head resting on his shoulder as he dragged her toward the rock she'd tumbled from. "Take it easy," he said. "You're okay. Just try and relax and it will be easier to get your breath."

Then the next thing she knew, he'd scooped her up in his arms and lifted her back to the rocky ledge. By then she'd thankfully coughed up the water in her lungs and was on her way to recovery.

"Lean back on me," he said as he joined her on the rock and pulled her into his lap.

"I'm all right," she said, although she still rested against him. "What happened?"

"It's complicated," she said, wanting to laugh and in some strange way wanting to cry, too. Why couldn't she and Sam have been this way together before? Maybe if they had he wouldn't have gone after Vasquez and gotten vampire bitten.

Now who was looking back with rose-colored glasses? Sam would have gone no matter what.

"Everything is complicated with you," he said dryly. "But a guy really needs to know why a woman almost drowns right before his eyes. Did you lose your balance? What?"

She pushed up from him and turned to face him. "You want to know what happened?" She pressed her finger to the center of the dark silky hair of his swoon-worthy chest. "That's what happened. Doona you realize you canna strip your clothes off and not give a woman fair warning of what she'll be seeing when she looks at you? You made me see stars and practically faint, Sam Sheridan—"

He paled and his eyes went flat before he looked away. "Damn. I'm sorry. I forgot about the scars."

"Scars? What scars?" Emerald blinked away the water dripping into her eyes to look closer at Sam. "Dear God. You were mottled with the shadows of leaves, Sam. I didn't even see them," she whispered, sliding her finger over the multitude of thin scars that covered him, chest, abdomen, shoulders, sides, and no doubt his back, too.

He brought his gaze back to search hers, eyes wide with surprise. "You didn't see them?"

"No." She swallowed the hard lump of emotion in her throat. "What happened?" she asked, though she already thought she knew. He'd been a prisoner. He'd been tortured. She just hadn't realized how badly.

"Vasquez's lash," he rasped. "If you didn't see them then what made you—"

"Light-headed? See stars? Desire for you. I want you so much that I almost bloody fainted from my need," she said softly.

"Damn, Em," he whispered. Tears filled his eyes as he cupped her chin with his palm, lifting her mouth to his. For a tentative moment his lips and tongue explored hers with a gentle sweetness that undid what little control she had left. She fell against him, demanding more, and his kiss turned explosive, so passionately deep that she felt him all the way to her soul.

She raked her fingers through the thick, short strands of his silky hair, pulling him closer. She wanted more, needed more, felt as if her life depended more on his next kiss than on her next breath. She knew his partially developed fangs were there, she could feel them, but it was such a small part of the total man that it didn't matter. Not now.

His hands were everywhere, caressing, exploring, setting her on fire with want. But it seemed just as she'd made her decision he began to slow down, breathing heavily as he backed off from a kiss. "Em, we should—"

She pressed her fingers to his lips. "We canna do anything else but this right now, Sam Sheridan," she said firmly. Then she tackled his belt buckle and zipper, pressing her full palm to the cotton-covered bulge of his erection. But before she could delve deeper, he groaned, as if in agony, then grabbed the hem of her shirt and pulled it up over her head. His mouth covered a lace-cupped nipple before she could bring her arms down. She slid her fingers into the silk of his short hair as his tongue set her on fire. She arched her back and he popped open the front clasp of her bra, freeing her breasts from their lacy prison.

He leaned back to look at her as he cupped her breasts and lifted them. "I'm dying here," he whispered. "Completely dying." He captured her nipple again, swirling his tongue around her aching peak until it beaded into a nub of pleasure that he sucked on. He cupped her other breast, molding and palming its fullness before rolling her nipple between his thumb and finger. The twin shards of pleasure shooting through her body, setting her afire, were more than she could stand. She arched her back, begging for more, and he gave it in full measure until she thought she was dying, too, her breasts pinpoints of throbbing pleasure that weren't enough to satisfy her starving need. She needed him everywhere.

Determined to give as good as she got, she grasped at his shoulders and pushed him back. Then she slid her hands across his chest, flexing her fingers into his supple skin, and teasing his hardened male nipples before she drew the tip of her nail down the silky trail of black hair bisecting his abs. She cupped the bulge of his arousal and he thrust hard against her hand, groaning deep in his throat. It was a wonder the seams of his fly didn't split open from the hard pressure of his erection. Leaning forward, she licked the water droplets lingering on his neck, planning to follow the wet path with her tongue all the way to the hot shaft throbbing beneath her palm. But she didn't get any further than the disk of his right nipple when Sam grabbed her waist and urged her back.

He'd changed. A dark lust radiated from him, primal in its intensity. His blue eyes were no longer cool and remote or warmly desirous, but hot burning flames of hunger. He breathed heavily, with his fangs resting against his sensual lip as if they ached to sink into something soft. He looked at her mouth, her neck, and her breasts before he came at her fast. Her heart paused then pounded as she prayed.

She'd known what might happen and she'd walked into the situation with her eyes open.

Chapter Five

WHATEVER CONTROL Sam had over his lust for Emerald was gone, evaporated like a mist under a scorching desert sun. He pulled her to her feet, consumed by the need to devour every inch of her. Her eyes were like the misty green forest surrounding them, abundant with life and dark with secrets. Her full breasts were beaded with need, their nipples satisfyingly suckled to a rosy hue. Yet her ragged breaths repeatedly thrust their lushness his way, begging for the more he was dying to give. Now drenched with water those jeans she wore clung even closer to every nuance of her body and her sex.

He could smell her arousal steaming the air around him. He could hear the pounding of her heart and the rush of her blood through her veins. Or was that his heart hammering and pulse racing? Leaning down to her, he brushed her lips with a sucking kiss and then licked his way down her neck, tonguing the throb of her pulse down to her collarbone. Cupping and lifting her breasts, he tweaked her nipples as he sank to his knees and trailed his tongue down the very center of her body, dipping eagerly into the well of her belly button. He abandoned her breasts for her zipper and peeled her out of her wet jeans and lacy thong, slipping off her tennis shoes. Sweet heaven, she was perfect. Soft curves and shapely legs that led a man right to the center of her desire. Silky curls covered her sex and it took him but a moment to spread her swollen lips and taste the sweet dew of her arousal. He groaned with deep satisfaction born not only from the years he'd been alone, but also from his undeniable longing for Emerald alone.

"Sam," she said, then gasped for air as she grabbed his shoulders, her body shuddering in response to the swirl of his tongue. "I need you now," she cried.

He paused to look up at her, a woman flushed and crazy with desire. Perfection. Sunlight lit her spiked blond hair in a madcap halo around her head. She was an angel made for love.

Though she had already unzipped his fly, the pressure of his clothing against his erection had become seriously painful. In fact anything other than being inside her wet heat would be painful. Had to have her or die.

Keeping a steady hold on her, he stood and slipped the condom from his pocket as he shoved his pants and Jockeys down his hips then kicked them aside. He ripped the condom open with his teeth, damn sure at the moment that he owed his life to Nick.

"Let me," Emerald said, her eyes all misty and hungry with pleasure and the anticipation of more to come.

He owed his life to her, too, Sam thought, and she gently and slowly slid the condom over his erection, teasing him as she caressed the length of him and cupped his balls, making his body jerk.

"No more!" he rasped, grabbing her and kissing her hard. "I'm going to go off like a rocket before we're ready to launch. The last time I was with a woman would have been before Vasquez took me prisoner."

"Dear heavens, Sam, that's been—"

"Eight years, Em. And well worth the wait." His heart thumped oddly in his chest and his body shook so badly with the urgency and power of his need that he wondered if his knees would hold. Snatching up one of the high impact vests, he put it on the hip-high boulder next to him then picked Emerald up and set her on it.

She opened her thighs and pulled him closer, urging him to come inside her. Instead he spread her legs wider and stepped back for one second, and the sight damn near brought him to an orgasm right then. Sunlight kissed her creamy skin and rosy-beaded breast to a golden glow. Her hungry emerald eyes promised heaven. Her full mouth was parted, impatient for his kiss. Her breasts quivered with each breath she took, a lush feast he couldn't get enough of. Her glistening wet sex lay open, so flushed and swollen with desire that the picture of her surpassed any definition of beauty he could give words to. All he could do was show her.

Moving between her legs, he lifted one foot and kissed her instep, working his lips up her calf to the sensitive dip behind her knee. Then he did the same with her other leg, ending with them bent at the knees and spread apart, ready to thrust into her welcoming heat. Giving her a long sucking kiss, he moved to devour her breasts one more time before thrusting into her. He'd no more than flicked his tongue over a hard nipple when she cried out, "You canna make me wait any longer to feel you inside me. I need you now!"

She hooked her knees around his hips and thrust up with uncanny accuracy. Positioned perfectly, he eased into the tight glove of her sex, and his entire body shuddered from the wash of pleasure flooding him. Gazing into her tender green eyes, he thrust home, feeling as if he'd finally arrived exactly where he belonged. Good thing the vest was high impact, they were going to need it.

"Sam," she said, sighing as if she, too, experienced the consuming rightness. He leaned down and kissed her, gently, reverently, absorbing her taste, inhaling her scent. She wrapped her arms around him, pulling him close to her heart. Then he moved inside her, easing back to thrust home again and again. With an increasing crescendo of passion he drove them higher and higher. She matched his every move, his every caress, his every kiss until a firestorm of exquisite pleasure overtook them both.

"Come," he rasped on the very edge of his orgasm. "Come for me." He thrust harder and deeper yet still.

"Yes, Sam, yes, yes, yes," she yelled then shuddered, coming apart in his arms. He kissed her hard, drinking in her cries of pleasure as her quivering sheath milked him to a mind-blowing orgasm. He felt everything more deeply than ever before. Her climax. His climax. Everything culminated into a sensual melding unlike anything he'd ever experienced.

He was in heaven wrapped in the arms of an angel.

At first he thought the whop of helo blades was the sound of his own blood in his ears, but as the distant chop drew closer, he realized it wasn't.

He leaned up and brushed Emerald's lips. "Hell, Nick's early," he said gazing into her satisfied eyes.

"Way too early," she said, smiling.

He had the deep need to say something special. Something to let her know just how straight to the heart their lovemaking had gone, but the words were stuck in his throat.

Suddenly Emerald flinched beneath him, as if she'd been hit hard.

"Dear God, Sam!" she cried, as if in deep pain. She pushed frantically against his chest.

"What is it?" He lifted off her as fast as he could, panicking even as his gut sank that he somehow had hurt her.

"It's not Nick," she said. "It's Wellbourne. I can feel the cold, the evil coming closer."

Sam didn't even bother to ask how. He stood, pulled her to her feet. "If you can feel him, can he feel you?"

"Yes. In a general sort of way. Like a playing hot/cold. I can feel his malice and chill. The closer he gets the more painful it becomes. And the same for him. He can feel my heat and the good. The closer he gets to me the more painful it becomes for him. And I canna put up another shield either, even if there was enough spiritual power in this place to help me. I can only do one at a time with my power at its peak. My power has been drained from maintaining the other one for so long. I've lost my visions as well."

He shoved her clothes in her hand and started jerking on his, kicking his ass all the way to hell and back. How could he have let his guard down so badly? It didn't matter that he'd thought they were home free, he should have anticipated Wellbourne would bring in more power and he and Emerald should have kept on the run. Then again, it would have been nice to know that she and Wellbourne had internal GPS systems on each other. Shit.

"Em . . ." Hell, Sam didn't know what he was going to do with her, but there was no use railing about it all now. They were both practically dressed and didn't have time for anything other than surviving. From now on he had to do whatever it took to keep his mind on that, or they both were going to end up dead. "Hiding from Wellbourne won't work, then. We're going to have to keep moving. Keep him guessing. But cover first. As soon as that helo dips into this valley, the downdraft from the rotors will wipe out the mists and leave us exposed." Grabbing up the bulletproof vest, he shoved them into her hands. "Stuff your feet into your shoes and get about ten feet into the trees behind before you put on the bulletproof vest, then wait for me."

"What are you going to do?"

"I'll be right behind you."

She nodded and moved. Sam shoved on his boots, slung the guns and duffel bags over his shoulder, and ran for the woods, just making cover as the roar and wind of a helo penetrated the steam of Silver Mist Falls.

He cursed himself every step of the way to Emerald. He'd been caught with his pants not down, but totally freaking off because he'd been more focused on her than on what he needed to be thinking about. They were at war with hell and now she just might die because he couldn't seem to think with anything but his dick. He should have realized when he heard the biker asking for Wellbourne that the Vladarian bastard would find a way to check out the crash. Looking over his shoulder, Sam spied a scrap of white on the ground. Emerald's thong.

Too late to go back for it. A lot of the mist was disappearing from the downdraft and if those creeps hovering in the helo had binoculars they'd tag him. He and Emerald needed to move fast. Reaching her, he called Nick, hoping like hell the flyboy hadn't left the camp yet.

Nick answered. "You two already at the falls?"

"Change of plans. We've got a copter after us."

"I'll pick you up at Hunter's Point, just on the other side of the ridge you're on. I can come in low enough to the ground they won't even see us."

"We'll be there."

Sam weighed the odds of being chased through the forest until who knew when against the dangers of having Nick come now. Wellbourne's and Emerald's paranormal GPS eliminated any options other than getting her back to the camp and beneath the protective shield.

"Follow me. We need to move fast. If you have any influence up above, pray Wellbourne lands the copter here to search for you."

"Hold on," Emerald said. "Grab the branch overhead for me."

Reaching up, Sam snagged the limb then watched with puzzled impatience as she removed one of the three bracelets from her wrist. "What are you doing?"

"The bracelets are my mother's, there's angel magic in them. Leaving one here will confuse Wellbourne's senses." She wrapped the bracelet around the tip of the branch. It gave off the sound of silvery bells as she let it go. "The wind will also keep shaking the bracelet. The pitch of the heavenly bells eventually drives the damned crazy. They can't stand it, especially demons."

"Just how many tricks do you have up your sleeve?" Sam asked dryly.

Emerald lifted a sexy brow at him. "Not as many as I have in my jeans."

He groaned, wanting every single trick she had treating him.

Behind him, he heard the helo throttle down, which meant the bastards were landing for a look-see. He hurried up the pace, grasping Emerald's hand to help her along. Keeping close to the cover of the trees, he led them over the ridge.

Nick was already approaching Hunter's Point, flying in dangerously close to the treetops. The least disturbance in the wind pattern or even a slight error at the controls and Nick would be in trouble, but Nick's skill as a pilot rivaled that of a Night Stalker, the 160th SOAR (Special Operations Aviation Regiment), night-flying, high-speed, low-altitude daredevil pilots who kept the military special op teams in business.

"Run for it," Sam urged. "When we get close, you go in low with your head down and keep it down until you're inside the cockpit. He'll be on somewhat uneven ground, and those blades will kill you in an instant."

"I'll follow you," she said and she did, keeping close and moving just as he did. Ten minutes had him shoving open the cargo door and urging Emerald inside. Nick lifted off the second Sam had his legs in. He was about to shut the door when he saw another helo top the ridge behind them. Nick saw it, too. He'd already throttled up, so he put the bird in motion, barely skimming the trees and banking sharply away from the mountainside.

Rotor and engine noise made talk impossible. He motioned for Emerald to buckle up in the seat. Then Sam grabbed an M-16 and wedged himself tightly into place in front of the partially opened cargo door. He positioned the rifle, ready to fire on the trailing helo at a second's notice.

As Nick dipped and cut into a ravine leading into another valley it became immediately obvious the pilot of Wellbourne's helo didn't have half of Nick's skill. The idiot dropped too low and then turned too sharply to keep the helo's flight smooth.

The bird rocked precariously before evening out. At that point the tight knot in Sam's gut eased some and the guilt of exposing Emerald to more danger loosened its choke hold just a little. He wouldn't let his guard down again. Period. No matter what.

Wellbourne held the lacy thong to his nose and inhaled, his gaze centered on the helicopter in front of them. The bastards were playing with them, teasing them with their fancy maneuvers. Just as the angel bitch and her vampire lover were teasing him. He'd no doubt she'd purposely left the thong for him to find.

A wailing moan from behind him screeched across his rage.

"Belt up or I'll toss you out of here," he told the Red Demons lying pathetically on the floor of the helicopter. Wellbourne would have already thrown them out, but he owed the ugly buggers some consideration. The Red Demons had been burned by the sun as they'd searched the valley and waterfall area for the angel bitch. Smoke had been puffing from them when they'd returned to the heavily tinted and protective glass of the helicopter. The only thing the idiots brought back with them was Emerald's white thong and the tale of angel bells that wouldn't stop ringing. Even now the memory of the bells had them rolling in excruciating pain on the floor of the copter. It would most likely drive them to extinction.

How had she escaped him? Less than a minute after he'd seen her in Twilight, he'd had the Hell's Devils gang after her. And the bitch's clever ruse of crashing hadn't set him off her trail for too long. As soon as he received the report, he'd commandeered one of the two helicopters at the Falls Resort and was on the scene less than ten minutes later.

"We have trouble, lord," said the Red Demon piloting the helicopter.

"What?" Wellbourne followed the demon's point to see another helicopter on their tale.

"Who is it?"

"It's from the Falls, lord. Have they come to help?"

"Valois," Wellbourne muttered. It had to be Valois. "The Royal bastard thinks he can get my angel. Turn around and warn them away," Wellbourne demanded.

"Lord?"

"You heard me." Wellbourne instinctively knew that unless he became the aggressor in the situation, Valois wouldn't hesitate to eliminate him to get to the angel. He'd have to keep Valois off her trail and find her later.

The Red Demon turned and made a beeline for the other helicopter. As they drew closer, Wellbourne stared in disbelief as two bullet holes pockmarked the windshield. Bullets wouldn't harm the undead, but if the bastard set the helicopter on fire they'd all die.

The Red Demons on the floor moaned again.

Wellbourne would teach Valois not to play footsie with him. If he could kill two birds with one stone, surely he could kill one bird with two demons. "Get above them," he ordered the pilot.

Emerald sat no more than three feet from Sam, but the distance between them grew by the second. She knew he was blaming himself that Wellbourne had found them and was most likely—in typical male fashion—going to go off on some macho philosophy of punishing himself by withdrawing from her. But it wasn't Sam's fault. It was hers.

The helicopter ride had her feeling like Dorothy in the middle of the tornado, except Emerald was leaving Oz and returning home. The twists and turns and dips and rises of Nick's evasive maneuvers had her slightly disoriented, but it was the events of the day that had her reeling off balance. Making love to Sam had shifted her world, altered her life as nothing else since her husband's death.

She couldn't pretend it hadn't.

Lost in thought, she startled when Sam suddenly moved

across the cockpit and tapped Nick on the shoulder as he pointed at something. Emerald leaned over to see. A second helicopter was after them. Not good. Not good at all. Leaning back, she shut her eyes and focused her senses on assessing the power level of the evil after them. Wellbourne was bad enough. This new element was equally as strong. Dear God. Maybe her gut feeling of dread this morning wasn't that some outside source was going to do him in. What if she would be the cause of his death?

Once again she reached deep inside, straining with all of the power she had to conjure a vision about Sam, about her, anything that would help her know how to help him. Her body shook and pain stabbed through her brain like an ice pick through her eye. And nothing. The future remained dark, closed, and a wave of despair hit her. How could she fight this darkness without her visions?

Suddenly she realized Sam was shaking her shoulder. He pointed out the window. The two helicopters weren't necessarily in pursuit of her and Sam but seemed to be playing "King of the Sky." She didn't catch much more before Nick dropped over another ridge and flew low to the treetops. She found it hard to believe, but her senses soon let her know they were gaining more and more distance from the chill of the damned.

Ten minutes later Nick landed at the camp. She climbed out of the helicopter and the world swirled. She grabbed Sam's arm for balance. Why did she feel as if she were still flying? Only now she was more like floating.

"I've got you," he shouted in her ear over the sound of the helicopter blades and swung her into his arms. Wind lashed at them as he bent impossibly low and ran across the field for the camp.

Once away from the punishing wind, Emerald shut her eyes and shook her head then opened them again. But the world was still tilted oddly and she felt lightheaded. "What's bloody wrong with me?"

Sam had straightened to his full height and walked with a determined stride. He wasn't taking any measure to prolong his contact with her or to make it romantic in any way.

"Probably a touch of flight disorientation," he said matter of factly. "It'll go away after you rest a little."

Emerald decided that she could insist on walking and stumble through her dizziness, or she could relax into Sam's embrace and try to tear down some of the distance he'd erected. The connection they'd made at Silver Mist Falls was very important to her and possibly the one thing that could save him. When Eric had become infected, Emerald had found a ritual in the ancient Angel Lore known as a Redeeming. Eric had refused to let her help him. His excuse was that it would have been too dangerous for her, but she soon realized that wasn't it at all. Eric had become addicted to the power that came with being damned.

She slid her finger along Sam's rough jaw. "So, I can still get into the Sheridan Mile High Club even if I get disoriented?"

He paused on the trail, met her gaze, and exhaled sharply. With that one look it was like he was buried deep inside her all over again. "If I had a club, you'd be *it*. But that isn't likely to happen. Ever. We've got to wake up and smell the undead—"

"Mom! What's wrong?"

Emerald looked up to see Megan running her way, with Annette trailing behind. "Set me down," she told Sam. He did but kept a steady hold on her arm until she'd gained her balance. Though still slightly dizzy, she held her arms out to her daughter. "Nothing's wrong, Meggie. Riding with Nick in a helicopter is worse than the bloody Ferris wheel at Duffy's Circus in Dublin."

Emerald squeezed her daughter. She felt way too emotional and vulnerable. Wellbourne was here, and Sam was right. But they had to do more than smell the undead. They had to destroy them, and she prayed that Sam wouldn't be among them when they did.

Chapter Six

UNABLE TO REST, Emerald paced the length of her room to the window. The distance Sam had set between them since leaving Silver Mist Falls added to the icy fear Wellbourne's swift pursuit had knotted inside her.

Sunlight bathed the camp and its surrounding forest in golden warmth, but night would inevitably come, creeping in to steal away the light. The wind would howl, and ghostly mists would blanket Spirit Wind Mountain as they did every night.

The mountain with its ancient worship site had long been known as a roaming place for restless souls caught in the twilit edges between this world and the next. From the time she'd arrived in Twilight until the spirit warrior Jared had finally appeared, Emerald had come to the Sacred Stones every morning at dawn. It was then she'd feel the spirits hovering near the goodness of the Sacred Stones and sometimes even hear their whispering pleas in the wind—cries from their souls of pain and loss and on occasion, warnings of things to come. She tried to open her mind to them now, hoping for a glimpse or a word as to what the future might hold. But as with her visions, her ability to hear the spirits had faded with the projection of the protective shield, leaving her with only her instincts to rely on.

Rubbing her eyes, she bit her lip to keep back a cry of frustration. She'd entered this fight fully believing that good would win out. But that was before she realized they were fighting more than just vampires, and before her glimpses into the future had gone blank.

Her vision of Jared last year—of his arrival and the ensuing battle against the Vladarians—hadn't given her any specifics as to how she and Megan fit into that battle. But she'd had little choice about coming to Twilight to help. The only way her daughter would ever be safe and have a life free of constant fear was to destroy the evil after them.

Emerald heard her door creak open and whirled around, heart leaping at the thought of Sam seeking her out.

Annette peeked inside. "Resting as ordered, I see," she said with a stern look. Considering the dark circles of stress and worry shadowing Annette's eyes it was a case of the pot calling the kettle black. Being a cardiac surgeon gave her the skill to save lives, but being unable to stop her sister from wasting away was taking a heavy toll. "Is all the dizziness gone?"

Emerald nodded. "Yes, but I canna close my eyes without feeling like I'm back on the helicopter. If the patients you two rushed to the hospital weren't already having heart problems, they'd have them after the ride for sure."

"You get used to it, but then I think Nick might fly a little differently with a patient on board than when escaping a pursuing vampire." Annette lifted a questioning brow and packed the room full with tension. "Seems like a lot happened today on your little trip to town. Now that Meggie's submersed in Harry Potter, start talking."

"It was . . . eventful."

"Eventful?" Annette threw her hands up into the air. "You leave on a wild hair. Get chased over the mountains by gun-shooting bikers and vampire-infested helicopters. Come back looking totally O-zoned." She lowered her voice. "I'm not talking atmospheric molecules either. And 'eventful' is all you're going to say?"

"Is it that obvious?" Wincing, Emerald moved to the mirror hanging on the wall. Her kiss-swollen lips and the sensual haze still misting her eyes were unmistakable. Great. They were all to meet in the dining hall shortly to decide what to do about the mushrooming black cloud over Hades Mountain and its effects on Twilight's citizens. Great.

"Scarlet letter lips? What do you think?"

"I think the bloody bugger has lousy timing." Emerald pressed her fingers to her mouth.

Annette grimaced. "Oh. Well, he . . . uh . . . it's probably been a long time since he—"

"Not *that* timing. He had to wait until he was vampire infected. Now I doona know if it's the vampire in him wanting me or if it's Sam who wants me."

"Of course it's Sam. He's had it bad for you for months but was just too much of a noble-headed fool to accept it. Besides, Vasquez didn't tap into Sam's jugular, and Sam killed the bastard within seconds. This whole vampire thing just might be nothing more than a scare."

"It's not a scare," Emerald said softly. "His fangs are developing. Within minutes of leaving the protective shield the infection started taking him over."

Annette frowned. "What do you mean? Jared said Sam's soul wouldn't be slave to a vampire master since he killed Vasquez."

"But he's still infected by evil, and that evil will claim him," Emerald explained.

The blood drained from Annette's face. "I hadn't realized." She moved to the edge of the bed and sat quickly, as if her legs were shaky. "I thought that meant he was free. But then I've been so wrapped up in Stefanie and Aragon, I didn't give it much thought." She paused a minute, absorbing, then narrowed her gaze in confusion. "How can you be so sure about this? Sam is about as tough and honorable as they come. There's no way in hell he'd ever become like Pathos and the Vladarians." She shuddered.

"He canna stop it, Nette. It will become even stronger than he can control."

"Have the Druids given you a vision of Sam turning evil?"

"No." Emerald sighed hard, burdened by the fact that she'd

had to lie to people who'd so readily befriended her and trusted her. "Nette, there's something that you have to know."

"What?"

Emerald sat next to Annette on the bed. "First, you need to understand what my visions are like. I never see enough to get any real answers. Just enough to scare the hell out of me and give me no choice but to act on them. And I don't get visions from the Druids."

"You came all the way from Ireland to Twilight on that?"

"No," Emerald said softly. "Over the past few years I saw glimpses of Vladarian Vampires gaining a dangerous amount of power in the world. Then last year I saw a warrior from the spirit world arrive at the Sacred Stones at dawn, and I saw him fighting the Vladarians. I had no choice but to come and help. You see, Meggie and I have been hiding for six years from a very powerful Vladarian. His name is William Wellbourne. He's connected to Cinatas."

Annette blinked, as if she'd been hit. "Good lord, six years? Why didn't you say something so I could help? So Sam could help? Why is this vampire after you and Meggie? And . . . what did you say about your visions of the future?"

"My visions doona come from the Druids, but from a much stronger force."

"What force?" Annette rubbed her temples. "You know, Aragon asked me about you and I swore up and down that you wouldn't lie about yourself." Hurt settled on her strained features.

"I'm part angel. My powers come from the spirit world. I had to lie about the source of my powers. The damned will go to great lengths to get their hands on an angel."

"Angel?" Annette's eyes widened in shock. "You're an angel?"

"*Part* angel. My father was human. My mother was a spirit being in heaven just like Gabriel, Michael . . . and at one time, Lucifer."

"Then how did she have you? Where you born here? I mean on earth?"

Emerald grinned. "Yes and in the regular way. Important spirit beings have physical manifestations on earth. My mother had become a fallen angel for a time, and while she was on earth, she met my father, fell in love, and had me. She was reinstated to heaven after God heard her case but delayed her return to stay with my father. When he died, she went back to the spirit world to be close to him there."

"Whoa. My head is spinning. Your mother was . . . well . . . how is she now back in heaven?"

"Right. There are two kinds of fallen angels. Those that rebel against God's plan who are banished forever and become demons for the damned. Then, like my mother, there are those that rebel against the antiquated order of the angel world. Those angels are sent to earth to do good works until their cases are heard by God."

Annette blinked. "With all I know, I shouldn't be stunned by anything but I am. You're an angel? And you never thought it important to tell me?"

"That's one way of putting it," Emerald said. "I'm sorry. When I first came here, I needed help. I also needed people to believe in my vision, but I couldn't trust anyone with the real truth of my heritage."

Annette stood and paced across the room. "I don't like it, but I can understand the necessity to lie in the beginning. Yet surely at some point you could have trusted us."

"I know." Emerald shrugged. "By then I didn't know how to tell you the truth. You're taking it better than I imagined. In my life, I've told less than a handful of people and most look at me as if I need a straitjacket."

Annette grinned. "We all might need one before this is over. But hey, I bet whoever you told wasn't engaged to a former werewolf either. It stands to reason that my best friend would turn out to be a secret angel." She made it sound as if she were saying "secret agent," which made Emerald smile.

"You're leaving something important out here. Who is this Wellbourne and . . . wait a minute. Was he the vampire after you today?"

"Yes."

"Why you specifically?"

Once again Emerald explained about Michael Wellbourne, but she didn't tell Annette about Eric.

Annette scrubbed her face with her palms. "You're saying that Sam will become a depraved creature like that? I just can't believe it."

"He won't be able to stop himself. His need for angel blood or for Elan blood will be too great, and he'll come after me, or Meggie, or Erin. It will happen by degrees. The first step is an inability to control his emotions and resist his desires."

"A case of damned if he did and damned if he didn't," Annette muttered.

Emerald winced. When Annette put it like that, it made Emerald feel as if she was being too judgmental.

Annette continued. "There has to be something we can do. Blood transfusions, something? We can't just let him . . ."

"The infection is in his soul. There is nothing physical to be done." When Eric had been bitten, Emerald had searched through heaven and earth for a cure. She'd found a possible answer, but Eric had refused to go through the ritual with her. She'd been willing, would have done anything to save him, but he didn't want to be saved. He'd liked the power infusing him and had been so sure of his strength as a Vampire Slayer that he felt he could never become like the damned. He'd gambled and lost. Now Sam was in the same jeopardy. Would he too become drunk on the power? Since Sam's fangs had appeared, she was pretty sure he'd get his first surge of vampire strength tonight.

"What then? There has to be something," Annette whispered.

"There is a ritual called a Redeeming from ancient Angel Lore. But it's dangerous even for a full angel to perform, and I'm only part angel. Both parties have to be willing to suffer through an agonizing cleansing by White Fire and there canna be any doubt in believing in it, or both could die. I haven't told Sam about it yet because I doona even know if I have the strength to do it and Sam always doubts everything."

Annette opened her mouth, as if she planned to argue, then shut it. There wasn't anything more to say.

After a long silence, Emerald sighed. "I haven't had a chance to see Stef today. How's she doing?"

Annette drew a deep breath. "Not good . . . she just kicked me out of her room. Risa is with her right now."

Marissa Vasquez had been a prisoner of Luis Vasquez, her uncle. She'd been rescued along with Stef after leading Aragon to Stefanie's prison in the jungle camp. Risa had barely left Stefanie's bedside since, spending her time caring and praying for her friend. The woman had a good and loving heart, but there was fear in her eyes. Emerald didn't know if the woman was haunted by hellish memories of her life as a prisoner or if she was afraid the horror wasn't over yet. Emerald turned her mind back to Stef and shook her head. "I bet you were trying to make Stef eat again, right?"

Annette nodded and blinked. A suspicious gleam of tears glistened in her dark eyes.

Emerald crossed the room and placed her hand on Annette's shoulder. "You're taking Stefanie's struggle personally and you canna do that. You're losing your medical perspective in the situation and thinking like a sister. Stef needs time to heal first."

"We don't have much time. One cup of pudding won't keep a bird alive, and that's all she's eaten today. I'm going to have to put her back on IVs and a feeding tube soon, whether she wants it or not." She pressed her palms to her temples, closing her pain-filled gaze. "What am I doing wrong, Em? How am I failing her yet again?"

Emerald sighed. If it wasn't for Aragon's solid presence, love, and support, she didn't think Annette would be able to keep it all together right now.

"You're not failing her. You canna save the world in a day, Nette. You have to stop trying to force Stef. She's the one who has to decide to recover and that might take a bit of time."

"If she does this for another week, she might go past the point of being able to recover. I can't just sit back and let her die." A tear spilled and ran down her cheek. "I can't fail her. I can't."

Emerald put her arms around her friend. They were a mad-cap mix. Annette tall and dark, and she short and blond, but they'd forged a friendship through the pain of Stefanie's kidnapping and had grown to be close friends.

"Luv. I doona understand it myself, but maybe you're hovering over Stef too much. Taking too much of the responsibility for her recovery, which makes it very easy for her not to. She's been through hell and you canna just make it all better with food and medicine."

"I'm not doing just that. I'm trying to open up any channel of communication with her I can, but she won't talk about anything. Nothing about memories from our childhood or of our parents. Nothing about what's happening now. Nothing about what happened to her in Belize. She won't even look at her drawings or pick up a pencil."

"You're trying too hard."

"So what are you suggesting?"

"Stop being at her side every moment."

"I'm not. I take breaks."

"One or two a day for what? An hour each time? Aragon's being more than understanding, considering the man just asked you to marry him and you've barely spent any time with him at all. Why don't you reverse your schedule? Keep tabs on her condition as a doctor, but only "visit" Stef as a sister twice a day. And don't stay longer than an hour. Let the rest of us carry some of the burden of seeing her. That includes Nick, too."

Annette shook her head. "Seeing Nick only upsets Stef."

"I doona think that's a bad thing. He might be the key to unlocking the emotions she has bottled up inside. Time alone might help that, too. With someone always at her side, she canna be free to think. So she stays on guard all the time. Also, leaving her alone might make her realize that she needs to reach out. Bringing down Sno-Med and Cinatas will help, too. To defeat the evil that hurt her will help her heal."

"If she holds on that long. It's just so frustrating. It's driving me crazy waiting to expose Sno-Med until we have proof of Cinatas's involvement in horrors like the experimental blood study Stefanie uncovered. I keep wondering what other killing experiments Sno-Med is doing."

Emerald squeezed Annette's shoulders. "We're doing the best we can. We canna save everybody all the time."

Drawing a deep breath, Annette cocked her head and arched a skeptical brow. "You going to do the same thing?"

Emerald frowned. "With Stef?"

"No." Annette waved her hand as if to encompass the world and mimicked Emerald's words back at her. *"You canna save the world."*

Emerald let go of Annette and paced to the window. "This isn't about me."

"Yes, it is," Annette insisted. "It's about both of us. I'm not blind. I can see the strain you're under. You can't keep expending yourself for this protective shield. The men are sure they can protect us. At least during the day."

"You doona understand. Guns and guards won't protect us from the damned."

"I'm not too sure about that. Flamethrowers will mow them down. My makeshift one stopped a Red Demon in his tracks. Sam says he has a shipment arriving soon."

"If you remember, fire only pissed Pathos off," Emerald pointed out. "Hell is a very cold place, and it's true that many of the damned canna take heat, but some can stand it more than others. I doona want our lives resting on a maybe. Besides, to cover them in fire, you have to see them coming. I'm sure Sam wasn't twiddling his thumbs in Belize when he was bitten by Vasquez."

Annette sighed. "We're supposed to meet in the dining hall in a few minutes. We'll have to hash this out with the men. There has to be some sort of middle ground with this protective shield. I'm going to go tell Risa and Stef where we'll be."

"I'll tell Meggie."

They both left the room, but Emerald carried her burdens just as heavily as she had before sharing them and she knew it was the same way for Annette. There were no good answers for any of them anymore. Emerald went to the common area where Megan was reading and peeked over her daughter's shoulder. "So what part are you at?"

Emerald thanked the stars that Harry Potter and his friends could whisk Megan away from the tension of their situation and bring some normalcy into her world.

"'He who must not be named' has just shown up!" Megan replied, too engrossed to look up from the book. She was curled up on the couch in the common area.

"Nette and I are going over to the dining hall to meet with the others. Risa is here with you and Stef. If she has any problems, you call me, either yell out the door or use your cell phone. We're only five seconds away, okay?"

Megan looked up from the book and rolled her eyes. "Mom. I'm almost eleven years old not two. I think I could have figured all that out. What are you worried about? Is something wrong? Is the shield all right?"

"The shield is fine. But it's a mom's job to worry. You know that." Emerald forced a smile. Wellbourne had Emerald feeling way too vulnerable, and Megan was picking up on it. "I know this isn't the fun summer you planned to have, but it's very important we stay together and fight this darkness threatening everyone."

Megan set Harry Potter down and got up, giving Emerald a huge hug. "It's okay, really. If I remember your stories right, the summer you began your angel visions wasn't much fun either."

"No, it wasn't." But Emerald hadn't had to face as great and dark an evil as the one hovering over them now. She hadn't told Megan about Wellbourne's arrival yet. Mentioning the Wellbourne name always gave Megan nightmares, and it hadn't been too long since Megan had stopped having regular nightmares over what happened to her father. Emerald gave Megan a princess kiss on her forehead and stepped back from the hug. "So do you think Voldemort is going to win or is Harry?"

"Geez! You're not supposed to say his name! And of course Harry will win. He has to. He's good and Voldemor—Arg! 'He who shall not be named' is evil," she said. "Can we have some hot chocolate tonight after dinner? The kind you make from scratch and not that yucky mix stuff?"

Emerald laughed. "Yes. Godiva and Ghirardelli are exactly what I need tonight."

Megan went back to the couch and her book, gluing her gaze to the pages.

"Tell me what happens later, okay?" At Megan's nod, Emerald went to get Annette. In about sixty seconds she'd see Sam again and she didn't know if the butterflies in her stomach were from anticipation or apprehension. His arms offered both heaven and hell, and a choice would have to be made soon. Maybe even sooner than either of them would be ready for.

Chapter Seven

WHOEVER SAID ignorance was bliss just didn't stick around long enough for it to bite him in the ass, Sam thought with little amusement. The sharp edge he'd ignorantly believed himself to be on this morning was nothing compared to the reality of his situation now—after having Emerald. Knowing the taste and feel of her, the sweetness of being inside her and seeing her come apart with pleasure only fed his hunger for her. He was five minutes late to the meeting he'd called because he'd been standing in a cold shower, trying to erase her scent from his body and take the edge off his need.

Talk about awakening a sleeping monster. His libido wanted to make up for eight years of celibacy. Now. And that wasn't happening. His mind and focus had to be on the situation in Twilight and dealing with this vampire crap infecting him. There was no denying it. Even if his emerging fangs hadn't marked him, the changes running rampant through his whole body made it clear. Every sense was heightened. Every hunger sharpened. Every need . . . desperate.

Sam assumed the black cloud over Hades Mountain had to be having a similar influence on the desires of the citizens in Twilight, and he was to blame. He'd been holed up at the camp for four days, and though he had been in phone contact with the sheriff's station frequently, it hadn't been enough. He'd called the station after he'd returned to the ranger camp. Myra had informed him that Michaels went home, since he didn't have a squad car to patrol in. Sandy was going to work a double shift because his wife had kicked him out. She didn't know where Carlton was, but he wasn't supposed to be in to work until tomorrow. She also said she'd been feeling extremely *ill* since Sam hadn't bothered to let her know he was leaving. So she'd be taking a sick day tomorrow and maybe the day after that as well. The safety and the well-being of the town rested squarely on his shoulders.

Sam knew he had to do something fast to stop the little hellfest going on at the Falls Resort before things got worse for everyone. But what?

Fire was the damned's biggest enemy. Unfortunately, getting his hands on incendiary weapons on such short notice had proved difficult. They weren't outlawed per se, but considering their sole purpose was to burn the enemy to death, they weren't necessarily an "approved and easy to get" weapon. The shipment of flamethrowers would arrive in the next day or two, but that wasn't *now*.

Four men going up against an army of damned didn't have a prayer. Without kick-ass fire weapons they had even less.

Bracing himself to see Emerald, Sam pushed open the door to the dining hall. Emerald, Nick, Annette, Aragon, Erin, and Jared were all there and in the midst of a discussion about how to stop the free health expos Sno-Med had planned—fronts for finding victims with Elan blood. Jared's and Erin's Internet investigations this morning had also yielded information about Sno-Med's worldwide activities and the real estate holdings of the known Vladarians. It would seem the lifestyles of the damned and infamous made the rest of the world's movers and shakers look like paupers.

"Sorry I'm late," Sam said, joining the others at the table, opposite the end where Emerald sat. Her arched brow told him his action hadn't gone unnoticed. He clenched a fist, already having to hammer down his response to her scent. It was like his entire system had not only become super sensitive but animalistic as well. Everyone, even at a distance, had a distinctive aroma to them. Part of it he recognized was man-made soap, cologne, or perfume. Another part was a scent unique to each individual. Then an even stronger smell made his mouth water.

It was blood. Acrid and tangy, except for Erin; she smelled sweet. But Emerald's was the strongest and most tantalizing. It was hard to describe, but the scent promised her blood would be the headiest wine, the sweetest dessert, the most arousing aphrodisiac. His fangs throbbed and a haze began to cover his vision. His nostrils flared.

"We started the party without you," Nick said. "Emerald gave us a recap of what's happening in Twilight with the black cloud. It's hard to believe."

Sam shook his head, mentally jerking himself out of the sucking whirlpool of his thoughts. In a blink of an eye it was as if someone—or some*thing*—else had taken over his mind.

He forced himself to breathe, noting that Jared gave him a hard look. Considering the warrior still retained some of his werewolf abilities, it was a good bet. Jared's iridescent blue eyes had a way of penetrating to a man's soul, and the silver streak in his long dark hair marked him, an acknowledgment from God that Jared was special, a Blood Hunter among warriors who'd been willing to sacrifice all to serve good. Aragon narrowed his obsidian gaze, giving Sam a once-over, too. Having given up his immortality and powers to be with Annette hadn't diminished Aragon's instincts or awareness. The scrutiny coming from the pair of six-foot-five-plus warriors filled the air with an uncomfortable tension and set Sam's fangs on edge.

He'd had to put up with their werewolf—well, ex-werewolf—stuff; they were going to have to get used to his vampire side. He barely resisted flashing his fangs. The desire to snarl at everyone around him kept digging at him.

Annette gave him the evil eye, too. But this time Sam was sure it had to do with what happened with Emerald. Great. Looks as if he was going to eat it on all fronts.

Sam looked at Nick and said, "If I hadn't seen and felt the difference in Sandy, Michaels, and Myra myself, I wouldn't believe it either. It's like none of them were aware of anything else around them but exactly what they wanted at that moment."

He left out the fact that he was experiencing the same thing.

"It's the way of the darkness," Emerald said softly, looking right at him. "Those that fall under the spell doona care about anything but satisfying themselves in the moment. It happens gradually and they doona even know they've become evil until it's too late."

Sam's gut clenched. She meant him. The townfolk, too, but mainly what would happen to him—what was happening to him. He could see it in her eyes.

"Which is why we have to stop," he said, looking her in the eye so she'd understand he meant her and him and what happened at Silver Mist Falls. "We have to stop the damned at the Falls or at least slow them down until we can make a full attack."

Jared grunted. "A good strike will slow down the output of evil. But you're going to face the same problem we did when trying to rescue Annette from Pathos. Anywhere the black cloud covers, the Underlings can go. If the cloud is larger, reaching the estate will be close to impossible."

The savage bloodlust of the jaguar looking bats—small cat-like bodies with black fleshy wings—still gave Sam the chills. He'd barely escaped being eaten alive by them. "Until the right firepower arrives, a ground assault is out of the question."

"Then we attack by air," Nick said, a satisfying gleam in his eye.

"You won't be able to see," Erin cautioned. "Not if the black cloud is as bad as Emerald and Sam say."

Nick grinned. "I don't need to see to fly."

Emerald groaned. "It's too soon for reminders." She looked as if she was still grappling with her helo-hangover—and more. Her kiss-me-blind lips had that ripe, well-loved look to them.

"Visibility might not be as big a problem as you think," Aragon said. "If this cloud is a larger version of the one over

Hades Mountain last week, then once you're inside its perimeter you can see clearly in all directions as if it wasn't there."

"Whatever we find doesn't matter," Nick said. "I can get us to the Falls Resort. Question is, what are we going to do to them?"

"Considering their numbers," Sam said, "guerrilla warfare is the only tactic that makes sense. We hit them as often as we can, where and when they're their weakest."

"Too bad I don't have a Cobra and a couple of MK77s," Nick replied. "Dropping hellfire on the bloodsuckers and their demons seems like it would be a match made in heaven."

"Ha, ha," Sam said, a grin tugging at the corners of his mouth as his mental gears unlocked. The overwhelming, seemingly impossible situation just developed a glimmer of light to it. "We could serve them Molotovs instead. Make them sticky, too."

"You want to put all of that in plain English?" asked Aragon, with both dark brows arched.

Erin laughed. "Yeah, you two lost even me with that lingo. The Cobra is a military helicopter but—"

"MK77s are firebombs," Nick explained. "Basically an updated version of napalm."

"A Molotov cocktail is a gasoline bomb," Sam added. "'Sticky' just means adding something like motor oil to the gas. The oil causes the fuel to adhere to the target area, giving a hotter and more effective burn."

"The Falls has a stone exterior," Nick said. "But the roof of that baby will burn nice."

"Yeah," Sam said. "Especially if we drop several loads of concrete blocks and break the surface. Then the burn will go deep faster."

"The Underlings might still be a problem," Jared cautioned. "They can fly circles around a helicopter."

"You doona know what you're talking about," Emerald said. "Nick will fly circles around them."

"He'll try," Sam said then ignored Nick's outraged snort. "The Underlings feed like frenzied sharks at the first scent of blood. I can wound enough of them with a M16 to keep the others busy feeding."

"If I knew more about the beasts, we could try poisoning them," Annette said. "We can lace bait with something."

"Use silver," Emerald said. "I canna say what ingesting it will do to the Underlings, but I know silver negatively affects the damned and a stake or a blade through the heart will kill them."

"Silver nitrate would be easy but too bitter," Erin said.

"A silver colloidal would work," Annette said, then frowned. "You know, I wonder if it affects the damned the same way it destroys germs? It bothered Pathos big time." Her voice rose, exited. "It would be interesting to conduct—"

"Yo, Annette," Sam said, before she could get sidetracked. "Lab rat later. Let's finish this so we can get the sticky bombs made. How long do you think it will take to do this silver thing?"

"How long do we have?"

"Until noon tomorrow," he said. "We'll hit them at their weakest hour." Even as he set the time, Sam wondered what sort of shape he'd be in tomorrow. From the questioning look in Emerald's eyes, he knew she was wondering the same thing.

He could feel the difference in himself after leaving the protective shield this morning, and he could tell after being back beneath it that the shield and the distance away from Hades Mountain did buffer him. Yet it hadn't put him back to what he would have termed this morning as being normal. And it didn't stop the occasional urges and cravings that struck him out of the blue. Urges that were becoming stronger and cravings that seemed to be more and more about blood.

"I'm sure the shield will hold, but everyone needs to be prepared that the Vladarians may make a move tonight," Emerald said.

"Sorry, I should have told you," Sam said, wincing. He'd been so wrapped up in himself that it hadn't filtered in his brain Emerald would be worrying about Wellbourne's next move. "Jared, Nick, Aragon, and I have talked it over. We've set up a constant watch, and all around the perimeter of the shield we've put up a few surprises for our friends. I can guarantee they'll leave with less than they come with."

Emerald didn't appear relieved, but it was the best he could do for now. That and get their attack for tomorrow equipped with some kick-ass cocktails.

The group split, men to make the fire and cement bombs, the women to prepare the silver-poisoned bait. Just before he left the dining hall, Sam turned to look at Emerald. As soon as he felt he could face her without dragging her into his arms, he'd have to talk to her about the way things had to be. With her back to him, she was in the middle of talking to Erin, so he quickly ducked out the door. But before he could even exhale in relief, a sharp pang of regret squeezed his heart. She didn't deserve his cold shoulder.

Come hell or high water, he was going to have to suck it up and talk to her tonight. Just as soon as he felt it was safe enough. For him. And for her. His fangs still throbbed.

Comfort and heaven came by the cup when chocolate was in the recipe, and Emerald was in desperate need of both. Emerald wasn't prepared to meet Sam's cold distance. Not after the morning they'd shared. He'd just walked into the room to share a cup with the group and she could instantly tell he was still camped out on the glacier he'd retreated to after they'd left Silver Mist Falls. He'd worsened as the day progressed. She wanted to rail at him, but instead she decided to drown her frustrations in drink. There was nothing better than the to-die-for concoction of Godiva and Ghirardelli cocoas, milk, sugar, and whipped cream to submerse one's sorrows in.

Sweet, delicious anticipation filled her mind and whetted her taste buds for the pleasure to come. A flash of Sam buried inside her and driving her to a heavenly orgasm suddenly intruded and deflated her desire for chocolate.

Bloody hell. Her eyes popped open. She shifted her gaze and locked onto Sam's. His blue eyes burned, licking her with heated flames all over as they raked down her body and then back to her face. The gackheaded bugger. Did he think he could turn on and off without a care to her feelings? She didna think so. Staring him right in the eye, she drank deep of the chocolate, sure to exhibit every nuance of its heady flavor in her expression.

Sam stood up so fast that he rocked the bench, making Jared and Aragon and Nick scowl and grumble. The three men had been waiting impatiently for Erin and Megan to finish with the whipped cream. Everybody turned to stare at Sam, wondering what was wrong.

Emerald smiled slowly. She knew exactly what was wrong. She stretched, subtly arching her back a little, fully aware of how closely her shirt would hug her breasts. *Bull's-eye,* she thought as his gazed centered on her chest.

"Perimeter check," Sam said, his voice hoarse. "My turn to make one." He stepped over the bench and headed for the door.

"Hey," Jared yelled, half standing. "I just did—" He didn't get to finish his sentence before Sam slammed out the door. Jared looked at his cup of chocolate, glared back at the door, and then sat back down with a shake to his head.

Emerald went back to her mug. Well, her little chocolate tête-à-tête to save herself was doing much more than she ever expected. Maybe even tempting Stefanie. According to Erin, who'd taken some hot chocolate and a tray of cheese and crackers to Stefanie and Marissa, Stefanie had awakened as the aroma permeated her room. And though she'd initially declined to have any, she was eyeing the cup Erin had left on the bedside table.

"Oh my God," Erin Morgan said as she drew a deep whiff of the hot chocolate. Everybody was having a similar reaction, except for Annette. Nothing but the killing sludge she called coffee did it for her.

Erin moaned aloud after her lingering sip. "I'm in love."

Jared furrowed his brow and studied Erin over the top of his mug.

Aragon elbowed Jared. "You've been replaced in the lady's affections, my friend."

Erin's gaze turned impish. "This is better than . . . anything. Than *everything*."

Annette laughed, and Emerald couldn't help but smile. They all so needed a few light moments.

Jared set down his mug, his devious smile spreading slowly. He elbowed Aragon back. "After the millennia we've been fighting together, don't you know that I always come out on top?" The look in his eyes practically stretched a trail of fire between him and Erin. She gulped the mouthful of chocolate she'd been lingering over and her eyes widened with clear mixture of curiosity and apprehension.

"It's all in the truffle," Jared said. "And how you play it."

"No," said Nick. "It's all in the—" He coughed and jerked his head toward Megan, clearly just remembering she was present. Emerald was sure they'd been about to get a euphemism for Nick's favorite four-letter word.

"What's a truffle?" asked Aragon, stepping into the conversation.

While everyone was distracted, Emerald went over and snagged Sam's untouched cup of chocolate. After all, she'd earned it.

Annette gave her an amused look and Emerald pretended that she didn't know what Annette was referring to.

"Truffles?" Erin cried out, catching Emerald's attention again. "What kind of truffles?"

"The only kind of truffle worth getting involved with from what I read on the Internet," Jared replied. "Belgium's House of Decadence's description of their chocolate was rich, melt in your mouth, and delectable."

Erin set down her hot chocolate. "What about these truffles?"

Jared's smile widened. "I expect they'll arrive from Belgium shortly. Ten pounds of them."

Emerald inhaled hot chocolate with her gasp and coughed. The wonders of the Internet. Just about anything they needed at the camp had come from Express Mail and or a delivery made by Barbara Cozie, the mother of Megan's best friend, Bethy. And everything the men ordered was currently being charged to Sam's credit card. Sam would blow a gasket when the truffle bill showed up.

"Ten pounds?" Nick laughed hard.

Erin's jaw dropped.

Annette laughed. "Holy hell, Jared, are you going to wear the truffles like chain mail?"

Jared frowned. "Hadn't thought of *that*."

"You're nuts," said Nick.

"They had those," said Jared. "Almond truffles. Pecan truffles. There were dozens. I didn't order that kind though."

"What were you thinking?" Erin asked.

"Should I have?" Jared asked.

"No. I mean what were you thinking to order so much?" Erin said.

Jared grinned. "You said the other night that you'd do absolutely anything for a chocolate truffle. So, I thought I'd order a few bargaining chips."

Emerald prayed that Megan was still too absorbed in Harry Potter to pick up on the conversation.

Erin blushed but pled her case. "No fair in using a woman's desperation against her. It was two in the morning and I was craving chocolate truffles like mad. You should just *share* your truffles with me. Not bargain with them." She sat back and gave Jared a woeful look.

"Maybe one," said Jared after a long drink of his hot chocolate.

"One truffle out of ten pounds of them?" Erin asked, outraged.

"That's quite a lot of bargaining chips," Annette commented, thoroughly amused.

"I've the appetite," Jared said, arching a brow at Erin, making her pink cheeks turn scarlet. She buried her face in her hot chocolate. He grinned, then added, "Besides, they just had so many flavors I wanted to try that I ordered one pound each of strawberry, raspberry, mint, peanut butter, orange, caramel, toffee, mocha, and two pounds of my favorite, peach."

"Mocha!" said Annette, her dark eyes gleaming.

"Strawberry? You said strawberry, right?" Aragon's face lit with interest. "Truffles are chocolates with flavors and they have strawberry?"

"Yes," Annette said. "Though technically truffles are a rare and expensive mushroom savored by the rich. It wasn't until the late eighteen hundreds that solid chocolate was invented, and the truffle became a confection as well."

"So," said Aragon. "You've a pound of the strawberry kind coming?"

"Yeah, I do," said Jared.

Aragon chewed on his bottom lip a moment. "How about you give your best friend the strawberry ones, sort of a show of camaraderie for all those times I had your back."

"Ha. It was me saving your ass as I recall."

"Hey, it's battle," said Aragon. "I did my share. You just happened to get lucky on the dramatic moments."

"Hmm. Half of the strawberry truffles then," said Jared.

"What?" cried Erin. "You'll give *him* half a pound of strawberry truffles, but you'll only *give me one*!"

Jared froze, obviously realizing he may have erred in his strategy.

"Bad move, friend," Nick said. "Now, if you'll give me some of the peanut butter ones, I'll help you out of this snafu."

Jared glared at Nick. "Why should I give you the peanut butter when all I have to do is give them to Erin and fix the problem?"

"That's not going to fix the problem anymore," Erin said, scowling harder.

"Why not?" asked Jared, totally perplexed.

"I told you you'd need me," Nick said smugly.

"There's trouble in the house of truffles," Annette said ominously. Then she leaned over and whispered into Aragon's ear. He shook his head no and Annette looked shocked then perturbed. "But the mocha ones are sure to be better. They're coffee flavored."

"Strawberry," insisted Aragon.

"You all are as bad as the Hogwarts' brat pack," said Emerald, laughing.

"No, Mom," said Megan, looking up from the book. "I think that even Harry and Ron would be smart enough to keep their plan secret from Hermione and Ginny until *after* they had the prized chocolate in their hands. As it is now, whoever gets the delivery gets the chocolate and will hold *all* of the bargaining chips."

All of the adults' mouths fell open as they stared at Megan, and Emerald burst out laughing so hard that tears fell. Then everyone was laughing. They all needed the relief.

Suddenly, a woman's scream cut through the air.

"Stefanie!" Annette cried, jumping up from the bench.

Before Emerald could set down the mugs of chocolate she held, the men were already heading out the door, Nick in the lead. Erin and Annette were fast on Jared's and Aragon's heels.

Megan had abandoned Harry Potter and was running hells bells for the door. Emerald grabbed her daughter's arm. "Slow down until we see what's wrong."

Megan pulled free, shaking her head. "No, I won't. You have to stop treating me like a baby. The protective shield is up, so we're safe. I'm sure it was Risa who screamed. She probably saw the black wolf again."

"Wolf?" Emerald asked, concern mingling with the stunning blow Megan had just given her. The last time Megan had delivered a rebellious refusal to cooperate was when she was a toddler in the middle of a temper tantrum. The protective shield would keep out the damned, but a natural predator incapable of evil intent would pass right through. "Megan Delaney Linton! You stop right now. What wolf? When did Risa see a wolf?"

Megan halted and appeared to be drawing a deep breath as if *she* was the one searching for patience. "Last night outside of her window, but she didn't wake anyone because she thought she was still dreaming. She's been dreaming about a black wolf almost every night. I have to go, she might need me. She's really frightened about a lot of things but feels too embarrassed to tell anyone." Megan dashed out the door. Emerald was left to race after her. Catching up to her daughter physically would be easy, but mentally and emotionally Emerald felt as if Megan had just pushed her into deep water. The child was nowhere near ready to start making decisions independent of what Emerald thought best. Not with Wellbourne here and the battle with Cinatas turning into a war against half of hell.

Chapter Eight

COME BACK *for me. Please. I . . . I . . . oh, Dear God . . . this world . . . I cannot live here. I cannot bear what happened.*

Sirius bowed his head, wanting to push Stefanie Batista's pleas from his mind, but he couldn't. He was a Pyrathian, one of the Shadowmen, who along with Blood Hunters were part of the shape-shifting warriors in Logos's Guardian Forces. He was a leader among his kind. He should be stronger than this. Yet Stefanie's heart and spirit were so imprinted upon his soul that he couldn't escape her even if he wanted to.

He'd broken the rules by breathing life into her twice, and now they were both paying the price.

Yet he would do it all over again to save her. Everything within him rebelled at what had happened to her at the hands of Vladarian Vampires. And although he knew he shouldn't, every particle of his being felt responsible for what had happened to her. The first Vladarians, the most vile of the vampiric damned, were fallen Pyrathians, his kind corrupted by evil.

Pyrathians breathed life into beings. Vladarians sucked life from them, either by draining their victim's blood or their spirit. Vasquez had had no need of Stefanie's human blood. She hadn't had the coveted Elan blood or even rarer angel blood that vampires preferred. But he'd fed off nearly every particle of her extraordinarily beautiful spirit through his tortures.

Logos was the only creator, thus all beings spiritual, mortal, and damned found their beginnings in the spirit realm. All of Heldon's Fallen once lived in the heavens or as Logos's creations in the mortal realm until evil found a way to turn them. Angels became devils and demons. Blood Hunters became werewolves. Pyrathians became vampires and so on, through all of creation. It was as endless as eternity.

One of Heldon's most effective tactics in his war against Logos was to bring death to a mortal before the fruition of the purpose Logos had given his creation. This act of destruction grieved Logos greatly. Pyrathians were charged to breathe life back into the mortal, foiling Heldon. They didn't always make it in time, and some mortals died that should not have been lost, but many went on to fulfill their purpose in life, often with a greater fervor than ever before.

There were rules to this great gift. The breathing of life was so intimate an act that a connection always formed between the Pyrathian and the mortal. It was a Pyrathian's duty to stoically break that connection after saving a mortal. And a Pyrathian was never to save the same person twice. Doing so would create an unbreakable bond between the Pyrathian and the mortal. Another Pyrathian could step in and do so if they were within range to save the mortal, but if not, the mortal must die.

This situation had happened before, rarely, but it had happened. And the wisdom of the Guardian Council had deemed it better for the mortal to die than to be trapped within the mortal world yet bonded to a spiritual being. And better for a Pyrathian warrior to bear the burden of a mortal's premature death than to be bound forever to a mortal.

He'd broken the rules and had saved Stefanie twice. Now he had to repair the damage. She had to live her life, and he had a duty to fulfill. He was a warrior bound by his oath to serve.

Determined to see this done, he crossed through the spirit barrier, appearing at her bedside. Her body had now wasted as much as her spirit.

"I hear you, Stefanie of the beautiful spirit. Now you must hear me," he said softly but firmly. Her shadowed blue eyes fluttered open, and Sirius's spirit wrenched painfully at the horrors haunting their depths. Making a fist, he forced back the need to touch her. He couldn't do anything to strengthen the connection between them.

He'd done too much already.

He also knew instantly she wouldn't choose to live for herself. Her spirit had been too decimated by the Vladarian. So how could he stop her from choosing to die?

Stefanie blinked several times at the naked man standing at her bedside. She had to be hallucinating. She knew she was in a safe place now. She knew Vasquez was dead. Herrera couldn't touch her anymore. It was only in her nightmares that they came to her. When she shut her eyes and could still see Vasquez torturing and killing her friend Abe Bennett, still feel Vasquez and Herrera raping her.

It wasn't night yet. Her eyes weren't closed. And she was in a protected place, a place safe from intrusion. So the naked man she saw standing in front of her couldn't be real.

Marissa, her blessed friend, had just left the room for some more *chocolate caliente*, and her sister had yet to reappear since she'd asked her to leave earlier today.

Her eyes drifted closed and she focused her mind on that one moment of ecstasy when a great powerful being had touched her soul and her agony had faded. It had only been a moment and she wanted it back. She wanted that being to come back and touch her again.

Come back for me, please. Where are you?

"Right here before you, Stefanie of the beautiful spirit. Open your eyes."

She flung her eyes open again, this time struggling against the weakness of her body to sit up and shove the confusion from her mind. With clarity came fear, the fear of being violated again.

Heart racing, she jerked her arms protectively about herself and pressed hard against the bed rail and the wall. She screamed, but weakness and panic made her feel as if she only gasped. Yet she still heard the cry, seemingly distant but loud.

The man was huge, powerful, with green eyes that blazed

with fire and a lightning bolt tattooed across the bulging muscles of his chest. His hair, a mixture of dark and light, hung to his shoulders. He had no weapon. He needed no weapon. His raw power was deadly enough without them.

"You beseech me to come, yet you abhor my presence? Do not fear me. I do not harm your spirit when you reach to me within my realm, I will not harm you when I enter your realm. Do you not recognize my voice?"

Stefanie heard him above the clamoring of blood roaring in her ears. She fought back the dizziness trying to overwhelm her.

"Where are your wings? And you were golden before," she whispered, looking him over, seeing nothing but a very large frightening male . . . everywhere.

"You saw me when I breathed life into you?" he asked, clearly surprised.

She nodded.

He shrugged and within seconds changed form, becoming winged and golden, and yet, in some strange way, like the naked man. His eyes still flashed with green fire and the room filled with a golden light. "Stefanie of the beautiful spirit, I understand your pain. I know your agony, but you must go on in *your* realm."

She shook her head. She didn't want to hear him say that. She wanted to hear him say he was here to take her from the pain. If he really knew what it was like for her then he would take her without question. Her hand shook badly as she slowly reached out to him. She desperately wanted to feel again that moment when heaven had embraced her and evil wasn't eating at her soul. "Touch me," she whispered.

He backed away. "I cannot deepen the bond between us," he said roughly. "I have already compromised all that I am. You must go on, Stefanie. I am a warrior with a duty to save others, too. You must . . . you must free me by fighting for yourself."

Stephanie curled her hand into a ball. Tears blurred her eyes, making the golden vision waver before her.

He groaned, moving toward her, reaching for her. The world seemed to shake as her gaze met the passionate fire in his green eyes. "Beautiful spirit, do not—"

The door to her room burst open and her golden visitor vanished, taking the golden light with him, leaving her once again alone with the darkness eating her soul. She shuddered and gasped at the loss, bereft.

Deputy Nick Sinclair stood in the doorway, looking fierce enough to slay dragons.

Stefanie burst into tears.

"Is this some sort of a sick joke?" Cinatas turned from the bright yellow Piney Garden Tours helicopter, and its green jumpsuited pilot to glare at Nyros. "What do you mean the Sno-Med helicopters are unavailable? I need one now! We have an attack planned for tonight!"

"Master, Wellbourne and Valois had an altercation in them, making the helicopters unsafe to fly. They are being repaired as quickly as possible, but there still may be a delay in the attack. This one was all I could get on short notice."

Nyros stood there calmly, as if there wasn't a thing in the world wrong with the transportation he'd set up. Had the Red Demon chosen such a visual atrocity on purpose? Arriving in that would murder his image. Image was EVERYTHING!

Cinatas thought the top of his skull would burst open from the rage. "I'm the head of an empire, not a fucking daisy garden! How dare you even think this would be acceptable! What did Wellbourne and Valois do?"

"Neither will say what they are fighting over, but I think it may be a woman, Master. Valois shot bullets at Wellbourne's helicopter, cracking the windshield and requiring some minor engine repair. Wellbourne dropped two demons into the rotors of Valois's helicopter, damaging the blades and nearly causing them to crash. This was during the day. The chopped demons were burned to death by the sun before they could regenerate. Wellbourne murdered my men. He will need to be punished and executed. They were demons devoted to Pathos and the Vladarian cause. I recruited them and have personally heard testimony that they had served Wellbourne well today, even harmed themselves in searching for the woman he was after."

Cinatas might very well eliminate Wellbourne; the insufferable bastard was too devious to keep around. But it would be if and when *he* decided to do it and not before he rid himself of Ny—

"A woman!" Cinatas exclaimed as a horrible thought hit him. "Wellbourne is after a woman *in* Twilight? Wellbourne and Valois are fighting over a woman in Twilight?" He grabbed Nyros's arm and shook the Red Demon. Why hadn't the inept fool put two and two together?

"Are they after Erin Morgan?" Cinatas demanded. "Are they looking to use Pathos's bastard offspring to usurp my position?"

Nyros's eyes widened as realization dawned. Cinatas figured out quickly, but still too late that he shouldn't have enlightened Nyros to Erin's possible uses. Releasing Nyros's arm, Cinatas brushed off the demon's sleeve and forced a smile. He'd have to keep a cooler head around the demon until Erin was dead. And he'd better see to her sacrifice fast. "What woman is Wellbourne after?"

"We've yet to discover that. No one seems to know, other than he saw a woman in town and then went after her. She was in the company of Twilight's sheriff and not with a Blood Hunter and it was said she had powers, so it may not be Erin."

Nyros notably left off saying "master", but Cinatas clenched his teeth and let the slight go. There was no way in or out of hell he was riding in that helicopter, which left him the choice of either a long ride in the limo or to cross through the spirit barrier. Time was of the essence. He flicked his hand at the helicopter. "Dispense with that atrocity and meet me at the Falls quickly. Once I've questioned the Vladarians, I'll expect news of Chateau Petrus."

He'd only crossed the spirit barrier once before, when passing from hell to earth with Pathos. They'd gone to the Falls, so he knew the necessary link—one could only cross to a place they'd been before. He knew how to transport himself, but still he hesitated, fear clawing up his throat until he forced the change, mainly because Nyros was staring at him with what seemed like disdain.

Somebody would pay. Somebody would pay for turning his undead existence into a bitch. Nyros, Wellbourne, and Valois were at the top of his list.

With a sucking pop he became agonizingly insignificant, just minute particles of matter in a universe of them. His importance disappeared into nothingness. Suddenly he found himself at the Falls but could not reform. He hovered in the Olympus room, seeing Wellbourne and Valois snarling at each other like two fanged pit bulls bent on death and destruction. Samir and Herrera had appeared as well and were going at it, too. It was chaos, and Vladarians were dividing themselves among the four factions.

But no one could see him. He could do nothing to anyone. This was worse than nothingness. It was like being locked into a glass tomb, unable to breathe, to move. He was consumed with terror and rage. Every particle of his being began to vibrate, becoming hotter and hotter. Flames erupted around him, searing him with a second of pain, a sharp reminder of his excruciating burns. Then the fire disappeared and he found himself standing in the middle of the room between Wellbourne, Valois, Samir, and Herrera.

When the smoke surrounding him cleared, he saw the gathered Vladarians and demons—all frozen in midaction—

staring at him wide-eyed. He thought they were gaping as one might at an inept fool, until he glared at the Red Demon closest to him and the creature fell to his knees, hands folded as if begging for mercy. Then Cinatas realized they stared at him in awe.

He felt different all over, more powerful than ever before. A quick glance at himself revealed he was standing on a smoking suit filled with ashes, like he'd landed on and melted the Wicked Witch of the West from Oz. His rubber mask had disintegrated, leaving his scarred face exposed. And his world class physique caused the seams of his clothes to bulge with menace.

Cinatas brushed a lingering speck of soot off his suit and then stepped away from the smoldering remains of what had to have been a Red Demon. The damned couldn't tolerate heat, but Cinatas apparently could take more than usual. He smiled with satisfaction over his inadvertently perfect entrance. He glared at Wellbourne to his right and Valois to his left, then pinned Samir and Herrera with pure murder in his eyes, baring his fangs at them all. How dare they tear down what little piss-poor army he had with their petty little disputes? "Do you all know what I do to problems? I burn them to death. You are all becoming a problem. And over what? Women? How can you be so stupid?"

"Vasquez promised Marissa and her oil shares to me," said Samir. "I have the contracts to prove it. When she is found, she is mine."

"He lies," yelled Herrera. "Marissa is mine. We are already lovers. I will find her first and all that Vasquez owned will be mine."

"Anybody who touches Emerald dies," Wellbourne snarled. "That angel bitch incinerated my Michael with a wall of White Fire, and so by right of Vladarian Law she and her offspring belong to me."

Valois laughed, taunting Wellbourne with a look of supercilious disdain. "Yours? When it comes to an angel, there is no law. It's every vamp for himself, first bite, first serve."

Cinatas immediately identified the angel as one of Erin Morgan's cohorts, along with Twilight's sheriff, Dr. Batista, and the two Blood Hunters.

Samir, Herrera, Valois, and Wellbourne began fighting again, and the rabid fever of hate engulfed everyone in the room, both the demons and the Vladarians.

"You're all wrong," Cinatas screamed at the group. "The women are not yours. I rule, therefore, I am the law, which means I come first. It's every vamp for me or no blood for you. The angel and Vasquez's heir belong to me first. After I've tired of them, we'll see. Perhaps whoever proves to be the most useful in the attack on Erin Morgan's camp, just might win one of the prizes, an angel or the heiress when she's found."

Any reluctance to participate in his plans evaporated. It was a toss-up as to which glare had the most malice behind it— Valois's infuriation that a Royal would be subject to Cinatas's dictatorial rule or Wellbourne's murderous rage that Cinatas had stepped in and claimed the prize. Whatever the response, they were all dancing to his tune, and the music was very, very sweet indeed.

Though the black wolf ran through the forests, his paws never touched the earth. The wind whipped through the trees, rifling leaves and fluttering branches, brushing the night creatures with its fickle breath, but never stirring the black wolf's sleek fur. For he had no substance, no real claim upon the mortal ground and his place within the spirit realm stayed just beyond his grasp. So he ran, racing upon the forest wind, desperately searching for a way to escape his twilight prison. He had to warn them danger was near.

Madre de Dios. Marissa Vasquez pressed her hand to her chest, looking to slow her racing heart. It was obvious from everyone gathered around her that only she had heard the howling of the wolf and only she had seen him. It was as if some dark force had conjured the wolf from her disturbing dreams to now haunt her days.

Was she cursed? Was she losing her mind?

They'd all rushed to her rescue after she'd yelled, yet the odd look in their eyes when she'd told them there had been a wolf that had suddenly disappeared made her feel crazy. Maybe she was *loco*. But she knew it had really happened. She'd left the sleeping quarters just a few minutes ago . . .

The shadows of the summer evening had deepened to an eerie twilight and she'd seen the faint twinkle of stars in the sky. She'd paused for a moment, to enjoy the fresh air, marveling in her new freedoms, still stunned that she could enter and leave a room when she chose, or eat when she wished, or even have more of something if she liked it. She'd only known the locked doors, barred windows, stale air, and tiny rations of the conventlike prison her Tío Luis had kept her and her *abuela* in.

The wolf had suddenly appeared out of nowhere.

Darker than the blackest night, *el gran lobo* had charged toward her, so fierce in its howling that she'd cried out in fear. Yet when it reached her, it hadn't attacked but had circled her, growling with menace at the forest at the edge of the camp, as if to warn her of something lurking just beyond her sight. Then, as soon as light spilled from the dining hall's opening door and the men ran toward her, the wolf disappeared as if it had never existed.

She'd first seen the wolf out her window several nights ago. Its predatory sleekness bathed in moonlight and mists had given it such a ghostly appearance she'd wondered if it was real or not. When neither Stefanie nor Meggie had heard the wolf's howling, she'd thought she'd imagined it. Then the wolf entered her dreams, filling her nights with a strange combination of unknown freedoms and apprehension. Surely to keep dreaming of a ferocious black wolf wasn't normal.

But she'd gone to bed each night, hoping the wolf would

come to her again, for its freedom fascinated her. She loved how a beast so large could run so gracefully through the forests. She loved the power and wild freedom that flowed through its every movement. Then last night the dream had changed and she was racing with the wolf, both of them unfettered and free, moving like the wind in the moonlight with the breeze brushing her face. It was the greatest feeling she'd ever known . . . until the chocolate tonight. That had been heaven, too.

A heaven she didn't want to lose. So as real as the wolf had seemed to her, she had to tell everyone that she'd imagined it. And she had, hadn't she? A real wolf couldn't appear and disappear instantly.

Nick and Annette, after seeing she was all right, ran to be with Stefanie. The others were with her, and Sheriff Sam had just arrived, breathing heavily and looking scary. She edged back, keeping a wary eye on him. She knew her uncle had bitten him and she knew what kind of monster her uncle had become.

Sheriff Sam had stopped her uncle from killing her during the escape and Marissa prayed for him several times a day, but she didn't believe it would help. Prayer hadn't stopped her uncle from becoming pure evil.

"Wolf?" Sheriff Sam asked, looking at Jared and Aragon in an oddly expectant way.

"There are no tracks," Aragon said.

"No presence either," Jared said.

Presence? What did that mean? Marissa was still trying to understand many of the things everyone said. She understood English, but sometimes the phrases confused her. Then, Jared and Aragon had a strange way of speaking sometimes. They were different from everyone, but she'd trusted them instantly when they'd stormed into the camp and freed the women from her uncle's prison.

Presence she did not understand, but *tracks* meant wolf prints. Even she could see there were none in the soft earth around them. Only her footprints and those of the others.

"Was it the black wolf?" asked Megan. "The one you saw out the window?"

Marissa shook her head, suddenly unsure of everything.

Since rescuing her along with Stefanie, these people had been wonderful. The care and consideration she'd received were unlike anything she'd ever known in her life. But it was all too good to be true and she feared it would all go away in the blink of an eye. She couldn't be imprisoned again. Never. *Dios mío,* what if they thought her crazy? Would they send her back?

"No, Meggie," Marissa said quickly. "I only dreamed of that wolf. He is not real. *Por favor,* everyone, please forgive me for frightening you. I was mistaken. It was just the shadows and I must have heard an owl cry."

"Are you all right?" Erin asked.

"*Sí,* but I feel embarrassed. I was only coming for more *chocolate caliente* and now I have disturbed everyone's evening."

Emerald placed a hand on Marissa's shoulder, and she felt a comforting warmth envelop her. "It's okay," Emerald said. "Why don't you and Meggie go back and I'll bring you both some more hot chocolate?"

"Stefanie, too," Marissa said. "I think she enjoyed the first one and the second will do her no harm."

"I'll bring more for everyone," Emerald said. "You care a lot about her and everyone appreciates how much you are helping."

Marissa sighed. "It is the least I can do. All of us who were imprisoned by my uncle felt Stefanie was Stefania like a saint because she gave us all hope. She believed her sister would come and rescue her and free us all and she was right."

"I am sorry things were that way for you and so very glad you are here with us now." Emerald gave Marissa a hug.

Tears flooded Marissa's eyes and her throat tightened with emotions she couldn't put into words. She could only nod in return.

"Do you need help with the chocolate?" Erin asked Emerald.

"No," Emerald said. "There is still some left in the pot. I'll only be a minute." She headed toward the dining hall.

"I'll do another check of the area just to be sure. I don't expect it to be a quiet night," Sheriff Sam said. He started to turn away, but then stopped to pin Marissa with a serious look. "If you see anything again, anything at all, do not be afraid to call out or to tell someone about it. There's too much strange paranormal crap happening for any of us not to take the least thing seriously. I don't care how many times anyone cries wolf or anything else. Do you understand?"

Marissa nodded, feeling the knot of worry that they would all think her crazy ease a little. Should she now insist she had seen the wolf and he seemed to be warning her of some danger? She looked at the forest the wolf had growled at yet couldn't see or feel anything wrong. Besides, Sheriff Sam was checking things again. She let it go for now.

"Aragon and I will join you," said Jared to Sam. He bent down and kissed Erin on the lips. "I'll see you in a bit," he said as he left.

The simple exchange of affection made Marissa's heart hurt. It amazed her that so large a man could be so loving. That all of the men here were kind. She'd known only cruelty from men.

"Come on," said Erin. "Let's go get ready for that chocolate. But I seriously think we need to come up with a better name than that for it. I've never had anything taste so wonderful."

"*Sí*," Marissa said. "I felt the same way." With one last look at the darkening forest, Marissa followed Erin back to the sleeping quarters. The only other heaven Marissa had known her whole life was the taste of wild freedom she'd dreamed of with the wolf.

Chapter Nine

THE BLACK WOLF *cried out, wrenched with frustration. He paced the ground outside the building, his heart racing and his body shaking. Danger was coming, evil was on the way and he could do nothing to stop it. He was a warrior, a battle-hardened Blood Hunter who'd fought mightily against Heldon's twisted minions for millennia and now he was nothing but a ghostly spirit trapped between worlds. He'd thought for a moment earlier that he'd found a way free.*

The woman whose spirit touched his in the Twilight when she dreamed had finally seen and heard him while awake. She'd heard his warning howl of danger before another presence broke the spell. He was sure of it. But it wasn't enough. She didn't understand and now it was as if she couldn't hear him anymore. His set his paws upon the windowpane, looking in, willing his whole spirit into the dreams of the sleeping woman inside, willing her to see the damned.

Wake up. Danger is coming. Wake up.

She didn't stir.

Sucking in deep breaths of the night air, Sam shuddered in revulsion, unable to wipe the nightmare from his mind or get a grip on the hungers clawing inside him. It was five in the morning. He'd been on watch up until an hour ago, fully expecting Wellbourne and Cinatas to attack the camp tonight. But they hadn't, which made Sam jumpy as hell.

He knew the root of it was much more terrifying than that. The vampirelike changes that had occurred in him when he left the protective barrier kept progressing even though he'd returned to the camp. He felt it in the depth of his senses—not only in his awareness of the scent of everyone's blood but also in his sensory perceptions of the world. Something inside him had shifted, split, becoming more animal than human. When Marissa had cried wolf earlier, he'd instinctively known without searching she hadn't seen a "real" wolf. Even though Jared hadn't sensed the presence of another Blood Hunter, Sam was certain Marissa had seen one. Otherwise, Sam would have detected a wolf's scent and sensed the violation of his territory.

An invincible predatory power had infused him—and it felt good.

That's what made the nightmare he'd just had such a horror.

Clutching his silver cross in his fist, he dug the angled edges of the pendant painfully into his palm as he grappled for some possible salvation from the forces seducing him.

The nightmare had begun just like his flashbacks. He was in Belize, hanging upside down in a tree, naked, the soles of his bloody, swollen feet being beaten by a hard stick. Just as Sam reached the screaming point, Vasquez began using the whip. Shards of excruciating pain slashed down Sam's back, across his chest and stomach, and over his thighs. "I'm going to kill you," Sam yelled as he writhed and dangled in a dance of torture that Vasquez repeatedly played out. He heard Vasquez's laughter of enjoyment and his taunting words "So, you think you've got the balls to kill Vasquez?"

Then the lash cut into his groin, into his genitals, just enough to make him scream and jerk uncontrollably and pray for a death that never came.

Everything in the dream had been an exact replay of the hell he'd lived for two years. Only tonight there'd been a twist. In the end, it hadn't been Vasquez doing the torturing. It had been Sam, and the man dangling at the end of the rope had been Nick.

Sam shuddered again as another wave of horror gripped him. Could he become a sadistic monster?

The nightmare had brought him to the forested edge outside Emerald's bedroom window. He desperately wanted to talk to her. Wanted her to tell him his dream wasn't prophetic. That he could stop this insanity. But he hadn't dared move a step closer. Whether it was real or imagined, he'd caught scent of her lavender fragrance and the heady sweet aroma of her blood and a hot surge of lust had gripped him, bringing him to such a sexual edge that he'd little doubt that he'd take her in a heartbeat if he went to her.

Why shouldn't you go to her? She's yours. You staked your claim on her today, drank from her honeyed desire.

Damn. He shook his head. What was wrong with him? He sank his fangs into the insides of his cheeks, tasting blood as he tried to inflict some painful reality into his mind. She wasn't a piece of property or a territory he could possess or call his own.

He needed to get the hell away from her now.

Instead of leaving, he crept from the shadows, moving closer to her window, his body trembling with the forces warring inside him.

A little sex, a little taste of her blood wouldn't hurt anyone. Nostrils flaring, he drew another sharp breath and realized he'd been sucking blood from his cheek and rolling it over his tongue, enjoying the tart tanginess, imagining himself tasting Emerald's blood as he climaxed inside her.

Son of a bitch! Sick with dread, he spat until his mouth was dry.

The air stirred behind him. He whipped around, only checking his deadly blow when he recognized Aragon's shadow.

"Easy," said Aragon.

"Sneaking up on a man can get you killed."

"You could try," Aragon replied, thoroughly amused. Topping over six five with the honed body of a warrior, it wasn't an idle taunt. Still, the feral power infusing Sam made him feel as if he could drop Aragon in a heartbeat. Aragon continued, "Jared and I both sense your struggle with the Vladarian poison and we're here to help if you need us. You saved Annette from Vasquez. I owe you, so I hope you realize you've nothing to fear from me."

Despite the gravity of his situation, Sam's lips twitched. When he and Aragon first met, the Blood Hunter had taken Sam to his knees in a flash, but with Sam's gun drawn and cocked in Aragon's direction they'd been at a standoff. A wary few days had followed before either of them had bought into the notion that they were on the same side.

"Yeah, I got that number," Sam said.

"Number?" Aragon asked.

"Sorry. I mean to say that I believe you," Sam explained.

Aragon nodded toward Emerald's window. "Why do you fight your want of her? The pleasure and love of a woman are the most amazing gifts I've ever known. If the warriors in the spirit realm ever truly caught wind of the delights of the flesh, I fear Logos would have a mutiny on his hands. All of the Guardian Forces would be here making love and not battling Heldon and his Fallen Army."

For a man who rarely said more that a word or two, Aragon sure dumped a load in Sam's lap. "I fight it because she deserves better than what I can give. Not only am I damaged goods, I'm probably also damned goods." Sam shifted, ready to move off into the night. He sure as hell didn't need a practically honeymooning happy advising him on what to do right now.

"Then you won't mind if I tell one of my brethren about her. He is—"

Sam rounded on Aragon and grabbed the man by the throat, flashing fangs at him. "If you tell anybody about her—"

The big grin covering Aragon's face slapped some sanity back into Sam. He'd been set up and had taken the bait, hook, line, and sinker. He walked off disgusted as Aragon's triumphant laugh rang out.

Eric! No!

Heart pounding, Emerald fled from the depths of her hellish nightmare, but the painful memories chased her from the tangled sheets of her bed. She stumbled across the room to open the window, desperate for a cool breath of the night air. Only her body trembled so badly she didn't have the strength to unlatch the old lock. Pushing aside the curtain, she pressed her fevered cheek and hot palm to the cool glass. The window fogged, blurring the darkness beyond. She didn't need to see in order to know Sam was out there. He'd grown worse since returning to camp. The coming of the moon and the night had brought the first surge of vampire power to him, and she could feel it.

The power of his presence was so strong that his pulsing desire hit her in almost painful waves of need. She couldn't tell if his surging lust was for blood or sex or both. She could only feel the potency of his growing power and the chill of evil taking root inside him.

The past was repeating itself, and she was terrified.

Curling her fingers tightly against her palm, she stared at her hands for a long moment, remembering with cold dread the horror that would forever stain her soul. She'd buried what happened with Eric deep, deep inside her in order to move forward with her life. Yet since coming to Spirit Wind Mountain and especially after Sam had been bitten, every time she closed her eyes she saw Eric burning alive within a wall of White Fire.

She hadn't been able to save Eric, the man she'd loved and who at one time had loved her more than life itself. What made her think she had a prayer of saving Sam?

Even before evil had gained a foothold on Sam, he'd rejected her help and given little credence to her magic. He'd been every inch the lone warrior, ravaged and in pain, yet still standing stoically strong against a great army. That unyielding, sacrificing courage was the same thing that kept him from her now and would doom them both in the future. The fool would stubborn himself right into the bosom of the damned and join forces with Dr. Cinatas.

She knew the path he'd walk.

He'd like the changes at first. He'd feel more powerful, more fit to fight. Then his control would go, making him a slave to his passions. His reasoning would slip next. He'd do the unconscionable, find excuses to justify his actions until he reached the point where he didn't care what was right or wrong. His soul would follow. The evil in him would twist his sexual desire to bloodlust, and he too would go for her jugular.

She was an educated, trained psychiatrist, a supposed bloody expert when it came to relationships. And here she'd let herself get all wrapped up in a man that she'd advise any woman in the world to drop hard and fast. She knew exactly what Bad Boy Syndrome was and how to avoid it. She didn't necessarily believe in love at first sight, but there was something about Sam that had grabbed her from the beginning and wouldn't let her go.

He'd worked himself under her skin. Ha. Most likely by pricking his way there, considering his barbed nature. Her heart wasn't listening to reason and her feelings were more than empathy for the torture he'd experienced in Belize. She'd wanted him even before she'd learned what had happened to him and she couldn't just walk away, but how could she go through the pain of losing someone she loved to the dark again? The pain of watching them become damned a step at a time. The pain of burning them alive with the power of her own hand?

Oh, Sam. She pressed her fingers to her lips, reliving the ecstasy of his lovemaking. Somehow she had to save him. She needed to tell him about the Redeeming.

Marissa shuddered in her sleep. Her heart pounded with fear. The wolf howled in her dreams, warning her, calling to her, but she couldn't listen. She couldn't answer his call. He wasn't real. She didn't want to go back to the deep pit of darkness that had been her life for so long.

Suddenly her Uncle Luis loomed over, his fangs flashing as he pointed a machine gun to her head. "You pray for your Tío Luis every hour like a good *puta, sí*?"

So dizzy she had to lock her knees to keep standing, Marissa nodded, her throat too parched to speak. She and her grandmother had had no water and no food for days because he wanted to make sure they were praying as fervently as possible for his continued immortality.

"*Muy bien.*" He shifted the machine gun as he looked through its scope at her. "If you fail me, your brains will decorate my walls. Now, let me hear what you pray and perhaps I will send you a feast tonight?"

Marissa began to force the words out, her throat hurting painfully. Only she and her grandmother were left alive. One by one, her family—her mother, her sisters, and her brother—had disappeared. She never knew exactly when, either. Her uncle had kept them all separated, letting them see each other only occasionally, when they'd performed as he wished. The last time she'd seen her brother, months ago, he'd told her that she would be the lucky one, that Tío Luis would marry her to an oil-rich man for her uncle's gain.

"Louder," he demanded as he brought the muzzle of the gun to her lips. "Speak louder for your Tío Luis, or there will be nothing for you tonight. That would be a shame, no?"

Marissa shouted out the prayer until she coughed up blood and fainted. But this time, in her dream, when she woke she wasn't back in her cell with her grandmother as usual, she was being chased through the jungle by her uncle, his machine gun mowing down everything and everyone around her. Blood and brains, bark and sap splattered her body, staining her soul with a horrid violence. But she wasn't alone. A black wolf ran at her side, urging her to run faster to escape the danger. His spirit filled hers with hope, made her feel as if she could be free. But she tripped, falling down, and when the wolf tried to help her rise, the machine gun ripped the wolf apart and he disappeared as if he had never existed, only the echo of his cries of pain could be heard. She was left alone to the mercy of her uncle, a man with no mercy, only evil in his soul.

Heart pounding and her spirit filled with dread, Marissa thrashed in her sleep, trying to shut out the painful howl of the wolf.

Misty gray shadows cast an otherworldly feel to the muted dawn around Emerald. The sun had yet to peek over the Appalachians, leaving the distant mountain ridges and nearby trees sin-black. Very little sound rose above the wind rustling through the leaves, so the racing thud of her heart filled the silence like a warning. Maybe she shouldn't have come. Maybe she should have waited for the rising of the sun when he'd be weaker, but instead of turning back, she quickened her steps.

She tracked Sam by sensing the power oozing from him, a power that had a chilling touch of the dark to it. With each step she called herself every kind of fool, yet she couldn't turn back. Something inside him wouldn't let her.

As she drew closer to the outer boundary of the protective shield, she grew worried, then frantic. Surely he wouldn't leave their perimeter of safety without letting someone know. Sam and responsible had always gone hand in hand.

That was before he was poisoned. He's a different being now.

Suddenly someone grabbed her from behind and jerked her back against a hard, hot body.

It was Sam. But Sam as he'd never been before. Darkness was weaving itself into the core of his spirit and eroding his control, making everything about him more dangerous than ever. His desire for her at a distance was potent, but nothing compared to being in bodily contact with him. Her heart thundered and she gasped for air.

"Looking for something, Em?" he drawled softly in her ear. "I might have what you want." Her body shuddered in response to the stroke of his penetrating, gravelly voice. He'd plastered himself to her back, her ass, her thighs, his every muscle wound to such a hair-trigger edge that it set *her* off.

She hadn't taken time to put on a bra and the full weight of her breasts rested against his restraining arm, leaving only the thin cotton of her T-shirt to separate hot flesh from hers. Her every breath brushed her sensitized nipples over the soft material of her shirt, sending darts of fire to heat the very center of her sex. The press of his arousal against her lower back in conjunction with the rasp of his breath in her ear melted her spine into a puddle. She wanted him now with a sharper, edgier need than she'd felt today—and that had been more than she'd ever desired someone before. It wasn't possible.

The animal in Sam seethed at such a high level of agitation that she knew the least provocation at that moment would push him into unleashing his lust.

"Sam," she whispered, reaching back to press her palm to his rough cheek. "We have to talk."

"You shouldn't have followed me." He slid his arm back until his hand cupped her breast and squeezed, turning her knees to mush with the hardened edge of his demanding touch. She leaned into him and he groaned deeply as she pressed her breasts upward for more.

He brushed his thumb over the peak of her nipple making liquid fire flood her every nerve, drowning her. She arched her back, moaning in response. She thought she would truly expire from the jolt of pleasure shuddering through her. He jerked up her shirt and cupped her breasts, pulling insistently on her nipples until she cried out from the feverish need. His hand rushed down, tugging her zipper open then shoving her jeans and her thong down her hips past her knees. Cupping her sex, he slid his finger into the groove to tease the nub of her desire. He was

136 JENNIFER ST. GILES

moving so fast that she couldn't think. All she could do was feel. Her head spun with the dizzying rush of raw desire.

"Sam," she whispered but didn't know if he could hear her above the sound of his own ragged breathing. A frantic wildness poured from him as he brought her closer and closer to a climax. He shifted and she heard his zipper. The next moment, he lifted her up, then locking an arm around her hips he pushed her forward, urging her to brace her hands against a tree. Her blood roared and bells rang in her ears. Warning bells. This Sam wasn't the Sam she knew at all. But it was all too late to stop the madness, a madness that had her body on fire and her senses inflamed with the edge of his desire as if he were seducing her into a dark realm where nothing but want and need mattered. He entered her from behind in one swift thrust. Then claiming one breast with one hand, he slid his other hand back to her sex and rubbed the wet groove with his every full thrust.

It was wild. It was animal. It was madness. Her orgasm came at her with the force of a freight train, she cried out from the mind-blowing rush of pleasure.

"Again, Em," Sam said harshly. "Come for me again, my angel. I want you again and again and again." He pumped harder, faster. She didn't think it possible but she was instantly thrust into another frenzied climb of pleasure, her whole being swept out into a stormy sea of insistent passion that had lost all reason. She came apart at the seams and spiraled out of control as wave after wave after wave of pleasure shook her to the very core of her being. Tears filled her eyes and her spirit reached out to him, needing him and the comfort of his soul. She felt Sam's rocking orgasm and on the heels of it a dark coldness that chilled her to the bone.

Evil was becoming more and more a part of him. She burst into tears.

"Em? Dear God, Em," Sam gasped, wanting to pull her into

his arms, but he was so stunned he couldn't move. He went from the throes of deep satisfaction to a chilling hell, as if someone had dumped him into a deep arctic sea. He was still buried deep inside her but the red haze of lust that had made him crazy was gone, leaving him with the cold reality of what he'd just done. He'd like to think she'd been a willing participant in the wild craze for sex that had possessed him, but had he really ascertained that before he'd attacked her?

More importantly, would it have made a difference to him if she hadn't been? He'd been in such a frenzy that he honestly didn't know. He seriously doubted it was every woman's dream to be taken against a tree with zero foreplay. He hadn't kissed her. Hadn't even looked her in the face. Just jerked off her clothes and slammed her into position.

What was happening to him? What was he becoming? Easing out of her, he hiked up his pants. Then, after pulling her shirt down, he picked her up in his arms and sat down on the ground. Cradling her close his chest, he buried his face in the tangle of her silky hair. Still weeping, she pressed herself into the crook of his neck, clinging to him.

"I'm sorry, Em. God, I'm so sorry," he whispered through the clog of emotion in his throat. "Did I hurt you?" The question tore at his gut. Tears stung the backs of his eyes. She had such a powerful presence that it was easy to forget how petite she really was.

She shook her head. Her hand slid up to his neck and she uncannily pressed her fingers to the very spot where Vasquez had bitten him. "Why the fook did you go and get a vampire infection, Sam?" she cried. Then she ran her finger down the silver chain around his neck until she reached the thick cross on his chest and fisted it in her hand. "Silver crosses can't save you and I doona know if I can do any-bloody-thin' to stop the evil in you from destroying us both. It's not fair." She let go of the cross to press her hand over his heart. "First Eric and now you."

The pain in her voice slammed into him. *Eric?*

Then the full impact of what she'd said hit Sam hard and took precedence over any faceless name from her past. The evil in him would destroy her? How? Was his nightmare as prophetic as he feared?

"Em?" he whispered, more afraid and confused than he'd ever been in his life.

She cried harder.

Sighing, he wrapped his arms around her and pulled her closer. After a time as he drew more head-clearing breaths into his lungs, he threaded his fingers through her hair and along the fine bones of her tear-dampened cheeks, seeking to soothe her. He kissed her forehead. Kissed her tears. Kissed her lips. Temper he could understand and deal with, but tears? They unmanned him. "Please, Em. You're killing me. Please stop crying. Yell at me. Hate me. Do anything but cry."

Emerald felt as if she stood on crumbling ground at the edge of the Grand Canyon. For the first time ever Sam dished out raw, tender Sam, and God help her, it completely undid her. He cupped her cheeks and brought her gaze to his. She wanted to cringe, knowing her nose had reddened and her face had blotched as it always did when she cried. But he wouldn't let her look away.

"Em, please," he said. "Stop crying." He blew out a harsh breath. "I . . . shit . . . I can't believe what happened. I'm sorry."

A hiccup of a laugh escaped her and she brushed at the tears on her cheeks, trying to calm her emotions. After several deep breaths she laughed again. "Sorry, Sam Sheridan? Sorry for fooking my brains out and giving me the orgasmic meltdown of my life? You bloody better not be."

Sam sighed. "The end result doesn't justify the means. I was so crazed, so lost in a surge of lust that I don't know if I could have stopped had you said no. Do you understand what that's doing to me inside? I didn't even use a condom. What if you end up pregnant?" He paused. "Geez. Tell me that you're on the pill."

"I'm not," Emerald said, grappling for balance. The thought of bearing Sam's child was a wondrous joy but would make his fall to the dark so much more agonizing. It was all more than she could think about at the moment; she was still too emotionally wrought up with everything that had happened.

"I'm sorry," he said again. "Nothing mattered to me but having you right that second." He paused, his expression ravaged with doubt. "Em, you have to tell me what you meant when you said the evil in me is going to destroy us both. Have you had a vision . . . about me?"

Bloody hell. This was Sam. Sam sounding as if his life depended on whether she'd had a vision about him. Her heart twisted at the fear in his voice. "Let me get dressed and we'll talk," she said softly. He helped her up and retrieved her panties and jeans. He held them up to the light and shook them vigorously.

"Doubt you'd get off on finding a spider in your pants," he said, handing over her thong, then he attacked her jeans.

She shuddered at the thought of a spider. "I'd never shed my clothes outside again if I did."

He held out her jeans, his hand trembling. "I didn't even give you a choice, Em."

She took her jeans and he raked his hands through his hair before turning away from her. "I had a dream tonight. I was back in Belize, but this time it wasn't me hanging upside down from a tree. It was Nick. And it wasn't Vasquez doing the whipping, it was me. You have to tell me. What did you see?"

The pain pouring from him flooded her. She went to him and pressed herself to his back, wrapping her arms around him. "I haven't been able to have a vision since I put up the protective shield. It weakens me too much. My instincts are all I have."

Easing from her hold, he turned around and grabbed her

shoulders. "Then what did you mean by saying the evil will destroy us both?"

"I know exactly what is happening to you. You canna stop it. Your desires will become your master and then evil will twist them. You want sex. You have to have it. You'll want blood. You'll have to have it. You'll want power. You'll have to take it. You'll want to hurt. You'll want to torture. You'll want to kill. And you will."

"Enough!" he shouted. "That's enough." His stark blue gaze, shadowed by the grays of dawn and fear, searched her face. "Without a vision, how can you be so sure I'll become such a monster, damn it?"

Emerald set her fingers over the twin puncture wound on his neck. "It's in you. I can feel it. It isn't you yet, but you will become it. The evil will take over, Sam. You canna pretend it's not happening. It's part of the sickness. The power. The uncontrolled desires. The denial. The feeling that you can handle it all, conquer it. But you canna. In the end you'll want mine and Meggie's blood, angel blood. Erin's blood, Elan blood. You'll crave it to survive."

He pushed her back. "No, you *can't* know everything. It isn't going to happen because I'm going to make damn sure it doesn't. Do you hear that, Em?"

"Yes, I do. But you canna do it by yourself."

Sam backed away. "I have to. Look what I almost did to you. Stay away from me, Em. Don't come following me in the night again. Do you understand?"

"No," she said. "That's not going to bloody work. You need me. I have to tell you about the Redeeming that may—"

Just then the chop of an approaching helicopter interrupted her. She turned around and shifted her focus from Sam to her surroundings. They were on the outer edge of her protective shield, where the barrier was the thinnest, and she sent her sensitized feelers out beyond the shield. Evil slammed into her in waves of icy, paralyzing wicked hate.

Unprepared, vulnerable, she cried out in pain and fell to her knees. The cold of the damned gripped her, froze her, and she stared in horror at the huge black helicopter that crested over the ridge right in front of her and dove her way, its bright floodlight shining directly on her.

She felt the Red Demons then. They were trying to break in, dozens and dozens of them surrounding the shield, which covered the camp to just about the treetops. She recoiled from the force of the malice. Five of the demons appeared about ten feet in front of her, lashing against the shield, but unable to get through.

"Emerald!" Sam screamed. His body slammed into hers, knocking her to the ground. He wrapped himself around her and rolled until they hit something hard, until they were beneath the thick overhanging branches of a huge pine. She couldn't see the helicopter anymore, but she could hear it hovering. Sam's intervention had snatched her consciousness back from the freezing concentration of evil.

"Come on," he said, jerking her to her knees, a deadly knife in his hand.

"The shield is holding the demons," Emerald gasped. "We're safe."

Sam peered through the tree branches. "Yeah. But what about the helo? If they have a rifle, are we dead? Will the shield stop a bullet? We have to change our position but stay hidden." The sounds of the helicopter doubled. There was more than one after them.

Emerald didn't argue. She followed Sam, crawling along the ground, scrambling across rocks and twigs and pine needles that bit into her hands and knees until they'd reached a more heavily forested section where they could stand.

"Let's get to the others," he said. "From the sound of it, the bastards in the helo are casing the area for us."

She grabbed Sam's hand. The painfulness of the attack and

the rush to escape had her dizzy. "We can slow up. We're within the full strength of the protective shield."

"And that does what?" he demanded. "It keeps the demons back, but does it stop bullets or bombs or lasers? Man-made shit meant to maim and kill? Have you tested it out? Do you know for sure? I can't believe I was so freaking gullible to buy into all of this crap and sit here for days, fat, dumb, and happy with mumbo jumbo over my head."

She opened her mouth to assure him that her shield was impenetrable, but then she snapped it shut. Was she risking all of their lives on a belief? She'd never tested it. Never thought to question it. What if the shield only held against the supernatural and not man-made dangers?

Suddenly, the shield above them wobbled like Jell-O and the ground shook, warping sound and movement. Emerald grabbed her head as a sharp pain slashed through her. "No! Doona do this to me. I canna doubt!"

This kind of doubt would kill them both during a Redeeming. She had to reinforce the shield before it shook more, failed, and the demons got in. Standing back from Sam, she started to spin in a circle, chanting the ancient words from Angel Lore and drawing deeper of the Sacred Stones' power. She spun, faster and harder, creating a whirlwind around her in her efforts to secure the shield stand against the evil. She wasn't sure how long she fought, how long she kept restrengthening the barrier, again and again, but she was too afraid to stop. Too afraid that another moment of doubt would have them all killed.

She spun until her world went black.

Chapter Ten

THE MAELSTROM of power whirled about Sam with near hurricane force. He stood a few feet from Emerald, shouting at her to stop. She looked desperate, out of control, past the point of exhaustion. It was all his fault and he had to stop her, but she either didn't hear him or ignored him. From the demon screams he heard at the perimeter of the camp, her defense was extremely effective, but at what cost? She looked deathly pale and her body trembled badly.

Pressed hard against the wind, he inched his way to her. His skin felt like it was being plastered to his bones. His eyes dried so quickly that his eyelids scratched every time he blinked. His ears hurt. Any minute he was sure his clothes were going to be ripped from his body. "Emerald! Stop!"

He reached for her, and the second his hand latched onto her arm she collapsed. He barely kept her head from smacking against the ground as he swung her into his arms. The wind immediately died and everything within the forest appeared perfectly normal. Morning had dawned at some point. The helos were gone and no demon screams could be heard. Birds chirped. Squirrels chattered. The storm of her power hadn't affected the forest at all, but it had ravaged Emerald.

She lay unconscious in his arms. All color had washed from her skin and her pulse raced wildly as if she were in shock. Her short and gasping breaths didn't seem to bring enough oxygen to her shuddering body.

"Damn it, Em. Damn it," he rasped, his eyes stinging. Pulling her close to him he blinked his vision clear and ran for the buildings. After a moment the shivering eased, but she still didn't wake. It wasn't until they were near the camp that she began to stir.

"Em, hold on. It's going to be all right," he said.

She shifted and then struggled against his hold. "Sam?"

She no longer seemed to be at death's door and only sounded really irritated. Breathing hard, more from emotion that strain, Sam paused. She was awake. Still pale though, and still ragged.

"The shield?" she asked, her eyes twin pools of worry.

"The damn shield is fine, Em. You're not. Turn it off."

"I canna. Need to have everyone safe. The helicopters? The demons?"

"They're gone now, Em. It's daylight." He searched for the strength not to yell at her. Did she never think of herself? Of what she was doing to herself by trying to protect them? Yep, she was the worst kind of stubborn ever. He started for the buildings again, not running now, but moving at a fast clip. "We'll argue about the shield later."

She immediately relaxed. "Just need to eat and rest and I'll be fine. Haven't been able to do either. Worried about you."

Sam bit down on the inside of his cheek. He didn't know which would explode first, his heart or his temper.

"I can walk," she said, trying to struggle up.

"I'm sure you can, but I can walk faster." He clamped his hold on her tighter.

"But—"

"The only butt up for consideration right now is yours. As in if you lay your ass on the line one more time like that, I'm going to hogtie you to a bed so you can't spin yourself into a grave. You're going to eat, rest, and then we're going to have a long talk about this shield shit."

She sighed and didn't argue with him, which raised his concern another notch. In fact, she settled into his arms just a little more, pressing her cheek to his chest, right where his heart thudded. Damn, but she felt so good against him. He wanted to tie them both to a bed, locked in time together so that nothing could happen but them making love over and over again. No vampirism. No battle with Cinatas. No Wellbourne. Nothing but each other.

Nick came barreling through the trees as if the devil had a pitchfork to his ass. "There you two are! We've been calling you both, searching. Didn't you hear us?"

"No," said Sam, surprised. Em always carried her Black-Berry. That she hadn't said a lot about her state of mind when she came after him. He knew he'd been too far gone in the nightmare and his lust to think about anything as innocuous as a cell phone or as important as a weapon, which he should have done, even though he'd thought it too close to dawn for an attack.

"Did you see it?" Nick asked. "The demons hit just before dawn. It was unbelievable. Jared, Aragon, and I were armed to the teeth, but it wouldn't have mattered if we'd all been holding limp dicks. The shield kicked ass. The demons were all over it and suddenly it turned white hot. They started smoking, bursting into flames, and screaming."

"We saw them hit but didn't stick around for the show," said Sam. "We were at the south end of the perimeter. They had two helos with them and I wasn't sure if the shield would stop a bullet or bomb or what."

"We heard the helos but never saw them." Nick studied Emerald's face. "What happened? Was she hurt?"

"I'm fine," Emerald said, trying to wiggle out of Sam's hold.

"Fine my ass. She blacked out after nearly spinning herself into a grave reinforcing the protective shield. It was her energy setting the demons on fire."

"Remind me not to piss you off," Nick said to Emerald. She shook her head. "Maybe you could tell your boss that."

Nick laughed. "I could say it, but it would take him years to hear it. Yet you're proof that there is hope and I'm eternally grateful it was you who got through to him and not Myra."

"What do you mean? What about Myra?" Emerald asked, her gaze narrowed at Sam.

"Nothing that bears repeating," Sam muttered. "Nick, shut up and disappear or more than demon asses will be frying around here."

"I don't think you can make it any worse than I'm going to make it," Nick said with a grimace. "Annette banned me from seeing Stef after Stef burst into tears last night when I walked into her room. I can't live with that. Whether Annette likes it or not, Stef and I have got to talk. Without a hovering sister nearby. There may be something I can say to Stef about what happened between us before she was kidnapped that can help her. I don't know what, but I do know that I have to try." Nick started to walk off but was headed the wrong way.

"Sleeping quarters are that way," Sam said, nodding to his left. "Just remember what I told you. All of you may be expecting too much from Stef."

"I haven't forgotten that, which is why I'm after flowers first. Meggie said there are pink ones in the direction of the Sacred Stones. She picked some yesterday."

Emerald gasped and suddenly shifted in Sam's arms, nearly causing him to drop her. "The pink ones are outside of the protective shield." Emerald looked at Sam, her gaze both angry and terrified. "Meggie did exactly what she knew she wasn't supposed to do. She could have been—"

"Don't play the what-ifs, Em," Sam said, his voice rough. If he hadn't left the camp then Emerald wouldn't have left and . . . they'd all be sitting here in ignorance while the town of Twilight went to hell. What-ifs didn't matter. Life had to be dealt with no matter how it was played out. "We'll both talk to Meggie and make sure she understands the danger."

Nick winced. "I hadn't realized she'd done that, and I was the one on watch, too. Meggie and Risa went out together and came back with a few flowers. We'll all keep a better watch.

Maybe one of us men should always go out with Meggie and even Risa, just to be sure they stay safe."

"Good idea. We also need to revamp security all around," Sam added. "Come see me after talking to Stef. Once we attack the Falls today, we need to be prepared for anything."

"Will do," Nick said, walking off.

"I need to be there for the meeting," Emerald said.

Sam grappled for patience. She didn't need to be at the meeting and he didn't want her there. He wanted to discuss setting up a security system that didn't rely on her magic and it would only upset her. But something had to ease the strain she'd put herself under and she wasn't likely to do it herself.

"No. You're to rest and let us take care of a few things. Em, we're men trained to fight, so let us, okay?" he said, giving her a quick, stern look. That was a mistake.

She had her bottom lip between her teeth again, worrying it. A habit that always undid him. He forced himself to keep walking. His desire for her now was just as strong as earlier. The only thing missing was the red haze over his vision, but even without the driving vampire urges, his control where she was concerned was threadbare.

She shook her head. "I have to—"

"No, and that's an order. Otherwise, I will tie you to your bed. And as much as I'd like to, it won't be so I can devour all of your charms unhindered."

She looked at him with surprised interest. Her pupils dilated and her mouth opened slightly, leaving that full wet lip available for sucking just inches from his mouth. Everything in him fired up like a launching rocket. He inhaled sharply and dug his fangs into his gums. Just a short time ago, he'd sworn to himself that he wouldn't come within ten feet of her again after what he'd done. Now he'd do it to her again in less than a heartbeat. Sam knew Emerald was in more danger from him than from anyone or anything else. God help them both.

* * *

"I told you the angel bitch was bloody powerful," Wellbourne said, leaning back on a sofa in the Olympus room. "Unless you cut off her power, you'll never get past her protection."

Cinatas thought the Vladarian's expression close enough to a gloat to warrant eliminating the bastard immediately. In fact all of the gathered vampires' attitudes bordered on insubordination. Unfortunately, Cinatas couldn't do without them . . . yet. A stab of pure hatred filled him. Pathos had created this problem. Had left his own son in the untenable position of having to grovel for everything. It burned Cinatas that Pathos had brought him to the Falls first after saving him from being a prisoner in hell. Pathos should have taken his only begotten son to Zion.

Pathos should have put Cinatas first and shown him all that he would inherit before dealing with the Sno-Med disaster and Erin Morgan's friends. Because Pathos hadn't, Cinatas had been forced to depend on the lowly Nyros for learning everything about the empire Pathos had built. It made Cinatas little more than a pig rooting for scraps. It was the same with the Vladarians. Being forced to rely on them for help was worse than death. Cinatas needed his own army in order to be effective.

"What do you mean?" Cinatas asked Wellbourne. He wouldn't put it past the bastard to have known the attack was doomed from the start.

It was all Cinatas could do to keep from annihilating the entire room of incompetent fools. The attack was a total disaster. The repair on the helicopters hadn't finished until almost dawn, giving them only a small window of time before the sunrise. Samir and Herrera had been no-shows, having apparently disappeared before the attack to search for Marissa Vasquez, each probably thinking the other would stay and fight. Both of them were going to pay a heavy price for going AWOL. Then the attack itself had been abysmal. The demons had gone at the shield like mindless sheep going over a cliff, employing nothing but dumb brute force. As for the remaining Vladarians, after one unsuccessful attempt to penetrate the camp's defenses, they'd all stood back and watched the circus with their thumbs up their asses.

This was to have been his victory. His bloody coup d'état. The attack was supposed to have been investigated and planned out *before* his arrival in Twilight. All he was supposed to do was head the invasion and get his hands on Erin Morgan. Her sacrifice and his coronation were set for tomorrow night.

"We are all wasting our time here," Valois said. Though the Royal Vladarian had muttered the comment to Rasputin, Cinatas heard it loud and clear, moving the vampire to the top of the death list. There might be few left among the damned by the time he rid the world of idiots. But to do that, he needed power—and maybe the angel would be the key. After all, Satan had angel blood. Cinatas would have it, too.

"Other than destroying Logos and the Guardian Forces," Cinatas snarled, "how can you cut off an angel's power?"

"She's in the physical realm and bound by the same rules that we are. To wield as much White Fire as she did tonight, she had to have an earthly source to channel it from Logos's realm. She drew from Stonehenge's power to destroy my brother Michael. There must a similar place of worship here that she is using. Destroy that and her bloody little power fest will be over."

"It must be the Sacred Stones," Nyros said. "On top of the mountain near their camp. But one would have to desecrate the site, and that isn't possible without Heldon."

"A desecration. A Black Mass," Cinatas whispered as a tingle of pleasure crawled over him. An image of him as the unholy leader of thousands filled him again.

Wellbourne paused, his eyes wide with interest. "A Black Mass would work. But none of us have enough power. As

Nyros said, we'd need Heldon himself, and it might take months to get him here."

Cinatas stood and paced the room. This was his dawning moment. What he decided now would set the course of his future. If he were ever to usurp Heldon's throne, he had to prove his own power by making this desecration himself. But how? Whose power could he steal? What could he possibly do . . . the news about the pope's plans flashed across Cinatas's mind. One man . . . worldwide power . . . power that Cinatas could easily tap into by stealing a simple blessed vase.

"You need to think outside the box, Wellbourne. Correct me if I am wrong, but to desecrate something holy, it must be used for the unholy, right? The more powerful the Holy the greater the desecration and the greater the desecrater's power. Isn't it rumored that is how Heldon become so powerful?"

"Yes. What are you thinking?"

Cinatas smiled. "Why not use sacraments blessed by the pope himself for our own purpose? There's a gold monstrance blessed by the pope being delivered to the St. Peter in Chains Cathedral in Cincinnati, Ohio, today. I think a Black Mass at the Sacred Stones using the blessed hosts is in order."

Nyros stepped forward. "Should you attempt such a feat, you still must have Heldon's permission. All things affect the balance of the war he wages against Logos and he must be aware of such a sacrilege. You cannot act without his agreement."

The nodding and agreement among the other demons and the Vladarians was sickening. No wonder Heldon had ruled for so many millennia. No one had the balls to go against his stupid edicts. Nyros was becoming intolerable.

Cinatas would be damned—ha, he already was—then *double* damned before he'd grovel for anything from Heldon. In fact, Heldon probably kept an iron hand on powerful desecrations because the beast didn't want another to become as powerful as he.

Sweeping his glance about the room, Cinatas took note of who appeared to agree with Nyros and who didn't think it was any of Heldon's business what they chose to desecrate. Wellbourne looked particularly put out, a reaction that fit nicely into Cinatas's forming plan.

Meanwhile he'd keep Nyros and the rest of the castrated Vladarians distracted with an additional plan. One that would draw the Blood Hunters out of the camp and make the women as easy to pluck as ripe cherries when the time was right.

"We don't need Heldon," Cinatas replied to the uproar as he stared Nyros down, letting the demon feel the brunt of his displeasure. Cinatas smiled. "We'll get to the humans another way. They're a camp full of crusading heroes. I'm sure we can find at least one person in this godforsaken, backwoods town that they'll come out of their rabbit hole to save."

The dawning enlightenment among the group was nauseating. He supposed he should make some allowances for lesser beings, since his sophisticated intelligence was so rare, but the tedium of coexisting with such "idiocracy" was pure torture.

"I want this done tonight," he informed the Vladarians.

"I can't wait to get my hands on that bitch," said Wellbourne.

"There are two things to take into consideration," Nyros said, standing up and interjecting himself into the conversation again. "Pathos spent hundreds of years doing all he could to hide the presence of Heldon's agents in the mortal world, from which the Vladarians have greatly benefited. He believed more was gained through anonymity than brute force and terror."

Cinatas could only see red as his throat clenched with fury. Nyros had gone too far. "That was Pathos's way and it is now time for a change. The recent attacks upon the Vladarians and Sno-Med make it necessary for us to retaliate in equal measure, lest we lose all the power that has been gained. I say we take over the sheriff's office and draw him out of hiding. That will get right to the heart of the town. If we can defeat their means of protection then we can control everyone."

This spurred a wild discussion among the Vladarians and sent Nyros off in a huff, an action that only solidified Cinatas's secret plan. A Black Mass was the only way to go, and Wellbourne wanted the angel bad enough to get his hands on the pope's consecrated monstrance. Cinatas needed more power and he needed it fast. He could feel his shaky hold on the damned crumbling.

Stefanie looked up as the door to her room creaked open. Marissa, who always made an appearance early in the morning, hadn't show up. And since she was alone, Stefanie couldn't help but wonder if the winged, golden man would come to her again. Ever since he disappeared so suddenly last night, her emotions had swung like a pendulum out of control, going from elation that he'd returned to despair that she'd never see him again.

"I have to talk to you, Stef," Nick said from the doorway to her room. He had a bunch of flowers in his hand and a look a terror on his face.

"No," she whispered. "I can't."

He did an about-face to leave, looking as if she'd slapped him. She started to call him back, but then didn't. Talk was beyond her. The pain was too much. She brought her arms closer about herself, trying to hold herself together.

"No, I can't just leave. You don't need to talk. Just listen," he said as he marched back into the room. He came to the end of the bed and set the flowers onto the blanket then ran a shaky hand through his short cropped brown hair. "Those are for you. They were meant to be an apology for everything that happened that night. I'm sorry, okay. The wine. The seduction. The sex. I knew in one look you weren't into casual. You've got lifer written all over your face. But I was horny and there was something about you, something that I had to know and touch. So I played you and it was wrong and I've regretted it every day since."

Stefanie stared at Nick, her whole being vibrating with so much pain that she couldn't even speak. Who she'd been six months ago was gone forever. It was as if that date and her shameful regret of having sex with a man she didn't love had happened to someone else. She'd been very lonely and had tried to fill that well with sexual attraction.

Nick exhaled harshly and fisted his hand. "I see the hate in your eyes when you look at me, Stef. It's killing me."

"Not you," she said, forcing the words from her closed throat. "Them. At Corazon. What they . . . they did to me by force . . . oh God." Her whole body shuddered. She couldn't think about this. She couldn't talk about this. Falling back against the bed, she curled into a ball on her side and tried to thrust the images of what Vasquez and Herrera had done to her out of her mind. What Vasquez had done to Abe had been even worse.

"Them, Stef? Dear God . . . you mean you were raped? By *them*? Jesus. I didn't know . . . your sister doesn't know either. She would have said . . . Dear God."

"Don't tell," Stefanie gasped over her choking tears. Annette had asked if she'd been abused that way, but Stefanie had denied it. She couldn't talk about it. Not even Marissa knew. Marissa knew her uncle had killed Abe, but she didn't know what else he'd done. She didn't even understand why she'd told Nick other than she could see he was blaming himself. "I can't talk about it, Please go away."

"No, I won't go away. You can't talk? Fine, don't talk. You don't want me to tell? Fine, I won't tell. But I'm not going to go away and pretend I don't know. I'm not going to sit here while you kill yourself by letting the shit eat at you."

Before she could move, or even uncurl to glance at Nick, he

scooped her up from the bed, sheets, blankets, and all. "No," she cried, trying to push away from him but she was too weak. She finally untangled herself enough to see his face. Logically, she knew she didn't have to fear Nick, but her heart still thundered and her blood roared in her ears.

"Yes," he said, ducking out of the bedroom. "I owe you one, and friends don't let friends die." Nick almost didn't look like Nick anymore. Lines of pain and a dead serious determination had replaced the playboy-with-revolving-bunnies demeanor she remembered from before.

"Just hold on, Stef," Nick said, shifting to hold her tighter to him. Marching across the common area, he headed toward the outside door.

"Nick! What in the hell are you doing?" Annette cried, coming from another room.

"Going to get some fresh air and have a little target practice." Spying paper and pencil on a coffee table, he leaned down and grabbed it. Stefanie was practically lighter than a feather.

"But she's too weak for this," Annette said.

"And she'll never get stronger wasting away in that bed. I won't keep her too long."

Stefanie didn't say anything. She was too dizzy and in too much pain. The effort to argue was too draining. She figured she might as well go with Nick for a few minutes rather than tangle with her sister on how little she ate.

"Tell everyone they might hear a few shots, but not to worry," he said then marched through the door into the sun. Stefanie had to cover her eyes from the brightness, but its warmth hit her face and felt good as it seeped into the chill of her skin. Morning air, fresh and fragrant, touched her, and she drew a deeper breath, remembering for a moment that this was her favorite part of the day—the time when she loved to either walk in the forest or sit and illustrate her latest story in the pure morning light. But that thought led her back to the morning she and Abe had been at the Sacred Stones with Rob Rankin. Rob had been a co-worker, a neighbor, and, she thought, a friend—until he'd kidnapped her and Abe at gunpoint, forcing them into the trunk of his car after she and Abe had discovered that Sno-Med was killing women in an experimental medical study.

She shuddered again. That had been bad enough. Then she'd been handed over to Vasquez, and she'd entered the gates of hell.

The nightmare filled her and she didn't know how much time passed before Nick stopped and set her on the ground. He shoved a writing tablet into her lap and then wrapped the blanket up her back and over her shoulders like a cape. Between her flannel pajamas and her covers, she wasn't chilled. But warmth was something she knew she'd never know again.

He knelt on the ground next to her and slid a pen into her fingers. "Put the mug of one of the bastards who raped you, hurt you, demeaned you, or abused you onto that paper. You don't want me to look at it, I won't. You don't feel like drawing, then don't, make a circle. Just put something on there that represents one of those sons of bitches."

Her hand trembled as she wrapped her fingers around the pen. It seemed as if she couldn't even remember how to hold it. "Why?" she whispered. Every time she closed her eyes she saw them. She didn't want to see them with her eyes open.

"Because," Nick said, reaching behind him. He pulled out a large, black pistol. "You're going to obliterate the bastard. You're going to put this gun in your hand and you're going to shoot and shoot and shoot. And we're going to do this every day until when you shut your eyes and that son of a bitch pops into your mind, you see yourself offing him. You aren't going to be a victim ever again, Stef. Not in your nightmares and not in life. This isn't a miracle cure, but empowering yourself even symbolically is a start. You were and are still a beautiful woman with a beautiful spirit, but they've buried so much shit on top of you, you can't even breathe much less see."

She looked Nick in the eye and saw his rage. Rage that hit a note deep inside of her. He wasn't trying to understand or empathize or tell her he knew anything about what she had been through. He was telling her it was okay to hate. Hate Vasquez and Herrera for what they had done to her. And hate them for what they had done to Abe. She clenched the pen in her hand as that rage bubbled up from its buried depths.

You must free me by fighting for yourself.

Stefanie gasped, looking quickly about for her winged golden man with the fiery green eyes, but saw nothing more than Nick, his gun, and the pen in her hand. Had she hallucinated it?

Vasquez's and Herrera's faces soon took shape upon the papers. Then image after image of the horror she went through began pouring out of her onto the pages of the tablet. She would do more than obliterate the bastards' faces. She'd obliterate what they'd done to her. Tears flowed as she drew, spilling onto the page, but she didn't stop, she couldn't stop.

It wasn't until she reached the last page of the tablet that she heard the strangled and ragged crying of another. Nick knelt next to her, watching. His face was twisted in rage, and tears were pouring from eyes filled with pain.

"God," he whispered. "Dear God."

She ducked her head in shame over it all.

He urged her to meet his gaze with a shaky hand. "You ready to kick ass, Stef?"

Only pain and anger blazed in his eyes. There was no condemnation. No pity. She nodded.

He handed her the gun. It was cold and heavy. She had to use both of her hands just to hold it. She could feel the lethality of it, too. Could feel that in a single second with just a tiny pressure from her fingers, she could potentially kill the evil that had destroyed her. She *would* end it. "I'm ready," she whispered.

"Good. I'm going to promise you something else. As soon as I can, I'm going back to Belize. Even though Sam swears he saw my father killed, I'm going to find out who is using the name Sinclair there. And when I go, I'm taking a list of bastards to hunt down. A list you're going to give me. Vasquez is gone forever, but if anyone else who did this to you is alive, or even if anyone stood by and watched this happen, one way or another they're toast. You can think what you want to about that. I've never killed a man before; spend most of my free time flying a helo to save people. But I'm telling you this. Evil like that can't be allowed to go unchecked so it's free to prey on someone else. Our laws don't reach into that jungle, but right can figure out a way to deliver justice. You read me, Stef?"

"Yes," she said. An image of the warrior-man she'd seen in her room came to mind along with an odd image of her fighting a battle at his side. Vasquez was already dead but Herrera wasn't and she wanted him at her feet twisting in agony from the deadly blows she'd delivered. Stefanie tightened her grip on the gun as power flooded her.

Chapter Eleven

"MOM, the pink flowers were just a couple of feet outside the barrier, and Risa was with me. Nothing bad happened," Megan said, her brow creased in a preteen's I-can't-believe-you're-making-a-big-deal-about-this frown.

"It doesn't matter, Meggie. You were told never to go outside the shield. You promised me you wouldn't and you did. You doona know all the bad things that can happen." Emerald set the last of the breakfast plates on the table and sent her daughter a sharp gaze.

Megan's frown deepened. "I've seen bad things," Megan said, her voice just barely above a whisper and her eyes filled with a knowing pain.

Megan had seen things no child should have to bear—murder, demons, death, things that made Emerald's heart ache. Emerald drew a deep breath to respond, but Megan continued.

"If something bad was going to happen with me and Risa picking flowers, wouldn't I have had a vision about it? Isn't that how you always decided what was okay to do and what was not?"

Emerald opened her mouth to deny that everything was that simple, then shut it and crossed the room on shaky legs. Scrying out the future before deciding to do anything is exactly what she'd done all of Megan's life. Now that Megan's visions had started, it would naturally follow that her daughter would expect to rely on them. Emerald wasn't ready for that, ready for her daughter to start making independent decisions that didn't align with Emerald's.

Megan was so young yet, and being able to interpret some visions correctly took experience.

Reaching her daughter, Emerald sat down and took her

hand. Megan had to understand that a lot more experience was needed before Megan could rely on her visions to guide her. And, truth be told, Megan should never rely on her visions as heavily as Emerald had.

"Meggie, you canna make your visions the sole basis for choosing to do something. I was wrong in that I never communicated the other factors that played into the decisions I made. There are rules in life, and breaking them means consequences, even if you haven't had a vision about it. If you were to go play ball in the middle of a busy highway you'd likely get hit by a car even if you didn't have a vision of it. The same holds true for the protective shield. If you choose to leave it, then evil can reach you. Having visions doesn't eliminate the consequences of your choices. They are extra stars to guide you in the darkness you face as an angel. Do you understand?"

Megan nodded slowly but didn't look entirely convinced. "What happens if I have a vision about something and to stop that terrible thing, I have to do what you told me not to do? If I'm really an angel and have angel gifts then shouldn't I do what they show me I must?"

Emerald hugged Megan. "You will be ready to do that someday, poppet. But doona be in too much of a rush. You doona have all of your angel powers yet and you've little experience in understanding your visions or the depth of the evil angels fight against. Until that day comes, your mother's word is law. Got it?"

"I suppose," Megan said, letting out an exasperated sigh. "Mr. Sam gave me a lecture, too. Nick said Mr. Sam was good at laying down the law. Mr. Sam has been doing it to him for years."

"What did Sam say?" Emerald asked.

"I'm still trying to figure it out," Megan said.

Erin bustled into the dining room from the kitchen. She carried a large bowl of scrambled eggs and a plate of hash browns. She deftly set the food in the middle of the table to accompany the grits, bacon, toast, and fruit already prepared. The men knew how to pack away food. "Everything is ready and I've already called in the troops. Are you two hungry?"

"I'm really hungry this morning," Megan said. "Mom, maybe you can ask Mr. Sam what he meant. He said that if I left the protective shield when I wasn't supposed to and put myself in danger again he'd switch me up one side of the holler and down the other." Megan drew her brows together hard. "Do you know what he'd switch me to?"

Erin laughed. "Ah, Meggie. That brings back fond memories. *Switch* means he'd tan your hide, as in give you a spanking. A *holler* is a valley between two mountains. He'd spank you down one side of a mountain and up another."

Megan's eyes bugged wide at Erin. "You're kidding?"

Emerald shook her head. "Sam wouldn't spank you, but I might. We've given you a very strong warning. Doona put yourself in danger."

"Okay, Mom," Megan said, then looked at Erin oddly. "How can you have fond memories of a spanking?"

Erin grinned. "My father always threatened to switch us up one side of the holler and down the other when I was growing up. And considering that the hollers in Nowhere, Tennessee, are twice the size of the ones here, it was no small punishment. He never did do it, even though I did deserve it a time or two. Especially when I drove his truck through the glass sliding doors into the kitchen."

Emerald laughed. "You canna leave the story there! You have to tell us more, right, Meggie?"

Emerald looked to Megan for support and felt the bottom of her world give out. Megan was holding her head, palms to her temples, as if she were in severe pain. Her whole body was trembling.

"Meggie?" Emerald reached for Megan and groaned at the

glazed, sightless look in her daughter's eyes. Megan was having a vision, and from the agony twisting itself across her features, it was a bad one.

Erin rushed over. "What is it? Does she have seizures?" Erin's nurse side had already kicked in. She briefly touched Megan's forehead for fever and checked her pulse at her throat.

"No. She's having a very bad vision." Gently, moving just a little bit at a time, Emerald pulled Megan into the circle of her arms.

"What can I do?" Erin asked.

"Nothing can be done. Not until it is over and then I pray to God somethin' can be done about what she's seeing now." Softly, so low that it could barely be heard, Emerald chanted to Megan a song from the angels that Emerald's mother used to sing, its ancient tongue a mystery to mankind. Megan, though still caught up in whatever horror, burrowed closer to Emerald.

Emerald tightened her hold on her daughter. Dear God in heaven, she wished she could spare Megan this. Just then the men entered the dining hall and Emerald met Sam's gaze over the top of Megan's head. Whatever he'd been saying to Nick died on his lips and he crossed the room in half a second flat, face blanching and blue eyes burning. Jared and Aragon immediately shifted into battle stance, their keen gazes searching.

"What's going on?" Nick asked.

Erin motioned for quiet, then pointed at Megan.

"A vision?" Sam whispered, surprising Emerald by how quickly he'd picked up on the cause of her daughter's trouble and had done it without a shadow of disbelief.

Emerald nodded. "A very bad one," she said. Whatever Megan was seeing now had her whimpering in fear. Tears fell from her blank eyes.

Sam shocked Emerald even more when he fell to his knees and set his hand over hers where she tightly held Megan's shaking shoulders, as if to gently add his comfort and strength to hers. Erin stepped away, going to Jared and Aragon.

"It's going to be all right, Em," Sam said. "Whatever we have to do to help, Meggie, we will do."

Emerald returned her gaze to Sam and found that the painful dread in her heart eased some as Sam's rock solid gaze didn't waver. She nodded, drawing in deep breaths. She and Megan weren't alone in this battle. With every passing day, the bond forming between her and her friends as they faced the evil threatening them all was building a cohesive wall of defense against the enemy, one she prayed would prove to be impenetrable.

Megan shook harder and Emerald held her tighter and chanted the song of the angels.

Erin, apparently having left the dining hall at some point, returned carrying a blanket. Annette was on her heels, doctor bag in hand, and behind her were Marissa and, miraculously, Stefanie. Sam took the blanket from Erin and spread it over Megan, then tucked it around Emerald, too. When he finished, he slid a chair next to her and Megan and set a supporting arm about them both, helping to hold Megan tighter.

Annette did the same as Erin; checked Megan's temperature with a touch and then her pulse. "Do you want me to give her something to make this stop?"

As much as the mother in her wanted to end Megan's suffering, she knew that seeking such temporary ease through drugs would eventually destroy Megan. Still, the only vision Emerald had ever had such an intense reaction to was that of her and Megan's torture and death. She hope to God Megan wasn't seeing something similar and prayed that as Megan matured her visions wouldn't take such a harrowing toll.

Suddenly Megan cried out loudly and jerked free of Emerald's hold. Emerald nearly fell, reaching for Megan, sure her daughter would harm herself. But Megan stood just a few feet away, her hands searching the air before her, as if she were blind and seeking her way. "They want me," she said, crying with pain. "They're going to take me."

"Oh, Meggie," Emerald cried, rushing to reach her daughter, but Megan shook her head and turned away. "They want you, too. Very bad things are going to happen. To all of us. To all of Twilight."

Megan went to where Marissa sat and touched her check. The woman had dark smudges under her eyes and her expression was strained, as if she hadn't slept at all. "There are many who seek to marry you only to kill you," Megan said. "There is nowhere that you can hide. You can't escape them. They are coming." Marissa paled and looked as if she would faint.

Megan turned to Stefanie who'd reached to comfort Marissa. "Only the fireman can save you and he has gone. Forever," Megan told her.

Then faster and faster, like a rapid-fire machine gun, she sought out the rest. She looked at Erin and Jared. "You canna live. He won't let your baby be born." She whipped around, her eyes staring blankly at Nick. "Your father will kill you." She stopped before Aragon. "You die trying to save the one you love, but she falls to the damned anyway."

"Meggie," Emerald cried, rushing to her daughter. "Stop. You have to stop." Visions were rarely this clear, this detailed, this final. They were as she told Annette, tiny snapshots, leaving you only guessing their meaning. Her daughter was so inexperienced at being able to interpret what she saw.

Megan rushed past her to Sam and started crying and hitting him on his chest. "Why do you kill my mother? My daddy also tried to. Why are you just like my daddy was?" Megan then screamed with terror and fainted.

Chapter Twelve

Sam caught Megan in his arms before she hit the floor. "Christ," he whispered, stripped of anything but a plea to heaven. Megan trembled all over, as if being ravaged by a chill. Even he was shaking in his black cowhides, and he hadn't been the one to suffer such a horrifying vision of the future. Everyone was dead silent and deathly pale. Nobody moved.

After a moment, Sam felt Megan stir in his arms. He looked down into her pale face. She opened her eyes, looking very sleepy and not at all as if she remembered the doom she'd just proclaimed. "Can I rest, Mr. Sam? I am so very, very tired."

Sam didn't know if it was exhaustion or if she honestly had no idea about what had just happened. All he knew was that he had to reassure her, had to ease some of the heavy burden she carried. "Yes, little sprite," Sam said. "You rest. Everything is going to be fine."

Megan closed her eyes, seemingly to fall instantly asleep.

Emerald moved toward them, wobbling as if she'd keel over at any moment. "Meggie," she whispered, holding out her arms for her daughter. She looked as if she'd fold were he to set Megan in her arms.

"I'll carry her," he said softly.

Emerald only nodded. Then she turned around, hands out in appeal. "Please, doona take what Meggie said as if it is written in stone. She canna know everything, and she can only see a small part of what the future will be. Choices made every minute can change the future. Please. You have to understand. She doesn't know how to handle her visions yet. She hasn't had time to learn and they are very bad for one so little. Doona be angry with her."

"Dear God, Em," Sam said, wondering what kind of hurt she'd been through. Though different, her pain had likely been as great as his. He swore softly. "Do you really think any one of us would hurt or condemn Megan? God help the little tyke. She's in a hell because of us, because of all this." He pulled Megan closer to his heart, wishing he could single-handedly rip apart Cinatas and the Vladarians.

"Evil brought this," Emerald told him. "You didn't. Not any of you. And were it not for all of you, then Meggie and I would likely be facing it alone."

"She's right," said Jared. "This battle began millennia ago. Aragon and I are here with you now because of that battle, and our might with yours will change the future because we will do whatever it takes to assure that."

"Agreed," Aragon said. "The child has given each of us a warning of what we need to guard against. We shall heed it." This freed everyone from their stunned positions. Nick immediately went to Stefanie and Marissa. Erin, Jared, and Aragon started talking as Annette approached him and Megan.

"If the damned think they're having any piece of me then they've got a hell of a lot coming," Annette said as she assessed Megan's condition.

Considering Annette had already scorched a demon and silvered a werewolf's woody with burn cream, Sam thought the odds were in her favor.

"Her pulse is strong and steady, slower than before," Annette said. "She's breathing easier, too. From what I can tell, she's sleeping now and needs to rest. I'll check on her again in about twenty minutes." Annette glanced toward Stefanie and lowered her voice to a bare whisper. "I'm watching a miracle in motion."

"I canna believe she's here either." Emerald gently brushed Megan's hair back from her face. "Doona push your sister," she advised softly.

"I won't," Annette replied. "Nick seems to have the right edge to reach her."

"Getting pissed off is a damn good start to recovery," Sam said under his breath. When Annette first learned that Sam had let Nick work on Stefanie's missing persons case and hadn't publicized that the two had been personally involved, she'd wanted to string both him and Nick up by the family jewels. "I told you he was a good guy," he added, then turned to Emerald. "Let's go settle Megan."

She nodded, swallowing hard, as if speaking was too difficult a task at the moment. The fear in her liquid green eyes flooded his heart and set his teeth on edge. At this point, he knew it wasn't fear of him but of the doomed future. And if Megan's words proved to be true, he was that future.

Annette hugged Emerald. "It's going to be okay," she said loud enough for everyone to hear. "We're all going to take care of each other and we're all going to be all right."

"Yes, all of us," Erin added. "A child. I can't believe it. That's why I've been craving truffles in the middle of the night." She pressed a palm to her stomach. The joy shining in her eyes was so bright that not even Megan's dire predictions could dim it. "With all of us standing together, we'll stop the evil from winning,"

"Count on it." Jared pulled Erin close to him. "Nothing will happen to you or the babe. Nothing."

Sam met Jared's gaze across the room. The warrior's nearly iridescent blue eyes burned with purpose. Yet the tense worry lining Jared's brow told Sam what he already knew, and his gut clenched even more. Nothing could guarantee how this fight would pan out and who would live or die. One thing was damn sure, though. Emerald wouldn't die by his hand.

He carried Megan to her room with Emerald right behind him. The moment he put Megan into her bed and Emerald covered her with a unicorn quilt, Megan sighed and snuggled into her pillow, as if she knew she was safe.

"We have to talk," Em whispered.

"Yeah, we do," Sam said, leading through the bathroom that connected Megan's bedroom to Emerald's.

"She's out cold, totally exhausted," Emerald said as she shut the connecting door and leaned back against it. "I don't think she remembers her vision right now. When she does, I'll have to help her understand that even if she sees certain things, it doesn't mean the outcome of them is carved in stone. I'm sorry for—"

"Don't you think it's about time you tell me everything? Explain what Megan meant by 'Why are you just like my daddy was'?"

Her eyes glistened with unshed tears and she drew a deep breath. "My husband's name was Eric. I didn't tell you about him because before you knew I was part angel there would have been too many questions I couldn't answer. And then once you were bitten by Vasquez, I didn't want to take the chance that you'd push me away." She pulled in another breath, this time shuddering as she exhaled. "There's no way to say this but to be blunt. Eric was from a long line of special fighters known as vampire slayers, men who fought for the good, killing monsters like Michael and William Wellbourne. We moved to Wiltshire because little girls with Elan blood were disappearing. Eric discovered Michael Wellbourne was the predator behind the disappearances and set a trap for the vampire, determined to kill him, but Michael bit Eric.

"Eric's fall into evil came fast, but you couldn't tell him that. He couldn't see how the vampire infection changed him in his heart and in his soul until it was too late. He refused to let me help him, refused to try a Redeeming, so sure that he could handle it all. But he couldn't. That last night we argued. He'd reached the point where he was more blood slave to Michael Wellbourne than he was anything else—husband, father, man, everything good in him had disappeared. It was Samhain, Halloween, and Eric left us to attend a depraved celebration at the Devil's Mound. I had a vision of vampires attacking me in my sleep and taking Meggie. Waking her, we quickly left our home to find a safe place to hide until I could figure out what to do. Our home was on the same road as Stonehenge and we'd just reached the worship site when Meggie and I were attacked."

Emerald shuddered again. Tears poured form her eyes, but it was as if she wasn't even aware that she cried.

"It was Eric," she said almost in a whisper. "And Michael Wellbourne along with an entire pack of Underlings. They attacked the car Meggie and I were in, busting the windshield, battering through the roof, trying to reach us. All I could do was race ahead and pray. There was a large gathering of Druid priestesses having a ceremony at Stonehenge to counter the darkness of Samhain. I drove off the highway and bumped through a field, right to the monoliths. Vampires have a damned form, a black winged beast with claws and fangs. Eric came at Meggie and me like that. He busted into the car, wild and crazed. He'd pledged Meggie to Michael for his perverted pleasures, and wanted me for the midnight blood sacrifice at the Devil's Mound. He clawed at me, trying to get to Meggie. I was fighting for our lives, our eternal souls. I had no choice. With my mother's help from heaven and using the energy from Stonehenge and the priestesses, I created a wall of White Fire. Eric, Michael, and the Underlings burned to death as I watched."

"Em," Sam said softly, deeply, wishing he could say more. She may have relayed the horror without falling apart, but he could see the ravaged pain in her eyes and feel it pouring from her heart.

"Sam," she whispered, pressing her cheek to his chest. "Don't you see? What happened with Eric is happening all over again." She touched her fingertips to where Vasquez had bitten him and looked up into his eyes full of pain. "The infection is in you."

Sam flinched, pulling back in horror. "No," he said, shaking his head. "No. That son of a bitch tried to give his daughter to a pedophile? A vampire? Do you think that I would ever do something like that, Em? Ever?"

Emerald placed her hand over his heart. "Not the Sam I know. But you will change unless you go through a Redeeming. If you don't, dear God, if you don't then—"

Her voice hinted at something so bad she couldn't put it into words. He could see everything in her eyes. The traces of their lovemaking. The horror she'd lived through. The pain she felt now and the dread. He also saw her resolve. She'd kill him too if it became necessary. His respect for her kicked up several notches, giving her about a twelve on a scale of one to ten.

Still he had to pull away from her. His muscles knotted with dread. "What is a Redeeming?"

"It's a ritual we would both have to go through."

He could see how important it was to her, but he really didn't want to have anything to do with any of this shit. It would be admitting that he was as depraved as Eric.

But you owe her that much. Just put her mind at ease. It couldn't be a big deal. He glanced at his watch. "I've got an hour before we take the helicopter and give the Falls a little fiery house party. We can do this Redeeming now." The words scraped through him like nails on a chalkboard.

She shook her head. "You canna do it like that. It's not that simple. It's a ritual that will take a long time and it canna be done just anywhere. We have to go to a very special spirit place. If all goes right, it can save you."

Something wavered in her voice. Deep emotion, fear, whatever it was it hit his alert button. "And what happens if all doesn't go right, Em?"

"Doona worry about that." She dropped her gaze, staring at his throat, making him more conscious than ever of the bite mark he carried. "The biggest problem is you canna doubt," she whispered.

He slid his thumb to her chin, edging along the delicate line of her jaw. Drawing in another breath, he savored the taste and smell of her still clinging to him. "Tell me, Em, or nothing's doing. What happens if I doubt?"

She met his gaze. The starkness of hers pierced right through him. "Then one or both of us could die."

He recoiled, releasing her, stepping back from her and shaking his head. "No. Oh, hell no. You aren't putting your life on the line for me like that. We'll find another way."

She grabbed his hand, latching onto him as if she were keeping him from going over a cliff. "There *is* no other way! Everybody's life is already on the line here, and we need you. Losing you would jeopardize us even more. Having you turn to the dark, having you come after me or Meggie or even Erin's Elan blood, would be even worse."

"No!" he said harshly. "No. We're not doing it. I refuse to let you endanger yourself for my ass." He backed away, heading to the door. "Stay the hell away from me. Do you hear? And if I come after you for sex, you kick me in the nuts. If I come after you for blood, you kill me."

Turning on his heel, he walked, ignoring the cry that tore through her and ripped him in half.

"I will not let you do this." Sven reached Navarre's chamber before Sirius could and blocked the doorway. They had been arguing since Sirius discovered Navarre was still stricken. "What happened is done. Navarre is already too weakened to return to battle. There is no point in you losing your warrior's power, too."

Sirius met Sven's protest with unwavering purpose. "It was on my orders that Draysius hurt Navarre. You would do no different, Blood Hunter, if you were in my place. Don't ask me, leader of the Pyrathians, to be less of a warrior than you are."

Sirius could see that his words struck true, but Sven still blocked the doorway. "There must be another—"

"The Pyrathian is right, Sven. You would do no less and most likely more," said York from inside the chamber. "And there is no other way to remove a Pyrathian's fire, except through Logos's own hand. If Sirius is offering to help our brother, why would you deny him?"

Sven sighed and stepped aside.

Sirius entered the chamber to find York's fiery countenance standing guard before Navarre. "I'm not here to harm him," he told the Blood Hunter.

"I know," said York. "There are those among the Guardian Forces, especially within the Shadowmen, who feel Navarre is lost to us and want the warrior to be given the peace of death while his dignity yet remains."

"What is this madness?" demanded Sven. "By Logos, are we to allow death because one is no longer strong?"

Sirius sighed. "It may be that we've forgotten how to be anything but strong warriors and when that fails us we've nothing left," he said, recalling how in his own mind his recent weakness had brought his worthiness as a warrior into question.

"What I want to know is why there have been so many losses among our kind in so short a time?" asked York. He looked at Sven. "With Navarre stricken and Jared and Aragon now permanently within the mortal realm, you and I are the only warriors left from our Blood Hunter unit."

"It is my failing that began it all," Sven said, turning away from them. "By wanting to save Jared I set this all in motion."

"No," said Sirius. "It's not just the brethren within your unit that are affected. I think the recent surge in the power of the damned and their growing presence within the mortal realm is the cause. This shift in the balance of good and evil in the mortal realm is rippling throughout the universe. There has been a sudden rise in the number of mortals needing a Pyrathian's fire and thus more of the warriors are spending time upon the mortal ground. Have you not seen the same within the ranks of the Blood Hunters?"

"Yes," said Sven. "It was noted at the last leaders' meeting."

"We're being more exposed to the influence of evil. Nor can we deny the growing tensions within the Guardian Forces," added Sirius. "What has happened is because of the damned's rise in power." What happened between him and Stefanie was part of it as well. Her kidnapping by the Vladarian vampire had resulted in Sirius breathing life into her twice. He'd gone against the rules to save her then, which created more problems now. Once one ideal fell then others followed.

Sven and York were both silent for so long that Sirius wondered if he'd spoken his thoughts aloud.

"Not to absolve myself of any blame for my part in the changes occurring," said Sven, "but I see the truth of your assessment, which means the Guardian Forces are in serious trouble if they can't restore a balance within the mortal realm."

"With so many rules limiting us, what can be done?" asked York.

"First," said Sirius, "I'll see to Navarre. Then we must gather the leaders of both the Pyrathians and the Blood Hunters to search for a solution."

York stepped away, allowing Sirius to approach Navarre. But before Sirius could kneel beside Navarre, he felt Sven's touch. "We're already doing one of the best things we can to fight against the effects of the evil," he said. "We are uniting rather than becoming divided."

And union required sacrifice, Sirius said to himself as he knelt, ready to compromise his warrior's power to give solidarity to the unity of their purpose. Absorbing more of Draysius's fire strike would likely weaken him past the point of effectiveness in battle. But when he set his hand upon Navarre's brow, he immediately realized that though the warrior was still in a coma, it was no longer from the pain and fever of a Pyrathian's fire.

"There is no more Pyrathian fire within him," Sirius told Sven and York. "And the damage done from Draysius appears to have healed."

Both of the Blood Hunters knelt with him beside Navarre.

"Then why has he not awakened?" asked York.

Sirius shook his head, but before removing his hand from Navarre, he sought a deeper connection with the Blood Hunter's mind and realized with a chilling fear that Navarre's spirit was far distant from his form, as if it were in another realm. Sirius pulled his hand back, shaken. He knew what Navarre was doing because he'd been sneaking off to do the same. He'd been watching the mortals too.

"What is wrong?" asked Sven, touching Sirius's spirit form with concern.

"Navarre's mind is with Jared and Aragon and those with them. He is watching them and is so caught up in what is happening with them that he cannot hear or see anything else. What gives me the gravest concern is that Navarre's spirit does not rest within his form. It is far, far away from him. But how is this possible? He's been nowhere but within the spirit realm since Draysius's strike."

"No," said York. "Unsure of how our skirmish with you and Draysius would end and knowing he couldn't chance capture, Aragon carried Navarre with him to the mortal realm. I found them there. Aragon was using his power to absorb Navarre's pain. I sent him on to rescue the mortals that were in danger and took over helping Navarre. But I immediately realized that Draysius's fire was too great for me to fight alone. Navarre was dying. I brought him back to the spirit realm and to Draysius, demanding that he help Navarre, and we argued. That's when both of you arrived and then Sirius absorbed Draysius's fire from Navarre."

"That must be the answer. Navarre's spirit left his form when he was dying in the mortal realm and when York brought his form back, Navarre's spirit did not return."

"Then there is only one thing we can do," York said. "Return Navarre to the mortal realm and see if he heals."

"The Guardian Council will never allow it," Sirius said, only to find Sven saying the same thing at the same time.

York's countenance rippled with anger. "Why do we need to involve the Guardian Council at all? They have not seen fit to offer their help to a loyal warrior. If you want my opinion, they only made the situation with Aragon worse. I see no reason to seek their council on how we choose to heal our brethren. They will only debate and delay the matter until it would be too late to save Navarre. We didn't ask the Guardian Council permission for Sirius to absorb Draysius's fire when the consequences compromised a Pyrathian leader. Why should we then ask when all it involves is Navarre himself?"

Sirius met Sven's gaze, instantly seeing the leader was just as torn. Never in their recorded history had an incident such as this presented itself. Was the issue as simple as York made it? Would they be compromising the integrity of the Guardian Forces? Or could their questioning be a rippling effect of the damned's surge of power?

"Saints in chains has a nice ring to it, wouldn't you agree?" Cinatas asked, clanking the heavy chain he had looped over his neck.

"Music to my ears," Wellbourne replied, dryly. He had to reluctantly admit that he was impressed. Cinatas had taken a humiliating defeat at Emerald's hand and was rising to the occasion with the most diabolical plot he'd had the pleasure of being a party to in . . . well, centuries. It wasn't every day he could pull one over on the pope. "I have to say, it was bloody good of you to include me in this."

"You were the only one in the room who doesn't have their nose stuck up Heldon's ass or their own."

Wellbourne chuckled, amused by Cinatas's derisive remarks. The man knew how to travel. Rather than suffering the tedious discomfort of crossing the spirit barrier, they'd taken a helicopter to an airport and traveled by private jet to Cincinnati. They drank wine, enjoyed ninety minutes satisfying any urge they chose to stroke, and now were walking down Desecration Alley. It was a better way for the damned to go.

Perhaps if things were any different, he and Cinatas would have made a dynamic team. As it was, Wellbourne was certain that in the end, he'd have to eliminate Cinatas in order to have Emerald. But in the meantime, he was willing to let Cinatas run most of the risks in case Heldon decided to weigh in on this plan to rob the pope—hell, who was the pope these days? Benedict? Constantine? Probably a Paul or a John or a Peter something. No, not Peter. St. Peter in Chains was the name of the cathedral they were presently stealing into.

It was 11 A.M. and the cathedral was already filled to capacity with parishioners eager for exposition of the Eucharist, where the papally blessed monstrance would be brought forth and the consecrated host would be given to each of the devout subjects in attendance.

Cinatas flung his hood back as he swarmed down the church hallway. His grotesque mug had women fainting and men backing away in horror. Wellbourne followed in Cinatas's wake and shouted in amusement, "Renounce God or die, you bloody fools! The Antichrist is here."

"Excellent idea, Wellbourne." Cinatas laughed, a full unholy roar that sent men, women, and children into a panicked stampede to escape the church. Screams echoed through the halls and the sanctuary as he made his way to the Blessed Sacrament Chapel. Parishioners held up crosses to ward him off, gesticulating madly as they called upon their precious saints. The gold monstrance stood at the front in a place of honor, framed by a gold-leafed altar. The presiding priest, draped in silken robes, moved protectively in front of the monstrance.

"Bless me Father, for I am Cinatas," said the monster with a smile.

"Begone, Satan. Get thee from the house of the Lord!"

"You'd think he was St. Peter at the pearly gates," Cinatas said. "There's only one problem. Do you know what that is, Wellbourne?"

"He's not being politically correct? These days everybody gets to go to the party."

"There is that, but we've our own party to make. No. The problem is our St. Peter here isn't in chains—and isn't he supposed to be upside down as well?"

"Bloody observant of you," Wellbourne said. "Peter was crucified upside down."

A handful of men rushed up to rescue the priest. Wellbourne flashed his fangs at them as he lashed out, breaking bones in a single blow.

Cinatas whipped the chain from around his neck and within seconds had it around the priest's neck, twisted in a choke hold. "Why don't you hold the monstrance so I can fix our fresh sacrifice to the altar?"

"Anything to help," Wellbourne said, admiring Cinatas's style. Wellbourne picked up the blessed monstrance. The priest fought wildly to escape as his face turned from red to purple to blue. Cinatas secured the man to the altar upside down then carved 666 on the man's forehead with a pocketknife.

"Perfection is a beautiful thing," Cinatas said as he stepped back from his artwork. "Bring the monstrance, Wellbourne. We've a desecration to attend."

Wellbourne had walked into the Blessed Sacrament Chapel with a smile on his face, but he left with a frown, feeling a bit too much like a flunky in Cinatas's wicked wake.

Chapter Thirteen

Emerald paced her room. Damn bloody man. How could he do this to her? Sam Sheridan didn't have to worry about being the cause of her demise, she was going to fooking kill him first!

She pressed her fisted hand to her heart, trying to numb the ache he'd left behind. Didn't he realize that his turning from her, his refusal of her help, was her worst nightmare?

She swung around, took one look at the bed, remembered the look in his blue eyes at Silver Mist Falls, and her heart wrenched. It had been like staring into the purest heart of a flame—mesmerizing, consuming, enslaving. She didn't think she'd ever been wanted so much, nor had she ever needed so badly. Eric had been her first love, her only love, and their relationship had sprung from the innocence of inexperience and blossomed into the tenderness and intimacy of marriage. There'd been passion and beauty, but the raw, elemental need storming in Sam and through her was unlike anything.

And when she'd gone to him in the twilight dawn, the rough edge of his dark desire had taken her to such a climax that no part of her wanted to leave the heaven of his arms—even though he was poisoned.

She shouldn't have told him about the Redeeming. One hint of danger to her and he'd gone all stubborn male on her. She should have waited until they'd made a stronger connection. She should have seduced him again. If he was making love to her then he couldn't be running away, and whether he realized it or not, contact with her made his human side stronger. He needed her.

He'd vowed to stay away before and failed . . . just what would happen if she went in full pursuit of him? What if she fought for him? Fought for him despite himself?

She sat up. He'd said it half right.

No. Hell no. There was no way in or out of hell if she was staying away from him. Not while there was the smallest seed of hope that she could save him.

Sam stood at the heliport, impatiently waiting for their pre-emptive strike against Cinatas to begin. Jared and Aragon were saying good-bye to Erin and Annette. Sam wasn't a happy camper with either of the warriors at the moment.

After leaving Emerald's room earlier, Sam had gone to Jared with one request. If Sam were to suddenly turn into an evil vampire, he wanted Jared to promise to off him immediately with the silver bullets or a silver blade. But the warrior had surprisingly waffled rather than readily agree. Jared's advice had been to listen to Emerald and go through a Redeeming. The man said he wished he'd listened to Erin when he'd been in trouble. Aragon, who was currently kissing Annette like they'd be apart for days rather than hours, hadn't cooperated with Sam's request to kill him either.

Biting back a frustrated curse, Sam turned away from his friends. He'd somewhat taken care of the problem. He'd loaded the silver bullets into his Glock, and just in case he found himself weaponless when the time came, he'd honed the bottom of the silver cross he wore into a sharp enough point that he could drive it between a rib and puncture his heart. Though he didn't know how much longer he'd be able to wear the cross. A reddened rash was beginning to appear wherever the silver came in contact with his skin. It was slight at the moment but would likely be increasing proof of his damned status—a litmus test for the growing evil inside him.

Turning away from where Erin hung on Jared's neck and Annette whispered in Aragon's ear, Sam headed for the helo and Nick. It was past time to give Cinatas and his Vladarian cronies a little housewarming at the Falls.

"Sam! Wait! Sam!"

He froze, barely hearing Emerald's call over the roar of the helo's rotors. In fact, he shouldn't be able to hear her, but he could. He could smell her, too, and his incisors throbbed just like everything north and south of his belt line.

Shit. Hadn't he told her to stay the hell away from him?

She wasn't only the worst kind of stubborn he'd ever met; she was the worst kind of crazy, too. The kind of crazy that put herself in danger for others. The kind of crazy that put herself in jeopardy for him. He turned around to see her running for him, waving frantically.

Though she was short and didn't necessary have to worry about the rotating blades, she was still breaking every damn safety rule in the book when it came to helos. He took off after her, catching her before she hit the danger zone of the spinning blades. Wrapping an arm around her, he scooped her up and carried her to a safe distance then planted her on her feet.

"What in the hell are you doing?" he yelled.

She grabbed his shirt, jerking him to her. Here eyes were narrowed with purpose. "You bring your ass back here, Sam Sheridan. Do you hear me? This thing between us is nowhere near fooking over and you damn well better not do anything stupid!" She planted a hard kiss on his lips, one that he couldn't stop himself from taking to the next level. Tongues and lips mangled into a hot number that had him breathing heavily by the time she pulled away. "You shove all that noble I-don't-need-you-or-a-Redeeming crap. I've already had one man who didn't have the guts to fight with me. You canna do it to me, too," she said.

His heart flipped at the passion in her eyes.

"Do you hear me?" she said. "Promise me you won't leave me, too."

He wrapped his arms around her, pulling her hard against his thundering heart. He couldn't say anything. How could he promise to do something that could cost her her life? He kissed her again and all of the angst and tenderness wrangling around inside of him turned that kiss into a heartfelt promise. Then he released her and went to the waiting helicopter.

Twenty minutes later, he stared at the black cloud roiling over Hades Mountain with dread. There was no mistaking the intent of the mushrooming darkness—it clearly was bent on engulfing all of Twilight in its evil.

And him. He could feel it happening again. Hyperawareness surged through him, empowering him. He could hear better, see better, differentiate every scent around him. It was almost as if he could even sense the molecules. He felt invincible, more powerful than anyone else.

Nick cursed as he flew the Life-Flight helicopter into the cloud.

"This is worse than pea soup," Nick said, his voice crackling through the headsets that Sam, Aragon, and Jared wore.

"We're going to be damn lucky if we don't slam into the side of the mountain," Sam muttered back, garnering a glare from Jared. The warrior was so antsy about being caged that Sam wondered if he would jump as soon as they opened the door to dump the fire bombs.

Nick sent Sam a disgusted look over his shoulder and patted the control panel. "If you were piloting, you mean. You've got number one ace in the seat here. I can handle this baby through just about anything. I'm popping back out from the cloud to get a better feel for the grade of the mountain and see if we can't slip underneath this cover by coming from the bottom up. My bet is that is doesn't go all the way to the ground once you're past the edges. Suckers wouldn't be able to breathe if it did."

"It doesn't," added Aragon. "When I came to the Falls after Annette, the cloud hovered well above the tree line."

"Then we'll soon be rocking," Nick said.

"Let's hope that's figuratively and not literally," Sam replied. "According to the building specs filed at the courthouse, the heliport is on the roof to the north end of the mansion. Hopefully their helos will be there and we can blow them first. Then we'll lay a ring of fire around the place before we dump the rest of the load on the roof."

"Here we go." Nick throttled up and thrust the copter along the contour of the mountain, shooting right into the roiling cloud. Within seconds they were engulfed in the choking black mist.

Sam clenched his teeth, unfortunately feeling the ill fit of his incisors. He had one hell of a bright future. Go evil or get really dead. Maybe he should just let the Underlings have his ass. Then there wouldn't be enough pieces of him left to do anybody any harm, much less cause Emerald to die.

You canna leave me, too. Emerald's cry tore through him again. Damn . . . what in the hell was he supposed to do about that?

Just when Sam thought he would scream from the tension building in him, Nick broke through the dense cloud and flared the copter sharply up to skim just above the surface of the trees. It was totally insanely impossible, but once they broke through to the inner part of the cloud, their visibility opened completely. Somehow, though the mist was still there, Sam could see for miles in all directions.

"Well, damn me," Nick said and whistled at the clear horizon. "This magic shit gets really weird, guys."

"I wouldn't even damn myself in jest these days," Sam said then directed Nick. "Hit the north end of the mansion up ahead."

"Mansion?" Nick asked. "That sucker's a mondo castle with enough spikes to make Vlad the Impaler do a happy dance."

"He was a Vladarian Vampire as was his father before him, Vlad Dracul," Jared said.

"No surprise there," Sam said with a shiver of dread. So that's what he freaking had to look forward to, being a bastard torturer of humanity. Maybe he would *bail* his ass out as bait for the Underlings, Emerald or no Emerald. But first things first.

"Time to get fired up, boys," he told Jared and Aragon. They simultaneously unbuckled their belts and Sam went for the cargo door, sliding it open. Wind whipped into the cabin like a tornado, carrying a stench so foul that his lungs burned.

There was more headroom in the Life-Flight copter than a conventional one, yet at six three Sam still had to bend over to maneuver. It put him off kilter even though Nick kept the machine as steady as a sniper's aim.

Aragon and Jared quickly brought eight of the homemade bombs to the doorway. Sam braced himself against the chopper door, where he'd be able to effectively launch the bombs. Nick dove down to put them into position.

They were in luck. The damned's black helicopter sat nice and pretty on the rooftop heliport, a prime target for the kind of damage they were aiming to cause. Sam nailed the copter from tail rotors to cockpit with five bombs. The subsequent explosion rocked the air and sent up a blast of heat so powerful that Sam could sense it in the air.

A horde of Underlings rose up from the trees, coming after them. Sam motioned for Jared to take over the bombing. He dumped out several buckets of silver-laced bait, and a large number of Underlings swooped down to get it like starved beasts. But more and more kept coming. After dumping the bait, Sam changed his position. He steadied the M-16 against the door's metal edge and waited for the suckers to come within range. He sprayed the Underlings with bullets, taking delight as they went wild. The frenzied feeding became a chaotic bloodbath that stopped nearly all of them in their tracks as they devoured the wounded in midair, tearing flesh from bone, in a macabre aerial dance of death. Their screeching of pain and triumph could be heard over the roar of the copter's engine and blades.

Nick adeptly wove the copter about the stone mansion. Sam kept at the Underlings, holding them at bay as Jared and Aragon dropped the firebombs. They managed to hit the large propane tank feeding gas to the house just before they dumped the final load onto the roof. Pulling back the M-16, Sam shoved the machine gun's safety home, but just as he slammed the helo's door closed, an Underling winged into the cockpit. The rank stench of decayed flesh inundated the small space. He swatted the Underling away with the butt end of the M-16 before it could tear into Aragon with its razor claws. The beast landed across the cockpit, rebounding fast.

Nick cursed loud. Several more Underlings planted themselves onto the copter, clinging to the windshield, blocking Nick's view. There had to be more all over the copter, because it listed to the side.

"Go up!" Jared yelled. "Get past the cloud."

Nick flared, fighting for control. Helicopters could turn on a dime and land on a quarter but they were the trickiest bastards to fly. One mistake could put them into an irrecoverable spin. Sam placed himself against Nick's back to make sure the creature didn't knock Nick off his game. Gaining any sort of advantage in fighting the creature when bent over like a rickety old lady was damn near impossible.

The Underling aimed for Jared. Weaponless, Jared feinted to the side and landed a solid kick to the creature's belly. The beast lashed out with a claw, ripping through the heavy denim of Jared's jeans. Blood instantly appeared, telling Sam the cut was deep.

Shit.

The Underling slammed against the side of the helicopter, but instead of being hurt or even stunned, it became enraged, screeching at an unholy decibel and lashing wildly. It launched itself at Sam with claws slashing and ice pick teeth dripping blood. The creature's fetid breath blasted Sam, so cold that it burned like liquid nitrogen. Sam swung with the butt end of the gun again, but the strap caught, killing the effectiveness of his hit. He dropped the gun and pulled his knife, managing a gut-splitting upward slash just as the Underling attacked.

The creature's blood was icy cold, making Sam's hand feel like it had been plunged into the blistering chill of the Arctic Sea. Stunned, he clenched his teeth against the searing pain. The creature's claws scratched Sam's arm as it slid down, dead. Sam's mouth watered and a surge of pleasurable satisfaction flooded him. Horrified by his reaction, he dropped the black bloodied knife and started wiping the blood off his hand with a windbreaker that hung over the back of Nick's seat.

He had little time to think about what was wrong with him on the inside. His right hand was burned, reddened, and blistered, as if he'd roasted it over a fire like a marshmallow.

"Here, let me," Aragon shouted above the roar of the blades as he grabbed a bottle of water they'd been drinking from and poured it over Sam's hand.

Nodding at the instant relief, Sam stripped off his T-shirt, wrapped it around his burned hand, and poured a second bottle over it, soaking his makeshift bandage. A choking stench rose from the creature's black blood, filling the cockpit, so acrid it burned his lungs like noxious smoke. Jared ripped off the lower leg of his jeans and wrapped the material around the gash on his shin to stop the bleeding.

Nick let out a blistering curse. Sam whipped around and felt the blood drain from his head. The windshield had so many of the beasts covering it that all you could see was black. The copter wobbled wildly, throwing Sam, Aragon, and Jared off balance. They grabbed for a handhold and Nick cursed again as he fought for control.

Shutting his eyes, Sam prayed they would make it rather than praying for death. Returning to Emerald's arms was foremost in his mind.

Cinatas blinked against the smoke and water stinging his eyes as debilitating fear burned through his mind. He stood frozen, staring at the flames licking their way to him. The hot tongues desecrated the purity of the ornate crown molding and the embossed walls. Its greediness devoured the golden silk curtains, raining down black, filthy ash. The Falls resort was on fire.

Suddenly his mind flashed back to the roof of the research center with Erin Morgan strapped to a stretcher, the taste of her Elan blood in his mouth, and Ashoden ben Shashur wasting away from the deadly cocktail of hemorrhagic diseases Cinatas had added to the vampire's blood transfusion. He'd been on the cusp of a winning high by his own hand. Then Erin and her werewolf lover had ruined everything. Agony had followed as a ball of fire engulfed him when the waiting helicopter exploded. He felt the fire eating the flesh of his face and arms and hands again, felt the pain that had driven him into insanity and beyond. His body shuddered violently.

It was happening again. His grasp on victory was being stolen from him by Erin and her cohorts. He and Wellbourne had returned with the pope's monstrance just a short while ago, and in addition to himself four Vladarians had been entrusted to take part in the Black Mass—Wellbourne, Rasputin, and Cuthbert, who insisted on Valois's being included. Cinatas had his doubts about the vampire and his condescending attitude—Royals were notorious for thinking their shit didn't stink.

Turning from the fire, Cinatas surveyed the utter chaos surrounding him. Heat from the fire had many of the Red Demons writhing weakly on the floor, tortured with pain—their intolerance to heat incapacitating them, despite the spray of the overhead sprinklers. Employees of the Falls, mostly depraved mortal souls seeking a place within the world of the damned, were dragging out as many demons as they possibly could. One had the nerve to jerk on Cinatas's sleeve, leaving a streak of smudged soot.

"Come, son of Pathos!" he said. "We must abandon the north wing before it collapses. There is no damage to the east mansion. All has been readied for you there, but the hall for your coronation has burned. We will need to postpone the ceremony."

Postpone? Rage replaced Cinatas's fear. Heads weren't going to just roll. Bodies were going to burn because all of Twilight would go up in flames. They'd know pain and fear and they'd bow to his name. Erin, her werewolf heroes, and her angel friends would be his. "Build a new hall. You have until midnight tomorrow." He thrust the man aside, uncaring that he fell closer to the flames.

Cinatas turned to his right to see Wellbourne approaching. "Where is the monstrance?"

"Safe in the east wing, but we have a problem. Nyros caught sight of it and immediately disappeared."

Cinatas grabbed the nearest demon and held him closer to the flames, to make him squirm with fear. "Go to hell. Find Nyros and bring him to me. If you fail, the Red Demons will feel the wrath of the Vladarians and we will choose another faction to serve us."

The ceiling began falling in. Cinatas threw the demon from him and the wary damned bowed then disappeared, hopefully on his way to get Nyros. Cinatas then headed for the exit, stepping over demons writhing on the floor from the heat of the growing fire.

"Take the hallway on the right to the eastern wing," Wellbourne said.

Cinatas suddenly had the strangest feeling that Wellbourne

wasn't there to assure Cinatas's escaped from the fire, but to escort him to a particular place.

His hunch was right. The moment he stepped into the eastern hall, he was met by the other Vladarians—Cuthbert, Valois, and the Russians. They were all in various states of duress and undress, having been in the middle of indulging their twisted appetites when the firestorm hit.

"When Pathos was at the bloody helm, shit like this never happened," Valois said.

"This sort of incompetence in leadership cannot be tolerated," Cuthbert condescended, his high-bred nose in the air.

If a man cannot control those who serve him, then he deserves to die.

"Gentlemen," Cinatas said. "I agree with you. The task of penetrating the defenses of Erin Morgan and her friends should have been dealt with *before* my arrival." He jerked Cuthbert's decorative silver dagger from his belt, and shoved it deep into the Vladarian's heart, where its silver purity would kill. The vampire dropped. He'd need to be burned to assure his nonexistence, where no chance of returning from the dead or undead existed.

"Now that I've exacted a price for the incompetence, does anyone have any other complaints that need addressing at the moment?" The group stared in silence. "None? Good, because we have work to do. I want the entire town of Twilight taken hostage by midnight tomorrow. We'll herd them like cattle to the high school and trap them in the gym. Heroes are all about sacrifice. We're going to give Erin Morgan and her friends plenty of folks to sacrifice themselves for."

"This might bring us more trouble than we want," replied Rasputin. "We only hold the positions of power that we do because we don't ever give the world any real evidence of our existence."

Cinatas sneered. "You all are so stupid. Pathos only used that as a measure of control over you. Besides, this little isolated town doesn't matter to anyone of importance. We'll quarantine it. Set up road blocks. Put out biohazard signs. Cut off communications, and if I don't get what I want from Erin Morgan and the rest, then the citizens of Twilight will pay. Perhaps they'll be victims of a biological terrorist attack. Small town USA will never feel safe again."

Wellbourne smiled. "Devious and ingenious."

Cinatas stomped on Cuthbert's head to make a graphic point. "There will be no incompetence permitted, understand?"

The Vladarians all nodded.

"Good." Cinatas walked passed the vampires, who quickly moved out of his way. Wellbourne followed him.

Seething, Cinatas rounded on him. "Are you lost?"

"Actually no. My doubts that you'd be able to fill Pathos's shoes with the Vladarians are fading. Between the Black Mass, your deft handling of the priest, and your show of strength against the Royals, it's likely Pathos's shoes will prove to be too small for you. I've never seen Valois cower down so fast. You killed one of his own right in front of him and he didn't say a word of protest."

"So what do you want for kissing my ass, Wellbourne?"

"I've helped you steal the monstrance for the Black Mass, but it's occurred to me you've yet to promise me what I want. The angel is mine." He bared his fangs. "I want the bitch that killed my brother."

"Of course. It goes without saying that you deserve her for helping me earlier," Cinatas assured the vampire, then turned and walked away with a smile. Deserve and get weren't the same things. Everybody knew that.

Chapter Fourteen

THE HELICOPTER yawed hard to the right. Sam struggled into a seat, grabbing the buckle and shoving it home. There were so many Underlings attaching themselves to the cockpit that seeing was the least of their worries. The creatures concentrated heavily on the right side, putting the bird off balance.

Shit, Sam thought, his stomach lurching as wildly as his heart raced. They were going to crash on Hades Mountain and the blame was his. He'd cockily written off the Underlings as mindless beasts incapable of acting together in any way. It never occurred to him they'd plaster themselves to the copter, hanging all over it like punks trying to upend a car in a violent riot. Nick would be hard-pressed to break free of the cloud and past the Underlings' boundary of existence, but if he did they just might be worse off than crashing. If all of these beasts incinerated at the same—

Suddenly fire mushroomed around them, putting them in what looked like a nuclear fireball. Intense heat reached him. Sam shut his eyes, bracing himself to die in an explosion of fire. He'd always thought that if a man had to go that would be the best way. Just boom. One quick instant of excruciating pain and then nothing. After suffering session after session of torture that drew out pain for hours and hours under Vasquez's cruelty, such a quick death had sounded like heaven.

Not anymore, though.

Emerald was it. Her misty green eyes and Irish burr. Her angry fire and her passion.

Of all the mistakes in his life, of all the things he'd done wrong, from getting captured by Vasquez to keeping Emerald at a protective arm's length for her own good, walking away from her without having the guts to admit his feelings had been the worst. That he would now die made it unforgivable. He wanted to take her slowly and tell her how much she'd burrowed down deep inside of him.

Nick's yell brought Sam's eyes wide open to face death head on.

Instead of fire and imminent annihilation, through the scarred and distorted cockpit shield he saw nothing but buckets and buckets of rain deluging the helo. He'd never seen such a heavy blinding rain before. Then suddenly, the rain stopped, leaving them with blue sky and sunshine.

An odorous cloud hovered inside the cockpit, fed by tendrils of acrid smoke rising from where the Underling's body had lain. The spontaneous combustion of its carcass had left a burn mark on the floor.

There were no cheers, no victorious war cries. They all sat in stunned silence as Nick maneuvered the beleaguered helicopter back to the ranger camp. Every one of them knew how close they'd come to dying, and none of them were in the mood for any false cheer. The deadly game they were in was too real, too vital, and nowhere near over.

When Sam looked back to see where the rain had come from, he found two miracles. The first was that the solid black cloud was now riddled with holes where plumes of white smoke puffed out. Apparently fire and its heat had a negative effect on the evil black fog. The second miracle was the presence of a lone, whitish rain cloud. It hovered and rained over a single spot of the murk encircling Hades Mountain. The exact area Nick just happened to fly them through.

Sam shivered.

They might still be flying because cocky-ass Nick Sinclair was the god of damn-good-seat-of-your-pants piloting. But they were still alive because of the miraculous hard rain located in just the right place at just the right time. Was the rain an answer to a prayer? Maybe. Sam had his doubts as to whether or not *his* ass was worth divine intervention, but the miracle sure made it feel like someone up there was on their side.

He wasn't feeling too good at the moment. Now that his gut had unclenched and his pulse had eased back to normal, he could tell that something inside him was really off, and it wasn't that his heightened senses were diminishing now that they were away from the cloud. Icy cold chills crept up his spine, making him shiver. Sam's hand burned with so deep a cold it had become numb. He knew the Underling had poisoned him, but even worse, he knew the vampire infection inside him was growing. He could feel a marked difference in himself. Proximity to the evil black cloud had made him feel strong and distance from it made him feel weaker. It was an ugly truth to have to face.

Before he even realized the time had passed, the helo set down on the ranger camp's helipad. The miracle of their survival became even more astounding as Sam exited the helo and saw that scorch marks and burned areas covered the entire bird. It was as if the copter had flown through the fires of hell itself—at least what the uninformed masses imagined hell to be.

He'd recently learned that hell was a place of burning cold. There was no other reason for the chill invading his body. It was now a question of when. How much time did he have?

Once they cleared the blades, Nick throttled up the helo, lifting to take the bird to the nearest repair hangar over in Arcadia, where hopefully they'd find the inner workings of the machine undamaged. Meanwhile, Sam would drum up more artillery supplies from his local military and hunting buddies. Sam's motto in warfare was "plan well and strike hard," but they hadn't had a choice in their attack today. Even if they hadn't accomplished anything more than putting a kink in Cinatas's day, it was the psychological advantage that counted.

The wind whipped with stinging force against Sam's bare back and shoulders as he moved away from the rising helicopter's downdraft. Emerald was waiting with Erin and Annette just beyond the blades' reach. The storm of wind kept him from seeing her clearly until he was right on her. But one look into her misty green eyes told him everything. They were as somber as his heart was grim. She knew the evil in him was stronger and yet she still came at him with open arms.

He couldn't hold back. Any strength to resist his need was gone. He let himself drown in her, pulling her into a tight, one-armed embrace and reveling in the feel of her against his bare chest.

How could he even begin to let her endanger herself to save him from damnation?

How could he not? After everything, how could he not fight to live . . . and . . . to love?

He didn't know what in the hell he was going to do, and right now he needed to focus on what came next. The Vladarians would retaliate once they recovered from their housewarming party, and it would be ugly.

Every instinct inside of him screamed he should send Megan and the women somewhere safe, somewhere the damned couldn't reach them, but he was fighting against an enemy who didn't follow any mortal laws of existence or combat, and his experience with the Underlings today taught him how costly underestimating the damned could be. There really wasn't any *safe* place, but they were *safer* if they all stayed together, under the cohesive efforts of everyone's protection. A large part of their safety and their ability to fight against such an overwhelming force of darkness was Emerald's protective shield. But what was that costing her and how long could she maintain it?

Until she depleted herself completely. Until she drew her last breath. She was just that kind of woman. She'd give her all for her daughter, for the group, for him . . . whether he deserved it or not. He pulled her tighter, burying his face against her silky hair and breathing in the heady nuances of her scent. Something inside him shifted at that moment. Something so deep in his heart he couldn't put words to it. He just knew that whatever it took, he'd do right by her until he drew his last breath.

His world changed, but then everything was exactly the same.

He could hear everyone around them talking. Erin's dismay over Jared's injured leg. Annette's assessment and medical recommendations for the gash. Jared's protests against stitches.

Being in contact with Emerald eased the chill, and his hand went from being numb to throbbing. But that discomfort was nothing compared to the frightening weakness stealing over him. Yet all he could do was hold her.

Emerald leaned back from him first, her expression grave. She touched his wrapped hand with her fingertips. "You're hurt, too."

"An Underling got them both," Aragon said.

"We need to hurry," Annette said. "From Aragon's reaction we know IV antibiotics and an antiinflammatory will help fight the Underlings' poison. The sooner we get you treated the better off you'll be."

"I was just slashed by its claw. Sam got the worst of it," Jared said. "The Underling's blood burned Sam's hand when he killed it."

"It's nothing," Sam said with a shrug. In terms of pain, he'd suffered a hell of a lot worse. The only thing getting to him at the moment was the cold. It was as if winter had stolen beneath his skin. "I'll check the perimeter—"

"Doona even think it, Sam Sheridan," Emerald interjected, clamping onto his good arm.

"But—"

"The only butt up for consideration is yours," she said, giving him a dose of his own medicine. "Now march." She urged him toward the sleeping quarters, where Annette had set up her medical supplies.

"I'll check the area for disturbances," Aragon said tightly.

Sam nodded, cursing the fact that he himself wasn't doing it. "Jared and I will join you just as soon as we're patched up."

Aragon shook his head, a sympathetic frown on his face. "Knowing Annette, that will be quite a while."

"Ten minutes," Sam muttered. "I need to arrange for the extra supplies so Nick can pick them up and get back before dark."

Aragon shook his head. "You're already delusional, my friend. Your injury is worse than mine was and you're human as well. At least I still had my spirit warrior strength, and an Underling's scratch nearly brought me to my knees."

Sam nodded, but in his mind he already knew he had one up on the Blood Hunter. Aragon had been pure to start with, so the poison would have hurt more. Sam wasn't. He could already feel his body accepting the cold.

Annette spoke up. "Aragon is right. We have no idea what the effects the Underling poison has on a human. So, Sam, that means you're mine until I say otherwise."

"He won't be arguing," assured Emerald.

Emerald led Sam to one bed while Erin guided Jared across the room to another. She'd felt the full force of the poison inside him when she'd wrapped her arms around him and knew he was in bad shape. Her heart hurt from the evil chill stealing through his body, a chill that the Underling's poison was strengthening.

"You're cold," she whispered, touching his good hand.

"You offering to warm me?" he joked under his breath, adding a half smile as his deep blue gaze met hers. There was something different about him that had nothing to do with the Underlings' poison or the evil chill trying to take hold of his body. He was no longer removed. Whatever filter he used to shove between them was gone. In his eyes was a heat that went beyond the sensual and into the realm of caring. Her heart squeezed painfully tight, then raced at the unspoken but very real emotion he showed her in a single glance.

"I'm glad you came back." She slid her palm against his, clasping his hand.

He tightened his grip, drawing her closer to him. "Me too, and I'll show you just how much the moment we're alone." The heat in his eyes and in his voice was undermined by a shiver that had him clenching his jaw.

"Let's get you warmed up," Emerald said, grabbing a blanket and spreading it over his shoulders. He sat on the edge of the bed, and she leaned herself against him as she arranged the blanket. Then placing her palms to his chest, she braced herself for the pain the chill in him brought and tried to infuse some warmth from her magic into him, but she wasn't very successful. She didn't know if there were too many distractions in the room or if the Underlings' poison was too strong.

Her heart cried out in dismay. Sam! Dear God he'd been through so much. How much more could he bear? She wanted to take his cold, take his pain, do anything to help. She wanted to touch every inch of his supple, muscled body, kiss every tiny lash scar that covered him. How could a human have taken so much and yet still be capable of the gentleness he'd shown her?

"Erin, clean Jared's wound with the antimicrobial solution on the top shelf there and set up the suture kit. I'll look at Sam's burn then get the IVs going," Annette directed.

Emerald reluctantly stepped back from Sam as Annette brought over a basin.

Annette lifted a corner of the blanket from Sam's shoulders and her gaze took in the scars covering his chest, arms, and back. "Jesus, this is what Vasquez did?" Annette whispered. "They cover you completely, don't they? This is the kind of torture Stefanie saw?"

"This and much, much worse," Sam replied.

"When you told me Vasquez gave regular lashings to his prisoners, I thought you meant lashes to the back, which are horrible enough, but this is . . . dear God . . . inhumane." She inhaled.

"It's over with for me," Sam said. "But it's going to take a long time for your sister to heal. What he did to the body is nothing compared to what he sucked from the spirit."

Annette nodded. "Better take a look at your hand." She gently set his hand in the basin and unwound the T-shirt.

Emerald winced. The burn pattern looked just like he'd been splattered with acid. The affected skin was red with a number of whitish blisters. To make matters worse, there were several long, bleeding scratches down Sam's lower arm. The Underling's poison would be in his bloodstream, too. The only good thing was that his whole hand hadn't been burned, just the back and a little of his forearm.

Annette sighed, but the sound was one of relief rather than despair. "This is good. We're dealing with first-degree burns mainly. There are some second-degree areas, but nothing deep enough for any muscle damage. You were smart to keep your hand moist," Annette told Sam.

Annette was only looking at the situation from a medical viewpoint. Emerald knew it was going to be worse. At this point the strength of the Underling poison in him made a Redeeming impossible. If they weren't able to stop it before it gave the vampire infection an even stronger hold on Sam, she might not ever be able to help him.

Hearing a gasp at the door, Emerald looked up to see Megan, Stefanie, and Marissa hovering on the threshold. When Megan had awakened, she hadn't remembered having a vision at all. The women had decided not to mention anything about it until Megan brought it up. It haunted all of them, though; Emerald could see the shadows in everyone's gazes. Stefanie said she didn't know a man of fire. Marissa said she would die before she went back to her old life. Annette claimed she'd make toast out of anyone who dared to touch her, and Erin concurred. The only exception to the haunted faces was Erin; she practically glowed at the thought of being pregnant with Jared's baby.

"What's happened?" Megan asked, her expression tight with concern.

"They've been hurt, Meggie, but it's nothing really bad. We could use a couple of basins of hot water."

"I'll get them." Marissa nodded and left. Stefanie stayed, and Megan's expression had turned from concern to fear. Before Emerald could reassure her daughter that everything was all right, Stefanie spoke.

"Where's Nick?" Worry etched Stefanie's beautiful, ghostly features. She was so pale, so haunted that she didn't seem to have any real substance in the world. Yet Emerald could see improvement. After eating half a sandwich earlier along with crackers and cheese, Stefanie had rested. Now she was up, taking an interest in the world around her. It wasn't recovery yet, but it was a solid step in the right direction.

Emerald directed her gaze to Sam. "Was Nick hurt by the Underlings?"

"No. He went to have the helo repaired."

Stefanie nodded. "Good. I'll help Risa with the water." She left.

Megan's expression had grown even more alarmed. Emerald now realized that Megan was staring at Sam and must be seeing his scars. She went to her daughter, who was growing paler by the second.

"Mom," Megan whispered. "I feel cold." She shuddered. "What's wrong with me?"

Taking Megan's hand, Emerald moved out into the hallway. She ran a sharp gaze over her daughter and touched her forehead to check for a fever. Megan's skin felt normal, but she continued to shiver. The temperature outside had to be in the eighties and not a whole lot cooler inside, which told Emerald the only "cold" Megan could be feeling was the Underlings' poison affecting Sam and Jared.

Bending down, Emerald hugged her daughter and whispered into her ear. "It's all right, Meggie. You're getting more of your angel powers. Sam and Jared were hurt by something evil and you are feeling that poison. They are going to be okay. You can feel the evil, but that evil can't hurt you here."

"More of my powers, really?" Megan sounded excited, but she still shivered harder and Emerald hugged her closer. From the degree of Megan's reaction it would seem that her powers weren't coming in easy, like the slow creeping of a calm tide, but were hitting her just like her visions had, in a stormy flood.

"Listen very carefully, Meggie. The power you have to sense evil is a gift to help protect you, but you have to learn how to stop the cold from taking you over. You canna let it overwhelm your mind or it will freeze you from being able to fight the evil causing it. When you feel the cold, you have to keep your mind strong and focused on good. This is very important. Just like your visions are powerful, it seems your sensitivity to evil will be high. That means you are going to have to practice hard to be strong. What you need to do while I'm helping Mr. Sam is go to your room, get all bundled up, and focus on good things. Songs, thoughts, ideas, stories, anything that warms your heart. Remember that nothing in here can harm you, so doona be afraid, and if you need me, just call and I'll be right there. You'll know you're succeeding when you're able to stay warm without being all bundled up, okay?"

Megan hugged her tight and stood back. She wore a wobbly grin. "This is like homework for angel school, right?"

"Right."

"Just you wait and see. Those men that hurt my da are going to be very sorry. I'm going to be a kick-ass angel."

Emerald's heart fluttered at the determination in her daughter's eyes. "Meggie, doona fight before you're ready. One of the first things an angel must learn is patience." Emerald gave her daughter another hug and prayed hard that Megan would never have to come face-to-face with the evil that had destroyed Eric. Emerald had really thought they would wipe out this faction of the Vladarians before Megan ever became old enough to fight. But after what had happened to Sam and now Jared, she wasn't so sure anymore. "You're already strong, Meggie lass. I'm very proud of you, doona ever doubt that. Now go do what I said, and I will send Marissa and Stefanie to you with something hot to drink, too. Okay?"

"More than okay," Megan said. "I'm finally learning to be an angel and I'll be able to help you. Just you wait." Wrapping her arms around herself for warmth, Megan hurried to her room. Emerald returned to Sam with a heavy heart that her daughter had to deal with so much. She was too young for all of this to steal away her innocence.

Annette had Sam's hand soaking in a cleansing solution, and she and Erin were setting up the IVs. Sam was on the phone talking about guns and ammunition.

Marissa and Stefanie returned, each carrying a basin of steamy water. They set one down on the bedside table near Jared and one near Sam. Emerald then told them Megan was feeling a little ill, and asked if they could take her something warm to drink and stay with her while Emerald helped Sam.

Agreeing, Marissa hurried off to the kitchen and Stefanie went to Megan's room.

"What can I do?" Emerald asked Annette.

"Get the electric blanket for Sam and then see if you can keep him in bed," she said. "He's already complaining because the IV antibiotic takes thirty minutes to infuse. Depending on how that works, we can give them more in four hours or start a regimen of shots after that."

"Shots?" Jared said. "No, thank you. I think I'll heal just fine without any human medicine." He still retained some of his powers from the spirit world, which helped his body to heal quickly. He sat up, his intimidating, hard-muscled bulk ready to hop off the stretcher.

"No you don't, buddy," Erin said. Unfazed that her man towered over and outweighed her, she planted her hand in the center of his chest, right over his warrior's amulet, which marked him as part of the Guardian Forces, and shoved him back down. "You're not going anywhere until Annette pumps you full of antibiotics, even if I have to sit on you to make that happen."

"You promise?" Jared asked, caving like a cream puff. The predatory gleam lighting his already glowing eyes left no doubt exactly where he wanted her to sit on him.

Erin groaned, turning a bright red.

"Hey," Sam said, setting his gaze on Emerald and wagging his eyebrows, "I demand equal treatment." That new warmth in his eyes was so bright it took Emerald's breath away. It went right to her soul, nearly wiping out the cold from the evil and gave her a whispering hope. Maybe, just maybe, if she could keep her focus on the light in his eyes, a Redeeming would work.

"Equal treatment?" Annette asked, dark eyes gleaming as she held up a scalpel. "You'll need a gash for me to suture up then."

Sam's frown tugged a laugh from Emerald. His cell phone rang and he mouthed the word "later" to her, giving her little doubt he wouldn't settle for less than exactly what he wanted. Emerald shut her eyes and prayed that they'd have a later.

Chapter Fifteen

FEELING DRAINED, Emerald slipped from the treatment room, shut the door, and leaned heavily against the wall. Sam wasn't responding to the antibiotics as well as they'd hoped, and electric blankets set to high couldn't keep him warm. His body temperature remained too low, but he was shivering less and less. His body seemed to be acclimating to the cold, which told her that the vampire infection had gained a deeper hold on him. He needed to fight the cold, not accept it.

Annette was now infusing a different antibiotic and a stronger dose of an antiinflammatory, but Sam's system had yet to respond. The warm light in his eyes was fading.

Drawing in several deep breaths, Emerald forced a calm into her soul that she was far from feeling. Once again she focused her mind on the inner place where in the past she'd always seen glimpses of the future. Nothing but darkness met her now and she quietly cried out in frustration. She had to do something to change what seemed to be inevitable, but just like Eric, Sam was sliding through her fingers despite her white-knuckled grip.

Currently, the men were gathered in the treatment room, planning responses to possible attacks Cinatas might make, and how to make the best use of what resources they had at the camp. She'd also learned the ins and outs of how the protective shield worked. This morning, after the attack, Sam— disbelieving Jared's and Aragon's explanation—had tested the shield.

The shield was like a supernatural filter of intent. It wasn't a barrier against everything but was a permeable spiritual barrier that worked according to the intent of whoever was trying to breach it. A bird could fly through without a problem. Even a test bullet aimed harmlessly at the ground would penetrate it. But point the gun at the bird, intent on shooting it, and the bullet would ricochet off. It was the same for Sam. He could walk right through the barrier with ease. Yet, when he was on the outside and had tried to stomp on a bug inside, the shield had thrown him back. The shield blocked anything and everything intent on causing harm.

The magic of protective shields was unique to angels and had garnered them the "guardian angel" reputation. Without drawing from another source of power like the Sacred Stones, she could only protect one being at a time, either herself or another. When she broadened the scope of her protection, she had to expend a tremendous amount of psychic energy, and she was feeling the effects more and more.

Even if she and Sam could disappear for a Redeeming now before he worsened, did she even have the strength to save him? She didn't think so. It was a moot point right now anyway. She wouldn't be able to do it and still protect the others—her daughter included. Heart heavy, Emerald pushed away from the wall, crossing the common room to Megan's door. Before she could knock, she heard a shout and a loud bang and she barreled into the room. A pillow smashed into her face, showering her with feathers. She inhaled with surprise and coughed.

"Mom! Are you okay?"

Emerald blinked her eyes into focus as she swatted at the feathers then blinked again. Megan, dressed in black from head to toe, held a thick stick, looking like a ninja batting at the World Series. "Wh . . . at are . . . you . . . doin'?" Emerald choked out, feathers flying.

"Nailing Red Demons," Megan said. "I was just showing Stef and Risa how. We're inventing a Quidditch game out of it. Watch this. Bomp. Bomp. Bomp. Another one bites the dust. Bomp. Bomp. Bomp. There are plenty of ways you can hurt a demon. And bring him to the ground," Megan sang as she flipped another pillow into the air. Then shouting "this is for taking my da from me," she did a 360 swing, nailing the pillow with her makeshift bat. Emerald dove to the side to avoid another feathery smash.

Stefanie and Marissa watched from where they were huddled on the bed. Feathers danced over their heads like sugarplum fairies. They both had their hands covering their mouths, doing a miserable job of hiding their laughter. It was good to see some of the worry lifted from their minds, if only for a few minutes. Still, Emerald grappled for balance both physically and mentally. When she'd told Megan to concentrate on good things to ward off the chill of evil, Emerald had envisioned her daughter singing some of her favorite songs from the *Sound of Music* or something while she cuddled up under her comforter, drinking hot milk. Instead she got the karate kid singing Queen and . . . feathers—a room flying with them.

She opened her mouth, searching for something to say, and a feather flew in.

"I'm not the least bit cold," Megan said. "Your cure is working."

"Good . . . job," Emerald managed to spit out, though "good heavens" had been what she'd been about to say. Megan's focus on avenging what happened to Eric was a concern to Emerald because it could potentially lead to a rash decision, something with greater consequences than flying feathers, but she didn't have the heart to discuss it with Megan now. "Only, you canna always destroy pillows to fight the cold. It would be a bit expensive, not to mention the mess."

"I know," Megan said with a sigh. She kicked at a pile of feathers and sent them fluttering into the air. "Feathers are just so much fun. They make me feel like I can spread my wings and fly." She gave an impish grin and added, "Fly like an angel."

Emerald shook her head and laughed. "Doona be jumping from the tops of buildings, thinking you can. Real angels doona have wings and doona fly. I'm going to be with Mr. Sam a while longer and wondered how you were."

"I'm fine. After I clean up the feathers, Risa promised to teach me how to make Belizean ganaches and fried dough crescents for dinner, but first I'm going to make peanut butter balls for a snack."

"I'm already hungry," Emerald said, surprised to see evening shadows looming over the day. She thanked Marissa and Stefanie for being with Megan.

Stefanie stood, a tentative smile on her pale face. "No, it's me who is thanking Meggie. She showed me that I could still smile and laugh—at least for Major League Feathers."

Marissa shyly added, "It is all right for her to teach me peanut butter balls, no? It will not cause a problem? Never in my life could I eat when hungry until I come here. It was not allowed. Your freedoms and blessings are so very great, they overwhelm me."

Megan gaped at Marissa. "You mean you couldn't just go get a snack or something when you were hungry? Why not?"

"My uncle allowed food only when he thought I earned it. Sometimes, he made me pray for many days before allowing a meal."

"That's terrible," said Megan. She went to Marissa and hugged her. "I am so glad you both are here now. When Stefanie was first missing, Dr. Nette couldn't eat she was so worried. It wasn't until my mom told Dr. Nette she had to be ready to be able to help her sister that Dr. Nette forced herself to become strong again."

Stefanie sighed. "I've been such a terrible sister. I know I've caused Annette a lot of pain, especially since she rescued me."

Emerald shook her head. "No. She loves you greatly and canna watch you suffer without doing everything she can to help you. That is the . . . way of love." Emerald's throat closed with the emotion flooding over her.

Sam.

You love him. Heart and soul you already love him.

She didn't just care about Sam, or lust for him. She loved him.

She felt as if the ground beneath her feet had disappeared and she was freefalling into an abyss of darkness where the despair of the past and all that had happened with Eric waited to consume her now. She wanted to take fate into her hands and twist it until the world was right again. Until Sam's soul and spirit were as pure as his heart . . .

Her breath caught and her heart pounded hard as she realized there was a difference between Eric and Sam. Eric's pride had been at the root of his withdrawal from her and his refusal to let her help with a Redeeming. It was different with Sam. He was trying to protect her and Megan. Sam was different from Eric, and she wasn't going to let the outcome be the same.

"Mom, did you hear me? I have to tell you something," Megan said.

Emerald blinked to find Megan in front of her, looking very serious and suddenly shivering. Stefanie and Marissa were busy cleaning up feathers.

"Meggie," Emerald reached out to her daughter. "What is it?"

"Remember when I told you that you couldn't let the bad men that got Dr. Nette get you or what was bad would be even worse?"

Emerald would never forget the call and the horrifying vision Megan had had. "Yes," she whispered, not wanting to hear what Megan would say next. Somehow Emerald knew this would be about Sam. "What did you see, Meggie?"

"Bad things. Bad people taking Mr. Sam and making him bad. You have to stay with Mr. Sam. No matter what. Maybe things will be all right then."

"They are gonna be all right," Emerald told her daughter fiercely, biting back a cry of frustration over her inability to see into the future.

"I feel nothing but icy cold from Mr. Sam. Can you help him?"

"I will," Emerald said, realizing the Megan could still feel the cold but wasn't letting it paralyze her. She hugged Megan. "Do you know how proud I am of you today?"

Megan hugged back and smiled. "I had help."

"Yes, Stefanie and Risa were a big help."

"And Grandma, too," Megan whispered. "Grandma spoke to me. She said she was here for me."

Emerald looked heavenward, but she couldn't seem to sense her mother's presence and no welcoming answer met her spirit. Still she sent out a thank-you and a plea that Sam might be saved.

"Do you think Nette will have time to talk to me now?" Stefanie asked, drawing closer.

Considering Emerald wanted to have Sam alone for a few minutes, she nodded. "Yes, just as soon as the rest of the antibiotics are infused, which should be any minute now."

Stefanie nodded, but the look in her eyes was still too haunted for Emerald to tell if Annette's sister's recent efforts to rejoin life would last. Emerald feared there would be setbacks.

Emerald touched her daughter's cheek, hoping and praying Megan would never have to know the depths of evil Stefanie had suffered. "I love you best," she whispered to her daughter.

"Can't because I love you bestest," Megan said, laughing. "Now I'd better help clean up feathers or there will be no dinner or peanut butter balls."

Emerald left the room and Stefanie followed. She carried a sketchbook and her expression had turned somber. "Meggie is so full of life."

"She's a wonderful person. I love her dearly. Just as I know your sister loves you dearly, too."

Stefanie drew a deep breath. "This is so hard for me. Coming here and having to be someone I am not. I'm not the same person anymore."

"No one expects you to be. Just be who you are now and Annette will still love you."

"Will she? I don't think I'm worth loving anymore. When I was first kidnapped, I prayed for life, but day after day death and despair filled me. Now when I pray for death, only life surrounds me."

Emerald slid an arm around Stefanie's shoulders. "I doona have an answer as to why evil exists and why it came into your life, but I do know that reason and purpose can be found no matter how devastating life becomes. Evil tries to destroy good, but it canna. Good will live on, especially within the heart and that is more important than anything within this world. Do you think anything at all could stop me from loving Meggie?"

"No," Stefanie said with a sigh.

"Nothing will stop your sister from loving you. Not even your death. That is the way of love. Just tell Annette how you feel. She will understand."

Stefanie nodded then folded her sketchbook under her arm.

When they walked into the treatment room, Emerald was shocked to find Annette by herself, slamming about supplies as she cleaned the room. She was clearly agitated.

"Where's Sam?"

"Gone," she snapped.

Emerald braced herself against the doorjamb. "What do you mean gone?"

Annette threw her hands up. "The men finished talking. Erin went to do some more Internet investigation. Jared and Aragon went to do something around the perimeter they'd decided on, and Sam said no battle had ever been won from lying in bed. He left in a foul mood, refusing to stay here wasting time! Wasting time! You'd think all I did in med school was twiddle my thumbs."

"The change in the medication worked, then?" Emerald drew a deep breath of hope.

"Some." She sighed, her shoulders slumping to show the heavy burden of curing something completely alien to the mortal world. "But I worry if it is enough. His temperature only rose two degrees. It's still too low in my opinion, and he'll likely go into shock if it drops again. But he won't listen."

"The gack!" Emerald muttered. "Death will only buy him a faster ticket to damnation!" She went marching for Sam, outrage winding her sails. The moment she stepped outside, she noticed the greenish cast to the evening sky, one that bespoke a brewing storm. She also felt with a shivering chill a change in the oppressive malice gathering about them. It was significantly stronger.

Damn! How dare he leave Annette's care! After a quick look around, she headed for the cabin he called an office and barreled in without even knocking on the door.

"Sam!" she yelled. "Sam!" She took two steps, slamming the door behind her. Everyone was fighting to save his ass and he could bloody well appreciate it by following Annette's medical advice.

She whipped around as the bathroom door on her right flew open, hot steam billowing. "Jesus, Em, what the hell is going . . ."

Sam stood in the doorway, buck naked, dripping wet, and gun in hand. *Armed and*—she raked her gaze down hard muscled and perfectly sculpted male everything—*dangerous.* Droplets of water slid over his honed chest and down the rippled planes of his abdomen. A trail of dark, silky hair led to his impressive sex already rising to the occasion as it jutted thickly toward her from the apex of his hard thighs. From what she could see, no place on his body had escaped Vasquez's lash. Everything in her ached for all he'd suffered and for what he was suffering now on the inside. It had to be no less painful. He still wore the cross around his neck even though the silver of it had chafed his skin. Then she saw that he'd sharpened the bottom of the large cross to a point that could easily puncture anything.

Swallowing hard, she refused to contemplate what he might be thinking and went to him. "Sam," she whispered, knowing her heart was in her eyes.

"You don't want to be here," he said roughly, almost angrily. He may have set his gun on the sink, but he was still armed—his temper seemed cocked and ready for a hard go, but so was his erection. He sucked in air fast, his nostrils flaring with each breath. He jaw was clenched and his eyes gleamed as every one of his muscles tightened to the ready, like a predator catching scent of its prey. There was no mistaking the changes in his awareness of her or what his body was demanding he get from her.

She ignored his warning and touched his bandaged hand. "Your bandage is wet. You need—"

"It's fine," he said sharply. "What needs to happen is you getting the hell out of here before I—"

"No, I'm not leaving. Are you warmer yet?" she whispered, lifting her palm to his cheek even though she already knew he wasn't. She had to touch him, make a connection any way she could. The cold radiating from him scraped painfully over her spirit.

"Em! Go!"

"You canna do this alone, Sam," she said, leaning closer to him. Her stomach brushed his arousal and he shuddered hard from the power of his need. She kept her gaze focused on him and the emotion warring with the desire in his eyes. "You need me."

"There isn't anything pretty here—or even human," he ground out harshly. He wrapped his good hand around her wrist, holding her palm captive to his cheek as he backed her to the bathroom wall and thrust his erection against her. Then he bared his teeth, grazing her palm with his growing fangs, showing her how sharp his incisors had become. Sexual desire darkened by a barely restrained primal hunger poured from him like an ill mist billowing from a witch's caldron. "I can even smell your blood now, Em. I can smell the sweetness of it and hear the hum of it singing in your veins, calling to me."

After a long moment, he drew a deep breath and stepped back from her, his body shaking from the force of his will. "Now go. It's too late for anything else. The Underling's poison has fed the vampire infection and the medicine isn't working. I'll die before I hurt you or let you get hurt trying to help me. Meggie's the one you need to be worrying about in all of this, so get the hell out of here and stay away from me."

Emerald's heart swelled and burned with the force of the emotions flooding through her. She sucked in the steamy air and shook her head, feeling stronger than she had in days. "No. You canna push me away. Evil took Eric. I won't let it have you. I'm fighting for you. No matter what it takes." She rushed at him and wrapped her arms around his neck. "You canna leave me, too, Sam. Fight, fight with me." She kissed him then, pressing her lips to his and sliding her tongue into his mouth to glide over his fangs. The chill of the evil in him scraped painfully over her senses, bringing a hard edge to the pleasure she felt in his passion. She willed every ounce of power and goodness inside her to him.

Color suffused his warming skin and he groaned as if in deep pain, making her realize the heat in her hurt him just as the cold in him hurt her. But he didn't pull away from her. He slid his arm around her back and drew her closer to him as his tongue met and tangled with hers, deepening the kiss into a whirlwind of desperation.

The kiss wasn't pretty. It wasn't simple. It was rough and so deep it reached to the center of her soul, pulling her from the inside out. It would have drained her completely but for the rising well of her love for him, an emotion so volcanic it flooded the very center of her being with heat—heat she then channeled through her hands to him as she sought to touch him everywhere.

"Hold on," he said, sliding his good arm around her hips to lift her hard against him and his urgent erection. She tightened her hold around his neck as he straightened. Kissing her relentlessly, he carried her with their bodies pressed tightly together. Leaving the bathroom, he walked to the back room where his desk and his bed were.

From the frenzy of need consuming them, she expected to be tossed onto the bed and thoroughly ravished, was eagerly anticipating a headlong rush into mindless passion. Instead, he set her on her feet and with a firm brush of his thumb along her jaw brought her gaze to his. The angles of his face were sharp with need and a burning, sensual hunger that was at odds with the doubt shadowing his blue eyes.

"Last chance to save yourself, Em," he rasped, quivering from his restraint. "This is a bad idea. I don't think you know—"

"Fook thinking," she said. "This is going to get in the way." She lifted the sharpened cross from his neck. "And so is this." Grabbing the hem of her shirt, she pulled it over her head. "I want nothing in the way of you making love to me again."

He cursed in protest, but before she could blink, his rough, capable hands had her bra, pants, and underwear on the floor and he had her falling back on the bed with him gloriously on top. The whirlwind of desperation that began with their kiss turned into a firestorm of give-and-take and need and want. His tongue ravaged her mouth with demanding thrusts and teasing strokes.

His fangs grazed her lips and tongue before he dipped to the pulsing tenderness of her throat. She could feel his heart pound and his body shake with the powerful urgings taking hold of his body. And knew from the way he hesitated and licked the path of her carotid that he hungered for the taste of her blood.

She arched her breasts against him and he left her neck to kiss a trail of fire to her aching nipples.

Groaning deeply, she undulated against him, desperate for him. Instead of filling her with the erection he brushed teasingly against her sex, he moved to her other breast and laved the same attention to it. He kept the first one inflamed, kneading with fingers that tweaked and squeezed with just the right amount of pressure to drive her crazy.

She kissed and caressed every inch of him she could reach, wanting him inside her so badly that her body shuddered with desperation and her sex wept with frustrated need.

"Sam, I need you now," she whispered.

"Not yet," he rasped sounding as if he, too, would explode if he didn't get inside her. "I promised myself that if I ever made love to you again, I'd do it slow and savor everything about you. No more wild tree hugging."

"But—"

"No buts," he said. Then licking his way down to one breast, he drew her nipple deep into his mouth and swirled his tongue around its hardened peak as he began the seduction all over again. In a fever gone wild, she gasped and clutched his shoulders, moaning and arching for more. He gave more, dancing his tongue all over her in between rhythmic sucks on her nipples that had her writhing beneath him until she could do no more than whimper with need.

She truly thought she'd reached the pinnacle of insanity due to pleasure when he moved lower.

Sam paused above the triangle of curls covering Emerald's sex and brought his gaze back to hers, loving the misty pleasure in her green eyes. She was beautiful all flushed with desire and need. Perfect. He breathed in the heady fragrance of her desire before spreading her legs and opening her pink sex to his gaze. He ran his tongue down the center groove of her sex, watching her react. Her hips thrust upward and her legs widened as she fisted her hands into the sheets. Her full mouth opened, wide and needy, and her green eyes went even more misty with pleasure. The hungering surge within him rocked him to the very edge of reason. Nothing mattered to him more than seeing that pleasure and fulfillment take the shadows from her eyes.

He dipped his tongue into the hot crevice of her, tasting the dew of her desire, then thrust in and out as he swirled around and around. She grew fevered, her back arching as she offered him every part of her. He slid the tip of his tongue to her little hard spot and flicked over it repeatedly. She thrashed her head from side to side, she moaned, she shuddered and cried for him to come inside her, but he gave her no mercy. He couldn't stop drinking from her as he licked and sucked her sex. She came in a shuddering climax that had both him and the bed shaking.

Emerald shook from waves of pleasure claiming her body and soul, but her spirit needed to feel Sam. "Now," she demanded, urging him. "Please. No more without you. I need you inside me now."

Groaning, his blue gaze fixed on her, he eased his body over hers and entered her in one hard thrust. She nearly came again from the wash of thrilling pleasure.

"You're so hot and so tight." Flexing his hips, he moved the hard velvety tip of his erection in and out. Then did it again, groaning deeply as he shook from the force of his control. It made her wild. Insane.

"More," she said, arching to him.

Spreading her thighs wider, she anchored her heels to his backside and arched her bottom off the bed. "I need you, as much as you can give, as hard as you can bloody give it. I canna wait."

"Em, I . . . oh hell, hold on baby." He grabbed her hip with his good hand and thrust deep.

Shards of hot pleasure shot through her. Their gazes met and held as he unleashed the full power of his passion. Both of them quivered from the impact of his thrusts. The ecstasy on his face and his glazed eyes told her he felt the same exquisite pleasure that she did as a frenzied storm of need consumed them both. The lovemaking was beyond anything she'd ever known. Her heart pounded, breathing turned ragged, and her vision blurred as the intense fever of desire flamed into a shattering climax.

Then suddenly his fangs flashed and he cried out as throes of his own release pulsed through them both and with a dark cry, he sank his teeth toward her neck, but thrust his own arm between his fangs and her and sucked on his own blood. Another orgasm convulsed through him and he sighed in satisfaction.

"I'm sorry," he gasped, wiping the blood from his lips when he finished. "I . . . I had to have blood." She could feel the thunder of his heart even as she could see the shame in his gaze. His expression was one of both ecstasy and agony.

"It's okay," she said reaching for him.

He pulled back, tears flooding his eyes. "I love you, Em, but it's too late. I'm damned."

"No," she said, wrapping her arms around him and pulling him as close as she could. "No. You bit yourself and you didna try and bite me. Sam. The good in you is still in control. We'll find a way."

I canna lose him. I just canna.

Chapter Sixteen

STEFANIE WALKED beside Annette. They'd left the treatment room and were following a tree-lined path that wound around the camp. She'd been struggling with how to tell her sister about what happened in Belize. The horror. The violation. Her despair. She'd started about ten sentences and hadn't finished any of them.

The peaceful surroundings were surreal compared to the churning turmoil inside her. Evening birds warbled. Bumblebees searching for one last sip of nectar droned and the wind gently rustled the leaves. But she knew it was all a lie. Evil hunted for them.

Nightmares of Vasquez and Herrera. Her own private hell of memories she'd never be free from. Closing her eyes, she recalled the hard kick of Nick's pistol as she pulled the trigger. Bam. Bam. Bam. Images of Vasquez and Herrera fractured as the bullets tore through them.

"Are you trying to tell me you're ready to see a doctor?" Annette finally asked. "I know some awful things happened, Stef. Things that you can't talk about yet, but maybe seeing someone who is trained to counsel victims of trauma could help."

"No," Stefanie said, her voice strangled with emotion. "I can't. Not yet."

Annette sighed. After a few more steps she said, "I'm sorry I've failed you so many times."

Stefanie sent her sister a sharp look of surprise and tripped over a tree root. Her sketchbook went flying to the pine-needled ground as she grappled for balance. Annette caught her arm, helping to steady her or she would have fallen on her face.

Once Stefanie gained her balance, she set her hand over Annette's. "How . . . how could you possibly say that, Nette? How could you ever think that you've failed me?"

Annette blinked, clearly shocked. "How could I feel otherwise?"

"Maybe because you've always been there my whole life, bandaging my scraped knees, pulling me back from the curb when a car raced by too close, keeping me together and holding me when Mom and Dad died. Dear Lord, you even risked your life to save me in Belize. So how can you possibly feel that you've failed me? If anything, it's the other way around. I've always let you down and I'm failing you now."

Annette pulled her hand back and turned from her, but Stefanie could hear the storm of emotion choking her sister. "You wouldn't have been working for Sno-Med. You wouldn't have ended up Vasquez's prisoner, and you wouldn't want to escape the pain of this world by starving yourself if I hadn't convinced you to get a 'real' job. If I had supported your desire to be artist and a writer you would have—"

"That's so not true." Stefanie grasped Annette's shoulder. "You were right. I had to have a job that supported me, but I didn't just give up on my dream. I submitted my story and artwork to a publisher."

"You did?" Annette swung around; her dark eyes shimmered with surprise and tears. She caught Stefanie's fingers. "You didn't tell me!"

Stefanie shrugged. "I didn't tell anyone, and it was just as well. I received a blunt rejection letter telling me I had pedantic prose and I would do well not to quit my day job . . . ever."

"What? Are they crazy?" Annette cried. "You tell fantastic stories about wonderful creatures! That publisher was not only blind, but also had zippo in the imagination department. We'll send it somewhere else. Someone will appreciate the magic of what you create." Marching ahead, Annette snatched Stefanie's sketchbook from the ground and opened it up.

Heart suddenly pounding, Stefanie rushed up to take the drawing of her winged warrior from her sister. Somehow, it seemed that she'd make him really disappear if someone besides her knew about him. But she was too late.

"Wow!" Annette said. "He's *amazing* . . . like he's going to leap off the page and kiss the daylights—" Annette's face flushed red. "He's wearing Aragon's amulet!"

"What?" A dizzying rush of disbelief made Stefanie's heart hammer hard before she shook the thought free. A lot of amulets looked alike. Just because her sister's fiancé had something similar didn't mean—

"Here," Annette said. Reaching into the collar of her shirt, she drew out a long chain with a round disk at the end. "It's Aragon's Shadowmen amulet. Jared has one, too. All the spirit warriors in the Guardian Forces have one."

Stefanie struggled for air, telling herself that she must have seen the amulet on Annette or Jared sometime during her illness and that is why she'd been able to draw one for her spirit man. She'd been so sick and so wanting to escape this life that much of the last month of her captivity and the days she'd been back were a complete blur. She'd heard of Masons and Shriners and Moose Lodges and stuff, but Blood Hunters? That sounded almost like vampire—she grabbed Annette's arm. "Please, Annette, please tell me Aragon isn't like Vasquez. A Blood Hunter sounds like a vampire. Does he have sharp teeth? Does he, oh God . . ." She shuddered hard.

"Stef!" Annette grabbed her shoulder and pulled her closer. "No. Never. I'm sorry I haven't explained things. You've just been so . . . well I've been so worried about you that I didn't think to tell you the whole story. It's unbelievable, but it happened. It's real."

Stefanie listened to her sister's tale, beginning with Emerald coming nine months ago, Jared and Erin's arrival in Twilight, and ending with Aragon and the love her sister had found with the spirit warrior from heaven's Guardian Forces. It was like she was hearing for the first time in her life that she wasn't crazy. That the dreams and imaginings she put to paper both in art and in writing weren't the wild musings of a woman with only one foot in reality, but those of a woman who could see more that others could. And if Jared and Aragon were real, then her winged warrior could be, too.

"May I hold the amulet?" Stefanie couldn't keep the excitement from her voice. It was as if fire surged through her body, awakening every part of her that had wanted nothing more than to sleep forever in a dark, numb void.

Annette took off the amulet and set it into Stefanie's hands. She traced her finger over the raised, twelve-point star, noting that it was four perfect triangles, one on top of the other. Several very tiny jewels peeped between the lines. Beautiful, golden, and iridescent in the light of the late afternoon sun, the amulet was heavy and extremely warm in her hands—like it was a living thing. "Do you have a fever, Nette? It's almost hot to the touch."

"No. It's just the nature of the metal. It's always that warm but it gets hotter." Annette laughed, almost as if she were a little embarrassed. "When I first found the amulet—Aragon had thrown it away, another long story for later—and I was holding it, thinking about who owned it, the medallion would become scorching hot and Aragon would appear out of nowhere. The amulet had the power to call him to me."

Stefanie tightened her hold on the necklace, her mind racing as fast as her pulse. Was the necklace a magical window into the spirit world? Would it call the winged warrior back to her if she tried? And if she did and he was real, would he say anything different from the painful words he'd said before?

You must go on, Stefanie. I am a warrior with a duty to save others, too. You must . . . you must free me by fighting for yourself.

She loosened her hold on the amulet. The spirit warrior had

said what needed to be said, whether she wanted to hear the truth or not. He should have said even more. That she had a duty to those living, too. Her sister, for one. Marissa for another. And Nick. What was she going to do about Nick? Annette was talking, and Stef turned her attention back to her sister.

"Wearing it makes me feel as if Aragon is always with me, but I wish he'd wear it himself like Jared does."

"Why won't Aragon wear it?"

Annette sighed. "He doesn't feel worthy, which is complete nonsense. He is worthy in every way, but the stubborn Neanderthal won't believe it. That's part of that long story I'll tell you some other time." She glanced at her watch. Her eyes widened and she laughed. "Good Lord. Do you know we've been gone for over an hour? I should get back and check on Sam. But I've missed us talking so much and don't want this to go away."

"It won't. I need to get back, too. I promised to help Risa and Meggie in the kitchen. They probably think I've chickened out by now." Handing back the amulet, Stefanie retrieved her sketchbook and closed it without looking at her winged warrior.

"You need to rest," Annette said. "You haven't been—"

"Nette." Stefanie shook her head, already hearing her sister's guilt and worry. "It's okay. I . . . I ate lunch, rested all morning and most of the afternoon. Peeling a potato isn't going to hurt me."

"Am I suffocating you?"

Stefanie nodded. "Just a little."

Annette breathed deeply and then sighed. "I won't do it anymore."

"Good. And you're also going to stop this failing-me nonsense as well. Because, I swear, every time I have ever needed you, you were there for me. Honest."

"I wasn't there the Friday night before you disappeared. I didn't return your call when I got out of surgery because it was late and I was tired. I'll never forgive myself for that. You were going to tell me what you and Abe Bennett had uncovered about Sno-Med and the experimental blood treatment Rob Rankin's wife was getting, right?"

"Maybe a little of it," Stefanie admitted. "I wanted to ask you a few questions about the patient records we'd uncovered. But mainly, I just wanted to touch base with you. Calling back that night wouldn't have made a difference in what happened Saturday morning. Abe and I would still have gone hiking. And while we had our suspicions the treatments Celeste Rankin was getting were deadly, we didn't have proof. Besides we had no idea Rob was trying to kill Celeste with them. We sealed our fate Friday morning when Abe and I went to Rob with our concerns. He plotted our kidnapping then and had us on a private plane to Belize by noon on Saturday."

"That's just it, Stef. Don't you see that if I had called you back Friday night, then I would have had a reason why you might have disappeared and would have torn Sno-Med apart looking for you? And it wouldn't have taken me six months to find you. Every time I think about what you went through . . . I die inside."

Stefanie pulled her sister into her arms and hugged her tight. "Me, too, Nette. I die inside, too, and I see you hurting for me and it makes it worse. I guess that's why I've avoided talking to you the past few days. I'm sorry."

"I'm sorry, too."

"Today, things are different for me than they've been for a long while." Stefanie wasn't sure if it was her winged warrior or Nick who'd had a hand in that difference. "The only way to explain it is I've found that parts of me survived the jungle. And when I think about good things, then those parts of me don't want to die. So, no more guilt allowed, okay? It just makes me feel bad."

Annette let out a choked, laughing cry. "Are you telling the doctor that she's making the patient sick rather than well?"

"Yeah. Now tell me about Sno-Med. How are you going to expose them? It just kills me that all of those women who died aren't going to get justice."

"Not true. We have Celeste Rankin's blood tests as some proof. Then the records you and Abe uncovered helped me find one of the patients from the study. Though she is a vegetable from the stroke the experimental treatments caused, she is still alive. And I'm sure we're going to be able to gather enough evidence to bring Sno-Med down. The big delay is in finding what we need to tie Dr. Cinatas directly to the study, so the peons under him aren't the ones to fry."

Stefanie sighed. "Nick thinks there's only one way for justice to reach monsters like Vasquez and Cinatas and that's through a quick and violent death. Six months ago, I didn't even believe in the death penalty, much less battles and fighting and war, but that was before."

"Before what?" Annette asked.

"Before I met evil face-to-face. Now I won't hesitate to obliterate it if I can."

"It's taking too long," York said, bursting into Navarre's room.

Sirius looked up from where he sat next to Navarre and guiltily pulled his hand from Navarre's temple. The sleeping warrior's consciousness still remained fixed upon Jared and Aragon and the humans with them, watching them all. This time Sirius hadn't connected to Navarre's mind to heal the stricken warrior, but to see the humans, to see how Stefanie fared. It heartened him that she was up walking. Though frail in body and damaged in spirit, her will appeared to have strengthened. But would it be enough to withstand what was to come?

She, Jared, Aragon, and the other humans were in grave danger.

Already an entire division of the Guardian Forces had gathered above the area known as Twilight. They were there to fight a huge faction of Heldon's Fallen Army that had advanced almost overnight. The heavens were roiling with suppressed energy, but the presence of the Guardian Forces wouldn't help Stefanie and the rest. By rule, Guardian Forces could only battle within the spirit realm. Only the Shadowmen—whose duties required them to take form in the mortal realm—were allowed to act within that world. Even then those actions were limited. Blood Hunters were permitted to fight only those who threatened Logos's Elan. And with few exceptions Pyrathians were only permitted to breathe life into mortals whom Heldon tried to destroy before their time on earth was over. If one of the Fallen tried to stand in a Pyrathian's way in the performance of his duty, then he could fight. These rules were placed millennia ago because the battles between the Fallen and the Guardian Forces had so disrupted the balance of life on earth that huge disasters fell, often wiping out life with either cold or heat. But that was before so many of the damned began to concentrate their efforts to rule the mortal realm. Something had to be done. Surely those on the Council would see the wisdom of his request.

"Has Sven been admitted to see the Guardian Council yet?" Sirius asked. Rather than ask specific permission to leave Navarre in the mortal realm and bringing the finality of an irrevocable decision upon the warrior's head, Sven had decided it would be best to make a general appeal to the Council that would allow the Shadowmen greater autonomy in helping the humans battle the evil pervading the mortal realm. If Sven could get permission for the Shadowmen to aid the humans, then as part of that permission they could take Navarre to the mortal ground to help.

York paced angrily. "If they were going to grant our request then it wouldn't be taking this long. They are delaying their denial with discussion so that Sven will feel his petition has received due attention, but the final answer will be no."

Sirius clenched his hand, frustration wracking his spirit.

Somehow in the blink of an eye the wisdom and sovereignty of the Guardian Council had lessened. "Considering all that is at stake, and the urgency of the matter, surely the Council will grant Sven special dispensation to act while they deliberate?"

"Maybe. But by Logos, what will we do if they don't?" York asked.

Sirius set his gaze on Navarre. The burden of being the one responsible for the loss of the warrior weighed heavily upon him and the need to heal him took precedence over almost anything else, except to cause greater harm. "We won't wait for an answer then," he replied as the decision to bear the full burden of Navarre brought a peace and acceptance to his spirit. "I'll take him to the mortal realm, to Jared and Aragon and the humans. With his spirit returned to him, he may yet recover enough strength to fight evil on the mortal ground even though he can no longer battle the Fallen Army in the spirit world."

"I'll come with you," York said, moving to Navarre's side.

"No." Sirius pushed York aside and lifted Navarre in his arms. "I alone will bear the punishment for this act should the Council deny Sven's request. Ask Sven if he would check on my brethren and let Draysius . . . tell Draysius that I'm seeing to a brother in need and will return as soon as I can."

York started to argue, but Sirius cut him off. "Let me see this deed done before it is too late. Navarre is mine to heal. You would do no less."

York paused, his fiery countenance flickering like a candle beneath a stiff wind. "Would I?" he whispered. "Were Draysius in Navarre's shoes and I in yours, would I?"

Sirius left, having no time left for talk. York had sounded devastated by the reflection. It was one Sirius knew well. Not long ago, he doubted he would have chosen this path either. He didn't know if it was because a new code of honor had written itself upon his heart, or if the imbalance of evil in the universe had set him on a path to ruin.

Chapter Seventeen

SAM LEANED into Emerald's arms and brushed his lips over hers for a last touch of heaven, then pulled back, his insides wrenching with as much pain as the pleasure he'd felt just moments ago. The bone-deep chill from the Underling's poison had almost disappeared beneath the heated magic of her touch, but it now returned with a vengeance the second the orgasmic rush of hot blood in his mouth faded. He shuddered hard. Blood from where he'd sunk his fangs into his own arm dripped upon the white sheets, staining the bed, just as his hunger for it had blotted the greatest experience of his life.

He had bitten himself instead of her, but the driving urge inside him to taste her blood hadn't let up yet. A red haze had crept into his vision, and his heart thundered with excitement.

He had to get away from her before he did something . . . like sink his teeth into the softness of her neck. Dear God, he couldn't believe how close he'd come to lashing into her vein. His orgasm had triggered a savage need for blood he hadn't been able to control. The orgasm he'd gotten from drinking hot blood during sex had come as a shock to him—not only its occurrence, but the nature of it as well. His climax with Emerald had been a unbelievable experience of body, soul, and spirit. The "blood orgasm" had been a dark release that had left him unsatisfied and desperately craving more. It was as if those small gulps had fed a beast within him that was roaring to be unleashed.

"Sam?" Emerald sat up, reaching for him as he reared back from her. "What's wrong?"

"Stay away," he said harshly. He managed to stand, his breaths ragged from his fight to control the urges pounding into him with sledgehammer force. She was naked before him, all rosy from sex and completely vulnerable to anything he wanted to take from her. He could even see himself doing her again, only this time drinking her blood instead of his.

"You're becoming really cold," she cried. "I can feel it." She shuddered with horror, as if she could read his thoughts. "You shouldn't have left the treatment room. Here, let me try and warm you while we get you back to Annette and more medicine."

She reached for him. God help him. In seconds he wasn't going to be able to stop what would happen next. He had to get out of there. Only Em would follow him. She would do anything to save him except realize that she needed to save herself.

Desperate to escape before he lost it, he pushed her back. "No! Stay there."

"Samuel Terence Sheridan, you canna fight this alone." She rolled toward him.

He spied a set of handcuffs on his desk a step away and didn't think twice. It was the only way to protect her from . . . him. In a flash he had her on her back on the bed and one of her wrists cuffed to the iron bed frame. He stifled her outraged cry with a hard kiss. "Listen. I only have the control left to say this once. I'm sorry," he whispered. "But you can't help. Not now. The beast in me wants your blood too much. Whatever happens, remember that I love you." It took every fiber of his heart and soul to pull back from her rather than take her again with his throbbing need. But he could still feel enough of himself to know that this time anything he did would have been to feed the growing beast in himself and not a need born out of his love for her.

He jerked on his pants.

"You leave here and the evil will only get stronger, faster," she said, strangely calm when he expected her to be railing at him.

He didn't respond but continued to gather his stuff.

"Going away won't make your hunger for me disappear, Sam. You have my scent in your mind, and as the vampire in you grows stronger, you'll come back for my blood. You won't be able to stop yourself. You canna fight this alone. Let me help."

Sam closed his eyes at the panic clawing inside him. She didn't understand. If she knew what was really going on inside him, she wouldn't be asking to help. He slung a duffel bag of weapons over his shoulder.

She sat on the bed with a sheet clutched to her. She didn't say another word but just stared at him with her big green eyes. Eyes that said more loudly than she could shout, *You canna leave me, too.*

He was damned. He didn't have a choice. It was the only way to save her. He tossed her the keys to the handcuffs, then turned on his heel and left. In twenty seconds flat, he made the run for his truck and took off down the dirt road that would lead him straight to hell.

For the first time practically ever, Marissa could have as much as she wanted to eat of something as miraculously delicious as peanut butter and she could barely choke down a bite. Her stomach churned. Shortly after she and Megan arrived at the kitchen in the dining hall, she'd heard the wolf begin to howl again, insistently crying out, as if desperate for someone to hear his warning.

Begging *her* to hear him. She knew it. She could feel his spirit reaching out to her as strongly as he filled her dreams. She didn't know how to answer him, not while awake. And even if she did know how to reach him, she didn't know if she dared to.

But *Dios mío*, ignoring the wolf *was* driving her mad.

"You don't add the raisins until after beating everything else together with the mixer," Megan said. "Got it?"

"Raisins and then beat," Marissa said, looking out the window, sure that as close as the wolf sounded he would appear again.

"Hey, are you all right? You got that wrong," Megan said. "It's beat then add the raisins." Setting down the mixer, Megan touched Marissa's arm. "You look as if you're seeing a ghost."

Marissa closed her eyes and drew a deep breath then forced a smile. "I am fine."

"It's the black wolf again, isn't it? Can you see him?" Megan rose on her tiptoes, straining as she peered through the window above the sink. "Is he out there?"

"It's nothing. I see nothing," Marissa said quickly.

"It's okay," Megan said. "You know there are spirits trapped on this mountain, don't you? My mother often spoke of them to me after she would come to the Sacred Stones in the early mornings. That is why they call this place Spirit Wind Mountain and why nobody from the town will live on the mountain."

"I hear him," Marissa whispered. "I hear the wolf." Leaning against the counter, she sighed in relief that perhaps she wasn't crazy after all. Yet as she considered Megan's words, a tight knot squeezed her heart. The wolf had to be a ghost trapped in this strange spirit world here, which meant that he was dead and all of her dreams of running free through the forest with him, beside him were just that—dreams of a wild freedom that would never be real.

"Then go to him," Megan said.

Marissa blinked. "How do you mean? How can I go to him?"

Both times that you have seen the wolf you were alone, right? And he was near the forest?"

"*Sí.*"

"Then you must go outside close to the woods where no one can see you. Maybe he will come to you again."

"Both times it was at night, or almost night. It is daytime

now. Ghosts don't appear in the day, and I would look *loco* to be searching for one as well, no?"

"Who says ghosts only show up at night? You think there're rules for ghosts like there are for Red Demons and vampires?"

"I don't know," Marissa replied. "I just assumed."

"And why would anyone here think you're crazy when it comes to things from the spirit world? We all know that just because we can't see something doesn't mean it isn't real. I tell you that if I heard a ghost wolf calling me, I'd at least go out and see what's up. It couldn't hurt."

Marissa gazed out at the oddly colored evening. The sunshine had dimmed to a specter of itself, gasping its last through the greenish clouds. The leaves fluttering in the wind were like panicked butterflies trying to flee an eternal trap—a visual of how she'd felt most of her life.

She wanted to cover her ears, not only from the increasing cry from the wolf, but also from Megan's simple suggestion to go find him. But the seed had been planted.

"*Madre de Dios,* I shouldn't go. I don't even know what I would do if I saw him again."

"Speak to him. See if you can help him. My mother says that sometimes you can help spirits find peace even just by talking to them and assuring them that whatever they are worried about here on earth is okay now."

"Will you be all right here alone?"

"Geez, you're as bad as my mom. Yes, I'm only going to add raisins to the peanut butter and dish up spoonfuls onto the pans. You're likely to be back before I finish."

"I'll hurry." She left quickly, before she could change her mind, before her breathless anxiety could steal away any more of her courage. Once outside she focused on the wolf's call, searching for which direction to take, only the sound seemed to be coming at her from all directions. She moved toward the forest edging the camp and closed her eyes, willing her spirit to feel the wolf's. It was the first time she'd opened her mind to him apart from her dreams.

Suddenly, a strange warmth filled her, made her body tingle all over, as if she were coming alive after being numb with cold for too long. And though she had her eyes closed, she could see the trees and the brush and the pine-needled ground rush by her, as if she were the wolf racing through the forest or she were seeing the world through his eyes. His cry changed from one of warning and desperation to one of relief and welcome, and somehow she knew which way to go. Opening her eyes, she ran toward him. She had no fear of him, even when he suddenly appeared before her. He was huge and as fierce as he was graceful. His glossy, thick coat of black fur covered him like a sleek, kingly robe. But it was his eyes that captured her. They were gold, pure gold, unlike anything she'd ever seen before.

Now that the time to speak had come, she didn't know what to say. Delaying, she held her hand out to him with her palm up. "Please," she whispered. "Let me help you."

He came to her and brushed his massive head against her palm, but her hand went right through him and she felt only the air upon her skin. She groaned. He was so beautiful, so magnificent that she found herself hurting because he wasn't real. She reached for him again, almost wishing he could be magical and gain substance from her touch, much like Sleeping Beauty had been awakened with a kiss from her prince.

Before she could touch him, he suddenly arched back. Suspended in midair he writhed wildly as a howl of pain roared from his throat. Her lungs seized and tears sprang to her eyes.

"No!" she cried out at whatever attacked him. "Leave him alone." She rushed forward, trying to reach the wolf, but he disappeared as if he'd never been, leaving the world strangely silent.

Dios mío, was it her? In trying to contact the ghost wolf had she caused him even more pain? She ran back to the kitchen, her heart aching.

Stefanie stared at the pine needles and crackling brown leaves on the forested path where she walked beside Annette. They'd each retreated to their own thoughts as they'd approached the camp. The wind had picked up even more, as had the shadows.

She sighed. The only time she'd found relief was when the warrior with fire in his eyes had touched her. She couldn't stop herself from wondering again what would happen if she were to use Aragon's amulet to "call" the spirit being to her.

The roar of an engine and the spinning of tires on gravel broke the silence like shattered glass.

"Oh, no," Annette said, worry and concern heavy in her voice. "That sounded like Sam's truck leaving the camp. We'd better hurry back." They quickened their pace.

Though out of breath and weak, Stefanie was holding up better than she thought she would. "He's really ill, isn't he?" she asked between breaths. "Will he become like . . . like . . ."

"Vasquez," Annette supplied. "I pray to God not. Knowing Sam as I do, if there's a way to kick evil's ass, he'll find it. He suffered too much and hated Vasquez so greatly, he'd never become what that monster was. Take my word on that, but something's wrong."

Stefanie thought about it and realized Nick's drive was the same—and maybe hers, too, now. She could still feel the heavy weight of the gun in her hand and the powerful kick it had given her clutched hands as she'd obliterated Vasquez's and Hererra's faces—mugs she was determined to forget.

As she and Annette rounded the bend, she saw a sudden flash of bright energy. A tingling awareness covered her body and she searched hard, having felt that awareness but a few times before and always when . . . She couldn't believe her eyes.

He was there! The spirit being who'd saved her life twice

stood in the shadowy distance ahead, in all of his golden, fiery winged glory.

And possibly a third time if she did as he'd requested and fight to live. Her fire warrior held a huge, dark-headed man in his arms, who looked like Aragon and appeared to be naked and unconscious.

"You're back. What happened?" Stefanie's shout brought Annette's head up. They both began to run. Dizziness dimmed Stefanie's vision and her muscles felt like pudding, but she kept running. She'd reach her warrior or die trying.

"Aragon!" Annette called out. "Who are you? What's happened to Aragon?"

The glittering being turned their way. His green eyes blazed across the distance, touching Stefanie with firey glow that felt almost like a kiss. For a brief moment even her skin glowed and she realized that he'd caressed her with some sort of energy. Her breath caught, her heart raced, and she nearly fell as her knees became mush. He was so much more magnificent and frightening than her half-dazed, hunger-starved mind remembered. She reached her hand out to him, but he shook his head and turned away, as if he'd revealed more that he should have and already regretted the supernatural touch he'd given her.

He placed the man in his arms on the ground and disappeared.

"No! Wait! I just want to . . . talk to you." But her cry came out as only a whisper. What little energy she had was ripped away. She stopped running and gasped for air as a heavy disappointment filled her.

Annette was still running, shouting Aragon's name, and Stefanie fiercely chastised herself for being so selfish. She hadn't given Aragon another thought. Annette's fiancé must be gravely hurt. He hadn't moved at all. Stefanie put her feet back into motion, hurrying to catch up to her sister. At that moment, Marissa and Megan came barreling out of the dining hall.

Marissa took one look at the naked man sprawled at her feet and flung out her hand to stop Megan. Then Marissa dropped to her knees, leaning over him as she put a cloth on top of him, clearly covering his privates from Megan's eyes. The Spanish Marissa spoke as she shooed Megan back inside was so panicked, Stefanie couldn't understand it.

"Annette!" Aragon shouted.

The call didn't come from the dark warrior on the ground, but from the forest behind.

Annette skidded to a stop, confusion furrowing her brow as she glanced toward the forest. It sounded as if a herd of elephants were crashing through the brush.

"Aragon?" Annette whispered as he appeared running toward them with Jared hot on his heels.

If Aragon and Jared were all right, then who was the huge, long-haired man on the ground?

"Bloody gack." Emerald was too mad for tears. Sam was a stubborn idiot who deserved whatever fate his hard ass landed in.

No he doesn't, her weeping heart whispered. *Yes he does,* shouted her mind, which was doing its best to cut her off from her emotions.

She'd just managed to unlock the damn handcuffs when Sam's truck had roared out of the camp. She'd been tempted to run after him naked as a jaybird, but there came a point when a man had to meet a woman halfway, didn't there?

As she dressed she steadfastly refused to recall anything intimate that had happened between him. He hadn't loved her all the way to heaven. He hadn't filled her spirit and her soul with a deep burning passion. He hadn't told her that he loved her. None of it had happened at all. All that mattered, all that counted, was that he'd left.

She slammed the cabin door and refused to look back at any of his belongings that filled the room.

But once out the door, she couldn't move another step. How could she let him go? How could she stop fighting to save him? Maybe it was just she who couldn't help him right this minute. His need for her angel blood in the throes of passion may have been too great for him to handle. Nick didn't have angel blood, and if anybody could find Sam it would be Nick. She reached in her pocket for her BlackBerry and realized it wasn't there. It was always there. Thinking back, she was shocked to remember that she'd left it in her room before breakfast that morning and hadn't given it another thought from the time Megan had had her vision of doom until now.

She ran the few feet to the sleeping quarters and snatched the phone off her dresser. She had gotten over thirty calls or texts from clients, and she blinked at the display, stunned.

Emerald dialed Nick. Her patients would either have to contact her partner or wait for a response.

Closing her eyes, she waited for the call to connect. *God, Sam. Where are you?*

"Yo, Dr. Em, what's wrong?" Nick said.

"Sam. He, uh, left the camp with some guns and, I—" She sucked in a deep breath. "I don't know if he's coming back."

"Whoa. What the hell? What do you mean he left the camp? He'd never leave everyone in a million years. He's probably going to do an in-depth recon. We both talked about the need to establish some kind of escape plan off the mountain. You know, just in case something with the protective shield went wrong."

"No, Nick. You have to believe me. Sam left the treatment room before Annette cleared him of the Underling's poison. He needs more treatment. The poison in him is feeding the vampire infection and I believe he is in real trouble."

"It's that bad?" Nick asked grimly.

"Yes."

"Shit. I'm in Arcadia, so my ETA is thirty and I've got to get hold of some wheels first. The helo is out of the picture for at least two days, which leaves us too damn vulnerable. Snoopy is lined up for a backup helo, but I don't want to use him to run me around. He needs to stay open for any medical emergencies."

"Snoopy?"

"Yeah, you'll know why when you see him. Annette knows him. He's a PI over here with a helo at his fingertips. He fills in whenever there's an emergency pinch with Life-Flight. I've had him on call since we commandeered Twilight's helo last week."

"I see. Doona let Sam know, but will you call me when you find him?"

"Will do," Nick said, then exhaled hard enough for her to hear. "Tell me something . . . is the shit like terminal cancer? Isn't there some way to stop it?"

Emerald paused, trying to find the right words and the resulting silence was like a nuclear bomb. "Honestly?" she whispered. "I don't know if anything can be done or not. Before the Underling poison I told him about a Redeeming ritual. It's a long and dangerous ceremony. I wouldn't be able to do it and maintain the protective shield at the same time. Sam refused to consider it. And now that the Underling poison has made his condition worse, I just doona know. And Nick?"

"Yeah."

"Night's coming. That's when the vampirism gets worse."

"I'll be in touch," Nick said then hung up.

In the middle of hanging up with Nick, Emerald heard Annette shout for Aragon. It was a cry of panic and pain. Emerald ran from the building toward the dining hall, her unshed tears drying almost instantly in the stiffness of the breeze against her face. As she looked up into the sickly overcast, evening sky, she realized that the oppressive cloud of evil filling Twilight's atmosphere had worsened. The darkness gathering at their gates hadn't been lessened with the attack on the Falls. With that realization, the dread that had sent her stowing away with Sam came back at her in full force and she wondered for the first time ever if her daughter would be safer with someone else, if there were anyone else strong enough to leave Megan with. Emerald suddenly couldn't breathe. She ran, but her lungs refused to work.

Taking Megan anywhere outside of a protective shield would leave her open to any kind of attack from the paranormal realm. Now that the damned knew there were angels in the program they would be hunting every nook and cranny for them. And then there was Wellbourne. With his capable network of murderous minions, both in the paranormal and mortal realms, he presented a greater danger than anyone else.

She rounded the corner to the dining hall, gasping for air. That's when she saw Marissa kneeling next to an unconscious, naked stranger and Megan standing next to her staring wide-eyed at the guy. Danger from the man didn't appear to be imminent. The only movement visible was the rise and fall of his chest. But it was a very scary concern to Emerald that he'd gotten here and she hadn't felt him cross through the protective shield. From the look of the man, all hardened muscle, massive size, and long hair, she thought he might have a connection to Jared and Aragon.

Looking like she was trying to figure out how to help the man, Marissa spoke in rapid Spanish as Annette and Stefanie with Aragon and Jared came running up. Annette bent down and began checking vital signs.

Erin came up behind Emerald, breathless from her dash from one of the cabins. "Who is it, Jared?"

Jared settled on his knees at the man's head and brushed the hair from his face. "It's Navarre, one of our brethren Blood Hunters. He will not harm anyone."

Emerald raised a brow at that. Both Jared and Aragon had been an intimidating package when they'd arrived, and in their werewolf forms, they'd downright scary. She did realize though that the reason she hadn't felt Navarre cross the protective shield was because he was a pure being from the spirit world, uncorrupted by evil or changed by humanity.

Aragon knelt at the Blood Hunter's side, his expression one of great sadness. "Navarre must still be injured, and this is my fault," he said quietly. "When I crossed the spirit barrier to search for news of Stefanie's fate, I was attacked and almost captured by a band of Pyrathians looking to capture or execute me according to the Guardian Council's decree. Sven, York, and Navarre fought to save me. Navarre jumped in front of me, taking a Pyrathian's fire strike that was meant for me. I brought him to the mortal world with me, but then York came and took him back. I'd thought he'd recovered. If he has been injured this long . . ." Aragon's voice trailed off, filled with anguish.

"Your fault, my friend?" Jared asked. "I know no Blood Hunter who wouldn't do that for one another, just as you would for every one of them. It was Navarre's choice." Jared placed his palm to Navarre's forehead. The man moved restlessly, moaning. "He's waking."

Marissa moved back a little, her gaze riveted to the man.

"Meggie," Emerald said, catching her daughter's attention. "Go get one of the tablecloths from the dining hall, okay? He might be cold."

Though Megan looked as if she didn't want to miss a single second of the drama, she nodded and ducked back into the dining hall.

"Navarre? Can you hear me?" Aragon asked.

Navarre groaned again, as if in pain.

Stefanie moved to Marissa's side and touched her shoulder. "Risa, are you all right?"

Marissa looked at Stefanie, gasped in air as if she'd forgotten to breathe, then struggled to speak, but no words came forth. About that time, Megan returned with a red-and-white-checkered tablecloth and handed it to Stefanie.

"Here," Stefanie said to Marissa. "Let me help you up and we'll cover the man."

Before Marissa could move, the warrior Navarre woke up

and grabbed Marissa's arm, pulling her toward him. He rasped one word. "Danger."

Marissa looked at the man and gasped loudly. "*Ojos de oro*," she cried and promptly fainted right on top of him.

"Risa," Stefanie cried. She tossed the tablecloth over the man and reached for her friend.

Navarre put his arm around Marissa, as if to claim her for himself. "Must save her," he said.

Jared and Argon looked at each other, brows raised.

"He acts as if he knows something very bad is about to happen," Stefanie said, quickly looking around the area.

The panic and fear in Stefanie's eyes grabbed at Emerald. She moved forward and caught Stefanie's arm. "I doona think he means the danger is now. I would know if any of the damned were trying to pass through the protective shield. I can feel everything that touches it with the exception of someone who is completely pure of heart and mind."

"Emerald is right," said Aragon. "Jared and I would both sense the nearness of anything we would need to fear. Navarre has just come from the spirit realm. The danger must be from there."

"No. More than just Heldon's Army," Navarre said. "A great gathering of the damned with the intent to destroy," Navarre said. He looked as if he was trying to rise but couldn't. His deep voice was rough and thick, as if he hadn't spoken for a long time and could barely remember how.

"Easy, Navarre," Aragon said, setting his hand on the man's shoulder. "Jared and I will help you save her. We are here. Let her go so we can help you get up."

"Aragon?" Navarre asked, moving his head toward Aragon. "I can feel your presence, but I cannot see you. Why the darkness here?"

Jared and Aragon exchanged a grim look and Emerald's insides clenched with empathy. Whether permanent or temporary, their friend was blind in this world.

Chapter Eighteen

"THERE is danger."

The deep voice rumbled through Marissa's mind followed by wild sensations that had her heart racing madly and her mind grappling for sanity. She lay upon a hard, hot body and her breasts tingled to the point where she couldn't remember how to breathe. Silky hair brushed against her cheek as he breathed and the supple velvet of his skin made her fingers flex with pleasure into the muscles of his arm and side.

The man was huge and naked and he was holding her tightly to his chest, as if he would never let her go. Yet she wasn't frightened in the least. In fact, for the first time in her entire life she felt completely safe.

But more astounding than anything else, the man's spirit and the wolf's spirit were one and the same. She'd sensed it the moment she'd touched him. She'd spent the last few nights with his spirit in her dreams and she knew the strength and feel of him. It was a soul as majestic and fierce as the wolf with all of its raw, predatory power. Even if she hadn't recognized his spirit, it had taken only one look into his golden eyes to know that both the man and the wolf were somehow the same.

"Let us help you rise, Navarre," Aragon said. "Release Marissa so we can help you both. She seems to have fainted, possibly in fear of you."

Navarre. His name was Navarre. It whispered through her mind like a gentle, cooling breeze, soothing, musical, yet powerful. Finally, she gathered enough presence of mind to breathe. Her lungs expanded, filled with blessed air. A second breath followed. Then a third until the havoc inside her settled and her body's life-sustaining functions fell back into their natural rhythms.

"She wakes," Navarre said. "Give her a moment to recover and we will both rise." The timbre of his voice vibrated through her whole body, making her feel things in more places than she thought possible. Her toes curled in her shoes.

Marissa lifted her head to look at the magical man, wanting him to look at her with his eyes of molten gold. But he didn't. He kept looking at the sky as he brought his free hand up to tentatively touch her arm. Then he trailed his fingers to her shoulder and through her hair before reaching her face. After he rested his palm against her cheek for a moment, he explored her features like one who was blind.

"Do you fear me?" he asked. His gaze was still directed over-head but not focused upon anything that she could—

Madre de Dios. He *was* blind.

"No, I do not fear you," she whispered, her heart flip-flopping even as her stomach lurched with concern. How was it possible? She knew the wolf spirit could see. There was no way she could mistake the intent gaze with which the wolf had studied her, and then there'd been the dreams. The running through the forest and seeing freedom from the wolf's eyes.

"Good," Navarre said. "Jared? Aragon?"

"We are here, my brother," said Jared.

Gripping her arms, Jared helped Marissa rise off Navarre's chest. Heat flamed her cheeks as she realized that she'd been lying upon the man, enjoying the sensation of being impossibly close to him while others had been watching her.

Once she eased back to her knees, Stefanie helped her stand. Together they stood back so Jared and Aragon could help Navarre.

With one warrior at each shoulder, they helped Navarre to sit up. But he suddenly grabbed his head with both hands and cried out, as if in great pain. "By Logos, what is wrong with me? I've no strength."

"Lay him back down," ordered Annette. "He must have a concussion, or worse. Is his blindness recent?"

"Yes," Aragon replied, his voice shaking with the guilt etched upon his fierce features.

"No time for rest," Navarre said, latching onto Aragon's arm, refusing to lie down. "I've been trapped in the Twilight, unable to see or be seen, hear or be heard. All I could do was watch . . . and pray. Great numbers of the damned have gathered upon the mortal ground nearby and the full focus of their evil intent is upon those of you gathered here. Their power is fed by an amassing of Heldon's Fallen Army overhead. It is the largest coordinated assault upon an area I've ever seen in my millennia of service. I must fight."

Though Navarre tried hard to stay upright, his body didn't cooperate. He wobbled off balance.

"Easy," said Aragon. "We know of the gathering darkness and are readying for a fight. But you, my brother, must heal. Annette?" The mighty warrior was clearly looking to his woman for what needed to be done.

"Get him to the treatment room. I can sedate him if necessary. Carry him as flat as possible."

"Must fight," Navarre said. Grabbing hold of Jared's and Aragon's shoulders, he tried to push himself to his feet, but then he cried out in pain and passed out. Jared and Aragon caught him and laid him back down on the ground. Marissa would have fallen back to her knees to do something, anything, to help even though she didn't know what, but Annette was there first. She quickly felt for Navarre's pulse and pulled a small flashlight from her pocket and checked his eyes.

"His pupils respond to light, but his pain, blindness, and repeated unconsciousness indicates this is serious," Annette said. "Get him to the treatment room. I'll stabilize him while we're waiting on the helicopter to the hospital for a CT scan. I've got connections and I'm sure I can get one done on the QT."

Marissa didn't understand everything Stefanie's doctor-sister said, but she realized that the magic man was badly hurt.

"I just spoke to Nick a few minutes ago," Emerald said, catching hold of Annette's arm. "The helicopter is out of commission for at least two days."

"Hell, I forgot it wasn't here," Annette said. "We need to go quickly. Maybe Sam in his patrol car—"

"Nick said a guy named Snoopy is sitting on go for any emergencies."

"He flies like Nick in combat mode . . . but we need to move fast," Annette said, dragging out her cell phone.

"I'll be riding shotgun" said Aragon. "The ride will be smooth and easy. Count on it."

Marissa hurried alongside the group. She wanted to touch Navarre, to hold his hand and help him, but realized she would only be in the way. Instead, she sent her spirit in search of his, just as she had when she'd gone to the wolf just a short time ago.

Nothing was there, not even the cry of the wolf.

Standing at the dining hall's entrance, Emerald, with Megan at her side, watched Navarre being carried to the treatment room. The tragic worry on Marissa's face as she hurried at the man's side didn't escape Emerald's notice. The way both Marissa and Navarre interacted had been odd, as if they were not strangers to each other but had close ties.

"Things are bad," Megan said.

Emerald turned to study her daughter's expression. "They've been better," Emerald replied. "I'm sure whatever can be done to help Navarre, Annette will make it happen."

"Yes," Megan said softly. "But I wasn't talking about him. The pure goodness in his spirit is so warm and beautiful, I felt like I was standing next to the sun in heaven. It was amazing. I was talking about Mr. Sam. He's gone, and it's bad."

"Dear heaven." Emerald caught Megan's hands and met her

gaze head on. "Have you had another vision? Doona be afraid to tell me about anything that you see. No matter what it is, I need to know. Even if you think what you've seen will hurt my feelings or make me angry."

Megan looked down, silently nodding. "I haven't had another vision, but . . . Mom, the cold and darkness coming from him hurt me badly. I could feel it no matter how hard I tried to shut it out. I know since Da was taken from us, you've had no one. And I so wanted you and Mr. Sam to be together, prayed for it. And look what happened." She kicked at the loose gravel at her feet, sending a spray of the pea-size pebbles and dirt into the air. "Evil takes him, too. It's not fair." Tears gathered in her eyes. "I know you love him, but when I felt him leave here, I was glad and relieved that the painful cold stopped. I'm sorry. Are you going to go after him?"

"Oh, Meggie, I'm the one who's sorry." Emerald pulled her daughter into her arms and hugged her tight, burying her cheek against the silk of Megan's moon-colored curls. She smelled like peanut butter and Ivory soap. Megan's rapid development was so frightening, and the only explanation for it was that Megan's father had been a Vampire Slayer and had supernatural powers of his own, which were passed down through the bloodline. Emerald wasn't ready for all of this to be happening now.

"When an angel's powers and sensitivity to the damned begin," Emerald explained, "It usually develops in small degrees so that you can learn how to handle it all. You should have told me it was so bad. I would have—" Emerald mentally smacked herself . . . twice. She'd been so caught up in Sam that she hadn't even thought of giving Megan the one thing that would help her deal with her hypersensitivity. It didn't matter that Emerald hadn't known had bad it was, she should have anticipated that it would be, considering the incapacitating power of Megan's visions.

"No. I'm not going after Sam. I'm praying for him, and if he comes to me I will try and help him, but there comes a point when an angel has to let go. I'm here with you, so you doona have to worry. And more importantly, I need to give you something that your grandmother gave me on my eighteenth birthday when I came into my full angel powers." Emerald released her daughter and unclasped one of the two angel bracelets left on her wrist. The third still dangled from its tree branch at Silver Mist Falls. She'd planned to retrieve it as soon as she could.

Her hands shook as she wrapped the chiming bracelet around her daughter's slight wrist. "There's angel magic in it," she told Megan. "It will enhance your powers with some of heaven's strength. And the tinkling it makes is at a frequency unique to angels. It causes the damned terrible pain, especially with demons because it sticks in their minds within seconds and drives them insane. After I've put it on for you, you need to kiss the bracelet, and then only you will be able to take it off. I'm sure your grandmother will also be giving you three bracelets when you turn eighteen."

"It is so warm," she said as she ran her fingertip over its silvery lengths. Then Megan looked up, wonder and awe and love glowing from her deep green eyes. "You're sure?"

"More than sure. What makes it so warm is that it is a special bracelet that gathers energy from around you to help you. Though doona think it is an invincible weapon and nothing can hurt you. It can only add power to your own. Now kiss it and make it yours."

Though Emerald could tell that Megan was as excited about the gift as she was stunned, she still hesitated. "Don't you need it? To help you with the protective shield? To help fight the bad men after us now?"

Emerald shook her head and caressed Megan's cheek. "I'll be fine, luv. I've learned to draw power from places like the Sacred

Stones, and someday you will, too. It will ease my heart knowing that you've a little bit of heaven's magic on your side."

Eyes wide, Megan brought the bracelet to her lips and pressed a kiss to it. The bracelet gave off a flash of bright light and then tinkled a hello to its new angel-owner. "Wow," Megan said. "Bethy isn't going to believe all of this. It's like . . . I mean I feel like I'm Harry Potter."

"Meggie, we still canna tell people about these things. All of this still must be kept secret. It's not safe for you otherwise."

"But Mom. It's Bethy. She'd never do anything to hurt me. It's not like I'm advertising in the newspaper or something."

"It doesn't matter. You canna take the chance that others will find out. When this is all over, the story won't be any more exciting than a camping trip on Spirit Wind Mountain."

"But you told. Mr. Sam, Dr. Nette, everybody here knows."

"Yes. I *had* to tell them. We're in a battle together. There's a difference between telling someone because it is important and telling someone just to share. There may come a day when you will *have* to tell Bethy or someone else who you are, but until that day comes it is better to keep our angel blood secret."

"She . . . she'll know that I'm not sharing with her and she won't understand."

The turmoil in Megan's heart pulled at Emerald. "I know. I've hurt others, too. Being who we are isn't easy and more often than not we end up standing alone." She didn't add just how hard that aloneness was sometimes.

"I don't know about you, but I could use something to eat. Did you and Risa make that Belizean dinner?"

Megan drew a deep breath. From the stormy emotions in her daughter's eyes, the subject was far from over, but she let it go for now. "We only got as far as the peanut butter balls. We were on the second batch when we heard Dr. Nette yell and everything went crazy."

Emerald wiped a smudge off her daughter's forehead. "Exactly what do you mean by crazy?"

Megan winced. "When Dr. Nette yelled, I accidentally lifted the beaters out of the mix. Peanut butter flew everywhere just like it did with the chocolate cupcake mix last Christmas."

Emerald laughed. It had taken hours to wipe that fiasco off the ceiling.

"This is going to sound silly," Megan said, "but I wondered when it happened if that's how you make a protective shield? By whipping good thoughts and magic around you so fast that they fling all about?"

Emerald held the door to the dining hall for Megan to go in first. Then she followed. "That's not silly at all, but really smart and somewhat true, though it is a little more complicated than that."

"Can you tell me?"

"First you must learn to draw on the power inside to protect yourself." Emerald explained to Megan how to search deep inside of herself until she felt she'd reached an awareness of her heart and spirit. Then to create a protective shield, she had to grasp the angel charm in her hand and spin around, building a shield layer by layer with the energy around her.

"Okay." Megan shut her eyes waited a second and then spun around and around.

After a minute, Megan came to a wobbling stop then looked about her. "Did it work?"

"I don't know. You canna see the protective shield. You can only feel it in your spirit and heart. There will be a special warmth all about you. Sort of like when you wrap yourself in your favorite comforter. Do you feel it?"

Megan scrunched her nose. "I don't feel anything different."

"Doona worry. I had to practice a step at a time before I could make a shield. Once you've learned how to do a shield then I'll teach you more. For now we better go clean up the kitchen. There's—"

"No better time than now. A chore delayed becomes bigger by the day," Megan interrupted, filling in the words Emerald had been about to say. Megan slipped her arm around her.

Shaking her head, Emerald stepped into the kitchen and felt peanut butter squish beneath her shoe. She lifted her foot to see the raisin-dotted goo.

"Oops," Megan said. "I forgot. Marissa dropped one of the trays when she heard Dr. Nette yell."

"It's all right, luv," Emerald said, a bit daunted. Peanut butter was literally everywhere. Yet in the scheme of things she wished that all of her problems were as simple as kitchen à la peanut butter. "I'll get the floor and you start wiping down the counters and cabinets."

Sam was in hell. Well, maybe not actually there yet, but he damn well was stuck between two hellish situations. The moment he'd gunned his truck's engine and flew from beneath Emerald's protective shield, he'd known he'd made a grave mistake. She was right. The assaulting malice in the atmosphere was ten times worse than it had been two days ago, and the burning cold of it was eating him alive.

The one thing that kept him from going back immediately was his hunger for Emerald. His craving for anything from sex to blood from her was too strong, and he had to stay away until he found a way to control his hunger. That wasn't likely to be soon, since night was approaching and everything vampire in him was at its strongest then—a terrifying thought considering the fang-throbbing state he was in now.

He turned onto the highway and headed toward Arcadia, thinking to put as much distance as he could not only between him and Emerald but also between him and the influence of the black cloud. Distance helped, but just minimally. He did reach a point of being able to think about something besides Emerald for fifteen minutes. Then the reality of the situation slammed into him. If the evil miasma over Twilight was as bad as he'd just felt it was, what the hell was happening to his town right now?

He whipped the car around and covered the distance to Twilight in record time. Coming to the edges of the valley, he thought he'd entered a war zone. A huge pile of burning rubber tires blocked the main road into the center of town. The sickening stench and smoke stung his eyes and made it almost impossible to breathe or see. From what little he could spot, debris littered the street, and the windows of the few buildings ahead were broken. Uncomfortable with abandoning the protection of his truck, he shoved into reverse, did a three-point turn, and flew back a few miles to an alternate route.

Though the back way in didn't have any destruction littering the ground, it still made his stomach crawl with dread. The houses were all boarded up, as if a category 5 hurricane was moments away and the dark cloud over Hades Mountain, while not that much bigger than it had been before, had thickened and turned crude-oil black.

Rather than driving his truck to the station's back entrance, Sam followed his screaming instincts and turned into a field about two blocks away, where he parked behind an abandoned barn. He suited up in a bulletproof vest and belted on the riot control gear. Then he checked his Glock and deliberated only a moment before slinging an M-16 over his shoulder.

One good thing he noticed was the more he focused on his sheriff shit, the more control he seemed to have over the vampire part of him. Years of regimental training seemed to bring his out-of-control ass into line. Either that, or he wasn't as far gone as he'd thought he was. Away from the overpowering temptation of Emerald and her blood, he could function somewhat, even though he could feel something in him give a welcoming response to the icy, malignant pulse from Hades Mountain. His fangs no longer throbbed, but they had grown, so much so that they now cut into his lower gum and cheek, giving him a constant, painful reminder of the beast he'd become.

As he neared the back of the station, he heard what sounded like a crowd shouting at a rally. The noise came from the direction of the main intersection of town, close to the high school. Keeping out of sight, he made his way to the trees outside the station and angled toward the road to see what had riled up the people in the town.

Numerous burning altars of rubber ringed the group, making it hard to see how many were on the ground. The stench was akin to that of a crisping Underling—so bad that even with his heightened senses, he could barely smell anything else. Spouting like a Hitler reborn, Mayor Stanton, a skinny, ineffectual man with a wire-brush goatee, stood atop a van parked in front of the Burger Queen Delight. Every man in the group gathered around him wore dredged-up camos and was armed with a mismash of weapons—rusted pitchforks and baseball bats included—and therefore more dangerous than an invading army. There were no women and children in sight.

"We the men are the minority," Mayor Stanton shouted. "And unless we take measures to assure our rule, we will spend the rest of our lives in powerless servitude, slaving away for others. Others who only exist to sponge off of our labors, and soak up our youth with their insistent demands."

The crowd shouted with outraged agreement.

"If we're the ones making the majority of the money then we should be king of our own castles. Women should never leave the home. They should spend their time solely upon our endeavors, our dreams. They should focus on readying themselves for us, waiting to serve our every need on bended knee as God intended for them . . ."

What the hell? Sam shook his head, wondering exactly what planet he'd landed on. He hoped this shit was just still talk and nobody was in serious trouble yet.

"This control of our lives and our destiny begins with ridding our town of strangers. To survive we must cut ourselves off from the world. And we must deal harshly with those who won't adhere to our view. Especially women who think to demean a man by trying to fill shoes God meant for man alone to use. We have one such woman tonight and I say we make an example of her. One that all women are going to remember."

Shit. Sam snapped to attention as Staff Sergeant Bond was pulled from the side door of the van.

"What the fuck is going on here?" Nick whispered as he slid into place next to Sam.

"Where in the hell did you come from?" Sam muttered.

"I tagged you on the road to Arcadia and hung back to see what's doing. Your mind must be a million miles away. You never saw me, even when you breezed right by me on your tail when you backtracked to the alternate route."

Sam only nodded. He'd been a million Emerald miles away. His obsession with her was going to cost all of them their lives. But he didn't have time to think about it right now. Bond was bound and gagged and fighting her captors every step of the way. It took three of them to bring her to the front of the group.

"Hell's what's happening here," Sam said. "And that shit over Hades Mountain is orchestrating it all. At least that's what I hope to God is going on."

"Who's the woman?"

"Staff Sergeant Bond."

Nick shook his head. "And you didn't let her lead you away in handcuffs? What's wrong with you? I'd let someone like that hijack me anytime."

"Leave it to you to think with your dick in a crisis. Haven't you realized yet that there are only two of us and dozens of them? We have to get her out of there and we have to find out where her sidekick is. They're Commander Kingston's stooges, and sending them back in a body bag will only mean more nails in my coffin."

"Her sidekick is up here," came a disembodied voice from above.

"Sergeant First Class Grayson. Nice to have you join the party," Sam said, spotting the man wedged on a solid branch of the sprawling oak tree above.

"I'm seconds away from dropping those bastards. What kind of shit town do you run here, Sheridan? It's like walking into a Stephen King novel gone bad."

"You've no idea," Sam said. "And be glad you don't. I suggest before we run out of time, that we pull back to the station and arm up on supplies. Guns are a last resort. I don't want anybody killed, so if a shot has to be fired, aim for a knee or a foot."

"There're no weapons left in the station," said Grayson. "I've already checked it out. No help there either. Empty as a ghost town. It was the first place I went when Bond was nabbed."

"The room with the black metal door down the hall?" Sam asked, just to be sure Grayson knew where to look.

"Busted open and cleaned out," Grayson said.

"What you carrying up there?"

"HK SOCOM .45," Grayson said. "Just so you know, once we get her out, I'm still hauling your ass to Kingston."

"You can try, but I wouldn't advise it," Sam said.

One of the revelers pulled out a thick rope with a nice noose looped at the end.

They were going to hang Bond.

Chapter Nineteen

THERE *was no Twilight. No forest. No moon. No sense of an-other's spirit anywhere. No real sense of his own, either. Writhing with a burning pain that ate at his soul, the wolf cried into the void, but no sound escaped. Bound so tightly he couldn't move, he fought to breathe, fought for freedom with all of his warrior's strength. But to no avail. He remained imprisoned and alone, sur-rounded by a cold blackness and pain.*

Was this then death?

Sirius knelt in the twilit edges between the spirit realm and the mortal ground, wrenched with pain and guilt. Dear Logos, what had he done?

Sirius had cursed what life Navarre had left. What use was a blind warrior? Surely Navarre would have preferred to have never awakened. The universe and everyone in it seemed to be spiraling to an inescapable demise. Especially him.

Rage at the evil converging upon Stefanie, Aragon, and he others as well as guilt over the ruination of Navarre's life tore at Sirius's spirit. He'd hoped Navarre might have recovered quickly upon the mortal ground and been able to stand against the damned. Instead Navarre was blind.

"By Logos!" Sirius cried out in anguish.

"I came to stop you," Sven said from behind him. "But I'm too late. Is Navarre, my brother . . . gone?"

Sirius rose to his full height, self-disgust and rage filling him. "No, but he might as well be. Navarre is blind," he informed Sven harshly. "And it is my fault."

"The news grieves me, but your fault, Sirius? I don't see how."

"I am responsible!" Sirius shouted, angry that Sven would take everything so lightly.

"Did you hit Navarre with a fire strike?" Sven demanded.

"No, but I led the band that—"

"Did you bring Navarre to the mortal realm when he was dying?"

"No, but—"

"Do you know the fullness of Logos's truth for all beings?"

"No, but—"

"Then you do not know enough to make Navarre's condition your fault."

Sirius couldn't accept Sven's logic any more than he could accept what was happening upon the mortal ground.

"It's more than just Navarre that worries you?" Sven asked softly.

"Yes," Sirius said, raging inside, aching to return to Stefanie's plea and stop the horror that was about to descend upon her and her friends.

"The energy you're expending with your frustration isn't helping those below."

Sirius whipped around. "Then what can be done to help them? What say the Council? Can we fight? Did they give us dispensation to break the rules set for us in the mortal realm?" he asked, finally getting to the heart of what he'd been afraid to face.

"They have decided to deliberate longer."

"Talk while mortals die and evil wins? They can't! How can the Council be so blind?" A lightning bolt charged by his frustrated rage shot out and streaked across the heavens.

Sven set a hand on Sirius's shoulder. "They want to be assured they are choosing the right course and not acting *rashly*. Your current state of mind would only validate their fears. A warrior's passion must be ruled by control or he is lost. The Council is also extremely wary of deviating again from Logos's set rules, since Logos censured them for ordering Aragon's execution."

Sirius pulled from Sven's touch and pointed toward the mortal ground. His lightning sliced through the sky and struck a rocky point near the Sacred Stones. "How can you be so calm? The humans need help now, not when the Council—"

He'd been about to say something scornful and barely bit the words back.

By Logos, when had he come to doubt the leaders he served? What right did he have to question their wisdom?

Logos and the spirit world were eternal. That knowledge had always brought calm to him, no matter how dire the battle. So where was his calm now? His control?

The answer to that lay wrapped up in the wounded yet beautiful spirit of the mortal woman with whom he'd forged a forbidden bond.

He couldn't be with her, but he couldn't turn his back on her either. He couldn't just let the sands of fate fall through his hand. Not when he had the power to act against the evil surrounding her.

If he was willing to pay the price.

He bowed his head, unable to look at Sven, for Sirius knew he would even sacrifice his allegiance to the Guardian Forces to fight the evil if he had to. "So this consuming conviction to fight the evil even if one breaks the rules to do so is what the Blood Hunters faced. What Aragon faced."

Sven's spirit touched his. "Yes. Know that we are one in this matter of helping the humans."

Sirius looked at Sven. "Then what can be done?"

"Have you forgotten? There is a higher power than the Guardian Council that I can seek when matters are grave."

"But Logos moves according to his own eternal time. And the mortals do not have that luxury."

"Logos is also moved by the heart. His judgment of Aragon renewed that truth for us. So I have hope he will see me immediately."

Sirius didn't want to wait. He turned away, wondering if Logos would strike him instantly dead for his rebellion.

"Looks like this party is going to get ugly," Sam said. Judging from the mob's rising excitement, his job just got ten times more difficult. "I'm going in to lay the law down on their asses. I think I can at least get close enough to Bond to knock her out of the way if any shooting starts."

"Disagree," Nick said. "Odds of getting her out unharmed are better if the two of us go in sporting our badges and that M-16. Grayson can play backup."

The man with the rope threw it over the traffic light pole and readied the noose.

"Time's up," said Sam. He shoved the M-16 at Nick, palmed two canisters of tear gas, and headed for the crowd. They didn't notice him until he was right on them.

"Mayor Stanton, you want to tell me what's going on here?" Sam shouted. Nick had closed in tight to Sam's side with the M-16 at the ready, making a bold statement to anyone who considered playing happy with their trigger.

"Mind your business, lawman," Stanton said.

Sam grit his teeth, his fangs cutting deep as his ire rose. "I'm doing just that, Stanton. Let the woman go and you all get back home or you're going to be my guests for a few days."

"You going to let him ruin our declaration of independence, men?" Mayor Stanton shouted. The crowd of men roared angrily.

"Wrong answer," Sam said. "Let's move," he added under his breath. While the crowd was still working themselves into action, he popped off the tear gas to both the right and left flanks of the rioting men. Any closer would put both him and Nick into the thick of the fumes with no masks.

He and Nick barreled their way past some stunned men toward Bond. She'd managed to keep the noose from her neck so far. Three men were still grappling to get hold of her.

He could tell the adrenaline rush pounding through him had kicked up his vampire side. Not only did he pick up on the different scents of their blood, but he also began categorizing them according to how appealing they were—something that had the real Sam part of him practically retching in revulsion.

The blood thing quickly morphed to a desire to just start shooting the sons of bitches for causing such a problem and trying to stand in his way. One man came at him, somebody he'd known for a good while, but his name wasn't important anymore. Instead of shoving him out of the way or sidestepping the bullheaded rush, Sam moved in with a nose-breaking blow. Then he turned and nailed another guy who was just standing there watching the fray.

"Shit," Nick said as they moved closer to Bond. "Ease up, before you set them off into using their hardware. These guys aren't playing as rough as they could be, considering we're two against thirty and they're armed."

"No," Sam said. "I'm not going to ease up. I've fucking had it with this shit. Get Bond out of here because I'm going to wipe the asphalt with their asses." Sam bared his fangs and went after the two men who had stepped in the way of reaching Bond. They saw his fangs, went white, and turned to run. Sam grabbed the back of their shirts, choking off their air as he brought them down from behind. The fact that they passed out before he could kill them or do any real damage just pissed him off even more.

"Holy shit," Nick said.

Sam didn't bother to look at Nick. Red had crept into Sam's vision and he had a thirst to spill blood. He turned on the three men holding Bond. They'd put a black plastic bag over her head. Sam screamed as he ran at them. They took one look at him, let go of Bond, and ran.

He went after them. One tripped on the curb, half a block ahead. The other two cut to the right.

Sam made a bone-crunching stomp on the fallen man's knee, then kicked him in the face. He didn't get up. Deciding to finish him off later, Sam went after the other two and caught up to them fast. They were trying to hide in the Laundromat. He began working them over as if there was no tomorrow, because . . . there wasn't. Ha-ha. The joke was on him.

All he could see was red. All he could feel was cold.

"Jesus, Sam. Stop." Nick's voice came at Sam, but he had no intention of stopping. These men needed a good washing. Who the hell were they, thinking they could hang a woman in his town? The damn washer was too small though, only the man's head and upper body were fitting. Maybe if he broke the bastard's back, he'd fit.

A cuff came down on his wrist, wrenching his arm back. Before he could bare his fangs and hammer the intruder, something slammed into his head, and everything went dark.

Cinatas stood in his snow-white suite where he'd been contemplating the victories of the day. The smoke and chaos in the valley below Hades Mountain was picture-perfect. He headed down to the dungeon with a spring in his step. Things were going marvelously well. He had four prized prisoners enjoying a taste of his damned hospitality. After checking them out, he'd inspect the magnificent sacrificial altar and coronation walkway the demons were building for tomorrow night's ceremony.

The malignant fever aggressively spreading through the citizens of Twilight was thanks to the demonic cloud roiling from the Falls. It had done its duty and then some. Slithering wisps of evil had polluted the community and paved the way into the hearts of the people for anything Cinatas wanted to seed.

Unfortunately, it galled him that he had to credit Nyros for the idea of the demonic cloud. That betraying, slippery bastard had yet to return from hell, where he was probably giving Heldon an earful about Cinatas's desecration and coronation plans as well as his possession of the pope's monstrance.

Cinatas closed his eyes a moment, wanting to hear a bevy of praise for his genius, but he heard only silence. All of this success and no one to share it with, he thought. All of his brilliance and no one to recognize it.

The Vladarians were, of course, fighting among themselves as usual. The Wellbourne and Valois factions were at each other's throats, while Samir and Herrera were secretly plotting to destroy one another.

Though Wellbourne had been making himself useful, it wasn't from any real adoration for Cinatas's greatness, but because Wellbourne wanted the angel. Angels . . . he can't forget there were two. One young enough to mold into anything he wanted.

Besides himself, the demons were the only ones interested in exacting revenge. They were pleasantly antsy for battle and would have gone out tonight. But the final act in his satanic drama hadn't come. Tomorrow at midnight, the crescendo would echo throughout the world of the damned.

He would not fail to get Erin. Not this time. His plans would work, and there'd be nothing Erin and the rest could do to escape him. The town would be cut off from the world by nightfall tomorrow. Telephone lines severed. Radio waves scrambled. Road blocks in place. And all of Twilight's citizens would march like sheep to a slaughter where Cinatas would kill them one by one until Erin and her gang surrendered.

The desecration would be his greatest feat, however. He had no doubt that he'd stumbled on the key to Heldon's powerful rule. And he'd been practicing.

In nomine Domini Dei nostri Cinatas Luciferi Excelsi. Ave Cinatas!

The Latin words of the Mass twisted to honor Cinatas had a really nice ring to them.

If he could break an angel's protective shield, then the

world of the damned would stand up and take notice and this pumped-up body would finally be imbued with real power.

A horrific scream from the dungeon made his mouth water and gave him an instant hard on. He hurried his steps.

Twilight's finest were below, enjoying the tender ministrations of his Red Demons. Crippling any law enforcement action or communication had been the order of the day, and the demons had done an excellent job. Three deputies and a woman, who he'd been assured "knew everything" about Twilight's sheriff and the department as well.

The demons had the prisoners chained to the wall. Two of the deputies were out cold, with blood running down their faces. A third was going wild against his chains, screaming obscenities at two demons fighting in front of a blond woman. She appeared to have fainted after giving such a delicious scream.

One Red Demon pushed another back farther from the woman. "I said leave her, Turk. Your duty is to stay alert and *watch* the prisoners. No one gets what they want from them until the master gets what he wants first."

Cinatas stepped fully into the room, pleased by the remark. "Who are you, demon?"

The demons jumped apart, startled.

"Bastion, master," said the demon.

"Bastion, you will now serve as my personal assistant."

"But Nyros—"

"Served my father. I choose you to serve me. Nyros may not live through his unauthorized leave."

Bastion's eyes widened as he replied, "Yes, master."

Cinatas nodded at the unconscious blonde. Firm, tanned breasts were practically exposed but for the ripped lace of her red bra. Though he wasn't necessarily attracted to her fake looks, her distress aroused him on a primal level, whetted his appetite. It had been a long time since he'd had a desire for any-thing more than the satisfaction he could give himself. "Have her prepared for my enjoyment and sent to my quarters."

It seemed he wouldn't be celebrating upcoming coronation alone.

Seething with frustration, Wellbourne stalked along the protective barrier. He could feel the angel bitch's presence. Even scent her heavenly blood on the wind. So bloody close and he couldn't touch her. He would, though. One way or another, he was going to outmaneuver Cinatas.

Wellbourne had no doubt Cinatas was going to screw him over. He could feel it in his gut. The condescending way the bastard had acted after Wellbourne had helped him get the monstrance made it clear. But the charade of being that maniac's patsy wasn't over yet. Dawn wasn't far away, which meant the desecration would be tonight.

What galled Wellbourne the most was that he hadn't dared give Cinatas the finger.

What if the psycho was right?

What if the real key to power in the realm of the damned was in desecrations?

Wellbourne didn't have a choice. He had to be on the inside track with Cinatas's Black Mass tonight. He wouldn't risk incurring Heldon's full wrath by actually doing the desecration, but he'd be there for the ride to see if Heldon either fried Cinatas's cocky ass or if Cinatas succeeded in breaking the angel bitch's shield.

If Wellbourne had kept going balls to the wall after her like he'd started out doing before Valois had butted in, Wellbourne might have had his hands on her by now. But who knew how long she could stay holed up behind her barrier?

One thing was certain. The second the barrier went down, Wellbourne's moronic backup team would get to the angels first. Maybe even get that nurse Cinatas wanted. Then Wellbourne would hold all the cards.

He paused before a patch of pink wildflowers and smiled, enjoying the fantasy of how that would play out. As he stared at the blossoms, he thought he caught a stronger scent of angel. Narrowing his gaze, he knelt down for a closer look. A good number of the plants were broken off at the stems. Somebody had been here picking flowers just recently. Somebody with an angel's scent.

His mouth watered and his blood surged. He could have his stooge in place before dawn, and just maybe the angel would come for more flowers.

"Tiptoeing in the tulips, Wellbourne. How droll," Valois said, appearing. He set the heel of his custom-made Bontoni on a flower and ground it into the dirt.

Wellbourne forced a smile. "What? No bodyguard, Valois? I would think that after the way Cinatas eliminated your lover, you'd be a bit paranoid about being next. Cinatas has no use for blue-blooded pansies."

"I brought Cuthbert along just so he'd have a fatal accident in our little war here. He made the mistake of bequeathing his estate to a very lovely woman with tasty charms. Soon my estate will be twenty times your net worth. The lower classes are so inept when it comes to amassing wealth. But then, when your mother was a barmaid, you can't expect much. In fact, I wonder what Cinatas would have to say about you sniffing around the angel's skirt without him? Planning something we all should know about?"

Wellbourne saw red ten times over. He was going to wear Valois's handmade Bontoni shoes home after he drank every drop of the bastard's Royal blood. Baring his fangs he went for the vampire's throat. He smashed into Valois, and they both flew into the protective shield. A lightning quick flash of heat enveloped them, then the vampire disappeared. Too caught up in his rage to think, Wellbourne followed Valois's track through the dark void of transporting to another place.

They ended up in the Olympus Room where Wellbourne crossed to the gold and diamond bottle at the wet bar and poured two glasses. It was Pathos's exclusive hundred-year-old cognac, made only from the Ugni Blanc grapes on the Dudognon's family estates in France. "Fighting between us is stupid, Valois. We need to join forces."

He handed Valois a glass. The vampire tossed back half of it in a single swallow, as if drinking million-dollar spirits was nothing.

"Join forces for what?" Valois asked.

"Power. If Cinatas's desecration is successful, we may need each other to defeat him. But a word of warning, mention my mother again and I'll be the one enjoying Cuthbert's widow on your grave. I saw you speaking to Nyros at length just before the demon disappeared. My guess is you sent him tattling to Heldon about Cinatas's little desecration plan, right?"

Valois's brows went up. "Maybe. As for a truce . . . we'll see."

Wellbourne only smiled and left the room. As soon as he could escape Cinatas's wrath, he'd get his men in place around the angel bitch's shield, especially near the flowers. His men would either get to the angels the second the shield went down before Cinatas could, or they'd get lucky and nab one during the day.

Chapter Twenty

SAM WOKE to a jackhammer working his head over like a UFC combatant on steroids. He must have one hell of a hangover, because he was practically numb with cold, and at the moment, he couldn't remember shit. He could smell though. The pine cleaner that always permeated the station house hung in the air, and the general aroma of all the mundane things that went with the job—stale coffee, sweat, gun oil, paper, Nick, blood.

Nick? Blood? Sam snatched his eyes open and groaned. He was in a jail cell at the station. It was dark, likely nighttime. A desktop lamp glared from the other room. "What the hell?"

"About time you surfaced," Nick said. "I was about to take you to the hospital, fangs and all. If I'd killed you, I would have never forgiven either of us."

Sam sat up. "What happened?"

Looking like twice-run-over roadkill, Nick scrubbed his head with his fingers, clearly agitated. He sat in the desk chair as if he'd been there quite awhile. "You don't know? You nearly killed several morons from town. I had to knock you out to stop you. One second you were Sam, coolheaded and leading the way to saving Staff Sergeant Bond from being hanged by a mob, and the next minute you'd turned into some kind of demonic berserker. You sent five men to the hospital. Doesn't look as if any of them are going to die, but that's purely by God's grace."

As Nick spoke, Sam's memory flooded back along with guilt and horror. The men who'd tried to hang Bond had deserved punishment, but that of the law he'd sworn to uphold, not from some unrighteous vigilante.

He wondered what it would take to blow the top of Hades

Mountain to kingdom come. Easing to his feet, Sam walked over to the locked jail door. For Nick to lock him up, Sam figured he must have been pretty damn scary. Still was, considering the amount of blood splattering Sam's clothes.

Sam expected Nick to meet him at the door with the key, but Nick didn't move, just sat there staring at him.

Sam rattled the door. "Let me out. We've got shit to do and I need to check on whether our weapon shipment has come in or not."

"No," Nick said.

Sam froze. "What do you mean no?"

"It's not dawn yet and your ass is staying there until the sun comes up. Then, at least, the chances of you losing it again are slightly lower."

"Are you shitting me? Listen, I'm fine, Nick. Look at me. It's me, Sam."

"Yeah. It's you all right, but it ain't you really and it's never going to be you again, is it?"

The stark pain in Nick's gaze slammed into Sam's gut. He nearly doubled over from the blow. Taking several steps back, Sam planted his ass back on the bunk.

"No," Sam said. "It's not."

Nick rested his elbows on his knees and hung his head down, as if trying not to pass out. "You know you saved my life back then. When you came back from Belize and hunted me up. I was so jacked up on booze and drugs it was just a matter of time before I landed in a grave. I'd been that way for years."

Sam started to brush off what Nick was saying until the word *years* hit him. "Years?"

"Yeah. My dad was a soldier first, Sam. He couldn't handle being off assignment and never stayed home for more than a month at a time once or twice a year. When you came back and found me messed up, that wasn't my first foray into the shit."

This was all news to Sam. "You were just fifteen. What in the hell are you saying?"

"That I'd been drinking since the age of ten. Along the way I added pot, some coke, 'ludes, and meth into the mix. I was pretty messed up. My dad didn't have a clue. He was too wrapped up in his guns."

"But your mom should have—"

"She drank, too. Don't remember her being sober all that much. She likely ran into the tree that killed her on purpose, though I don't think she meant to off herself. I think she was just trying to get my father to stay home longer. He couldn't leave if she was hurt, right? I heard them arguing that night. Things worked out okay for my dad though, don't you think? He handed me over to his mom and then went right back to work after my mother's funeral."

"Nick, I don't know what went down, but I know your father loved you and your mother. He never stopped talking about either of you."

"I don't doubt that. He'd die in a second for us. The problem was he couldn't *live* with us. Not for any length of time. He was addicted to adrenaline."

"Why haven't you told me any of this before?"

Nick shrugged. "You idolized my dad. He was your mentor. Your hero. As I got older, I also realized you were forcing yourself to live so he wouldn't have died in vain."

"Reed was a hero. He took on the world to save me. You see, Vasquez was the driving force behind the SINCO oil cartel, the only power forcing OPEC to keep the price of oil consumer friendly. What were a few men left in the hands of a torturing monster compared to the economic well-being of the whole country?"

"So my father found you by accident then?"

"No. Reed's honor wouldn't even let my ashes rest on foreign soil. He hunted through the jungle until he found the helo's crash site and realized something was seriously fishy about the whole setup. He started asking some hard questions of the locals and of the military. The locals told the tale of Vasquez's American prisoners. The military told Reed to forget it. He didn't. He went against orders, put an independent team together, and came after me and my men. By then . . . my men had died. Reed's team got me out, but Vasquez was hot on our trail. Everyone separated and planned to meet back up at the rendezvous. Reed and I made it to within a mile of the site, thought we were home free. Then Vasquez moved in. He mowed us down; machine-gunned us in the back. A bullet grazed my skull, knocking me unconscious. I don't know how long I was out. It could have been minutes or hours, but by the time I crawled over to Reed, he was dead—no pulse, no breathing, nothing. So the claims that Marissa made about a Sinclair drug lord in Belize's jungle can't be true. Somebody has to be using Reed's name."

"How did you make it out of there?"

Sam shrugged. "I crawled for a long while, slid down a cliff, landed in a river, and tried to swim until I passed out. A villager found me delirious but alive in the muddy banks. I sent him back after Reed, but he couldn't find the body. They did find the other men at the rendezvous point. The rest of the team searched for Reed's body but couldn't find it or the site where Vasquez ambushed us. By then my medical condition was too grave to delay returning. Kingston was waiting for us in the states and took us into custody. The long and short of it was I had to vow to keep my mouth shut about everything, stay out of Belize and away from Vasquez, or face a court-martial and spend the rest of my life in a military prison. In return, your father won a posthumous Medal of Honor instead of a dishonorable discharge." He paused. "I kept my word until I learned that Vasquez was a vampire. In my mind, that coupled with Stefanie being Vasquez's prisoner voided my vow to Kingston."

Nick whistled. "Do you think the government is aware of this whole vampire and demon stuff?"

Sam shrugged. "Before Belize, I would have said no. Now, I'd say I'd be surprised if they didn't know and a vault full of X-Files is buried under the White House's rhetoric."

"I'm glad Reed got you out. You became the dad he could never be."

"You don't know that. Saving me wasn't worth the price he paid. Hell, look at me now."

"I'm looking, and I'm not going to fucking take it sitting down," Nick said. "We're getting you back to Emerald and you're doing that Redeeming. Period."

"She told you."

"Yeah."

"Did she forget to mention the fact that she could die?"

"What? She mentioned some danger, but she mainly said she couldn't maintain the protective shield and do the ritual, too."

"I don't know the specifics, but if things during the Redeeming go wrong, it could kill her. I'm not willing to take that risk."

"Roger that. Then we find another way," Nick said. "We go to every corner of the earth, talk to every somebody and every nobody about stopping the vampirism or controlling it. Somewhere there's a way to save your ass and we're going to find it."

Nick sounded like Emerald had at some point along the line. Sam knew there was no miracle cure to be found in Tibet or in the shake of a shaman's fist. Nick didn't know squat about the paranormal, but his fierce purpose touched Sam's heart. He'd known Nick cared but hadn't realized just how deeply. "Okay. Once we knock out Cinatas and his gang, I'm all yours."

"We'll see how long we stick around. If this doesn't wrap up fast, I'm not waiting to find a cure. We can just take everybody with us and make Cinatas go hunting for a while."

"That might have worked before we wiped out Vasquez's camp, but then we didn't have a choice about that because he had Stefanie. You're forgetting Cinatas is trying to take the whole town of Twilight. We can't take everyone."

"Fuck the town, Sam. We'll evacuate. Everybody has somewhere to go. We'll leave Cinatas holding an empty shell until we get you fixed. Got me there?"

Sam sucked in a deep breath. Nick was serious as hell and made it all sound so simple. It was kind of hard not to catch a little bit of the hope in his eyes. Was that whole impractical scenario really possible?

Sam tilted his head. "By the way, what happened to Bond?"

"She was one pissed lady," Nick said. I got the plastic off her head and got her loose, but she clocked me before she realized I was her knight in shining armor." Nick pointed to a slight black eye. "I got her back though, before I dumped her on Grayson."

"You hit her?"

Nick recoiled. "No. I kissed her. As for where they are now, I don't know. I told them to get the hell out of Dodge. Then I had to go after you. And now here we are. You've got a bit before dawn so you might as well take your boots off for a spell. I'm going to get about two hours of shut-eye on the couch in your office."

"You can't just leave me in here, Nick. I'm cool now."

"Good, then," said Nick, getting up and walking away. "You can rest and so can I. Yell if you need anything."

Sam felt his ire begin to bubble and his fangs throbbed in rhythm to his head. He suddenly had the urge to—

He fell back on the bunk as the need for violence and blood sucked the heart and soul right out of him. God, what had he become?

He didn't want to sit here and wait for the dawn. That would leave him alone with his thoughts and Emerald. *You canna do this alone. It will only be worse if you leave here.*

Sucking his own blood had been minor compared to the shit he'd loosed on the town. What if Emerald was also right about him reaching the point that he'd come after her? The cold that shivered deep inside him had nothing to do with the evil stealing into his soul and everything to do with the woman of his heart.

"Sssacred Stones . . . Sacred Stones . . . mmmust, Sacred Ss-stones," Megan said, talking in her sleep, moving her head back and forth as if pained. She was all cuddled in her quilt, curled up against Emerald's side. Megan shivered and so did Emerald, but not from any chill in the predawn air.

Wellbourne was near. He'd been close for nearly an hour now, circling the shield, never touching it, never testing it, but just there—a predator waiting for the kill. Though she knew he couldn't get in, the familiar dread filled her. Of all the enemies she faced, she feared him the most.

Careful not to wake her daughter, Emerald smoothed Megan's brow and hummed the song of the angels, hoping to ease her daughter's troubled sleep.

Since Sam had left, everything had felt different, as if the very heart of her desire to battle evil had suffered a crippling blow. She felt empty and in some way, resigned. Sam would follow the same path as Eric, and the end would be inevitable.

She hadn't heard from Nick since he'd called to say he'd caught up to Sam and was tailing him into Twilight. She'd asked Nick to call her back and let her know how Sam was when he could.

Nick hadn't called, and that told her one thing—Sam was in bad shape.

Annette and Aragon would be back at sunrise with Navarre.

The CT scan showed minor brain swelling. In human terms such an injury wouldn't necessarily account for Navarre's blindness or continued loss of consciousness. But ruling out a severe traumatic brain injury in a human didn't address how minor swelling would affect a spirit warrior. Perhaps their bodies were so sensitive that Navarre's injury was catastrophic. Only time and medication would tell.

"Mr. Sam!" Megan screamed, a horrific cry of terror.

Emerald jumped. At that moment, evil slammed into the protective shield with such force that her body contracted in pain. The air flew from her lungs and her vision faded to stars. Just when she thought she'd lose consciousness, the attack on the shield and her pain ended. Wellbourne and whatever entity had amplified his power had disappeared.

"Mom?" Megan cried.

"Right here, Meggie." Emerald reached for her daughter. "Everything is fine. You just had a nightmare."

A solid knock sounded on the door. "Is everyone all right?" Jared asked.

"Yes," Emerald said. Giving Megan's shoulder a squeeze, she rose from the bed and opened the door.

Jared's reassuring bulk with a sleepy-eyed Erin at his side filled the doorway.

"What happened?"

"Nightmare for Meggie." Emerald lowered her voice. "Wellbourne's been circling the barrier for a while. He's gone now."

"You didn't wake me," Jared muttered.

"I would have if he'd made repeated attempts to break through the barrier, but he only hit it once just a second ago and then left. With the men all gone I didn't think you'd be going Rambo tonight."

"Going Rambo?" Jared cocked a questioning brow.

"She means foolishly going off to attack Wellbourne by yourself with no one to watch your back," Erin explained then looked at Emerald. "He wouldn't have. I would have made sure of that."

"I know who and what Rambo is," Jared said. "I'm just insulted that she thinks my skills are so lacking. I'm going to run a check around the perimeter and try and control my Rambo urges."

Megan, with her comforter wrapped around her, joined them, and Emerald pulled her close.

"Are you all right, luv?"

Megan nodded.

"You want to tell me about it? The nightmare?"

Megan wrapped her comforter tighter. The haunted look in her eyes hurt Emerald. "Can I have some hot chocolate? I'm cold."

"Hot chocolate it is," Emerald said, forcing a smile.

"I'm in," said Erin. "I've been craving the heavenly brew at least once a minute since you introduced me to it."

Stefanie and Marissa came stumbling out of the room across the hall. "What's wrong?" asked Stefanie.

"We're making a hot chocolate run," Erin said. "You two in?"

"Make it a double," said Stefanie. "Neither of us has been able to sleep."

"The wolf?" Megan asked, looking at Marissa.

"He is gone," Marissa said, her eyes welling with tears.

Emerald was surprised not only by the question but also by Marissa's response.

"Come on," Stefanie said, taking Marissa's hand. "Who needs wolves and dragons when we've got Emerald's chocolate?" They moved down the hall.

Megan, barefoot followed them. "Dragons?" she said looking at both the women. "What are you not sharing?"

"Wish we knew the real answer to that question, Meggie. Marissa and I did discover something in the closet of my room tonight, though."

"What?" Megan gasped.

"Feather pillows. A whole stash of them."

"Really?"

"I heard that," said Emerald.

"What's with the pillows, wolves, and dragons?" Erin asked frowning.

"I can tell you about the pillows, but the wolves and dragons I doona know anything about. We're going to have to do some investigating. I have a feeling there're a few secrets lurking in the shadows around here lately."

"Not good," Erin replied. "Secrets in the shadows are deadly. Last time I saw secrets in the shadows and went looking, I found four dead bodies and Cinatas. Sometimes I get this overwhelming feeling that I'm never going to escape him. Even with all of you here, Jared at my side, and the protective shield standing over me like a guardian angel, the dread won't go away. Especially now that I know I'm pregnant with Jared's baby."

Emerald caught Erin's arm in a squeeze, and they started walking toward the dining hall as they talked. "Believe it or not, I know that dread inside and out. I feel the same way about William Wellbourne. The Vladarian has been hunting me and Meggie for six years and almost caught us." She paused a moment, drew a breath, and then plunged ahead. "So you're certain that Meggie interpreted her vision right? You're pregnant?"

Erin blushed and smiled slightly. "I hope it's not just wishful thinking on my part. And Jared's, too. There's no physical proof yet. It just . . . well . . . it just feels right. Do you know what I mean?"

"I think I do. I knew in my heart I was pregnant with Meggie long before the doctor confirmed it." Before Emerald even realized what she was doing, she pressed her hand flat against her stomach, thinking about what consequences her passionate encounters with Sam might bring.

In short order, they had the chocolate into mugs. Jared

showed up for his share, declaring he could smell it from the other side of the camp. He and Erin got into another truffle tussle while Stefanie and Marissa, yawning repeatedly, excused themselves to try and sleep for another hour. Emerald carried the dirty pots and cups into the kitchen and Megan joined her.

Still wrapped in her quilt, she fiddled with some magnets that had been left on the refrigerator door. Emerald ran water into the chocolate pan. When she turned the water off, she could hear Megan's sigh all the way across the kitchen.

Emerald held her breath and waited, though in her gut she knew what was coming.

"Did you mean what you said about telling you everything?" Megan asked.

"Yes, I did, luv." Emerald braced for the blow but turned to give her daughter a reassuring look filled with love. "Doona be afraid to tell me, Meggie. No matter what it is."

Tears filled Megan's eyes and she ran across the kitchen and wrapped her arms around Emerald's waist. "Oh, Mom. There's a terrible, terrible storm. Wind. Cold. And a sea of demons. And blood. So much blood. And Mr. Sam is drinking the blood, Mom. He's looking at the demons, smiling and drinking the blood. And all of the horrible things that I saw yesterday about everyone come true. Erin, Risa . . . you."

Heart crushing beneath the burden, Emerald pulled her daughter tight. And for the first time Emerald wondered if the reason she hadn't been able to glimpse a vision of the future is because that future was too horrific for her to see.

"Meggie, listen to me. Visions can be warnings to help us know what to stop from happening. This is very important. Sometimes an angel has to hope when there is none. Sometimes an angel must walk where none will follow. And sometimes an angel must believe and act on nothing but faith alone. Believe, Meggie. Believe like an angel that you can take the darkness you see and turn it into light."

Chapter Twenty-one

MARISSA LOOKED up as Erin's hand brushed her shoulder. She'd been hovering around Navarre's room, ever since he, Annette, and Aragon had returned from the Imaging Center. It was hard, being near, wanting so badly to help him but being unable to do anything except pray.

"Call me or Dr. Annette if he wakens or even if he becomes restless, okay. I'll be across the hall, hunting down more information on the Internet."

"I will," Marissa said then drew a sharp, bolstering breath. "Would it be all right to . . . to hold his hand?" She couldn't believe she was being so forward. He was, after all, a stranger to whom she'd never been properly introduced. But with the absence of the wolf's spirit and her insane conviction that this man and the wolf were the same, she had to touch him. Deep in her heart, she hoped she could reconnect with his spirit by doing so.

"Yes," Erin said. "Touching patients who are unconscious, speaking to them, singing to them, is very important. I've heard it helps bring them back to consciousness because they know they are being cared for . . . and loved in some way. Call me if anything at all worries you, okay?" She gave her an encouraging smile, then left the room.

Alone with Navarre, Marissa studied the man who'd become a part of her life in such an abrupt and magical way.

He lay on his back, unmoving, yet still loomed so vibrant and large in the small room that he made her feel as if he were in a battle stance with his sword raised to strike a blow against the darkness she'd known all of her life.

His hair, black and thick, hung to his shoulders and gleamed in the sunlight streaming through the window. It reminded her of the wolf's sleek coat. His features weren't what she would call beautiful. His strong brow, hooked nose, and square jaw were too sharply angled and almost predatory for beauty. But they were majestic and . . . dangerous, she thought, finally settling on two words that fit him well.

The thick-chained, golden bronze amulet he wore hung in the center of a sculpted chest sprinkled with dark silky hair. She knew the feel of it, the warmth of him. She tingled from her head to her toes, remembering yesterday, her cheek and palms against the hot supple heat of his firm body. Drawing a deep breath, she squeezed her hands together to keep them still.

His chest rose and fell in slow, measured breaths and the beat of his heart showed as a pulsing light on a monitor next to the IV pole. She'd prayed so hard all night that he would return well.

"Navarre, can you hear me?" Her gaze returned to his face, hopeful. No answer came, or movement.

As she slid her palm against his, she noticed how long and thick his fingers were. His hands were twice the size of hers. Refusing to think about what she was doing, she slid her fingers up his arm, gently pressing against the corded muscles as she followed the sinewy contours to his shoulder. He was hot, as if fevered, and even though Erin had said a Blood Hunter's body temperature was higher than hers, she still felt a jolt of concern and worry.

She ventured to his corded neck and shoulders. When she touched the chain of the amulet, she was surprised to feel how unusually warm it was. She traced her finger down the chain to the large disk, which was even hotter.

The engraved star on the amulet had twelve points and three tiny jewels inset into the gold.

"How is he?"

Marissa quickly pulled her hand back and looked to find Stefanie and Megan in the doorway. "The same," she said softly.

Stefanie and Megan joined her at Navarre's side.

"He has an amulet," Stefanie said. "Like Jared, Aragon, and the fire—"

The sad emotion in her friend's voice brought Marissa's attention to Stefanie's face. There were tears in her eyes. Marissa reached for Stefanie's hand. "What is it?"

"Nothing." Stefanie shook her head then met her gaze. "He's the magic wolf man you spoke of last night, isn't he?"

"*Sí.*" When neither she nor Stefanie could sleep last night, they'd stayed up and told fairy-tale stories. Marissa had told one of a majestic wolf, king of his pack, who'd saved the life of a poor peasant girl. The girl vowed to love the wolf forever, and every night beneath the moonlight, she would run free with the wolf in the forest. But years later the girl became very sad because, though she loved the wolf, she was also very lonely. The wolf found her crying one night and after learning of the girl's sadness, he sent her from him to go find happiness with one of her kind. Then every night the wolf would cry out his pain to the moon. The girl tried to find another, but no man matched the majesty of the wolf and she cried every night as she listened to the cry of the wolf. Then one night there was a knock upon her door, and when she answered, she found a man with the eyes of her beloved wolf. A man who told the story of loving a woman so much that he gave up everything to become a man she could love. Stefanie had told the story of a fiery dragon warrior who lived in a spirit world and of a woman who lived in a world with darkness. The woman had been killed twice, but the dragon spirit kept saving her and told her to fight the darkness in her world just as he fought the darkness in the spirit world.

"He must be hurt very badly," said Megan.

Erin popped her head into the room. "I thought I heard voices," she said, smiling. "The test last night ruled out any serious head injury by our medical standards, but things for spirit beings may be different. Annette and I are still trying to understand how Navarre was injured according to Aragon's retelling of what happened. Apparently a Pyrathian's fire strike is like being hit by lightning and that's what hurt Navarre."

"*Dios*," Marissa said as she automatically reached out and placed her hand on Navarre's chest. Her heart ached from the pain she imagined he'd suffered and the blindness and weakness that imprisoned the warrior now."

"Fire strike?" Stefanie said. She grabbed hold of the bed railing, wavering on her feet as if she were stunned.

Erin shrugged. "That's what Aragon called it. There are different units of Shadowmen in the Guardian Forces. Blood Hunters are one, and it would seem Pyrathians are another. I'll have to ask Jared if there are more."

"Pyrathian," Stefanie said, her voice almost a whisper.

"I dreamed about lightning last night," said Megan.

Everyone turned to look at Megan, faces expectant for some great revelation of the future.

Megan shook her head. "It was a dream, a silly dream I'm sure, because angels don't have wings and fly and they did in my dream. The angels were taking stones from the Sacred Stones and putting them upon a dark-haired man who had died. One on his head, one in each hand and on each foot, and then on his chest around his heart. When they finished, lightning struck the stones and the man came back to life. But this time he had fangs and he killed the angels that had saved him by spilling and drinking their blood. There was so much blood."

Nobody said a word.

"Come on," Megan said. "It was just a nightmare and not as bad as some that I see on the television."

Erin exhaled loudly. "It might have just been a nightmare, Meggie. It's just that when Jared came here he'd been badly poisoned and was afraid he would do terrible things if he let himself live. He went to the Sacred Stones to die. He was struck by something like lightning and he did die, but then I gave him CPR and he lived but had no more of the evil poison in him. Your dream was the opposite of that though. I thought all power of the Sacred Stones was for the good and not to turn someone bad."

Suddenly the muscle in Navarre's shoulder tightened. Marissa looked at him to find he was thrashing his head back and forth. The monitor measuring his heartbeat raced, making her heart thunder.

Erin rushed over to him. "Navarre," she said firmly. "Can you hear me?"

She reached for a cloth, dipping it into the nearby basin. Wringing out the extra water, she set the cloth on his brow.

"Let me help," Marissa said, taking over for Erin. As she spoke softly in Spanish to Navarre, his head turned her way. He exhaled sharply and then became calm again.

"I think he's responding to your voice," Erin said. "That's a great sign."

Marissa's cheeks grew warm and her heart fluttered with hope.

Both Megan and Stefanie moved back toward the door to be out of the way.

"We'll go in case our talking disturbed him," Stefanie said. She stepped from the room, but Megan didn't immediately follow. She looked at Erin. "Do you think the nightmare was more than just my imagination?"

"Maybe. The Sacred Stones are very powerful. I know that much at least. One way to look at things is that they played a part in saving Jared, but then they also were part of the power that had killed him, too. So I could be wrong about the power always being good. If they brought someone evil back to life then that would be bad."

"I think I understand," Megan said then went after Stefanie.

Marissa wondered if the Sacred Stones would help Navarre.

It would be so easy to go over there and get nine of them. They weren't that far from the protective shield, just a little ways past the pink flowers she and Megan had picked for Stefanie the other day. Dampening the cloth again, Marissa bathed Navarre and thought more and more about Megan's dream. There was still time left in the day to go for a short walk.

"What in the hell is going on up there?" Sam asked, easing the rented U-Haul to a stop about a hundred yards back. A weird feeling had been eating at his gut all day and it mushroomed into dread as he saw the barricaded road up ahead. Half a dozen folks in white, helmeted space suits were blocking the way back into Twilight.

It had been one thing to leave the camp but remain close by and be able to help if things went to shit with Cinatas and the Vladarians. But it was another thing to be hours away from reaching Emerald and Megan and the others. His soul may be going to hell in a handbasket, but his heart was all tangled up in Emerald.

The call had come in for the weapons that Sam had put out an emergency signal for, but there'd been a hitch. He and Nick had to pick them up, and the long trip had been no picnic.

As Sam watched, one of the suits turned to do something to the barricade behind him. That's when he saw the Sno-Med emblem on the back of the spacesuit, four blue triangles, positioned north, south, east, and west, with their tops facing one another.

"Cinatas!" Sam exclaimed with a curse. "Wanna bet there're *D-e-m-o-n-s* in those *S-n-o-M-e-d* suits?"

"You're preaching to the choir. I'm curious as hell to know if they're stopping everyone from going into Twilight or if they're looking for us."

"I say we don't stop and ask." Sam put the big truck into gear. Though the bulk had been a bitch to maneuver through the mountain passes, he welcomed it now. "You ready?"

"More than ready," said Nick. "Let's haul ass and kick demon butt."

Sam floored the gas pedal. Gravity was on their side as well. They'd hit a downhill patch just after the last bend. Any official human setting up a haz-mat roadblock would have caution signs up and orange traffic cones a hundred yards back. There would also be more official-looking vehicles parked on the side than two black Humvees with dark tinted windows.

Ten yards out and going eighty miles an hour, Sam blew the truck's horn. Demons or not, the goons had plenty of time to get out of the way and they unfortunately did.

All of them dove for safety before Sam hit the red and white wood barricade, decimating it into toothpick-size pieces. He eased off the gas enough to make the next turn then pushed the pedal to the metal. The two black Humvees were hot on their exhaust.

They didn't have a choice but to head directly for the ranger camp and the protective shield. They needed the hardware and ammo in this truck and couldn't take the chance of it ending up anywhere else.

Sam braced himself to see Emerald, hoping to hell—nope, praying to God—that he had more control over himself than he had before. The day was almost over now, and he was going like a bat out of hell right back into the devil's pit that had almost claimed his soul last night.

Cinatas seethed. Something odd was going on with Well-bourne and Valois. Their two factions of supporting demons were barely restrained from killing each other, but it seemed to Cinatas that a thin veneer of civility had developed between the Vladerian leaders. Bastion's spies reported seeing them sharing a drink in this room earlier.

Cinatas wondered if the two were forming an alliance to overthrow him. It would bear some thought and swift action, but not tonight. Evening was approaching, and he was anxious to leave anarchy, death, and destruction in his wake as he paved a sure path to ruling it all.

"Bastion, is the message ready to be delivered?"

"Yes, Master. The deputy is already in the helicopter."

"Good. We go now."

"Master, the sun hasn't set as of yet. Another thirty minutes—"

"No. I can take the heat. Everyone else must suffer. I doubt the demons in their suits are comfortable as they block the roads and herd the townspeople into the high school. There is no time to waste. Once we return, you are to assure everything is perfect for tonight's ceremonies. First my coronation as emperor of the Unholy Empire and afterward the blood sacrifice to me. Erin will need to be prepared as soon as I arrive with her. Also make sure the chains on the altar and the walls surrounding it can withstand a Blood Hunter's strength. I plan to have a number of reluctant spectators with me. So we go now."

"Yes, Master."

"Where are you going?" Wellbourne asked, edging closer and lifting a drink to his lips.

"To give your angel and her friends a message," Cinatas said.

Wellbourne frowned. "So early?"

The Vladarian sounded odd. Did he have something to hide? Cinatas smiled. "I want some daylight to scope out the area and locate the buildings."

"I thought Wellbourne already did that for you," said Valois, joining the group.

"Oh, really?" Cinatas asked. No question about it, something was up between the warring vamps.

"Just a ground check earlier today," Wellbourne said, quickly. "Wanted to see how far the Sacred Stones were from the camp and if the angel bitch would have time to escape before we reached them. But an aerial view of the camp would be invaluable. Seen Nyros lately, Valois?"

"Nyros?" Valois replied, a model of innocence. "No."

"What about Nyros?" Cinatas demanded, looking between the two vampires. The glare Wellbourne fixed on Valois was more than satisfying. No doubt about it, they were up to something but damn well didn't want to be. So who was coercing them into it? How were they involved with Nyros and his unauthorized jaunt to Heldon? Was anyone else in on the conspiracy?

Cinatas looked about the room. Only two people had their attention focused his way. Samir and Herrera. The four of them had better not be plotting to ruin tonight's ceremonies.

"Wellbourne, you and Valois are coming with me," Cinatas decided.

"I'll meet you at the helo pad." Wellbourne tossed back the rest of his drink and set the empty glass on the polished table, but Cinatas noted his hand shook.

As they left the room, Cinatas saw that Samir and Herrera watched carefully. He leaned toward Bastion. "Order two of your most trusted to follow Samir and Herrera, then meet us at the helicopter. Hurry, I do not wish to be delayed."

"Yes, Master." Bastion split off from the group, running like an Olympic sprinter.

Cinatas wanted to kill all of the Vladarians. He and all the worlds would be better off without the scum, yet it galled him to no end that he *needed* them. Dependence was so un-godlike as to be insulting. He was more than anxious to see if tonight's desecration would empower him.

Marissa couldn't get Megan's words about the Sacred Stones out of her mind. If the stones had magic power to them, surely they could help Navarre. Even if they didn't, at least she would know in her heart that she'd tried. Erin and Annette were with

Navarre, administering a new medication. This would be her only opportunity to go to the Sacred Stones before night came.

After giving a quick glance about the area, Marissa hurried into the forest, taking the path that would lead her to the wild-flowers she'd picked with Megan. The Sacred Stones were supposed to be a short distance up the mountain from there.

She didn't want to be away from Navarre for too long so she quickened her pace almost to a run and suddenly felt as she did in her dreams with the wolf. Her long hair flew in the breeze that brushed her cheeks and a sense of freedom rushed through her.

Are you there, my wolf? Can you come fly with my spirit in the forest?

Maybe if she ran free as he had, his spirit would come to her. Running faster and faster, she reached the white wildflow-ers then left the protective shield and rushed through the pink flowers on her way to the Sacred Stones. To do things as Megan said, she would need nine stones.

"Why looky here!"

Something caught Marissa's hair and jerked her back off her feet. She hit the ground with a bone-jarring, brain-numbing thud.

A tattooed bald man with piercings in his eyebrows, nose, mouth, and ears leaned over her. "Another pretty little toy. Betcha the boss will give us this one to play with as a little ree-ward for sittin' here all day."

Marissa rolled away from him, but a kick to her thigh from the opposite direction kept her from getting to her feet. She looked up to see another man, hairy and scarier, holding Megan hostage with a beefy hand covering both her mouth and nose. Megan struggled, as if she couldn't breathe, and Marissa felt as if she would explode from the fear and worry that filled her.

"Megan?" Emerald called, peeking into her daughter's bed-room. When Emerald had passed by earlier, Megan had been nose deep in the Harry Potter book. Finding the room empty, she crossed over to Stefanie's room. She could hear Erin and Annette talking softly in the treatment room.

Before Emerald could knock on Stefanie's door the Black-Berry in her pocket vibrated. Digging it out, she saw she had missed a call from Barbara Cozie. The bloody thing never rang. Emerald connected to her voice mail.

"Listen," Barbara's voiced hissed in a frightened whisper. "Everyone is being forced from their homes by men in biosuits. They say we have to evacuate to the high school because there's been a toxic leak. The phones are down. Do you know what's going on? No one answers at the sheriff's station. I'm scared. Call—"

Barbara's voice ended abruptly and Emerald shivered with dread. She quickly dialed Barbara's number but got an *all circuits are busy* message. Whipping around, Emerald went to the treatment room. Megan wasn't there, hopefully she was with Stef and Marissa. "Nette, you've got to hear this message I just got."

"Hold on a sec." Annette punched a few more numbers on the IV machine then turned. "Is it from Nick and Sam?"

"No," Emerald said. "But it might mean they're going to run into some serious trouble on their way back. Listen." She punched the speakerphone and replayed Barbara's message.

"Toxic leak?" Annette said, eyes wide. "Let me find out what's happening." She pulled her phone from her pocket, blinked twice, and pointed it in two different directions. "It's telling me there's no service, which is a first for here."

"Let's try outside. I'll call you." Emerald got the busy recording again and Annette still registered no service.

Emerald tried calling Sam's number. Same message. Nick's, too. Just as she was about to dial a number outside of Twilight's area code a sharp pain squeezed her heart and she doubled over, dropping her phone.

"Em!" Annette grabbed her. "What's wrong?"

"Hurt. Canna breathe. Something's wrong. Where's Meggie?"

"I'm sure she's fine. Come on, let's get you inside."

"No. You doona understand. Meggie. Must find. Something's wrong with Meggie."

Annette opened the door. "Megan!"

Erin and Stefanie came running. "What's happened?"

Emerald gasped for air. Why couldn't she breathe? "We have to find Meggie. Did she say anything to either of you about going anywhere? She was just in her room reading."

"No. Risa isn't here either," Stefanie said.

Erin frowned. "Risa said she was going to lie down and rest for a while."

Stefanie shook her head. "She decided to take a walk. Maybe they went together."

"Flowers." Emerald gasped, feeling light-headed. "They picked flowers outside the protective shield the other day."

"Oh God," said Erin. "What if . . . Oh God. I didn't even think. The Sacred Stones. Megan had a nightmare about the Sacred Stones last night." Erin told Annette and Emerald Megan's story. The more Erin said the more Emerald's panic grew even as her heart broke. Erin described part of the Redeeming ritual that apparently had a horrifyingly gruesome ending. But she couldn't think about that right now.

"Megan!" Emerald called, clutching her chest as she ran toward the Sacred Stones.

Emerald felt another slashing sharp pain in her chest, then nothing.

"Megan!" she cried. "Dear God. Meggie, please be all right."

The man holding Megan went to kick Marissa again, this time in her ribs. She grabbed the man's boot and rolled away from him. The man holding Megan went off balance into a split, like he'd stepped on a banana peel. He screamed. Megan fell from his arms as the man tried to stop his fall, one hand going for the ground, the other for his groin.

Marissa gave the boot another hard jerk before getting to her feet. The man screamed louder.

The bald man roared. Head down, he came right at Marissa. She was up against a tree, hemmed in by branches. She couldn't see Megan, but she could hear the other man still moaning in agony. With no place to go but up or down, Marissa ducked into a ball at the last minute. The man plowed into the tree and she darted between his legs to get away.

At the sound of Megan's grunting, Marissa turned to see her hit her attacker in the head with a heavy blue sack. He fell to his side, groaning.

Marissa grabbed Megan's arm, pulling her in the direction of the protective shield as she picked up a dead branch for a club. "Go," she urged Megan as the bald man came after them with a roar.

Marissa turned to face him, her weapon raised.

The sound of a jarring electric guitar cut through the air. And the guy stopped to pull a phone out of his pocket. He pushed a button then cursed with words she'd never heard before. "Boss says to abort now. Cinatas is coming. We get seen here we're dead."

"What about the girl and the bitch—"

"Ain't nobody knowed we caught 'em, unless you tell. We haven't seen anybody all day, have we?"

Marissa couldn't believe her eyes or her ears. The men were hobbling off the other way. Part of her wanted to chase after them with the club and hit them a few more times for scaring her so badly and for hurting Megan, though Megan looked as if she'd recovered fast enough. Another part of her wanted to go and get at least one of the Sacred Stones to help Navarre. But she had to tell the others that Cinatas was coming.

Body shaking, Marissa hurried after Megan. She ran into Annette first and was relieved to see Megan in Emerald's arms up ahead. Nobody said anything until they'd all returned to the safety of the protective shield.

"Where are the bad men Meggie is talking about?" Annette asked, gasping for air.

"It is crazy," Marissa said. "They got a call that said Cinatas is coming and they had to leave or their boss would kill them if Cinatas saw them."

"Cinatas is coming here?"

"*Sí*, they say he comes now." Marissa blinked, shocked to see how swiftly and silently Jared and Aragon approached. If she hadn't been looking she wouldn't have known they'd arrived.

"I'll run ahead and tell Aragon and Jared." Annette turned and plowed into Aragon.

The man wrapped his arms around Annette and pulled her hard against his chest. Marissa could see the love and the worry gouged into his fierce features. "If you ever run into danger again and not wait the minute it would take to get me first I will . . . I will . . ."

"Forgive me again," Annette said.

"With Cinatas coming," Jared said, "until we see what he's up to, I'd like for all of you to wait inside."

"We're going right now," Emerald said, taking Megan's hand.

"Mom," Megan said. "I had to go to the Sacred Stones. You told me to believe. That an angel sometimes has to walk where none will follow and act on nothing but faith alone."

"Later, Meggie. I canna think right now." Suddenly Emerald stopped in the middle of the path and her body shuddered, as if chilled to the bone. "Sam's back," she said. She reached for Jared's arm. "It's bad," she said. "It's verra, verra bad." She hugged her daughter again. "Doona do *anything* without telling me first. Go with Risa while I go see Sam. And we will talk about the Sacred Stones and your dream later."

Marissa took Megan's hand and shivered, too. Emerald's eyes were windows on a world of agonizing pain.

"Get ready to bail," Sam told Nick. With the Humvees trying to muscle them off the road and Sam doing everything he could to keep the demons eating his exhaust, there wasn't going to be time to slow down and let Nick take the wheel before crossing through Emerald's protective shield. He'd seen the way she'd fried some of the demons with the shield and wondered if he'd gone so far over the edge that the shield would nail him, too.

He could feel the cold rage stirring inside him as he wrestled the Humvees for the road. Red crept into the outer fringes of his vision. It was just like last night all over again.

So though his intentions were good, he wondered if he'd still be alive in two point five seconds. They hit the protective barrier and hot fire flashed through him. He cried out in pain, fighting to keep the truck on the road as he slammed on the brakes.

An explosion behind them rocked the truck.

"I don't believe what I'm seeing," Nick said. He bailed out of the truck without explanation, but Sam had been screaming too loudly on the inside to see anything.

Shaking from pain as heat seared at the cold inside him, Sam got out of the car. One Humvee was engulfed with flames in the middle of the road, looking as if it had plowed into a brick wall, but there was no visible barrier there. The other Humvee had slid sideways in an apparent attempt to stop, went off the road, and plowed into a tree head on.

Not a demon was stirring.

Sam guessed he wasn't damned yet.

He turned back to the truck, but out of the corner of his eye he caught a movement about ten yards to the right of the road, behind a pile of brush that looked just a little too conveniently placed.

"We've got more company," he told Nick.

"More?" Nick asked.

Ignoring the burning Hummer, Sam walked along the edge of the protective barrier until he was aligned with the brush. "Might as well come out and go home, Grayson and Bond. I thought after last night, you'd have the intelligence to get the hell out of here."

Bond stood, rifle aimed at him. "Don't move," she told Sam. "Cover my ass, Grayson," Bond said and started running for the crashed Hummer.

Grayson cursed, surfacing with his rifle pointed Sam's way. "Move and I'll shoot."

Sam held his hands up but still yelled at Bond. "Stop! If any are left alive, they'll kill you."

Bond was almost at the car when the door barreled open and a Sno-Med–suited—demon came out.

"Shit," said Sam and ran to the back of the truck. Grayson threatened to shoot Sam twice as Sam flung the back open, tore off the canvas tarp covering the weapons, and snatched up a flamethrower.

Space suit advanced on Bond then pulled a spiked club from behind his back. It was attached to his wrist with a thick chain. Bond had had the sense to aim her rifle at the demon, but Sam knew it wouldn't do her any good. The demon threw the club about the time Nick plowed into Bond, knocking her off her feet. The club missed by a whisper as Nick and Bond went rolling.

The demon reeled in his club, heading after them.

Grayson fired on the demon, aiming for the bastard's legs, but he kept coming. Grayson pumped more lead into the demon's chest. Bullets ripped and the demon regenerated, unstoppable. But the sun was still out, barely. And where the bullets tore the suit, smoke rose from the demon. Not even that deterred him from going after Nick and Bond, though.

"Hey," Sam yelled at the demon as he ran forward. "I've got something for you."

The demon whirled his club overhead, gearing up to nail Nick, and Sam fired off the flamethrower. He covered the demon with fire then aimed at the Humvee, sure there was another demon inside. The suckers rarely traveled alone.

Screaming, the demon still tried to throw his club, but his arm fell off midswing as he disintegrated. The club and chain fell to the ground with the burning arm still attached.

Nick and Bond got to their feet, coming his way.

Sam motioned to Grayson. "You coming with me or waiting for more of them to show up?"

"What was it?" Grayson asked, holding his rifle up in surrender.

"You don't want to know," Sam said.

Bond passed through the protective shield but when Grayson reached it, he hit a wall.

"What the hell?" Grayson yelled.

Bond whipped around, looking apprehensive, then relaxed when she saw Grayson, behind her, unharmed, and standing alone. "What's wrong?"

"Come here," Grayson said.

Bond moved back to Grayson's side and Grayson did a double take, reaching out and touching the air space Bond had just walked through. Grayson came up against the invisible wall again.

"This isn't a time for jokes," Bond said with exasperation.

"Who's joking," Grayson said.

Bond moved forward with ease. Grayson hit the wall. About that time Sam heard two things that put his gut into a knot. The chop of a helo coming closer and the feel of Emerald rushing toward him, her heat scraping his insides raw.

"Drop the gun and see if you can pass through," Sam shouted at Grayson.

"Are you crazy?" Grayson said.

"No, but you are if you stay out there," Sam told him. "Here that helo? Odds are more of those bloodsuckers in suits are about to descend and you don't want to be caught by them."

Grayson cursed. "Why does Bond have hers then?"

"Simple. The shield knows she doesn't intend to kill me, whereas you do."

Grayson dropped the gun, and Sam pulled him through the barrier. The helo drew closer. Jared and Aragon rushed up. Emerald had to be right behind them

"Cinatas," Jared shouted, pointing up to the sky. Clearly their favorite doctor was paying them a house call. As Sam paused to study the weather, his heightened senses picked up on the dank smell of a brewing storm and the oppressive pressure bearing down on him. Tornado weather.

"Sam?" Emerald whispered.

Adjusting his gaze, he saw Emerald step from behind the former Blood Hunters. Everything else escaped his mind. He thought he could fake indifference. The scent of angel's blood and lavender overpowered everything around him. His fangs responded with an aching throb. He wanted her every way possible a man and vampire could want a woman who inflamed his every hunger.

"Em," he said, emotion strangling him. Nothing could stop him from opening his arms, and his heart came to a standstill when she didn't even hesitate to come to him.

She entered his embrace with her body shivering. He knew he was the reason for her trembling and it wasn't because love had her shaking. It was his darkness and cold she felt, just as her heat tore at him. After squeezing her tightly and brushing a kiss to the top of her silky head, he stepped back, releasing her.

"If that's Cinatas then we really shouldn't be standing here as an easy target."

Emerald grabbed his hand. "It's Cinatas and Wellbourne. There are others, too."

The helo flew over and Sam stepped in front of Emerald, trapping her between him and the truck to keep Cinatas and Wellbourne from even seeing her. He shielded his eyes from the setting sun's glare, and as he stared, something black separated itself from the helo way up high, dropping their way fast. What the hell? "It's a man," Sam yelled, his heart thundering. The sons of bitches had thrown someone out of the helo.

Instinct had Sam going for the canvas tarp by the truck. Nick had the same idea. They grabbed opposite ends and dragged it beneath the falling body. Catching on, Jared and Aragon latched onto the two other ends, pulling the tarp taut.

If Cinatas planned to bomb them with demons, the shield would keep them out. If the body was human, then Dear God, Sam prayed the trampoline plan would work.

The body hit the canvas hard, jerking the rough material from Sam's hands. It pulled from Nick's grip, too, but Aragon's and Jared's hold held. The body bounced into the air then plopped off the canvas onto the ground, landing faceup. Chains attached to the man's wrists and feet clanked.

It was Deputy Michaels, covered in blood, with a note literally pinned through the skin and muscle of his left breast.

Surrender to me, or the townspeople will die one at a
time beginning with Twilight's finest. You have until
one hour after sundown.

"He's dead," Sam said. The helo made two more passes, as if to gloat, then echoed away.

The rage was back, bubbling with icy resolve inside Sam like an arctic volcano about to explode. All he could see were shades of red. All he could feel were degrees of cold as Emerald's warmth was smothered. He fought for control, fought to shove the monster inside him back into a dark cave.

Emerald came closer to him and he clenched his fangs. He smelled her blood and his mouth watered in anticipation of her sweet taste. His incisors and groin ached.

He wanted to make love to her one more time. Drink from the well of her desire, show her how much he felt for her. But even if they had the time, he was too far gone to trust himself alone with her. He could barely restrain his appetite for her in a crowd of people.

Chapter Twenty-two

THE MOMENT Emerald laid a comforting hand on Sam's shoulder as he stared at the body of his friend, she knew she had lost him as surely as she had lost Eric. The cold hard knot in Sam's center burned her, but she didn't pull away. She couldn't.

"Michaels," Nick said, stumbling forward to the body and searching for a pulse, though death was obvious. "They manacled him, then beat him to—death." His voice choked with grief.

Sam pulled away from Emerald's touch. He bent down and unpinned the blood spattered note. Though his every movement was controlled and deliberately calm, Emerald could feel the suppressed rage oozing from him.

At some point between when he left the camp yesterday and now, Sam had crossed the line. The darkness had empowered him and he had latched onto it, drawing upon its cold strength. Eric had done the same, grabbed onto the power of the evil and made it his.

And now she felt as if Sam had closed himself off from her. She nearly cried out, wanting to rail at both heaven and fate.

"Fuck this," Nick said, standing, going face-to-face with Sam. "I'm going to town and I'm burning every one of those bastards' asses and you aren't stopping me."

"We'll both go," replied Sam.

"All four of us will go," said Jared, and Aragon grunted his agreement.

Emerald would be going, too, but she kept that to herself. What the men didn't know wouldn't hurt them. There might be part of Sam left, but a larger part of him was too far gone. Anything could send him plunging into Cinatas's hands. Though death seemed to be the inevitable outcome, if she was with Sam, she might be able to do something to help. Something that would prevent Megan's nightmare about the Redeeming ritual from coming true.

No, she knew what Megan had seen last night was a vision. Emerald had never mentioned or described a Redeeming ritual to Megan and there wasn't any other source from which Megan could have gotten a description of the ceremony.

"Someone want to tell us what the hell his going on around here?" Bond asked.

Nick turned to the woman. "Hell is what's going on. Those suited bozos were demons. The bastards in the helo are vampires. And that black cloud over Hades Mountain and Twilight has poisoned everyone's soul in the town. Possibly even yours and Grayson's, considering you two are gunning for Sam even after he saved your asses last night."

"Bullshit," Bond said, but it was clear from her troubled frown that Nick had hit a nerve.

"That is the unvarnished truth," Sam said, his fangs flashing. Bond brought her rifle forward, and she and Grayson took several startled steps backward. Thankfully Sam didn't advance on them as he vented. "You two barged into the middle of a battle with the corrupt Sno-Med Corporation. It's run by an insane doctor and owned by bloodthirsty vampires who use demons as their errand boys and feed on innocent mortals. They've taken my town hostage, murdered citizens, and are planning to pile up the bodies unless they get what they want, which is the lives of everyone here, including a child. And if you aren't careful, you'll end up damned and sporting some shiny white fangs like me."

"That's . . . it's . . . impossible," Grayson said, shaking his head. "I mean I know I saw those—"

"Demons. Red Demons. Spell Sno-Med backward. Then Cinatas. Talk to everyone here, and then you tell me what's not possible. Better yet, why don't you ask my dead deputy?"

Grayson stared at Nick and Sam a minute, shook his head then asked, "Who's helping with the fight? I mean, if what you're saying is true, then who knows about this? Surely the military or the government mu—"

"Must know?" Sam asked. "My thoughts exactly. Why don't you ask Commander Kingston next time you see him? He protected the vampire bastard who tortured me and my men for two years. It's possible the U.S. brass had a 'no touch' policy because they didn't want to upset Vasquez and SINCO, but I doubt if that's all of it. They have to know about the other shit, or be deaf, dumb, and blind. We're on our own against these suckers."

"SINCO? Vasquez?" Bond said, her frown deepening. "You're saying the head of the oil cartel was a vampire?"

"We're saying *every* SINCO cartel member is a vampire," Nick said.

"Which doesn't matter worth a crap right now. We have to figure out where Cinatas is holding the rest of my men and then keep him from getting his hands on Twilight's citizens," Sam said.

"Too late." Emerald pulled out her BlackBerry. "They've been evacuated to the high school." She played Barbara's message for them.

Everyone fell silent after Barbara's plea for help.

"Having everyone at the high school might play in our favor," Sam said at last.

"Yeah," said Nick. "We take out the demons holding them hostage and then we're halfway in control of the game."

"Not quite," Sam said. "Cinatas is ruthless enough to blow the whole building up with everyone in it. We need to move folks. The underground tornado shelter will work. We'll firm up the plan once we get a visual of the situation. I suggest everyone do what they have to do. We leave in thirty minutes."

Emerald turned to Sam, her emotions roiling. Thirty minutes. That's all they had. It wasn't enough. Forever wouldn't be enough. Before she could say a word, Sam spoke to Nick. "Let's put Michaels in the truck and take him to the camp."

She bit back everything she wanted to say. Now wasn't the time. There would be no time.

She left the men and took a solitary path back to the camp where she and Megan were going to have a heart-to-heart about obeying, no matter what. Emerald walked alone as she'd done most of her life, but now alone had an edge more painful than anything she'd ever had to bear.

Sam stood in his makeshift office doing a last-second review before meeting Jared, Aragon, and Nick in the dining hall. From there, they'd head to town ready for battle. He checked the silver-tipped bullets in his Glock. Packed with every incendiary he could carry, he'd likely explode from contact with a spark of static electricity.

The flamethrowers, grenades, and white phosphorus grenades they'd trucked in were designed to cause the maximum amount of burn damage. Once they secured the town's citizens they'd move in on the Falls for a crispy demon-fried Underling, flame-broiled Vladarian extravaganza. He was determined to twist fate into a sword sharp enough to slay the evil threatening Emerald and Megan and everyone else he cared about.

Giving the room a once-over, his gaze slid over the bed he and Emerald had shared. Blood still stained the sheets, and he walked over to snatch them off the mattress, planning to dump them in the trash. Instead, he brought them to his chest and drew in a deep breath of her lavender scent.

A bittersweet flood of need and regret washed over him. Images of loving her flashed through his mind, the tenderness and hope of her touch, the sultry seduction of her mouth, the drowning depths of her emerald gaze, and the sharpness of her wit. He wanted, needed her more than he needed life. And he couldn't have either.

He dropped the sheets in the trash and moved over to his desk, picking up a pen, but putting the turmoil of his heart into words wasn't working. He ended up writing one simple sentence, sealed the envelope. After writing her name on it, he placed the note on the desktop. Then, taking his silver cross from around his chafed neck, he set the cross on the envelope.

He wouldn't be needing the cross where he was going, and he wouldn't be coming back.

Half of him yearned like hell to see Emerald before he left. The other half prayed to God that he wouldn't see her. He wanted to hold her one last time, draw as much of her scent into his lungs as he could. He wanted to feel the essence of her spirit in his soul one more time. He wanted to look into her eyes and tell her he loved her. But then he feared she'd see the finality of his purpose in his eyes. That she'd know he wasn't coming back and she'd ask him again not to leave her, to fight, to go through the Redeeming ritual. And just like Reed had given his life to save Sam, Emerald would do the same. He couldn't let it happen.

The wind had picked up sharply in a short amount of time, and the feel of the approaching storm had grown heavy with menace. As the wind whipped and whirled, a howling moan echoed up from the valley, sounding like lost ghosts wailing for something dear that had been lost. Just as he secretly cried inside. He'd lost. Emerald had lost. But he was going to make damn sure the damned lost even more.

As he approached the dining hall, he could hear the voices of Erin, Jared, Annette, and Aragon inside, and his gut twisted. He was happy, that they'd found a way out of the darkness and continued to find love in each other's arms, but Sam was also filled with bitterness that he and Emerald had a different fate.

The warriors' tones were solemn. This was no hoo-rah bat-

tle to get pumped up over. They weren't going out on the of-
fense and striking a blow. They were the one and only line of
defense to protect everything they loved, a fact that drove the
fragility of their existence like a stake into their hearts and made
every moment as precious as life itself.

There'd been nothing but grim determination and a heavy
sense of do or die as they'd gone through the weapons. He and
Nick had wrapped Michaels in canvas and put him in the large
kitchen freezer. It was the best they could do to keep his body
from deteriorating in the heat. They had taken the shackles off
his wrists and legs.

Sam reached the dining hall door but didn't open it. He
needed to brace himself in case Emerald was inside.

As he stood there, he heard approaching footsteps and the
arguing voices of Bond and Grayson.

The unsolved matter of Commander Kingston's little escort
party was becoming a pain in his side. Sam needed assurance
that the military wouldn't stick their noses into things, for he
had no doubt they would invade, take over, and make labora-
tory rats out of Jared, Aragon, Emerald, and her daughter. Any
might the military could bring to the battle didn't make up for
the ill they'd perpetuate. Short of killing these two, Sam had to
get them on his side. Currently, they were arguing.

"I'm going and you're staying here," Grayson said angrily.

"Why? I'm a better shot than you are. Logic demands that I
go help or we both go."

"There's nothing logical about any of this shit, much less
you putting your life on the line when we don't even know
what monsters we're facing. Damn it, Bond. I can't let you do
it. I'm ordering you to stay."

"Then court-martial me. If I were a man you wouldn't be
doing this right now. Admit it."

"You're right. So tough. Facts are facts. Women can't be in
combat because a man will jeopardize himself, the mission, and

his team trying to protect the weaker sex. It's instinctual. You might as well cut out my heart and soul if you ask me to flush my need to protect."

"Buddies protect buddies all the time. Men jump on grenades to protect their team. They go to extreme measures to save a buddy and will often face death themselves just so they don't leave one of their own behind. To protect others is instinctual no matter if that person is male or female. I don't buy into the military's line on that one."

"That's different."

"How?"

"Because . . . shit, there isn't time for this. You're staying, Bond."

"I'm going."

"You're both coming," said Sam, interrupting their spat.

"No, she's not," Grayson said.

"Good," Bond said. "I'm ready to fight."

"I didn't say you would be armed," Sam replied. "See, I've got a little problem. You now know something that threatens people that I care about. Word of this getting out to anyone could be disastrous."

Grayson narrowed his eyes, and his body tensed as he widened his stance. "I would think any help in your fight would be welcomed. What are you hiding?"

"Let's just say I don't trust Commander Kingston. Sno-Med is huge. SINCO is huge. There are bad men in high places. With just us fighting, at least we know the battle is being fought and possibly won. The military steps in here and no one will know if they're aiding and abetting Cinatas and the vampires or not, because they'll remove everyone here to 'protective custody' and take over."

"Take over what?" Grayson asked.

"Do the math," replied Sam. "Their medical corporation has the world feeding from their hands. Their oil cartel has weakened OPEC and may be strong enough now to put a stranglehold on the world's energy supply. Their power and control is global. What do you think they want to take over?"

Bond gave a short laugh. "You sound like an 007 movie. It would be impossible for any one group to take over the world."

"Is it? Sam asked. "A week ago, I wouldn't have thought my whole town could be taken hostage. Yet they've done it. We're dealing with immortals here with unlimited resources and this is just the tip of the iceberg. You can't just shoot these creatures. Fire works on the demons, and silver through the heart can take out a vampire. But you tell me, how most of the sheep in the world are going to react when a monster gives them the choice of saying baa and being fed or being slaughtered? Sure, there'll be factions of rebels, but the general populace likes its comforts. So that leaves me with a very big problem." Sam bared his fangs. "Luckily my desire to drink blood hasn't taken control of me yet. But that could change . . ."

Grayson stepped forward, his jaw clenched and hands fisted. "Threatening us isn't going to—"

Bond elbowed Grayson in the side. "I'm reserving judgment on everything until I have a better idea of the situation, which means participating in what's going down tonight. If I see there's a remote chance that you're right, then you'll have not only my silence, but also my allegiance as well."

Grayson cursed. "Why don't you give us a few minutes to talk this over?"

Sam stared at them both a long moment. Did he have any other choice? He didn't have more time to waste on it, and maybe letting them see just how real this battle was would turn the tide in his favor. "Okay. But leave your weapons behind because they aren't going to do you any good. Nick will arm you with what you'll need—and just know that since I am already headed toward damnation at some future point, I won't hesitate to take you out if you betray us."

Leaving it up to them to follow him into the dining hall, Sam turned and entered. Surprisingly, Emerald wasn't there. Annette was with Aragon. Her brave face was so precariously pasted on that a single unshed tear would wipe it off.

Annette cupped Aragon's cheek, angling his face down to plant a kiss on the end of his chin. It was as high as she could reach. He grinned and caught her against him, leveling a hard kiss on her mouth.

She pulled back. "I've only a minute. Marissa is sitting with Navarre. But I had to see you."

"I would have come to you before we left and you know I will be back."

Annette nodded, seemingly swallowing the lump of emotion in her throat. "Yeah, I'm adjusting to that one. Sometimes . . . well sometimes—"

"You think it's all going to go away?" Aragon said.

Annette nodded.

"Come here." Aragon pulled Annette closer. "It's not going to happen. We know what to watch out for and we shall make sure that vision doesn't come true, yes?"

Annette kissed Aragon in answer and Sam's augmented hearing picked up Jared and Erin's conversation. She didn't look any calmer than Annette. She was wringing her hands and pacing the floor in front of Jared.

"I've been doing this for thousands of years, Erin. I don't understand this worry."

"You've told me enough about your life that I know battling up there and battling down here are two different things."

"You don't think me capable?" Jared asked, a mixture of outrage and odd amusement on his rough features.

"No. I'm just saying . . . oh . . . damn it. Be careful! Please!" She rushed to him and wrapped her arms around him and he pulled her close.

"I'll be more than careful. Have to show our son how to catch a woman as beautiful as his mother."

"And if it's a girl?"

"Then I'll have to teach her to wield a sword so she can fight off the men."

It was too painful, hearing their promises and plans. Sam shut them out and went to Nick. He stood alone at the other side of the room, staring out the window at the gathering storm that had now turned dusk into an early night.

"This is tornado weather," Nick said as Sam walked up.

"Not surprising. Everything is all twisted to hell and back anyway." After a moment, Sam explained the situation with Grayson and Bond, including what he feared the repercussions would be if the military or government caught wind of everything. "You need to be prepared to handle it."

"With Bond involved that won't necessarily be a hardship," Nick said. "And after hearing about those goons nearly stealing Meggie and Risa—"

"What?" Sam's question exploded in the room, and he lowered his voice. "What are you talking about?"

"You didn't hear Jared? Maybe you'd already left by then. It happened just before we got here. Meggie and Risa left the protective shield and two thugs got hold of them. Emerald thinks they were working for Wellbourne."

Sam felt the blood drain from his head and he braced his hand on the wall. "We need to set up some ultra-high-tech security around this whole mountain. I want you to call in my military IOUs until you get what you need, but being Reed's son, you won't even need them."

"Where are you going to be?"

"Have you taken a good look at me, bro?" Sam bared his fangs.

"I see the fangs, but you're still you, man. You're beating this rap. I'd feel it if you weren't you, if you know what I mean."

Sam thought about arguing with Nick but didn't see the point. Nobody could really understand his need to end things before the evil in him reached critical mass, not unless they were in his shoes and could feel the cold taking over. Sam's only solace in the situation would be taking Cinatas and Wellbourne down with him.

The door opened. Bond and Grayson entered with a gust of wind, and on their heels was Emerald. The desperation in her eyes jerked hard on his heart. God. How he wanted to soothe her fear and tell her everything was going to be all right and he'd be back to hold her by the sunrise, just like Jared and Aragon were telling Erin and Annette.

"Do me a favor and gear up Bond and Grayson while I talk to Emerald," Sam said. "We'll just have to keep a sharp eye on them. When you're done, we'll go."

"You got it," Nick said then lowered his voice to a whisper. "You know, if you were as bad off as you think you are, she wouldn't be so much in love with you."

"Yeah, she would. She's not only too stubborn, but her heart is too big and fearless for her own good." A fact that only made the emotions swirling inside him even more painful. She didn't deserve for things to go down as they would. Leaving Nick, Sam met Emerald halfway across the room.

"How's Megan?" Sam set his hands on her shoulders, feeling her heat immediately seep in. His fingers painfully tingled, as if the circulation had been suddenly restored. "Nick just told me what happened. God, if Wellbourne had gotten her I'd—you don't want to know what I would do."

Emerald leaned into his touch, seemingly drawing comfort from the contact. "Meggie's all right. I've just finished giving her the lecture of her life though, so she isn't happy with me right now. She's wrestling with what she's supposed to do—like stay within the protective shield—with what she thinks she must do as an angel to fight evil. No matter what it is, she has to come to me first. She's also really worried about you." Emerald brought her hands up to grip his arms and looked deeply into his eyes. "And I am too, Sam."

"Come with me," he said, taking Emerald's hand and leading her from the room. Once outside, he faced her. "Tell Meggie that none of it is going to happen. Nothing she saw about me hurting you is going to happen. I'm making sure of it."

Emerald shook her head, tears filling her eyes as she placed her palm against his cheek. "You're wrong. You canna lone wolf this one, Sam. It's going to take fighting together to survive this."

He wanted to pull away, vent his frustration with a number of choice words. Everything inside him was telling him that his gut decision to take out Cinatas and Wellbourne in a one-man suicide mission was the best thing for everyone. Her determination to save—but she hadn't said save this time, had she? She'd said survive. What had changed?

Suddenly, she narrowed her gaze at him. "What exactly does, 'making sure of it' mean?" She studied his face a second then grabbed his shirt. "You aren't fooking planning to come back to the camp, are you?"

Sam stared at Emerald for a long moment. How could a man want to kiss and throttle a woman at the same time? The raw pain in her eyes stole his breath. He met her gaze and brushed his thumb over her lips.

"You and I both know it's too late, Em. Stop pretending otherwise."

That she didn't argue with his assessment spoke volumes and put the final nail in his coffin.

This wasn't how he wanted things left between them. Sliding his hands up her neck, he cupped her chin and brushed his lips over hers before saying, "There's only one thing you have to keep in mind. Only one thing you need to concentrate on and remember. I love you, Em. No matter what happens tonight, or what goes down in heaven or hell, nothing is going to change that. I love you."

The tears spilled from her eyes. "Bloody hell. I love you, too."

She pressed her palm over his heart, and he felt her quiver. Was it from the emotion filling her or from what she was feeling in him? He didn't want to know.

"Em, oh damn, I—" Unable to speak through the thick knot clogging his throat, he caught her up in his arms, kissing her as he backed her to the cold wall of the dining hall. She wrapped her arms around his neck and gave him all she had to give, meeting his passion with a fire of her own. It was so fierce that he could feel the heat, but it didn't reach deep like it had before. His center stayed cold.

The door to the dining hall swung open and Sam reluctantly ended their kiss. She let him back from her embrace, but before he could speak to the others, she stopped him, pressing her fingers to his lips. "And there's one thing that you have to concentrate on. I am with you. No matter what."

He nodded and she left, taking what was left of him with her.

Chapter Twenty-three

DRIVING his truck while the others followed in the U-Haul, Sam ruthlessly shoved all thoughts of Emerald from his mind and focused on the maze of back roads that would take them from Spirit Wind Mountain to Lookout Ridge. There they'd have a perfect view of the town and what Cinatas was up to.

The strength of the approaching storm made the empty road and dark houses he passed even more eerie. It was as if everyone and everything had disappeared. Not even a dog barked.

Sam parked on a widened shoulder of the road and waited for Nick to pull the big truck over behind him. Then he led them on the fifty-yard hike through the scrub and foliage to the point. The wind stung his face and made his eyes water.

Their bird's-eye view showed hundreds of cars parked at the high school and demons in the white space suits standing around the perimeter of the building—two on each side that he could see. Light showed from the windows of the school and, surprisingly, at the station. The rest of the town was dark.

"Geez, all Cinatas had to do was send out a party invitation and everyone in Twilight walked right into his trap," Nick said.

"Can't help but think this is my fault," Sam replied. "When we discovered how corrupt the head honchos at Sno-Med were, we should have alerted everyone here."

Nick cursed. "Don't go chopping your head off for things you couldn't have changed. With no proof, what do you think you could have said to anybody that wouldn't have landed all of us in the loony bin? Not a damn thing."

Aragon stepped up to Sam's side and glared at Nick. "The only heads that need to come off are demon heads and the Vladarians. Not Sam's. No matter what he asked you to do."

Nick frowned. "I didn't mean—"

"Figure of speech," Sam told Aragon, then changed the subject. Nick didn't need to know that Sam had asked the warriors to kill him when the vampire infection took over.

"I wonder what's going down in the station," Sam said.

"Whatever it is, we'll have to hit both the school and the station at the same time," Nick said.

"It would be even better," Sam added, "If we could get one man into the high school before we hit it. That way we have a chance of stopping any demons who might be inside from trying to hurt the citizens should the outside demons set off an alarm."

Jared grunted. "As fast as I move with my were abilities, I can eliminate the demons on the inside at the same time they are being brought down on the outside."

"There are only eight demons on guard. Aragon and I can take the outside," said Nick. Pointing at the area below, he drew out a plan. "The school is a rectangle. By carrying two flamethrowers, each with a hundred sixty-foot target range, one of us can approach the northeast corner and the other the southwest. Aiming a flamethrower along each wall, we could try to fry all the demons at the same time."

"You're forgetting you've got help here," Grayson said.

"With us two you'd have four. We can each take a side," Bond added.

"No," said Sam. "I need one of you with me to take control of the sheriff's office at the same time they secure the outside of the school, and someone needs to stay hidden in the tree line at the back of the school to take out any arriving demons."

"Bond can watch our back," said Nick. "Then she can help check the rest of the buildings in the town."

"Wait a minute guys. Just because—"

Sam could hear Bond working back into her able-bodied argument. Whether fair or not he was with Grayson on this one. A woman in danger would always be a distraction to a man. If she had as good an eye as she claimed, then putting her as look-out was the best job.

"Grayson, you're with me, and Bond will back up Nick and Aragon," Sam said, ending the matter. "By the time you four are in position, I'll be ready at the sheriff's station. Once the high school is secured then you can lead them along the dark fence of the football field over to the elementary school and the tornado shelter underneath it. We might be able to keep them hidden from Cinatas and the demons until the sunrise."

"We'll meet you and Grayson in town before going after Cinatas," Nick told Sam.

"It's a plan, then." Easing back from the lookout's ledge, Sam led the way back to the truck.

It would take Nick, Aragon, and Jared at least twenty minutes to move the citizens to the tornado shelter. By that time, Sam would have left Grayson at the sheriff's station and be well on his way to taking out Wellbourne and Cinatas at the Falls.

"Are you crazy, Em? You can't do this!" Annette planted her backside against the driver's door of her BMW. "How can you risk leaving Meggie an orphan to go after Sam right now? At least give them time to make an initial attack on the demons holding the town."

Emerald shook her head. "You doona understand, luv. It will be too late then. I have to be there to stop Sam one way or another. If not, Meggie and I will be—" Emerald sucked in air, unable to put into words the deep fear inside of her. She lifted her hand to Annette's shoulder and squeezed. "Please understand. I have to do what I can to fight against the visions. I canna do any less."

"Then I'm coming with you," Annette said, shrugging off Emerald's hand as she stepped away from the car and opened the driver's door. "I've a score to settle, and frying a few demons will help even it out."

"You canna and you know it," Emerald told her, wanting to both smack and hug her friend. "You've a patient that needs you. I'm the one with the power to help Sam. Besides—" Emerald swallowed hard. "Besides, I need you here, Nette. I need to know that if I am completely wrong about this and I doona come back, you'll be here to take care of my Meggie."

Annette paused then looked up at the sky, blinking hard. "Shit. Damn it, Em. Is there really no other way?"

Emerald shook her head and Annette cried out as she pulled her into a hard hug. "You had better come back and bring Sam's stubborn ass with you. You should have told Jared and Aragon what you were planning."

Emerald gave a choked laugh against Annette's shoulder and stepped back. "And risk them going to Sam? If you haven't noticed, they're forming quite a me-Tarzan-you-Jane club when it comes to battle."

"Mom!"

Emerald turned to catch her daughter in her arms, surprised to find that Megan carried her pillowcase with something heavy weighing it down. Emerald bent to meet Megan at eye level, brushing her daughter's silken hair back from her damp forehead. "What is it?"

"I forgot to give you these when we . . . well, talked."

"You mean when I lectured and you argued," Emerald said softly. "I was only angry because I love you so much and I don't want anything bad to happen to you. It almost did today."

"I know."

"We'll talk more later about how you can be responsible to your angel side and still be safe, okay?

"Yeah. I'm sorry. But you need these," Megan said, reaching into the blue pillowcase. She pulled out a round stone about the size of an egg and held it out.

"From the Sacred Stones?" Emerald asked.

"Yes."

Emerald took the stone, feeling a deep heat emanating from it. She'd been to the Sacred Stones every day for months and they'd never felt this warm. But then she'd only come at dawn, after the chill of the night.

"They're from the ring around the center pillar of the Sacred Stones."

"You've more in the pillowcase?"

Megan nodded. "Nine. You'll need them all. And it's very important that you bring them all back."

Emerald took the gift. She didn't have the heart to tell Megan that inanimate objects could be imbued with magic or channel magic but weren't magical in themselves. As far as Emerald understood, any stone would work in a Redeeming because the power came from the heavens not the earth.

Forcing a brave smile, she hugged her daughter, then got into Annette's car. She dropped the bag of stones on the passenger's front floorboard.

"Be careful," Annette called out. Emerald promised then cranked the engine. Finding she still held one of the Sacred Stones, she stuffed it into her pocket as she drove away. As Megan and Annette disappeared from her review mirror, all of Emerald's resolve quivered like Jell-O.

Bracing herself for the evil she could already sense bearing down upon her, Emerald left the protective shield and drove without headlights toward Twilight and Sam. It wouldn't be hard to find him; she could sense him whenever he was near.

The roads were dark with no traffic, and as soon as she pulled onto the highway leaving Spirit Wind Mountain, the rain began to fall. Leaves and small branches ripped from the trees by the wind hit the windshield, forcing Emerald to turn on the wipers full blast just to see.

The ominous chill of malice in the air grew colder with every mile. Her body shivered and her heart raced with fear.

Would she have to kill the man she loved? She prayed not,

but so many things seemed to be racing to that inevitable end. Megan's visions. Sam's actions. Fate. The damned. Everybody seemed to be lending a hand to Sam's demise. And nothing seemed to hear the cry of her heart.

As she drew close to the town, she was so lost in thought that a flash of headlights on a bend in the road startled her. She had a sick feeling in her stomach, and without questioning it, Emerald whipped the car down the first dirt road to her right, braking to a sharp stop. She pulled the emergency brake to keep from rolling and killed the engine. Then popping the headrest of the set to its highest position, she lowered herself behind it, turning so she could get a look at the passing car.

The wall of icy cold that hit her as a white Hummer limo passed left her shaking from the pervasive chill. The Sacred Stone in her pocket became surprisingly warm in contrast, so much so that she pulled the stone out and wrapped her hands around it for a few minutes.

Whatever evil was in the limo wasn't on its way to the Falls. That was in the direction of town. Trouble was, they could be headed anywhere—Spirit Wind Mountain, Cinatas's Sno-Med Research Center in Arcadia, or even the municipal airport.

She hated thinking the possible destination could be the ranger camp, but she couldn't turn back now. The shield had held, and she had to get to Sam. Putting the stone back in her pocket, she restarted the car and made a three-point turn to get back to the highway. All too soon she found herself a block from the station and parked next to the trucks Sam and the others had driven to town.

After several bolstering breaths and a number of prayers, she opened the door and moved into the night where the pervasive chill of the damned and the whipping fury of the wind stole her breath. She shielded her eyes with her hand as she pushed against the wind to make her way closer to the station. The lights were on.

Staying deep in the shadows, Emerald eased ahead, even though her every instinct screamed for her to run away from the darkness bombarding her. Sam was here. So were a lot of demons. She knew it, but somehow with so much cold attacking her from so many directions, she couldn't tell which direction he was in.

A frozen hand landed on her shoulder, and she screamed as the cold knifed through her. It wasn't Sam. It couldn't be Sam. Dear God, it just couldn't be.

Hunger and rage burned in Sam's gut. From what he and Grayson had been able to figure out, the station house was going to be the demons' headquarters for executing the citizens. They had two people tied inside, a high school football coach and a waitress at the Burger Queen Delight. The demons had already been beating them. Sam could smell the blood and the fear, and his reaction to it sickened him.

He enjoyed both of the sensations.

The maleficent chill in him had mushroomed out of control. He was stone cold, like a block of ice, an indomitable glacier, capable of slaying anything in his path. Even the chill rain falling on his skin felt warm. His fangs ached until he had to gnash his teeth to ease the pain. Blood welled in his mouth, and he sucked on the salty, smooth flavor.

Nick, Jared, and Aragon had to make their move soon. Sam didn't know how much longer he was going to keep it together. He and Grayson were positioned to come in through the front just as soon as—

A small whirlwind, littered with damp leaves and debris, funneled from the back of the station to the front and flung the scent of lavender and angel in his face. His body instantly reacted, everywhere, as a hard-edged desire sliced through him. Son of a bitch, surely he was mistaken, but . . .

He took one step, then heard Emerald scream. The fear in

her cry reached deep into the cold. "Stay here," he told Grayson. "If we get captured, go to the high school and connect with Nick. Let him know that Emerald brought her ass to town."

Rain splattering his face, Sam ran, surprised at how quickly he could move as he pumped around the corner of the sheriff's station. Rounding the corner, he wiped his eyes clear of rain and his heart twisted hard as everything in him roared with animalistic fury. A demon had hold of Emerald, and two more were coming out the back door of the Station. She was his and all he could think of was annihilating anything in the way.

Aiming the flamethrower at the two demons coming out the door, he let it rock. A stream of yellow-orange flame mushroomed into a blast of fire that engulfed the demons and instantly set the back porch of the station on fire. Knowing the intense heat would keep other demons from exiting behind him, Sam turned to Emerald. The demon had his arm around her neck, angling her back and up so that she had to stand on her tiptoes to keep from being choked. She didn't even have her hands up trying to loosen the demon's hold on her throat but was digging into her pocket with one hand and shaking her tinkling bracelet near the demon's head. The demon was moaning as if in pain, but was doing his damnedest to choke Emerald before he succumbed to any weakness.

Sam let the flamethrower drop to the ground at his side and held both his hands up to the demon. He didn't need the weapon. He'd wipe out the demon with his bare hands and fangs. "Let her go and you can take me instead. She's not important. I am."

The demon laughed, sounding like a legion of men in hell, speaking all at the same time. "No. He wants the angels, both of them. Now that I have her, you're going to bring me the daughter or she will die."

Emerald shook her bracelet wildly and the demon screamed in pain, but wouldn't let go of Emerald. "No . . . canna . . . get Meggie."

"Who wants the angels?" Sam asked the demon.

"Wellbourne and now the Master. They both want the angels."

"But I will be the one who gets them," Sam told the demon and flashed his fangs at him. "The angels are mine."

The demon's eyes widened. "Who are—"

Whatever Emerald was digging for in her pocket, she clearly found, because she suddenly cried out in anger, pulled her hand from her pocket, and slammed that fist behind her, hitting the demon in the head.

The demon's scream of agony shocked Sam. The creature instantly released Emerald. Instead of escaping, Emerald swung around and hit the demon with her fist again. This time in the chest. The demon clutched his chest and went over backward. His body convulsed then went suddenly still.

Sam didn't know what in the hell Emerald had done, but he didn't have time to reflect on it. Grayson came running, yelling, "They've made the move at the school and demons are escaping out the front of the station." He didn't wait for an answer but rushed back to the front, flamethrower at the ready.

Sam grabbed his flamethrower and Emerald's arm, but the heat radiating from her burned him so badly, he had to let go. "Come on," he told her, motioning in the direction Grayson had gone.

"What the hell is that thing you hit the demon with?"

"A stone from the Sacred Stones," Emerald said, running beside him. "I'll explain later."

When they reached the front corner of the station, he cautioned her to wait behind him. Grayson was out at the street, dousing two demons with flames. But he was in trouble. One demon was coming at Grayson from the woods behind, looking to take the man out, and suddenly another one appeared from thin air on Grayson's side—too close to Grayson for Sam to take out with the flamethrower.

"Stay out of sight," Sam told Emerald. Running, he aimed the flamethrower to the right side of the demon who'd just appeared. The heat radiating from the flame was enough to cause the demon to scream and twist away, thus alerting Grayson. Grayson swung around and nailed the demon with his flamethrower. A beautiful sight. Sam switched the direction of his flame, setting the demon coming from the woods on fire as well as the trees behind.

The incendiary weapon was effective if not exact. Collateral damage was unavoidable in close quarters. He turned back to Emerald and let out a stream of curses as hot as the fire. She hadn't stayed put. She was walking with her hands up toward a demon who stood at the doorway to the station with a knife to the captive woman's throat. Emerald shook her bracelet and the demon whipped his head back and forth in pain.

The waitress, clothes torn and face bruised, appeared to have been driven past the point of terror. She stared at Emerald with no emotion showing. She didn't struggle nor was she breathing heavily as one would whose life was seconds from being ripped away. Sam slung the flamethrower behind him and held up his hands, wondering how in the hell he was going to get both women out of this situation.

"I'm the bloody angel the Master wants," Emerald said to the demon, moving to within feet of him. "Hear my angel bells?" She jangled her bracelet and the demon cried out. Then she spoke sweetly to the beast. "I'll come with you if you let her go."

"He wants both of us," Sam said, walking with his hands up, his gut churning. "I killed Vasquez and the Vladarians want my blood. I'll come, but you have to let the woman go."

The demon shot his gaze from Emerald to Sam then back. "I'll let her go. Go all the way to hel—"

Emerald threw something at the demon, hitting him in the middle of his forehead hard and stopping him from slitting the woman's throat. The demon fell back, his knife clattering to the concrete along with a stone Emerald had thrown. The woman just stood there as if in a trance.

Sam rushed up and pulled the woman out of the way. He pointed the flamethrower at the stunned-looking demon. "Get up," Sam demanded. He couldn't use the weapon this close with the women right behind him.

The demon smiled at him then disappeared.

Grayson ran up. "How in the hell can you fight shit that can do crap like that?"

"Pray," Sam told him. "Guard the women, I'm checking out the station."

He found the place on fire and empty of demons. The football coach struggled against his bonds. The scent of blood turned Sam inside out and made him want to die. He had to bring his sleeve up to his nose and breathe through the material of his shirt to tamp down the urges pulsing inside him.

He dug out a knife and cut through the man's bindings then helped him outside to the fresh air. "Let's move everyone over to the high school," Sam said. Grayson and the football coach helped the stunned waitress. Sam kept a sharp eye on Emerald. She had one hell of a penchant for trouble.

Her showing up put a large monkey wrench in his kamikaze plans to take out Cinatas and Wellbourne. They were halfway to the high school when it hit Sam in the gut. Claiming the town back from the demons, while not a piece of cake, wasn't proving as hard as Sam expected. Cinatas wasn't in town.

"Stay behind me and as close as you can get," he told Emerald, grimly. "If you see anything moving, you tell me and whatever the hell I tell you to do, do it without question. Got it?"

"Yeah. You bloody Tarzan me Jane, but that's okay."

It was more like a bloodsucking cannibal and a ripe, mouthwatering lamb, Sam thought, looking at Emerald's lushness and craving everything about her. He turned and shoved his sleeve in front of his nose and bit hard on the inside of his cheek with his fangs, trying to lessen her scent and suck on his own blood.

Chapter Twenty-four

WITH EACH STEP through the icy rain, tears fell silently in Emerald's heart, tears of pain and sadness at their fate, tears of anger. Sam was so cold that even walking next to him ripped at her like claws tearing her apart. She could feel him fighting the surging power of the darkness, but heartbreakingly, she could also feel him losing the battle. For as much good as he wanted to do, the evil kept tempting and twisting his urges, poisoning the rightness in him.

Why was she so caught up in believing Sam's infection was like Eric's? At every turn Sam acted differently than Eric had.

Because no matter what the path, the journey ended the in the same place.

And that was the inescapable doom. No matter how much she loved Sam. No matter how much Sam loved her. No matter how much she wanted to fight for him. No matter how much he might fight alone, the vampirism would grow until he became her mortal enemy, until he stood for all things of the damned. He couldn't stop it. He couldn't control it. And neither could she.

"Get down." Sam pulled her toward him and dove for the ditch alongside the road. Emerald hadn't even been paying attention to her surroundings. She'd almost reached the point where she didn't care, almost reached the point where all she wanted to do was pull Sam into her arms and just hold him until fate tore him away, even if it meant she would die, too.

"Grayson," Sam hissed.

"We're good," Grayson whispered from somewhere to their left.

Blinking rain from her eyes, Emerald huddled under Sam's protective arm, coming to the quick realization that if she didn't kick her own ass out of this pity party, somebody was going to do it for her. Half a dozen demons, all with clanking medieval weapons, piled from the back of a van parked on the side of the street, and she hadn't even been aware of their presence because she was feeling too fooking sorry for herself. They turned toward the high school, clearly intent on a fight. Another van pulled up and six more demons exited. They followed the others.

"Stay here," Sam said then leapt up to the road.

"Hey, bozos," Sam shouted at the demons. "Anybody ever tell you all that you're uglier than hell?"

All twelve of the demons turned on Sam and spread apart, apparently intending on surrounding him.

"It's D-day for demons," Sam said then laughed. It was a laugh of exhilarated excitement that bordered on hysterical, not at all like the calm, make-my-day Sam Emerald knew. He gave them a moment to advance closer to him, then he loosed the flamethrower.

On fire, the demons went screaming and roiling into the night.

Sam laughed hard and chased after them, dousing the demons with more fire. Emerald's gut sank and she covered her ears, refusing to watch any more. She understood the necessity to kill in this battle between good and evil. And she understood the demons didn't deserve to live in the first place, but Sam's almost hysterical pleasure was wrong.

Sam returned, smiling and pumped up, high on his power. "Come on," he said, motioning her and the others from the ditch. Emerald almost stayed where she was rather than watch more of Sam's deterioration.

Fook it, she thought, rushing up from the ditch and grabbing Sam's arm.

"Move closer to the high school," she told Grayson. "We'll catch up in just a second."

"What the hell?" Sam said, trying to pull away, almost belligerently angry. "We don't have time for—"

She sent a mental blast of heat and goodness at him, refusing to let go when he shuddered and tried to jerk his arm loose from her grip again. She sent another and yet another wave at him, refusing to let up, even though she knew that both her touch and her power were hurting him. Finally, Sam shook his head then looked at her with a sad question in his eyes. "Em? It's happening isn't it?"

"Yes." The tears in her heart filled her eyes and she wrapped her arms around him, pulling him as close to her as she could.

He wrapped his arms around her, too. "I'm sorry, Em."

"I know. We need to catch up to Grayson."

He didn't say any more but grasped her hand and led the way. They wove between cars, stealthily approaching.

As they neared the high school, they caught up to Grayson, the man and the woman next to him huddled quietly together.

"Anything?" Sam asked Grayson.

"Some heavy fire toward the back of the school when I first got here. But quiet since."

"Okay. You all stay here while I check it out."

"I'm coming with you," Emerald said. "Please." She didn't have to say it for him to realize she was afraid the darkness would take him over again. To her surprise, Sam agreed. Ducking low, they traveled alongside a hedge until they made it to within twenty yards of the front of the school.

"I smell Nick," Sam whispered. "To the left." Moving in the deep shadows, he skirted an outside courtyard area with benches then paused to give a low whistle before turning the corner of the school.

An answering whistle came and Nick appeared. The Bond woman was with him.

"Where are Jared and Aragon?"

"Jared's still inside. We're waiting on his go. I'm sure that quietly taking out the demons one by one isn't as easy as torching them. Aragon's covering the other side of the school. More demons keep showing up, so we haven't been able to help Jared yet."

"Em, that evil meter still working good? Can you sense where they are?"

"Lead the way," she told Sam once she got over the shock of him asking. Less than a minute later, he helped her slide in a side door to the school. The school was eerily quiet. Emerald didn't know if it seemed so because of the storm outside, or if she expected noise from the gathered townspeople. Were she to be evacuated under strange circumstance, she'd be demanding answers, loudly. So would Bethy's mother, Barbara. God, she prayed they were all right.

Shoving her worries to the back of her mind, Emerald focused on locating demons by the feel of their evil cold. She motioned Sam to follow her. Moving up the hallway, about three rooms down from the cafeteria, she pointed to a door on the right and dug the Sacred Stone from her pocket.

Silently, Sam eased the door open, but he didn't have to worry about being quiet. The three demons inside were too busy to notice or hear Sam. They had a blindfolded woman gagged and tied to a chair. One demon, who was also blindfolded, was apparently cutting the woman's clothes off while two others raucously directed him. Sam's justice with his jagged silver blade was swift.

Emerald untied the woman and removed the gag, but the woman just sat there as if in a stupor. Shock?

Helping the woman rise, Emerald led her to the door. There were several coats hung on hooks along a wall and Emerald snatched one up. The woman was still like a zombie as Emerald help to slip it over the woman's shredded blouse.

"You two step outside. I'll be just a minute more," Sam told Emerald. "Jared told me earlier that if I couldn't burn a demon, I had to cut its head from its body or it will regenerate."

Emerald led the woman into the hall and had just shut the door when the sound of pounding steps and cold assaulted her. She looked up to see a demon running right at them. She set her bracelet tinkling, which caused the demon to slow up and twist his head from the pain. Then she nailed him in the chest with the Sacred Stone. He went down like a ton of bricks.

When Emerald turned around, Sam was exiting the room and the woman had left them, going directly for the cafeteria. The woman didn't look around or yell for help. She just opened the door and went into the cafeteria, as if she'd only gone for a bathroom break.

"It's like she's in a trance and doesn't even know what happened to her," Emerald said.

"The waitress the demons had at the station was the same way," Sam said.

"I've heard they're adept mind controllers but haven't ever seen them in action."

"Is there no end to the damned's reach?" Sam said with disgust. "Can you sense any more of the bastards?"

Emerald nodded as she concentrated. Feeling her way, she led Sam down another wing and pointed to a room. Inside two demons were playing on computers. Sam eliminated them in a flash. Around the next corner, they found Jared. He gave a rundown on the areas, he'd already cleared.

"As best as I can gauge, this wing is the last of it. Once it's clear, we have to take out the three in suits with the citizens and move the people to the shelter. I have a feeling we need to get to the Falls as quickly as we can. Cinatas isn't here, but he feeds off watching his own work. Something else must be going down."

The rest of the wing was empty. Jared went to the other side of the cafeteria to enter through the west doors, and she and Sam lined up to enter the east doors. Spying through the glass-windowed doors, Emerald saw a demon stationed at each of the exit. Another stood at the front of the room with his arms crossed and legs wide, like a jail warden. All the citizens sat unnaturally quiet in the chairs.

Opening the east door, Sam grabbed the demon from behind and dragged him from the room. He took him out in seconds. Jared did the same on the opposite side, and then all three returned to the cafeteria.

Sam moved on the third demon, who decided the jig was up and disappeared. "Shit, he's gone for reinforcements." Sam ran to the front of the room. "Attention, everyone!" His voice cut through the quiet cafeteria like a knife. Everyone looked at him put showed little to no emotion in their expressions. Emerald saw Barbara and Bethy at the back of the room and headed in their direction.

Sam continued to speak to the crowd. "There is no time for questions. A tornado is coming and everyone must walk to the tornado shelter next door immediately. Exit through the west door and go single file along the football field fence. Go now."

For a moment nobody moved. Then the people closest to the west door began filing out and the others followed suit without saying a word. Emerald's stomach gave a sickening lurch. Was everyone under some sort of demonic spell?

She reached Barbara and Bethy. They managed to make it from their seats and stood at the line for the door. "Barbara? Bethy?"

Both of them looked up, but their expressions remained blank.

Emerald set her hand on Barbara's shoulder, searching with her angel powers into Barbara's spirit. It was as if her friend was buried in layers and layers of freezing cotton. "It's me, Em. We're here to help. Do you understand what I'm saying?"

Barbara only nodded and moved forward in the line. Bethy followed.

Moving to catch up with them, Emerald reached for Barbara's hand and immediately sent out heat and goodness from her spirit to Barbara. Barbara shuddered hard, blinked, then whipped her head up, suddenly alert.

"Em?" she cried. "What's happened?" She looked around. "How did I get here? Why are we at the high school?" She saw Bethy then and reached for her daughter. "Bethy? Are you okay, honey?"

Emerald set her hand on Bethy's head and sent the child the same energy that she'd sent to Barbara. Bethy reacted the same way, quickly coming out of the demon-induced trance to her usual bright-eyed cheerfulness.

"Mrs. Em! Where's Meggie?" She glanced about and started to frown then looked at her mother. "Mom? How did we get here with all of these people?"

More and more people were filing out the door like sheep on autopilot.

"It's a long story," Emerald told them. "What we need to worry about right now is getting to the tornado shelter as Sheriff Sam has ordered. It's tornado weather."

Barbara's expression turned to alarm. She looked over and saw Sam directing people out of the room. "Is there anything I can do to help?" she asked, taking up Bethy's hand.

"Just help the others get there," Emerald said. "We'll talk about everything later, okay? I'm going to see if others need me now."

Barbara nodded and moved forward in the line.

Emerald walked along the line touching people, imbuing the heat necessary to break the demon's spell. Every one of them instantly reacted, but she alone couldn't get to everyone. She needed help in order to project her power to more than just one person at the time.

The heat of the Sacred Stone in her pocket registered, and she pulled it out. Bolstering her strength, she closed her eyes and focused on forming a wave of spiritual heat. To her amazement the small stone amplified her energy, and as she moved toward the door, everyone she passed by began waking up.

Sam kept directing everyone to the shelter and caught up to her.

"You're doing it," he said. "You're bringing everyone back from zombie land. How?"

"They must be in a demon-induced trance. I'm using the same heat you feel from me, only the Sacred Stone is enabling me to project it to more than one person at a time. Sort of like the Sacred Stone site enabled me to put a protective barrier around the whole camp instead of just one person."

"Move on through the line to those outside, and I'll keep directing everyone to the shelter."

Emerald circled around the cafeteria then headed outside into the wind and rain. Aragon, Bond, and Nick were standing at the west doors with Jared. Grayson was there, too, and Emerald noticed the football coach helping the woman from the station toward the tornado shelter. She ran adjacent to the line of people, fighting the rain as she made her way to the first person. As people woke from their stupor, she pointed toward the funnel cloud hovering over the valley and directed people to the shelter. Most of them didn't even need to be told. They took one look and hurried ahead, but in an orderly way, helping the others around them. When she returned to the high school, she found the last of the townsfolk exiting the cafeteria and Sam in discussion with the others.

"Either Cinatas has left town and is running scared, which I seriously doubt. Or he is up to something more than tonight's takeover of the town. It was a whole lot of effort and show for him not to be here backing it up," Sam said.

Emerald groaned. "Maybe he did leave town. I meant to tell you, but there hasn't been even second to think. On my way into Twilight a white limo passed, heading east on SR44."

"Damn it, Em. Cinatas must be on his way to the camp! The town was just bait."

She shook her head. "But the shield—"

He grabbed her shoulders so hard that her breath caught with surprise. "Don't you understand? Nothing is foolproof. What if they've found a way to get past the protective shield?"

Emerald grasped Sam's shirt, needing to tie herself to him to keep from jerking away from the icy pain his touch brought. "God, Sam. They canna. I would feel it. I would know—"

A loud roar exploded through the valley, like a hundred freight trains converging. Whipping around, Emerald saw the black funnel cloud of a massive tornado hovering over Twilight.

In the heavens above the mortal ground where Sirius paced in seething frustration, Logos's Guardian Forces clashed in a brutal dance of war against Heldon's Fallen Army. The atmosphere above the mortal ground roiled beneath the battle, twisting and turning as the very foundations of the universe shook from the ferocity of the warring armies.

The iridescent blood of his comrades fell heavily, small drops that soon became a heavy shower, and Sirius knew that before the battle ended, a torrent of spirit blood would fall upon the mortal ground. It would bring life to all those in the mortal world; as with all things in Logos's creation, nothing ended without bringing life to another.

By Logos! Lightning flew from him as he clenched his fists. He knew in his mind that the mortal realm mirrored the spirit realm, but he couldn't accept that this would be Stephanie's fate. Turning, he was thrown back by a blast of energy from the spirit realm. Flinging his arm and wing in front to protect himself, he staggered to keep his balance.

"Tell me it isn't true!" York cried, radiating red-gold from his shimmering anger. York had barreled into the mortal realm with such fury that he appeared like a fireball from the heavens as he landed. "Navarre is blind in the mortal realm?"

"That is what Sven and I witnessed," Sirius said, lowering his wing.

"How then can he fight the descending doom?" His voice was raggedly harsh.

"Look," Sirius said, lightning scattering a wide arc as he flung out his hand. "How can any of them survive this? I'm not waiting for the Council's decision or for Logos's answer to Sven's direct plea, so you may wish to go back and not be associated with my defiant intervention."

York lifted his sword. "Back to back we'll eliminate every damned spirit we can find and face the consequences together."

Sirius shook his head. "This is my responsibility. Sven will—"

"Sven will join you," said Sven himself as he pressed through the spirit barrier.

"You spoke to Logos?" Sirius asked, amazed at Sven's swift return.

"In a way," Sven said. "I couldn't speak to Logos, but I did speak to Elohim."

"The Guardian of Hosts," Sirius whispered. As it was with Logos, speaking to Elohim directly was a great honor.

"I simply asked for dispensation to address the large surge of evil within the mortal realm as deemed necessary by the Pyrathian and Blood Hunter leaders."

"And he agreed?" York asked.

"Somewhat," said Sven. "The rules with mortals still apply, but should we encounter a large faction of the damned"— Sven grinned—"we have free rein to send them back to hell."

Sirius drew his weapon, but as he surveyed the situation before them he feared anything the Shadowmen could do would be too little too late. Arming themselves, Sven and York turned their backs his way and he put his back to theirs. Together, weapons out to slash and maim, they began to spin in a powerful circle, drawing upon the energy of the universe.

Faster and faster they swirled, their destructive force cutting through the ill spirits converging in the atmosphere, sucking on the evil forces.

Demons, mutated creatures, and legions of the undead would do everything possible to stop their demise. They'd throw obstacles from the mortal ground at the Shadowmen—houses, cars, anything and everything. They'd even throw innocent mortals at the Shadowmen. Sometimes, to their heavy sorrow, the warriors would fail to save the innocent, but they'd make sure every one of the cowardly damned paid for their crimes. None would escape the whirlwind of their wrath.

Electricity crackled all over Cinatas's body, burning in its intense heat as the supernatural power of the ancients who'd worshiped Logos within the Sacred Stones fought to thrust him from the circle of their holy ground. But he didn't shrink back, as the Vladarians with him had.

He walked to the center of the Sacred Circle, carrying with him the golden monstrance filled with hosts blessed by the pope. Perhaps the Blessed Sacrament he carried buffered him from the worst of it. Perhaps his defiance in conducting a Black Mass had empowered him, or he'd fed off the Vladarians' awe. For by the time he reached the center, they'd fallen to their knees, amazed.

When he'd first entered the circle of the Sacred Stones, he'd panicked and wanted to flee from the agonizing heat, but his desperation to save face in front of the others had kept him rooted to the spot. Then he'd realized, he'd been burned before and survived. He had known the agonizing lick of fire, the searing of his flesh, and had survived. He could do it again.

At the foot of the center pillar, he set down the monstrance. Taking a knife, he cut his palm, allowing his damned blood to

328 JENNIFER ST. GILES

fall upon the blessed host. It immediately ignited into a tower of flames that shot high into the air and sent sparks everywhere. In his mind he willed himself into power and Heldon into insignificance.

Raising his hands to the roiling heavens, Cinatas yelled, *"In nomine Domini Dei nostri Cinatas Luciferi Excelsi."* The ground vibrated beneath his feet, a slight tremor that shook the center pillar of the Sacred Stones. Pebbles fell from tiny cracks in the stones.

"Ave Cinatas!" Wellbourne, Valois, Rasputin, Yaroslav, Samir, and Herrera shouted back as Cinatas had instructed them.

With each verse of the Black Mass Cinatas uttered, the Vladarians replied, *"Sanctus, sanctus, sanctus Cinatas! Cinatas in excelsis!"* The quaking of the ground increased until the outer stone pillars of the Sacred Stones swayed off balance and crumbled. The center pillar alone remained standing. Feeling all-powerful, he slashed his other palm and pressed both of his bleeding hands to the center pillar, allowing his damned blood to drip down its sacred stone.

"Consummatum est," he yelled, and a hot wind exploded from the direction of the protective shield like a popped balloon. Then a lightning bolt shot down from the heavens and struck the stone pillar, creating a mushrooming circle of power that surged through Cinatas and hammered each of the Vladarians.

Chapter Twenty-five

EMERALD STOOD stunned even as her heart raced at the ferocious power of the tornado hovering over Twilight's valley. The top of the funnel cloud was huge and gray-blue in comparison to the black cloud over Hades Mountain.

The townspeople began to run to the shelter. Sam and Nick shouted directions, and Grayson and Bond helped people move along. With the roaring monster hovering over the valley, there was no need for stealth.

Before Emerald could react, or do anything to help, agony ripped through her and she gasped in stunned disbelief.

"Sam!" she cried, rushing toward him. "The shield! The shield . . . Dear God . . . it's gone."

Sam grabbed her shoulders, helping her stand as another wave of horror shook her to the core. The protective shield was down, invaded by evil, and part of Emerald wanted to crawl into a ball and die. How could she have been so wrong?

"We've got to get to Meggie. We've got to get to her!"

"Easy, Em," Sam said, holding her tighter. "Tell me what's happening."

"The protective shield is gone. I don't know how, but I felt Cinatas's presence, as if he'd invaded my body and the shield disappeared. We have to get to Meggie. We have to go back to the camp now."

Sam looked up at the tornado crushing down on the valley. "No, Em. We can't."

Marissa soothed Navarre's brow with the damp cloth, but nothing she did seemed to ease his agitation. He'd cut himself twice on the metal side rails as his muscles jerked in the throes of nightmares.

If only she'd gotten even one of the Sacred Stones.

Unfortunately, her quest would have to wait until morning.

The night was too dark and menacing for her to even think about leaving the camp. A fierce storm had descended just a short time ago. She didn't even want to leave Navarre's side.

The door to the treatment room was open, and she could hear Annette, Erin, Stefanie, and Megan talking. They were all working at keeping each other distracted as everyone's hearts and minds were with the men and Emerald.

"Danger!" Navarre suddenly yelled. Marissa jumped. Navarre's eyes were open, his golden gaze confused and unfocused. He fought at the bindings.

Marissa set her palm to his cheek. "Navarre. It is all right, we are here. Everything will be fine. You need to rest."

Annette came running into the room. "He's awake!"

"No," Navarre said loudly. "Must save you. Must save all." He fought the bindings and broke them in seconds. Sitting up, he pulled the IV from his hand. Blood spattered the sheets and the heart monitor shrilled as the wires were jerked from its casing.

Navarre wasn't waiting for anyone or anything. He leapt over the safety rails and grabbed Marissa's hand. When she looked at him, his eyes were shut, like someone in a trance.

"Come now," he said, pulling her hand.

Annette had a syringe and a vial in her hands. She looked up. "He's too big and powerful to try and stop. Keep him happy until I get this ready and let's pray he doesn't do anything to hurt himself."

Marissa let Navarre pull her from the room, wondering how he knew which way to go. "All must come now," Navarre said. It was amazing but he walked to Megan on the couch, grabbed her arm, and started pulling her out the door, too. Not roughly, but firmly.

"Let her go," Stefanie cried.

"Must escape. Must hide. Danger here."

Navarre released her hand to open the door. Megan cried out, frightened, and tried to pull away from him. As Marissa looked over her shoulder, she saw Annette with the syringe and Erin cautiously advancing on Navarre, clearly intending to drug him.

Suddenly Marissa felt and heard the spirit of the wolf. The creature howled, and she peered through the rain to see the black wolf at the edge of the forest directly ahead of them. It cried again, reaching into her soul.

"Wait," she cried. "Don't drug him!" But her warning came too late. Annette had already plunged the syringe into Navarre's arm.

Navarre pulled Annette in front of him and pushed her forward, gently. "Must go. Danger." Then he staggered slightly. Marissa reached to steady him.

Megan screamed. "I'm cold! Oh, God so cold." She shook so badly that she couldn't stand. Stefanie rushed up to help, but Navarre caught Megan in his arms.

Suddenly the earth shook. She and the others fell to the ground. But Navarre kept moving, struggling for balance.

Marissa was sure they'd just made a very big mistake.

The earthquake knocked Stefanie to the ground. She blinked at the stinging rain, struggling to her feet. In a quick glance she saw her sister and Erin rising as well. Navarre was still standing. He held a crying Megan in his arms and had pulled Marissa up, but he had thrust her behind him.

Stefanie turned to talk to Annette and came face-to-face with a nightmare from her past. Herrera's face. She choked on the malevolence filling the air and scrubbed at the rainwater in her eyes. Surely she was having a flashback to the jungle. But Herrera's horrifying presence loomed larger as he walked to her, his fangs flashing.

"Run, Stef, run," Annette yelled.

But Stefanie couldn't move. All she could do was scream as a torrent of fear paralyzed her arms and legs. Even her heart felt as if it had stopped beating.

"*Qué, querida?* You are not happy to see me? I have missed my *putica*. Had I known you were here with the almighty Cinatas, I would have come sooner." He grabbed her arm, twisting it behind her and pulling her sickeningly against him. "Where's Marissa?"

Staggering, Navarre groaned and fell to his knees, still holding Megan.

Marissa cried out, and Herrera turned to look. As if she were watching a nightmare in slow motion, three other vampires appeared and captured Annette, Erin, and Marissa.

"Ah, Herrera, look what I've got." The vampire held Marissa trapped in front of him. "My fiancée. And to think I've been scouring the jungle for my little jewel."

"You lie, Samir," Herrera shouted. "Vasquez promised her to me. Tell him, *mi novia.*"

"Let the mortal women go, now!" Navarre said, his voice slurred as he tried to stand.

"I'm sorry," Annette cried. "He was trying to warn us."

"Oh, God," said Erin. "Run, Navarre. Take Meggie and run."

Navarre struggled to his feet, took two steps toward the forest, but another vampire descended. He threw a knife, embedding it in Navarre's back. Navarre yelled in pain and twisted to protect Megan as he fell to the ground. The vampire jerked Megan away from Navarre, and Megan screamed as if she was in pure agony.

"My little angel at last," said the vampire.

"Nice little party we have here, but this rain is killing my mood." The demonic voice came from behind Herrera, and it sent a deathly chill all the way to Stefanie's soul. "Get them in the limos."

Megan screamed, fighting the vampire holding her.

The demonic voice spoke again. "If you can't even handle

the brat, Wellbourne, how do you expect to be vampire enough for the mother? No wonder she took out your brother."

Wellbourne snarled with rage. He shook Megan like a rag doll and flung her over his shoulder. Stefanie could see the child gasping for air.

The man with the demonic voice entered the circle, and Stefanie flinched at his hideously scarred face. He looked like some grotesque creature from the depths of hell itself. Navarre hadn't moved, and the vampire set his foot in the middle of Navarre's back. "My good fortune just gets better and better. A Blood Hunter to serve me." He snatched the knife from Navarre's back.

Marissa cried out, struggling to free herself.

"Cinatas!" Erin said. "Jared is going to kill you."

"Not before I kill you, dear sister," the demonic man said. "Let's get to the Falls before their heroes realize they've been had."

"Don't call me sister, you insane bastard," Erin spat. "Let the child go. She has nothing to do with this."

"*Au contraire.* Angels are in high demand, especially young and tender morsels. And as much as it disgusts me, you're only one of my half sisters. You see, Pathos was a brilliant sperm donor. We've thousands of siblings, but you were special. Royalty of sorts—and therefore you'll have a beheading fit for a queen."

Erin turned deathly pale. "No. You lie."

"Don't believe him," Annette said as she kicked and screamed, trying to stab the vampire holding her with the needle she still clutched in her hand.

Stefanie tried to wrench away from Herrera, but he wrapped his arm around her neck and squeezed until the world faded to black.

Every time Sam thought things couldn't get worse, they did. Tenfold.

"I doona care about the tornado. I have to reach Meggie or die trying," Emerald cried, trying to pull back from him.

He tightened his grip. "Screw the storm, Em. Nothing's going to stop me from getting Meggie. But we aren't going back to the camp, because that's exactly what they'll expect us to do. We're going to the Falls. We can either take it over or if they show up with Meggie and the rest, we'll ambush them."

"What if Cinatas keeps them at the camp?" Emerald asked.

"Cinatas is a creature of habit," Jared said, his voice ragged. "He will take his hostages back to his own ground where he is king, just as he did when he kidnapped us before and took us to Sno-Med's Research Center. We've no time to waste if we're going to have the advantage."

"Agreed," Sam said. "Let's move out. Grayson and Bond can stand guard at the shelter in case any demons show."

The area between the high school and the station was eerily demon free. Sam feared he knew exactly why the demons had seemingly disappeared. They were all gathering around Cinatas, now that the protective shield had been destroyed. His stomach clenched as doubt ate at him.

They spent a few minutes putting together an assault plan based on their aerial memory of the resort. The big-ass truck that he and Nick had hauled the weapons in would work, not only to carry everyone back in but for better cover as well. Everyone armed up—flamethrowers, silver knives, and grenades would be their main defense. Sam gave Emerald his pistol load with silver-tipped bullets just in case. It wouldn't help much against the demons, but she had the Sacred Stones for that dirty work. However, a silver bullet would stop a vampire in his tracks if she lodged it in the bloodsucker's heart.

Or in his, Sam thought.

Nick, Aragon, and Jared, sitting in the backseat of the truck, continued discussing possible assault plans, which left Sam a moment to speak to Emerald. After a moment's hesitation, he gave his better judgment one last shot before they headed for the Falls. "Em, considering what we'll face at Cinatas's resort, I wish you would stay here. The thought of Wellbourne sinking his fangs in you kills me. I promise to get Meggie out. You can trust me on that one."

Emerald shook her head. "My safety isn't the issue, Sam. Power's the most important thing to consider now. You canna deny the power I have or deny me the right to use it in saving my daughter."

Sam sighed. "That's what I figured. But knowing what you can do doesn't make it easier to accept you in danger."

Sam backed the truck up then hit the brakes at Emerald's cry.

"Wait. There're more stones in Annette's car. We need them."

"Hurry," Sam replied, surprised that he could feel as good about having a few stones on his side as he did ammo and guns.

"Stones?" Nick, Jared, and Aragon all asked incredulously.

"Yep. She's been popping off demons with one of them and then used it to break the trance the demons had over the town. Which beats me. I've been to the Sacred Stones more times than I can count and they've been nothing but rocks on a mountaintop. But then, they practically executed you, Jared."

"It wasn't the stones themselves," Jared said. "They only channeled the power from the spirit world. It was the purity of the ancients destroying the Tsara's poison in me that took my life, and Erin's love that saved me. For Emerald, the stones not only channel her power, but amplify it."

Emerald returned and Sam let the conversation drop. Keeping the truck on the road as he drove through the treacherous storm to the Falls proved to be a challenge. By the time they reached Cinatas's bastion of depravity, he could feel the pulsing cold sinking its poisoned teeth deeper and deeper into his soul with every mile.

Hades Mountain and the cloud weren't cowed by the tornado, but stood in malevolent defiance. Underlings milled about the edges of the cloud, but at least there were dozens rather than hundreds. Sam didn't know if the silver poison had eaten into their numbers or if more were waiting out of sight to devour intruders. Sam stopped the truck just shy of the Underlings' reach, and the men set up flamethrowers out of each window for maximum protection.

Seeing prey, the Underlings went into a wild frenzy, forming a wall of snarling beasts gnashing their fangs in hunger.

"Now we know why chariots of fire were necessary," Nick said. "It's the only way to keep crap like this from hitching a ride to glory."

Sam shook his head and signaled Emerald to take off. "Whatever you do, don't stop until you get to the top."

He'd been right to worry. As soon as Emerald drove beneath the cloud, the bombardment of evil was greater than ever before. His fangs swelled and his hunger coalesced to a point so sharp he felt his soul splitting apart.

Going into kill mode, he doused the wall of Underlings with fire as they plowed up the side of Hades Mountain. The beasts flew off screaming, then crashed like burning meteors. Nick, Jared, and Aragon kept the heat coming from their ends as well. Emerald drove the gauntlet to the Falls like a drag racer with the cops on his tail.

Things were strangely screech free by the time they reached the resort's massive circular drive. It was no longer the posh picture of decadence. Fire from the sticky bombs they had dropped had damaged most of the main building.

"Cinatas and Wellbourne aren't here," Emerald whispered. "Either they're not back yet or . . . they're not bringing Meggie and the others here."

"First we gain control, then we'll reassess," Sam told her, using all of his willpower to keep it together. He could do this. He had to do this. Save Megan. Kill Wellbourne and Cinatas and then he could free himself from the hell he'd become. "The psychological advantage of losing the town as hostages and losing their home base will put us in a position of power. And power is one thing a guy like Cinatas can understand." Sam parked the truck so that it was as hidden as possible from any approaching cars.

Emerald had the sack of Sacred Stones tied to the belt of her jeans. Sam, Nick, Aragon, and Jared were loaded with ammo. They left the truck, skirting the edges of the buildings and the woods as they entered the resort through a broken window in a fire-damaged section.

No guards were out front or in the burned section they invaded. Like shadows, they moved with quiet stealth, dropping low, fanning out and closing back in as they made their way through the damaged portion of the building. As they neared the end of that wing, Emerald motioned to them.

"Demons," she whispered, pointing to a door.

Sam, with Jared and Aragon, made the assault into the room. One demon rushed the sheriff, going for his throat. Sam dropped and rolled, knocking the demon off his feet. Then coming to a crouch, he readied his machete, and when the demon charged a second time, he relieved the beast of its head in a single swing of his blade. Jared and Aragon had taken out the other two demons.

"Jackpot," Sam said, looking around. It was a surveillance room with a wall of monitors that gave them live feed of every room as well as a computer-generated diagram of the entire resort—their road map to victory.

"This is why it was so easy getting in tonight." Sam pointed to a number of blacked-out monitors. Five of them were labeled for the front entrance. "The fire damage from our sticky bomb strike took out their security cameras."

Sam scanned across the views, shuddering. From the accessories visible in the "bedroom" suites, all manner of torture and decadence appeared to be available. Thank God they were empt—

Sam's fangs throbbed and a red haze edged into his vision. "Son of a bitch! They have Sandy, Myra, and Carlton chained in a dungeon."

Sam set his hand on Nick's shoulder. "We'll get them out of there."

Nick nodded, swallowing hard.

"Cinatas is definitely coming back here," Jared said.

"They are gathering for something outside," Aragon said, pointing to a monitor on the lower right.

Sam turned to see Jared and Aragon focused on a row of monitors revealing a single gold throne resting at the center of a white carpeted stage. Behind the throne was a white marble wall equipped with a line of black manacled chains placed for the neck, arms, and legs to hold prisoners spread-eagled. There was room for six victims along the wall. In front of the throne was a solid gold block about two feet wide and six feet long, taller at the back and lower in the front where a scoop was carved out. Just right for a person's neck. From the scoop a slide ran down into a gold, wide-mouthed urn. Black manacles lay ready for its victim. The design of the block and the jeweled double-headed ax lying on top left no doubt of its purpose. It was to behead and drain victims of their blood.

"Dear God," Emerald said as she walked up.

"Fuck," said Nick.

"Doubt Cinatas plans to use that for himself or the demons," Aragon said.

Sam agreed, though this time he wished he was dead wrong. That sacrificial altar was for humans, either Sam's employees in the basement or Erin, or Annette, or Stefani, or Marissa, or . . . Megan. Sam's stomach heaved, reassuring him that evil hadn't taken all of his soul yet.

As they watched, demons began appearing out of thin air. The manageable dozens quickly grew to hundreds and began chanting, "Hail, Cinatas the almighty! Hail, Cinatas the almighty!"

Dressed in black tie, a vampire walked on stage, motioning for quiet.

"The desecration of the Sacred Stones, a feat requiring unbelievable power, has been accomplished tonight by one being. A being who stood strong in the purest of flames and walked through fire. I ask you, legions of the damned, who can do such a thing? Heldon from his icy realm? No. I tell you of a greater power, a greater being—Cinatas!"

The crowd went wild again. After the momentum built, the vampire motioned for quiet before continuing. "From this day forth there is to be a new order in the world of the damned. You shall now have an emperor to worship. To commemorate his anointing he will offer a special sacrifice, a beheading. Everyone here will be given a taste of the sweetest Elan blood known. All here shall drink the blood of his sister, Erin Morgan. Afterward, he will introduce your future queen. What better partner for the king of the damned than a tiny angel?"

Chapter Twenty-six

EMERALD LOCKED her knees against the threatening dizziness and leaned into the steadying arm Sam wrapped around her. She knew evil. She'd faced it before, had battled it all of her life, but never had its true hideousness been more real to her than it was at this very moment. And she'd only *heard* what Cinatas had planned for tonight, not seen it.

A howl of rage roared from Jared and reverberated throughout the room. Emerald stepped closer to Sam. Jared was a formidable warrior, but the raw savagery pouring from him took on a whole different level. His iridescent blue eyes now glowed white-hot, so bright it was like looking into the sun.

Then he changed right before her eyes. She'd almost forgotten Jared wasn't completely human and hadn't realized exactly what he could become. He still held some were traits from his Blood Hunter spirit. Though he no longer became a wolflike man covered in a silver coat, he grew much larger and more deadly. His muscles bulged, ripping the seams of his shirt and the legs of his pants. His beard grew thick and black as did the hair on his chest. His hands enlarged, becoming clawed weapons that gave her little doubt he could tear anything apart, limb by limb. Breathing heavily and seething with hot rage like a pulsing laser beam, Jared turned and headed for the door without saying a word.

Aragon planted himself in front of Jared. "We go together, brother."

Jared growled and started to shove Aragon to the side, but Aragon grabbed Jared's fist and slammed it against his chest. "Cinatas has my heart, too. We fight together to win. Always have. Don't turn your back on me now."

Jared inhaled, and Emerald could feel him fighting for control, fighting the need to vent his rage against the damned unencumbered by the weakness of a mortal at his side, for Aragon was now mortal.

"Change of plans," Sam said into the seething silence. "Jared, you, Aragon, and Emerald are going to wait out front for Cinatas to arrive with the women and Meggie. Nick and I will hit the dungeon and free Sandy, Myra, and Carlton. Nick, you bring them to the front while I head for the amphitheater. As soon as you extract Meggie and the women and have the deputies and Myra ready to leave, set off a grenade. That will be my signal to make the demon bastards in the amphitheater eat fire. Once I rain hell here, I'll cut over to old man Hatterfield's place. Nick, you can pick me up from there when it's safe. Now let's move."

"I'm coming back and blowing this joint with you," Nick said.

"Nope," said Sam. "Getting seven women and two injured deputies off Hades Mountain is going to require everything the rest of you have. There's no telling what's going to come after you." Sam flashed his fangs. "I'm hoping my vampire status and guerrilla tactics will buy me enough time to burn this place to the ground. Anyone else with me will blow my cover. Now there's no more time for talk."

Sam pushed them, leaving no room for argument. Emerald stared at Sam's back. It was logical, but her heart was choking on the suspicion that Sam had no plans to escape. He expected to go down in the flames with the damned here at the Falls.

Before Sam split off, Emerald grabbed his arm. "Promise me," she whispered. "Promise you'll walk away from here, Sam. You may not be who you were before Vasquez bit you, but there's no way in hell you're at Cinatas's level. There's more to the Sacred Stones than I knew. They're powerful enough to make a Redeeming work, even at this late stage."

"I promise I'll never come close to being what Cinatas is," he said.

"That's not what I bloody asked you to promise me," she said, her heart sinking at the hard resolve in his blue gaze.

He finally gave in, pain cutting across the cold in his eyes. "Em . . . I . . . shit. I don't know anymore. If you could feel what was happening inside of me, you wouldn't be asking me to come back. All I can promise is that I'll try and keep my options open. You focus on saving Meggie right now, okay?"

Biting back a cry, Emerald nodded, and Sam left with Nick. She followed Jared and Aragon back to the front of the resort where the warriors mapped out their attack.

Emerald eased into her hiding place. The turbulent wind and rain were no match for the storm of fear, hurt, and anger whirling inside her. In her mind, she kept playing out Megan's nightmare of the Redeeming ritual and its bloodbath ending. How could she ensure that it wouldn't happen? She had to find a way. Love wouldn't let her give up on Sam, and she could tell Sam wasn't giving up his fight against the darkness.

Ten long minutes later a limo rolled into sight. Evil pulsed so strongly from the car that her head throbbed with stabbing pain. She braced herself.

The limo came to a stop at the entrance, but before a door opened, vampires and demons began to appear out of thin air, all crowding around the limo. Emerald wanted to scream. She, Jared, Aragon, and Nick were now more than grossly outnumbered. They were facing impossible odds. The demons chanted, "Hail Cinatas the almighty! Hail Cinatas the almighty!"

The vampires motioned for silence then moved forward, opening the car doors. The first thing Emerald heard was Megan yelling, but she wasn't crying out, mindless with horror. "The Dark Angel is coming," she cried. "The Dark Angel is coming!"

"Shut her up!" The demonic yell of rage directed at her daughter nearly had Emerald rushing from her hiding place.

She probably would have if Aragon hadn't clamped a hand on her shoulder.

"Easy," he whispered. "We can't attack now. We must wait."

Wellbourne laughed as he emerged from the limo, dragging a struggling Megan with him.

A man whose face was hideously scarred came flying out of the car and grabbed Wellbourne by the throat, sending sparks of static electricity flying everywhere. "Laugh again and you die."

"Forgive me, almighty Cinatas," Wellbourne said in a strangled voice.

Megan watched wide-eyed at the exchange and thankfully kept her mouth shut. At a closer look Emerald could see Megan was terribly pale and shivering to the point that her lips were blue.

Cinatas released Wellbourne's throat, then brushed his hands off, as if he'd dirtied them. He grabbed Megan's face, and she screamed in pain. "Gag this monster for the ceremony and chain all the women in the theater to watch Erin's beheading. I'm sure they'll appreciate a little taste of what's in store for them if I don't get what I want."

"Not the Vasquez woman. She is mine," said a vampire exiting the limo. "Besides, Samir doesn't have the brains or the guts to head SINCO. I do."

Another vampire exited. "Marissa is mine, Herrera. I have the contracts to prove Vasquez gave her to me."

"You lie, Samir," the vampire called Herrera said.

Cinatas whirled around. "I will decide who gets who if and when I think it's time. This is my triumph, and anything or anyone that diminishes it will die. Do you understand, Herrera?"

Herrera only nodded, his demeanor nowhere near as subservient as Wellbourne's.

Cinatas turned to the vampires and demons who'd lined up

to greet him. "Legions of the damned, I come to you with power and greatness!"

"Hail, almighty Cinatas!"

"Tonight my rule begins with a celebration of blood. The first of many sacrifices to me for the enjoyment of all."

The demons cheered.

At the sound of a struggle, Emerald directed her gaze back to the limo. Demons pulled out Erin, Annette, and Stefanie bound and gagged. Four demons each carried the women over their heads, and the crowd cheered again.

Suddenly, chaos broke out. Herrera jumped into the driver's seat, revved the engine, and shot the car forward, nearly hitting the demons carrying the women as the limo veered sharply to the right.

Marissa must still be in the car.

The other vampire who claimed ownership of Marissa ran after the limo. "I'm going to kill you, Herrera," he shouted. Then he disappeared into thin air.

The crowd went crazy, some cheering for Herrera, some for Samir. Chaos looked imminent and nobody was focused on Cinatas. Emerald watched Wellbourne, who still held Megan captive. His gazed darted in every direction, giving Emerald the distinct impression that he was considering running off with Megan like Herrera had taken Marissa. Megan shuddered hard and appeared to faint.

Emerald moved, ready to attack all of hell to get to her daughter. Aragon's heavy hand locked onto her shoulder and pushed her back down again. "Wait."

Cinatas screamed with rage and held up his hands. Electric sparks zinged from his fingertips, silencing the crowd with awe.

"Herrera and Samir die tomorrow," he decreed. "Tonight is mine, and nothing will stop me."

He marched like a king into the crowd. Wellbourne, carrying an unconscious Megan, followed Cinatas. The demons with Annette, Erin, and Stefanie went next. Then the horde of demons followed, chanting a hail to Cinatas.

Nothing will stop me. Nothing will stop me. Cinatas's voice rang over and over in Emerald's mind. She found herself wondering if anything could stop him.

Madre de Dios. The limo shot forward like a bullet and jerked hard to the right. Marissa, bound hand and foot and gagged, rolled helpless across the floorboards. Her head and shoulders slammed against the wooden bar, bringing tears to her eyes. Glass clanked and tires squealed.

What was happening? One minute she'd been packed like a sardine with Erin, Annette, and Stef; the next, they'd been taken away and she'd been left alone. But the fear and pain she felt were nothing compared to how deeply she ached for Navarre. All she could see was him lying in the rain, blood gushing from his wound when a monster too hideous to describe jerked the knife from Navarre's back.

She struggled desperately against ropes so tight her hands and feet were numb. The driver raced like a madman as she tried to wedge herself between the leather seats, but couldn't quite twist her body enough to stop the bruising punishment of being thrown back and forth. But nothing compared to the torture of being unable to help Navarre. Even the prison she'd spent most of her life in was heaven compared to her powerlessness now.

He'd tried so desperately to save her. He had warned her, but she hadn't listened. She'd failed him and because she had, he was . . . She couldn't bear it.

Her heart and spirit searched for him, searched for the black wolf, but her plea went unanswered—a cry of pain that echoed to the center of her soul.

Suddenly, the car jerked to a stop, and moments later the door opened. She turned her head and would have screamed if she could.

Herrera stood in the doorway looking down on her, his cruel, dark eyes gleaming in triumph. "I am much smarter than Samir, no? He thought he had you and now you are mine." The twisted smile on his satanic features gave just a whisper of warning to the malevolent viciousness of the man. She'd seen what he'd done to animals, heard what he'd done to women, and believed he alone of her Tío Luis's men was responsible for the disappearance of her family.

"Your home awaits you. You are eager to be my bride, are you not, my little *novia?*"

Marissa just glared at him.

"You will be," he said, then reached down, grabbed her breast, and squeezed until her vision went black with agony.

From the moment Sam slid into the dungeon with Nick, he knew he was a goner. The three demons on guard were in the middle of working over Deputy Carlton like inquisitors from the Spanish Inquisition. Sam saw pure red. His body went arctic cold and he did nothing to hold back the rage pumping him to invincibility. Wielding two machetes, he took off the heads of all three demons in a double strike and didn't stop hacking until their bodies were a pile of minced meat on the stone floor.

Through the thunder of blood roaring in his ears, he heard Nick calling his name. "Sam. Dear God, Sam. Can you hear me?"

Sam looked up. His vision was still washed in shades of red. He saw Nick standing across the room with his flamethrower and machete raised, prepared to defend against an attack. He was facing Sam. Behind Nick, Sam could see a horrified Sandy supporting a bloodied Carlton. Myra stood with them, wrapped in some kind of sheet, her face expressionless. Sam hoped for her sake that she was in some sort of demon trance like the townspeople and wouldn't remember what went down here.

"Go," Sam said. "Get them to safety. I'm taking this place down, okay?"

Nick nodded.

"I won't be going to Hatterfield's. So there's no point in coming after me. You understand?"

Sam forced a smile. "Tell Em. Tell her she brought heaven to me. A man can't ask for more than that. I'll wait for the sound of the grenade before I rock this joint to the ground. Meanwhile, I'm going hunting for black blood. So don't come back here."

Nick didn't even nod; he turned and herded the others out of the dungeon. Sam bowed his head and focused on drawing deep breaths of the stench. Black demon blood didn't carry the appealing aroma of human blood. That was one thing to be thankful for, surrounded by the undead; he didn't have to worry about sucking blood before he gave himself a farewell bonfire.

Stefanie's heart pounded so painfully in her chest that she was sure a coronary was but a beat away. Corazon de Rojo hadn't been hell on earth after all, because she was there now. There'd only been two vampires at Corazon—Herrera and Vasquez—and no demons. Now she was covered in demons. Their burning cold hands had practically touched her everywhere as they'd carted her like a trussed up pig to slaughter.

She hadn't seen Marissa since being dragged from the limo and Stefanie's soul cried for her friend.

Stefanie knew Nette and Erin were in the same helpless spot she was, though she hadn't been able to speak to them since Herrera had gagged and tied her at the camp. His depraved touch crawled like a poisonous spider in her soul. A hundred years of pulling the trigger on Nick's pistol and decimating a portrait of the bastard wouldn't be able to erase the memory of what he'd done to her. Killing him wouldn't either. She'd have to thank Nick anyway, because instead of shrinking into herself and wanting to die, she was burning with the need to see Herrera and the rest of these bastards brought to justice, whether through God, the law, or from her own hand.

Maybe then, just maybe, she'd feel a small measure of the peace she'd experienced briefly when the winged fire man had touched her back to life. She knew it was real and not imagined. She'd felt it twice now. And she now knew *he* was real, too. One of the Shadowmen. A Pyrathian.

Hear me? I'm fighting! Her spirit cried out to him wherever he was in the universe. And she would fight. Just as soon as she found her way out of this hell before it swallowed her and everyone she loved alive. *I'm fighting!*

"I know." The deep voice washed over her like a comforting caress, calming her. Her fear eased and her heart beat softer. She was not alone.

Chapter Twenty-seven

M*EGGIE! MEGGIE!* Emerald silently cried, desperate to reach her daughter with her spirit, but Megan didn't respond. Dread turned Emerald's heart into a painful knot that could barely beat. She couldn't think. She couldn't breathe. Her daughter was in the hands of monsters and she couldn't do anything to stop them.

It wasn't until Emerald saw the last of the demons disappear into the resort that Aragon released his hold on her shoulder.

She stood on cramped legs and gulped in deep breaths of air, fighting the panic that practically had her running after Megan. She had to think. She had to concentrate. Power. She'd need more power than ever before. The demons paled in comparison to the beast Cinatas had morphed into.

Now the shield was down, the energy of her visions returned. She closed her eyes as the future flashed through her mind. Cinatas stood upon the four corners of the earth, an abomination breathing fire and spewing ice across a wasteland of destruction. He led armies of depraved creatures in raping the earth and annihilating life. And like an unholy Joan of Arc riding at his side, projecting wave after wave of spiritual death, was Megan—a twisted and broken Megan.

Emerald shuddered against the dizzying flood of horror. No. Not her Meggie. Never.

"Emerald?" Jared grabbed her arm. Comfort and strength flowed in his touch. "Do not fear. We will save them all. Megan will be all right. We need to get to Nick and Sam."

Emerald couldn't speak, not yet. She nodded and followed Jared and Aragon down from their hiding place.

As soon as they reached the first floor, Jared sniffed the air. "Nick?"

"Right here," Nick answered, easing from the shadows. Deputy Sandy—wide-eyed with fear at Jared's semi-werewolf form—moved in protectively behind Nick.

"Don't worry," Nick said. "He's on our side." Nick looked at Jared. "I saw what went down out front. I didn't see Marissa, though."

Aragon grunted. "Marissa was taken by the vampire called Herrera."

"The sooner we get out of here, the sooner we can go after her," Jared said. "Plan B will have to be the amphitheater." He looked to Nick. "Where's Sam? We're going to need him."

Nick hesitated before answering and glanced Emerald's way. She knew in that one look that Sam had broken his promise to her. He wasn't keeping his options open. He was lone-wolfing it on a suicide mission, just like the vision she had of him when she first met him. The single warrior, beaten and bloody, facing an entire army of the damned on a glacier and eventually being dragged into the horrors of hell.

"Sam's hunting down Cinatas and Wellbourne while he's waiting for the grenade to let him know we've cleared out of here with the women," Nick said.

"The bloody gack isn't even trying to make it out of here, is he?"

Nick inhaled and Emerald caught a glimpse of pure haunted pain in Nick's damp eyes. "He's not himself anymore."

Emerald wanted to scream. "He canna know that for sure yet. He canna." She grabbed the Sacred Stones hanging from her belt and shook the bag, feeling emotion clog her throat. "He didn't even give me a chance."

Nick froze a minute, then began. "I've got Myra and Carlton, but they're barely functional and need to get out before the shit hits the fan here." Nick turned to Sandy. "If you can't find keys in one of the vehicles or hot-wire one, wait in the U-Haul. You'll find enough weapons in there to keep a small army away.

Just remember that fire fries demons and silver through the heart will drop a vampire."

"I can handle it," said Sandy. "As soon as I get them out, I'll be back. I've more than a few scores to settle with the bastards here."

Nick set his hand on Sandy's shoulder. "Take care of yourself first. You've been through hell."

"I'll be back," Sandy insisted.

"By then I hope there won't be anything to come back to because we will have burned this baby right back to hell."

"Let's move," Jared said. "We're running out of time."

Emerald tightened her hold on the Sacred Stones, realizing she just might have all the power she needed to save everyone. As they rushed to the amphitheater, her mind raced through the possibilities, from protective barriers to walls of White Fire. Her pulse kicked into high gear, and renewed strength followed on the heels of the confidence flooding her spirit. Good would triumph. It had to.

Sam left the dungeon, hating the damned and loathing himself. Emerald had given him heaven and all he'd dished out in return was hell. Still seeing nothing but shades of red, he went demon hunting with a vengeance. Around every corner, he found two or three as he made his way to the amphitheater. Every group of demons he came across was taken by surprise as Sam went right for their heads. His machetes and his burgeoning evil power turned him into a quicker-than-lightning killing machine. But the violence did little to help him escape his real demons. Emerald's voice still haunted him.

I've already had one man who didn't have the guts to fight with me. You canna do it to me, too.

The good in you is still in control. We'll find a way.

Bloody hell. I love you.

Promise me. Promise you won't leave me, too.

"I didn't have a choice," he yelled into the empty corridor, slamming the blood-spattered machetes against the stone floor. The clang of metal echoed with his voice. "You didn't give me a choice," he shouted again, this time directing his gaze toward heaven. "You hear me?"

"I think the whole bloody world can hear you," Emerald said, appearing around a corner. "Are you trying to get yourself killed, Samuel T. Sheridan?"

Sam blinked twice. He was seeing Em, feeling Em, and smelling Em—every sweet blood-scented ounce of her. Em was here! Sam surged to his feet, anger and disbelief and love all tangling into a knot in his stomach. "What in the hell are you doing here?"

"Good to see you, too, luv." She may have sounded exasperated, but hurt, worry, and fear filled the misty green eyes that always drove him crazy. He wanted to drown himself in her warmth.

"God, Em. You shouldn't have come." It was too late. Wasn't it? He didn't know whether he was cursed, or if this was a second chance. The red was already easing from his vision, as if her presence had the power to suck him back to sanity.

"She's not alone," Nick said, joining Emerald. "We're all here. Plan A didn't work."

Aragon and Jared appeared, their faces grim.

Aragon explained what happened when Cinatas arrived with the women.

"We're making the attack in the amphitheater," Jared said. "The damned will all be concentrated in one small area and distracted with Cinatas's theatrics. We can take out dozens at a time with the flamethrowers. We'll just have to be careful and not point them in the direction of the stage. Cinatas ordered the women to be chained in the theater along the back wall behind the throne. Erin will be chained to the altar."

"It'll work if the bastards react by fighting first and don't immediately try and kill the women when we move in," Aragon pointed out.

Sam's mind kicked into gear, going over the layout of the amphitheater. Feeling more human than not now, he tucked his machetes away then moved closer to Emerald and the others. "It'll work better if we all drop down from above with flamethrowers and form a line of defense between the women and the damned. We'll likely only have to worry about Cinatas on his throne then."

"Once I have the stage in sight," Emerald added, "I'll put up a wall of White Fire for as long as I can."

"You've mentioned that before. What is it?" Sam asked, bracing himself for the blast of painful heat he'd get when he touched her, but he couldn't stop himself. He brushed his hand down her arm, drinking her in.

She shivered but caught his fingers in hers and brought them to her lips. Burning as hotly as the love in her eyes, her lips were searing upon his chilled skin and cold soul. "It's a shield of purity so hot that if anything damned touches it, they immediately incinerate."

"I'd better stay the hell away from it then." Sam pulled his hand back. "That's part of the Redeeming ritual you mentioned, where you, me, or we both die if things don't go as they should. Right, Em?"

"Sam you have to give me and the Sacred Stones a chance, please."

"First we get Meggie safe. Then we'll see." As much as he wanted salvation, he wasn't willing to risk her life for it. Carrying Reed's death on his shoulders was already more than he could handle. He'd die if Em died, and he'd damn himself if they both died.

A second-story balcony ended up being the best place to maneuver from, and they were just in time for the party. He couldn't tell what was happening with the tornado, but he could hear a distant trainlike roar above the chant of the demons, and the oppressive atmosphere sucked the air right out of his lungs.

The sight of Annette and Stefanie gagged and chained to the wall nauseated him. Erin struggled against the two captors chaining her to the altar. And worse, an empty child-size chair sat to the right of the throne. Megan was nowhere in sight, which meant they had to hold off on their attack. Their plan to form a line of defense between the women and the audience looked as if it would work perfectly if Megan was brought to the small chair.

Unfortunately, the party was much bigger than even the amphitheater could hold. From Sam's surveillance angle, a host of Vladarian Vampires sat up front, and then came the demons. They spread like a grotesque sea all the way to the forest behind the resort.

He moved over to Emerald. She'd placed the Sacred Stones in a pyramid at the bottom of a planter. She'd set one stone off to her right. As she worked, she glanced below, obviously looking for Megan.

"We'll get her out of this," he said softly.

Emerald brought her gaze to his. "I know," she whispered, but she bit her lip, clearly anxious, her eyes brimming with unshed tears. How often had he watched her worry her lip, longing to be the one sucking on her mouth? He looked out over the sea of demons, wondering again how they were going to get out of this. Was there anything different he could have done?

God, he prayed. *Please see them out of this alive.*

He cleared his throat. "How wide can you make the wall of fire? How long can you hold it?"

"I canna tell you. I've only created a wall of White Fire once before. It all depends on how much the stones will amplify and channel my power. Cinatas is also a wild card. He's become a beast unlike any other of the damned I've ever known. You should have seen him when he arrived, electricity crackling over his body and shooting from his fingertips."

He ran his gaze over the redwood patio furniture on the balcony. "Be right back."

It took him less that a minute to break apart a table and pull two solid sides off a lounge chair. Everyone looked at him oddly. "Wood doesn't conduct electricity. If Cinatas has gone neon, you're going to need it." Since Nick and Aragon would concentrate on freeing the women and he and Jared on taking out Cinatas and the vampires, he gave Jared one side of wood for a shield and he took the other. Then he gave everyone except Emerald a hefty club-size plank from the table. "Remember. Get the women and exit through the back as quickly as possible. There are too many demons to defeat."

The roar from the crowd below signaled that Cinatas had arrived. Robed in gold and velvet like a king, he entered the theater, pompously sauntering to the stage as he nodded at his damned subjects. The demons practically bowed at his feet. The vampires looked disgusted. Behind Cinatas was Wellbourne, who—thank God—dragged Megan alongside him. She looked dazed and frightened, gagged with her hands tied, but otherwise appeared unharmed.

Sam got into position, prepared to strike.

Meggie! Emerald's spirit cried as she sent her senses into the depths of the depravity below to connect with her daughter. She knew the second Megan felt her because Megan lifted her head and straightened her shoulders, looking around the crowd. Wellbourne also paused a second and searched the amphitheater, forcing Emerald to pull her spirit back.

For the first time in the twenty minutes since Megan fainted, Emerald could breathe past the choking fear in her chest. They'd gagged Megan and taped her arms together, hindering her from using her angel bracelet against them.

Cinatas reached the stage and went to the gold throne. Wellbourne brought Megan up and sat her in the smaller chair, then stood behind her with his hands on her shoulders, anchoring her to the seat. Three other vampires remained on the stage, two of them standing behind Cinatas's throne and one holding the double-edged ax. The demons launched into a wild celebration as Cinatas waved his hand and shot tiny sparks of into the air.

"Guys ready?" Sam asked and received three go's. "Em?"

Fearful that in the next few minutes fate would rip them apart forever, she met his gaze and mouthed the words of her heart. *I love you.*

He gave her a half smile. *Me, too.*

"Now I'm ready," she said.

"Shit. I'm not." He crossed to her, kissed her hard. "That's forever. No matter what happens."

"Let's do it," Sam said and didn't look back as he launched the attack. Jared, using his were-strength, lobbed a dozen or more firebombs to the back of the amphitheater in rapid secession, exploding fire, chaos, and death in the demon ranks while Sam, Nick, and Aragon jumped over the railing. The men landed on the stage below with their flamethrowers already pumping out fire over the crowd in front. Cinatas stood on his throne, screaming at the vampires and demons to attack. Sam landed next to Megan. Aragon near Annette and Stefanie. Nick beside the vampire holding the ax. Jared by Erin. With everyone in position, it was Emerald's turn to act. She'd get the White Fire burning and then join the fray with the Sacred Stone she'd set aside. Sam would blow his gasket, but there was no way she was sitting up here all cozy while her daughter and friends were in the battle of their lives.

She covered the Sacred Stones with her hands and reached deeper into her soul than ever before as she focused her gaze on the front of the stage. White Fire erupted, spreading a line that went all the way across the theater. The flames were tiny at first but grew as she focused more and more of her energy.

Emerald gave one last burst of power, and the tongues of White Fire soared head high. The demons running toward the stage disappeared in a puff of gray ash the second they hit the white flames. Then Emerald slowly eased her hands back from the Sacred Stones and breathed a sigh of relief that the wall held. It was the best she could do, but it wasn't going to be enough. Demons were already searching for ways to get around the wall, since they couldn't get through it. It wouldn't take them long to realize that all they had to do was exit the amphitheater and go through the woods to bypass the White Flames.

Below she saw Cinatas turn his rage on Erin, whom Jared had just freed from the altar. Bolts of electricity shot from Cinatas's fingers at her. Jared blocked them with the redwood shield and advanced on Cinatas.

She glanced Megan's way, hoping Sam had her free but instead encountered the heart-stopping sight of Wellbourne holding Megan at knifepoint, at a standoff with Sam. Wellbourne backed slowly away from Sam, moving to the right edge of the stage, which put him in a good position to escape through the back of the amphitheater.

Suddenly a loud roar filled the night and the wind went wild, sucking and pulling at her.

The tornado. She whirled about, searching the sky. Then with awed horror, she saw trees and stone and demons at the back of the theater being sucked up by a twisting maelstrom of death. Looking down, she saw another vampire attack Sam from behind.

Wellbourne jumped off the stage with Megan, running to escape.

Fighting the sucking wind, Emerald raced across the balcony, taking the steps to the lower level two at a time where she could intercept Wellbourne. The pull of the wind wasn't as strong on the ground as it had been on the balcony.

She had the Sacred Stone in one hand and Sam's gun in the other. Wellbourne was looking back over his shoulder and Emerald planted herself in the middle of his path. Megan, pale as a ghost, had tears streaming down her cheeks but bore no sign of physical harm. Emerald leveled Sam's gun at his head and shouted about the wind. "Let my daughter go, Wellbourne. I'm the one you want. I'm the one who killed your brother."

Wellbourne whipped around and smiled, unfazed by the gun. "About time you and your heroes showed up. I knew you'd sense the shield go down and get here fast." He laughed. "What Cinatas didn't know didn't hurt me at all, did it? I have you both now, just like I planned. Serves him right for the shit he's made me eat playing his lackey."

"Let her go," Emerald repeated.

He laughed again. "You don't quite understand how things are. Shall I explain?" Reaching down he grabbed Megan's arm and twisted it until Megan moaned in pain, making Emerald die a little inside. "If I have her, then I have you, and you will do everything I want when I want. Now drop the gun and turn around. We're getting out of here. You delay, she pays." He twisted harder and Megan nearly doubled over from the pain. He brought the knife closer to Megan's throat. "Do you understand the situation now, angel bitch?"

"Dear God," Emerald whispered. She couldn't just turn around and leave with the monster. She couldn't shoot him and she couldn't hit him with the stone yet. One wrong twitch could kill her daughter. Emerald's eyes burned so badly that she thought at first the dark shadow behind Wellbourne was only tears welling in her eyes. But the silent shadow grew larger.

Sam.

Coming from behind, Sam grabbed Wellbourne's knife

hand, knocking him hard enough to buckle his knees. Emerald threw the Sacred Stone and hit Wellbourne in the face. He yelled as his damned flesh sizzled and smoked. His hold loosened enough that Megan tried to escape, but he fisted his hand in her hair before she could. Emerald rushed forward to free Megan.

Wellbourne twisted away from Sam's grip and slashed out with the knife.

Emerald screamed and her heart stopped as the knife plunged toward Megan's head.

Sam jerked Wellbourne back and shoved himself over Megan. The knife went into Sam's back once, then again as Wellbourne raged. Sam cried out, arching against the pain, but kept pummeling Wellbourne's hand with his fist until Megan was free.

Emerald grabbed Megan away as Sam and Wellbourne went tumbling to the ground in a snarl of knives and fangs.

Emerald wrapped her arms around her daughter and pulled her to safety by a large bush ten feet away from the fighting men. Tears streamed down Emerald's face as she gently removed the gag and untied her daughter.

"I'm okay. I'm okay," Megan said over and over, yet she kept crying. "I remember what you told me. 'Sometimes an angel has to hope when there is none. Sometimes an angel must walk where none will follow. And sometimes an angel must believe and act on nothing but faith alone.' I believed, Mom. I believed in good and it saved me from their evil."

"You're so brave and strong." Emerald pulled Megan close to her heart. She knew Sam was hurt and desperately prayed he'd break free from Wellbourne so she could shoot, but it wasn't happening, and from the way the fight was going, she feared Wellbourne would kill Sam. "I need you to hide behind this bush a minute while I go help Mr. Sam. Doona come out until I come back. I mean it, okay?"

"Okay. This fighting evil stuff isn't as easy as Harry Potter makes it seem."

"Real life things are never easy, luv," she said then saw Megan safely hidden before she ran to where Sam and Wellbourne were still tangled up. Wellbourne was on top and had a knife inching toward Sam's throat. If she shot Wellbourne in the heart from the back, the bullet could go through Wellbourne and hit Sam. She had to do something or Sam would be killed.

They were so embroiled in their battle that they didn't see her coming. She moved around to Wellbourne's left side, bent low to angle the gun up from the ground, and shot Wellbourne twice in the heart at nearly point-blank range.

Wellbourne looked up in shock.

"Silver bullets," Emerald said.

"You bit—" Wellbourne died before he could finish his sentence.

She felt no satisfaction or triumph, only relief that Sam was alive and that she and her daughter were free of a predator that had hunted them for so long.

Sam pushed Wellbourne's body off him, took the vampire's knife, and shoved it into the bastard's heart. Then, moaning, he rose to his feet.

Emerald reached to help him, but he pulled away. "Sam. You're hurt. What do you think you're doing?"

"I'll be fine. Wellbourne hit vest and muscle with his knife. Nothing vital." He moved several steps, as if testing himself, then walked over to the edge of the trees and picked up his flamethrower and machetes.

Seeing the Sacred Stone next to where Wellbourne lay, Emerald pocketed it, remembering Megan had said it was important to bring them back. "You came after Wellbourne unarmed?"

Sam strapped everything in place except for one machete.

"My knife is still stuck in a vampire on the stage, and the machetes and flamethrower would have slowed me down. Neither of them would have helped in a hostage situation. There's no way Wellbourne was going to disappear with Meggie." Sam moved closer. "Where is she? Is she all right?"

"Yes. It's okay to come out, Meggie." Megan slipped from behind the bush and ran to her.

Emerald took Megan's hand in hers then leaned into Sam. She pressed her cheek to his heart. He may have been cold but deep inside, he was still Sam. "Thank you."

Sam touched Megan's head lightly then brushed a kiss to Emerald's lips, and gave them his heart in his touch.

Suddenly the sensation of icy cold invaded her senses. "Demons!" she said, twisting to the right.

Sam instantly spun and set the flamethrower off as three demons appeared from the woods. They disappeared in a ball of fire, but then the stream of fire stopped and Emerald realized he was out of fuel. Sam ditched the flamethrower.

"You two stay close behind me," he yelled, moving back toward the stage.

The demons had found their way around the White Fire, and Emerald wondered if everyone was now trapped. The stage came into view and Emerald, who'd known magic and miracles all her life, felt her jaw drop. The tornado had inched forward until it whirled in the middle of the amphitheater, sucking everything into its vortex. But the wall of White Fire was shielding their friends from its force. Onstage the tableau appeared to be over. Nick and Aragon stood by, Annette, Stefanie, and Erin on the ground just ahead.

"You three okay?" Emerald asked.

"Now that we see Meggie is all right, we are," Annette replied. "Where is Marissa?"

"Herrera kidnapped her," Emerald said.

"No!" Stefanie cried, grabbing Annette's arm for support.

"No . . . he . . . he'll— Oh, God. He'll hurt her. He's . . . awful." Her breathing turned harsh.

"Breathe deep," Annette said, wrapping an arm around Stef's shoulder.

Nick cupped Stef's chin and brought her gaze to his. "I'll get her back, Stef! I'll get her back fast. You believe me, right?"

Stefanie nodded and clasped Nick's hand. "We'll get her back."

Jared was onstage, dousing everything that would burn with fire.

"What happened?" Sam asked. "Where's Cinatas?"

Nick cursed. "Jared went after the chicken shit and he up and disappeared with another vamp he called Valois."

A crumbling roar reverberated through the air. The tornado moved, dancing in a wider circle as it ate up forest then a corner of the resort. Bodies of demons and debris twisted around and around in its circling wave of death.

"Let's get out of here," Sam yelled, launching everyone into action.

"Hop on for a piggyback, Meggie," Nick said, bending down. Megan latched onto his back and they took off with Erin, Annette, and Stef. Jared and Aragon followed.

As everyone cleared out to a safe distance, Sam threw a grenade onto the stage, blowing everything away, erasing any chance that the stage could ever again be put to use.

Emerald fell into step with Sam, not wanting to let him out of her sight. They were actually going to get out of there alive. It was a miracle—

"Wait." Emerald grabbed Sam's arm and ground to a halt. "The Sacred Stones, I canna leave here without them."

"Stones, Em? We've a tornado on our ass in case you haven't notice. There're more stones at the site."

"No time to explain. I canna leave without them."

"Go," Sam shouted at Jared and Aragon. "Leave if we aren't there in one minute. I'll get her out another way."

Jared turned back. "I'll stay, too."

"No," Sam said. "She's mine. I'll take care of her. You take care of yours. Do you understand?"

Jared nodded.

"Tell Meggie I went back for the stones. She'll understand."

"Let's hurry." Sam grabbed her arm, and they raced for the balcony stairs about fifty feet away.

The stones in the planter with the blue pillowcase anchored under it were the only things left on the deck. The wind of the tornado had taken everything else. A Emerald loaded the stones into the bag, the White Flames disappeared, loosing the force of the tornado in their direction. She almost went over the railing, and would have, if Sam hadn't caught her.

He wrapped his arms around her and had to practically drag them both across the deck and down the stairs. The wind whipped with bruising force, sucking away breath and strength. The way around the resort was much harder now, and every inch of ground they gained was a battle that only eased a little when they turned the corner. But she and Sam were together and they were making it. She had the Sacred Stones. Everything was going to be all right. It had to be.

Chapter Twenty-eight

H IS GLORY. His greatness. His moment of triumph had incinerated to ash. And it was all *her* fault, Cinatas raged. Not Erin's. That worthless bitch didn't have any power and he'd been a fool for focusing on her. She and her were-lover would still die. But he had something more important to do first.

It was Wellbourne's angel bitch's fault. She had destroyed his victory. Angel power! Angel blood. The one thing that he lacked. He wasn't leaving here tonight without it. And only the mother would do. The child he'd get later. For now, he wanted an angel with experience.

Watching from the rooftop, he saw the group race along the edge of the resort. They'd be headed to the vehicles, which meant they'd have to pass one at a time through the gate and she was practically at the end of the line. Perfect.

"Is there anything else, Master?"

"No, Bastion. Take the monstrance to Zion and wait for me there. Now that I know desecrations lead to power, we have a lot of work to do. Tonight was but a minor setback. The world is my oyster and I'm going to eat it raw."

Glass exploded and twisting metal screeched, adding to the howl of the advancing tornado. The resort was being torn apart brick by brick. Sam fought the wind, holding on to Emerald. The stab wound in his back from Wellbourne hurt like a son of a bitch. He could smell the blood dripping down his spine. His body was growing colder and colder by the second.

The pain and Emerald's nearness had kept his mind sane and the heavy red haze at bay. But the evil insanity was still there, lurking in the darkness in his soul and in his mind. It gnawed at him just as hard as the fact that Cinatas's ass wasn't in the dirt with Wellbourne's. Emerald, Megan, and the others wouldn't be safe until then.

Sam could already see the hope of a future in her gaze as she struggled with him. It touched his heart deeper than anything, but it also made him sick inside, because he didn't share that hope. She had the Sacred Stones, they would soon have the opportunity for the Redeeming Ritual, but that didn't erase the risk to her.

He didn't know—

Emerald's hand was ripped right out of his grasp. He spun around, expecting to see her struggling against the wind or on the ground. Instead he found her in the grip of a hideous monster. Electricity crawled like spiders all over his scarred face and hands. Emerald struggled, shuddered, and cried out, clearly tortured in the monster's hold, which had to feel like being zapped by a stun gun.

Cinatas.

Sam smiled, baring his fangs as his vision turned bloodred. The son of a bitch didn't know who he was dealing with. Sam lifted both his machetes and ran right at Cinatas.

"I'll kill her." Cinatas juiced up more, making Emerald scream in pain, but Sam didn't stop. He hit Cinatas like a ton of bricks, sure of two things. Cinatas wanted Emerald too much to kill her, and as long as he had hold of her he was going to hurt her. All three of them went flying back, and Emerald fell free of Cinatas's grasp when Sam sliced his machete through the bastard's shoulder.

"Run." Sam's shout was only a gasp as he brought both of the machetes up and pushed to his feet. "Get the hell out of here!"

"You die!" Cinatas screamed. With both hands he shot a double bolt of lightning at Sam.

"No!" Emerald screamed.

Sam ducked and rolled. He was going to kill Emerald himself for not leaving. The tree behind him exploded into splinters, and shards of wood embedded in his legs. The sharp pain sapped his strength.

"Guess I'm not making your day after all," Sam snarled as he whirled at Cinatas, both machetes in action. He landed a slicing blow to Cinatas's side and back, receiving another stunning jolt of electricity. This time Sam felt his heart stop for a few beats before it kicked back in, leaving him dizzy.

A quick glance at Emerald showed she was nowhere in his immediate sight. Shit. Now he was even more worried. He needed a forty-meter clearance on all sides to detonate his last WP grenade and send himself and Cinatas into a really hot hell. He'd been saving it for the bastard. But he couldn't set it off without knowing where Em had gone. Too many shadows of bushes and trees rose in the darkness. She could be hiding close and would be killed in the fire.

Cinatas let loose another bolt and Sam rolled to the side. Another tree bit the dust, leaving a deadly javelin of splintered wood at his feet. Sam snatched it up and let it fly. It hit Cinatas in the chest. The beast fell to his knees, raging as he shot another bolt to Sam's right. The tree split and the trunk came crashing toward Sam.

Cinatas hit him with the next bolt. Sam went down, all his muscles twitching. He struggled to rise, to hold Cinatas at bay longer so Em would have time to get well away. Cinatas laughed, as if he knew he'd won. Sam got to his knees and threw the machete. It lobbed end over end through the air. Cinatas knocked it aside, but it still sliced into his arm. Sam's heart seized a moment, pain shooting deeply through his chest.

Cinatas aimed a killing blow and Sam rolled to the side. Then suddenly a wall of White Fire erupted between him and Cinatas. The monster bolt boomeranged off the White Fire, hitting Cinatas in the head.

Em. Damn. She was still here. Sam's heart beat crazily now

making his chest quiver. His hands and feet were going numb. His vision dimmed. He struggled to rise, but his muscles wouldn't work right. "Run . . . Em. Please . . . God . . . run."

"No bloody way," Emerald cried, reaching him. "I'm not leaving you. You're coming with me. I love you." Tears poured from her eyes and he went crazy that he'd never drown in her misty greens again.

"Not . . . leaving . . . me. You're . . . taking . . . the best . . .of me . . . with you." A sudden pain seized Sam's chest and left arm. He gasped for air and the world went black.

"Sam! No! You canna leave me. You just canna." Blinded by tears, Emerald searched for a pulse and felt none. Body shaking and heart breaking, she pressed on Sam's chest, counting out beats then angled his head and neck to blow air into his lungs.

She heard the roar of the tornado, felt it sucking on her, but she never looked up. She worked on him until it hurt to move, until she couldn't breathe herself, until her own heart pumped painfully in her breast. Then she cried. Face buried against his still chest, she cried like she'd never cried before. He was gone from her in this life and he'd be separated from her in the next because he was damned—

Sometimes an angel has to hope when there is none. Sometimes an angel must walk where none will follow. And sometimes an angel must believe and act on nothing but faith alone.

She rushed to get the Sacred Stones. She'd redeem his soul. She didn't care if no angel before had done something so bold. She didn't care what the cost. She wasn't going to let his soul go to the damned. Sam was a good man. Slowly the tears cleared from her eyes and she beheld the moonlit world around her in disbelief.

It was gone. All gone except for the tiny patch of trees where she stood next to the wall of White Fire she'd erected. The resort had been leveled. No trees or structures remained on top of Hades Mountain.

Cinatas was gone, too. Had the tornado taken him? Had he escaped? It didn't matter right now. Sam mattered the most.

Emerald ran to the pile of Sacred Stones. They were hot. Taking them carefully, she brought them back to Sam. Kneeling at his side, she placed the stones. One in each hand. One on his forehead. One on each foot. Then four over his heart.

She set her hand over the Sacred Stones, covering his heart and recited the Redeeming Vow. "What you are, I am. What I am, you are. I'll suffer your burning cold hell and you'll walk through the purifying fires of my heaven. Now and forever I bind our souls together. Amen."

Emerald braced herself, ready to be thrust into hell with Sam, to pay whatever price was needed to redeem him. She felt herself being lifted from her body, and somewhere in the darkness of it all, she sensed Sam's spirit and moved toward him. It wasn't the vibrant pulse of a living man, but the whispering breath of a ghost hovering in the twilight edges between worlds, a spirit trapped between the realm of the good and the realm of the damned. Pain filled her heart. *Sam. Oh, Sam.*

Opening her eyes, she found his writhing spirit lying before her, naked and ghostly. He was in agony. Pain poured from his spirit, washing over her and breaking her heart anew.

They were upon a sea of mists, and in the sky above there were no stars. There was no sun, no moon. No color. Nothing light. Nothing dark. Nothing black. Nothing white. All was shadowy shades of gray. She placed her hand over his spirit heart and repeated the Redeeming Vow. But nothing happened. Her heart began to pound. She couldn't be wrong. She couldn't be—"

"Emerald, daughter of my heart. You cannot redeem him."

Emerald looked up to see her mother, shining a glorious blue and gold. "I must. There has to be a way."

"You misunderstand, child. He has already redeemed himself. His selfless sacrifice to stop evil and to fight it within himself saved his soul."

"Then why is his spirit in such agony?"

"Because he refuses to leave the mortal world and embrace that of the spirit world. He'd rather live in pain and haunt the earth with his spirit to be closer to you than to embrace the peace of the heavens."

Emerald closed her eyes, searching to reach past her personal agony. "I love him. Why did I have to lose him?" The spirit and comfort of her mother's touch surrounded her but did little to lessen her pain. "I love him as you loved father."

"The journey of love is never easy. I can tell you his name is not yet written in The Book."

Emerald opened her eyes. "And that means?"

"What has been written cannot be unwritten."

Emerald's mind searched for her mother's meaning. "Then . . . then he could yet live?"

"With the breath of life from a Pyrathian, if Logos wills it to be so. Take his spirit with you, daughter of my heart. Return to the mortal ground. If it is to be so, you will not have long to wait. But if his name appears in The Book then you will have to let his spirit go. Tell him to embrace the heavens then and live in peace until your spirits meet again.

"I am always with you, child. And with Megan. She will be greater than me or you, but she will need direction and protection. She has great power, and the wrong influence could take her into a darkness from which she might never surface. But we will guard her well—for we love her bestest."

Everything around Emerald exploded in a bright flash of gold and blue light and she felt herself falling. Unable to stop herself, she fell faster and faster until pain slammed into her, from her head to her feet.

Groaning, she opened her eyes and saw a golden winged man with fiery green eyes hovering over her. He wore an amulet like Jared's and Aragon's and he had a lightning bolt emblazoned on his chest. One of his hands rested on her forehead, and as she cut her gaze to the side, she saw his other hand pressed to Sam's forehead. She looked back to the man but he was gone. Sam groaned, moving.

Dazed, Emerald sat up. As she reached for Sam she noticed odd piles of rubble surrounding them. The moment she felt his warm skin beneath her hand and the steady beat of his heart she started to cry. He was alive! Sam was back and the evil had been purged from him.

She shivered and realized her clothes had also somehow disappeared. The mountain night air blew lightly over them with a refreshing chill, for the oppressive evil that had hovered in the atmosphere was gone. The cool grass beneath her, though soft, had been dampened with dew.

"Sam?" she whispered. As she moved closer to him, she found that a pile of round, warm stones lay between them. The Sacred Stones. Then she did a quick double take. They were no longer on Hades Mountain. They were on Spirit Wind Mountain, in the circle of the Sacred Stones—but only the center stone was left standing.

"Sam!" She shook his shoulder hard. "Wake up! We have to go find everyone." They had to be safe, she knew it, but she wouldn't rest until she had Megan with her and everyone together.

Sam groaned, reached for her, and pulled her down on top of him. "In the morning, angel. I'll do whatever you want in the mornin'. This night's not over yet." He slid his hands down her back, grabbed her bum, and drew her even tighter to him. He was rock hard, and moving quickly he kissed her so thoroughly she saw nothing but stars.

"Oh, bloody hell, Samuel T. Sheridan. I love you, but we canna make love now."

He opened his eyes. Then as he stared at her, she saw reality dawn. She felt him wiggle all over, as if feeling himself out

"Em?" He looked around and shook his head. "What's happened? Where are we? Where's Cinatas? How . . . Why are we here naked?"

She quickly explained what had happened on Hades Mountain. "I doona know if the tornado took him or if he escaped. We're naked because clothes canna pass into the spirit world. When you died, you crossed over."

"Em," he whispered with tears in his eyes. "You're naked, too. Did you sacrifice yourself to save me? Did you die, too?"

Emerald started to shake her head, then she remembered what her mother had said about the Pyrathians. That winged golden man she'd seen with his hand on her and on Sam . . . had she died? "I doona know and canna think about it now. We have to get to the camp and find everyone else. I have to see Meggie.

"Are you hurt?" she asked, still awed by everything.

He sat up. "No . . . I'm fine. I love you, Em. More than life itself."

"I know." She leaned forward and kissed him. "You fought for us, for me. You dinna leave me even in death, and I dinna leave you either."

Standing she picked up some of the Sacred Stones. "Bring the others," she said as Sam gained his feet. Then she went to the place where the center pillar, now scorched black with fire, stood and placed the stones in a circle around the pillar. Sam added his and reached for her hand.

"Anybody ever tell you that naked in the moonlight is your thing?" he asked. "You're always beautiful, but in the moonlight you're magical."

"Look," she said, pointing to the stones. "There's the real magic."

A white mist rose from the stones, forming a circle around the center pillar. And as it rose, it erased the black, leaving a sparkling white to glow in the moonlight.

Epilogue

Later that day.

"I TAKE BACK what I said earlier." Sam reached up and pulled down the tree branch so Emerald could retrieve the angel bracelet she'd left a few days ago. He'd lived a lifetime since then. They'd arrived at Silver Mist Falls thirty minutes ago to get her bracelet but had gotten distracted.

Everyone—Annette, Aragon, Jared, Erin, Stef, Nick, and even Megan—had been working on tornado cleanup in the town all day, and getting Emerald naked and into the soothing water had been more than he could resist. He'd stripped her, tossed her into the water, and made love to her as if there was no tomorrow. And considering her nude, damp state and his hard, ready one, he was about to do it again.

"If you said something nice, you canna take it back," Emerald replied as she unclasped the bracelet from the branch and replaced it on her wrist, the sound of bells tinkling as she raised and shook her wrist. Sunlight gleamed off the silver just as it did off her spiky moon-glow hair. "Only bad things can be retracted."

He lifted a brow, marveling anew at her love. She was a mystifying mixture of strength, power, and vulnerability that gave full credence to who and what she was—an angel who delivered heaven to his heart. "Is that written in some heavenly rule book?"

She turned to look at him, her green eyes still dreamy with pleasure. Yep, he was 100 percent going to make love to her again, and if she lowered her gaze, she'd know it, too.

"No," she said softly, placing her warm hand his chest, sending a jolt of delicious heat all the way to his toes. "It's written on my heart, where I treasure your words and your love."

His breath caught and his heart thumped hard. Oh man, he was so gone. He'd done his damnedest to keep from her, to do right by her, sure he was nothing but bad news. He'd been wrong. She'd fought for him and loved him at his worst, always believing, never giving up, and he was hers forever. He snaked an arm around her waist and pulled her flush against him, relishing the brush of her nipples on his chest and how his aching erection nestled against her softness. "Then let me amend my earlier statement when I said being naked in the moonlight is your thing. So is naked in the sunlight. Hell, naked and any kind of light."

She laughed. "That's because you're male, and female naked anything goes." She wiggled her hips, making him groan.

He shook his head. "Nope. Only you. You kissed the darkness from my soul." Grabbing her bottom, he lifted her up, positioning himself against the wet, welcoming heat of her sex.

Wrapping her arms around his neck, she hooked her knees on his hips and brought her lips to his. Taking his time, he ran his tongue over her lush bottom lip then sucked on it softly before delving into the velvet warmth of her mouth in a passionate give-and-take that had him drowning in pleasure. The miracle of being redeemed, of being alive, of being with her was almost more than he could take. Nothing else mattered. So even though many dark and difficult things hovered over them now and in the future, it didn't steal away his joy in the moment.

The buzz of his cell phone and the tinkle of her BlackBerry did, though.

He ended the kiss with a groan. They had to get back to reality.

"Let's not answer just yet." She hugged him closer.

"I wish I could, but I'm expecting to hear from the governor about declaring Twilight a disaster area, and Nick has the APB out for Marissa and the limo." They couldn't put one out for

Navarre, but Nick was also checking all flights out of any airport for a match to Herrera, Marissa, and Navarre.

"You're right." She sighed, and he let her down but kept hold of her hand as they returned to their pile of clothes. The sun made rainbows throughout the mist-filled valley. It was a beautiful, green piece of heaven that he and Emerald would come back to again and again. Maybe even buy the land and make a home there with Megan and a child of their own, if that was in the cards. But all of that was in the future. The here and now had to be taken care of first.

Besides clearing the top of Hades Mountain and obliterating the Black Cloud, the tornado had taken a hit-or-miss pattern through the town and the valley. The sheriff's station as well as a number of businesses and homes had been destroyed, but miraculously no one had been hurt. Deputy Michaels's death at Cinatas's hands and the men Sam injured were being attributed to the storm. Carlton and Sandy were the only two people in the town who had any recollection of everything that happened. Apparently, demon trances wiped out memories. Not even the mayor or the men who'd participated in the lynch mob remembered anything, though Sam was going to keep a sharp eye on them.

Bond's and Grayson's memories were intact and they were still in Twilight, helping out with the tornado relief. They'd basically turned their allegiance over to the cause and to Sam as well. They'd return to Fort Bragg and Commander Kingston, but would be changing the rules of Kingston's game. Apparently the commander had personal dirt he wanted kept under the carpet, which Grayson was going to use that as leverage.

By the time Sam reached his phone, it had stopped ringing. Seeing Nick's number, he punched the call back button and Nick answered.

"What's up?"

"We've got a lead on Marissa. The limo has been found at a

small airport outside of Nashville. I'm getting them to fax over information on all the flights out of there."

"Fast work."

"Doesn't seem fast enough though." Nick sighed. "Only the slight possibility that Herrera might take Marissa to somewhere besides Vasquez's decimated camp is keeping me and Stef off a plane to Belize."

"As soon as we have a solid destination, we'll move. Together."

"Also, the governor's secretary says he will be calling us at six this evening. Something about wanting to set up a press conference first, but it looks like it'll be a slam dunk to get the relief funds."

"Excellent. We'll be back to town shortly."

"Take your time. The cleanup crews are done for today and the Burger Queen Delight is giving out free food. We're all over here, drowning in cholesterol. Jared and Aragon have discovered the existence of cheeseburgers and peach and strawberry milk shakes. It may take them a millennium or two to satisfy their appetites."

Sam hung up, shaking his head.

Emerald was still on her BlackBerry and laughing hard at whatever the other person was saying. He decided her nipples needed some attention and came at her from behind to cup her breasts and tease. She leaned into him, her laugh ending in a moan.

"Gotta go," she said and disconnected. "That's not bloody fair. I canna think when you do that."

"Sorry, I didn't think. I just couldn't keep away. We're you on a professional call?"

"No. From now on until I can turn my patients completely over to my partner, I'm only going to take calls one day a week. That was Annette."

Frowning, Sam stopped teasing Emerald and swung her

around to face him. "You're not giving up your practice, are you? I know I've made comments, but . . . hell . . . they were asinine and I'm sorry. I was jealous of the attention others were getting. You can count on that not being an issue. Just know that I'm available for research purposes."

"Research only?"

He cleared his throat. "Any purposes. Now what about your practice?"

"Not giving it up, but definitely restructuring everything so I have more solid blocks of uninterrupted personal time. I won't be returning to Ireland, so I'm making arrangements for that, too. But just now Annette called to say she made a truffle interception."

"A what?"

Emerald explained what went on in the truffle discussion after Sam had left the dining hall the other night.

Sam's mouth gaped. "Ten pounds of chocolate?"

"Guess Jared thought he'd get a tussle for every truffle." Emerald wrapped her hand around Sam's erection. She not only had magic powers, but magic fingers, too.

Sam died and went to heaven when she gave him the magic of her mouth as well. When he could stand no more, he pulled her up, kissed her forehead, eyes, nose, and cheeks as he explored his way back to her lush, kiss-swollen lips. Delving into her mouth, he fed on the heady taste of her, drinking in the scent of lavender and musk. He moved along the line of her jaw and the slim column of her neck before dipping down and sucking her nipples to needy, hard points of arousal.

On his knees, he parted the pink lips of her sex, inhaled her erotic fragrance, and kissed the glistening, swollen flesh until she quivered with his every lick.

"Sam, I need you now. I canna wait," she said.

"Then don't," he replied as he stood and laid back on a flat rock by the misty falls. She climbed over him, hugging his hips with her knees and bracing her hands on his chest. Sam thrust upward into the hot glove of her core that perfectly cradled his erection. Back arched high, he filled her completely and held on to the heaven of the sensation for just a moment before taking her for the ride of their lives. She moaned, her desire-laden gaze fixed on him. She was hot and beautiful in passion. Her mouth open and needy. Her body moving to the rhythm of his desire. Damn but he wanted to be touching, sucking, and kissing her everywhere.

"Thirty," he said.

"Hmm?" She looked at him in dazed confusion.

He flicked his thumb over the nub cresting her sex, repeatedly, loving being between a rock and her little hard spot. "Thirty pounds," he said. "Jared should have ordered thirty pounds of truffles. A month."

"Talk later. Canna think now. Can only feel." Emerald moaned, rocking against him.

"Feel me then." Looking into her pleasure-filled eyes, he went crazy, thrusting up hard until she cried out his name and her body convulsed as she climaxed. Her hot sheath clamped down on his shaft and sent him flying to heaven.

She fell into his arms and he pulled his angel close. Heart, body, and soul, they were one.